A GIFT
OF LIFE

Also by Henry Denker

NOVELS

I'll Be Right Home, Ma
My Son, The Lawyer
Salome: Princess of Galilee
The First Easter
The Director
The Kingmaker
A Place for the Mighty
The Physicians
The Experiment
The Starmaker
The Scofield Diagnosis
The Actress
Error of Judgment
Horowitz and Mrs. Washington
The Warfield Syndrome
Outrage
The Healers
Kincaid
Robert, My Son
Judge Spencer Dissents
The Choice
The Retreat

PLAYS

Time Limit
A Far Country
A Case of Libel
What Did We Do Wrong
Venus at Large
Second Time Around
Horowitz and Mrs. Washington
The Headhunters
Outrage!

A GIFT OF LIFE

Henry Denker

William Morrow and Company, Inc.
New York

Library of Congress Cataloging-in-Publication Data

Denker, Henry.
    A gift of life / Henry Denker.
      p. cm.
    ISBN 0-688-08762-0
    I. Title.
    PS3507.E5475G54   1989
    813'.54—dc20   89-31773
                                                      CIP

Printed in the United States of America

First Edition

1 2 3 4 5 6 7 8 9 10

BOOK DESIGN BY BILL BURNER

To Edith, my wife

The Author wishes to express his deep gratitude to The Transplant Unit of Columbia-Presbyterian Hospital in New York City for their unstinting cooperation in the research involved in writing *A Gift of Life*.

1

EXCEPT FOR HIS sharply focused blue eyes, Dr. Christopher Slade's face was covered by a green surgical mask as he leaned over the open chest cavity of the patient on the operating table.

An intense light was focused on the new heart Slade was suturing into place. It appeared to be a good, sound, healthy heart. The fit, while not exact, was close enough, after he had trimmed the circumference very slightly and adjusted the patient's aorta so it joined perfectly to the new heart. With extreme care, he proceeded to complete his suturing.

Around him the rest of the transplant team went about their duties with quiet proficiency. Second Surgeon Boyd Angstrom stood ready to assist at any moment, if it became necessary.

The scrub nurse and the circulating nurse were ready with instruments, sutures, pads. The two anesthetists kept watch on their oscilloscopes, across whose screens danced rhythmic electronic impulses which revealed the vital signs of the patient.

At the heart-lung machine two perfusionists diligently tended their complicated mechanism, observing the flow of blood through its colorless plastic tubing. Until the patient's new heart could assume the burden, this ingenious invention had to continuously oxygenate and circulate four liters of blood through the patient's body to keep him alive.

Slade tied each suture with immaculate care as he joined the patient's aorta to the implanted heart. A few careless or inefficient sutures could give way and bring on bleeding and, possibly, death. Chris Slade never approached the operating table without being painfully conscious of the admonition of the surgeon from who he had learned the technique of heart transplantation.

The transplant surgeon is the only person who, each time he lifts his scalpel, deals with life and death. He must be bold and sure, self-confident, sometimes even overbearing. But always humble in the knowledge that the simplest error on his part can cause death.

Slade finished tying his last suture. He was ready now for the ultimate test.

Each time, no matter how precise and successful the surgery, how healthy the new heart, how perfect the fit, there came the moment when, like all other transplant surgeons, Chris Slade had to face the ultimate test: Would this new heart function normally? Or, as sometimes happened, would it fail?

Having checked out all details and all sutures once more, Slade started to release the clamp that would slowly restore normal blood flow to the patient's coronary arteries and thus stimulate the new heart to begin beating.

As the fresh blood flowed into it, the new heart began to convulse erratically in irregular fibrillations.

Usual reaction, thus far, Slade considered. But when the fibrillations continued, he requested, "Countershock."

Boyd Angstrom passed two flat, electrified metal panels, which Slade placed alongside the struggling heart.

"Shock," Slade ordered.

Angstrom activated the electric shock to the panels. The heart jumped in response, but did not assume a normal regular beat. No cause for alarm. Not yet. It often took two, sometimes three shocks to stimulate a transplanted heart out of its erratic pulsations and into normal rhythm.

After the second shock, the heart assumed a more even, less convulsive beat. Slade was neither relieved nor satisfied. This heart, only four hours ago taken from another body, seemed to limp along instead of regaining the firm healthy beat that transplant surgeons like to see.

He decided it was time to impose the ultimate test: to slowly wean the patient off the heart-lung machine which had been sustaining life during the course of the transplant, thus gradually imposing the entire burden on the new heart. The need for gradual transition was a mandatory protection. If during the procedure the new heart failed, it would be necessary to quickly put the patient back on full bypass.

The first step in the transition was to reduce the flow of oxygenated machine-fed blood from four liters to three. If the new heart reacted well, then to gradually cut down the machine feed to two liters. Then down to one. Finally, if the new heart beat robustly under its new responsibility, the final step would be to shut off the heart-lung machine completely.

If this new heart cooperated, it should require only fifteen minutes to go from four liters to complete shutdown.

Slade became aware that he was sweating more than he usually did at this stage of surgery. He half turned to his nurse. She mopped his face dry. He wondered at his profuse sweating. Was it caused by some hunch, some thorn of intuition, that warned him that this case would not go according to plan?

He signaled the perfusionists to turn off the flow from the heart-lung machine. The new heart, lying in its strange surrounding, stitched to an unfamiliar cardiovascular system, should now function on its own. No one in the O.R. spoke. There was no sense that the crucial phase of the surgery was completed. That all that remained was tidying up, suturing up the pericardium, reuniting both sides of the rib cage, closing

up the chest. Slade's premonition of failure had somehow
infected the rest of his team.

He stared down at the heart, watching each pulsation as
the red muscle, crisscrossed by arteries and blue veins,
continued to contract then expand, contract then expand . . .
contract . . . then expand . . . contract . . . then expand.
Slowly. Then even more slowly.

Slade faced a critical decision now. Should he put the
patient back on bypass, which was not without some risk, or
resort to drug therapy? He held out his hand and demanded,
"Epinephrine!"

"Yes, Doctor," the scrub nurse replied, starting to fill a
hypodermic.

"Find McCandless. Get him up here!" Slade ordered.

At once an assisting nurse started to the wall phone.

The scrub nurse passed the hypodermic to Slade, who
injected the drug into an exposed artery. After some moments,
the infusion appeared to take effect. The heart picked up its
pace and assumed a more steady rhythm. Still Slade was not
reassured. He watched, and as he feared, the heart began to
dwindle again. He reached his surgically gloved hand into the
chest cavity, under the heart, and began to assist it with his
own rhythmic pumping. The heart felt spongy to his hand, not
as robust as this muscle should feel. A healthy heart from a
twenty-two-year-old donor should have more tone, be more
vigorous.

Where the hell is McCandless?

Lean, dark-haired and lanky, Cardiologist Allen McCandless
was described by some people as Lincolnesque because he
gave the impression of being a dour man when, as at this
moment, he was puzzled and thoughtful. Actually, most times
he gave the impression of being a pleasant and optimistic man.
He had to, to deal with the many potentially terminal patients
he treated as Chief of the Transplant Unit of the University
Medical Center.

At the moment, he sat across the desk from Harvey

Strawbridge, Hospital Administrator. Strawbridge, ruddy-faced, sporting a very neat white mustache, prided himself on being in command of one of the most talented cardiac staffs in the nation. Though the Medical Center was not located in New York or Stanford, Pittsburgh or Boston, he still took great satisfaction in the fact that it deserved to be ranked with the finest medical institutions in any of those larger cities. One day, Strawbridge felt confident, that would be acknowledged.

What Strawbridge had just revealed to Allen McCandless caused the puzzled cardiologist to respond, "If this mysterious patient really needs a transplant, there are centers a lot closer to Washington, D.C., than we are."

"Exactly the point, Mac," Strawbridge pointed out, his florid face lighting up with a faint provocative smile.

"Doesn't make sense," McCandless said. "If the patient lives in the Washington area, works in Washington, why send him a thousand miles here to the Midwest for a heart transplant? He's going to need family and emotional support while waiting for his new heart and afterward. All patients do."

Strawbridge leaned closer across his desk, as grave as if about to impart an important national defense secret. When he chose, Strawbridge could become a man of dramatic presence. A polished, adept executive, he had a deliberately subtle way of exercising his power so that he could never be accused of being either ruthless or manipulative. But it was understood by all who worked with him that, in the long run, it was usually the better part of wisdom to accede to his requests.

"Mac," Strawbridge began, as if welcoming the cardiologist into a conspiracy, "when the White House calls—"

"The White House," McCandless repeated, surprised.

"Yes, Mac, the White House," Strawbridge continued. "When they call and say they want this man transplanted here, to protect him from the snooping, prying, overactive, overcurious news media that invade the capital like locusts, it's not my job to question."

"But, for the patient's own welfare, there are non-medical factors that must be considered," McCandless pointed out. "Factors vital in every heart transplant. Patient attitude, family situation, habits . . ."

"I explained all that to the White House. They told me his wife will be coming with him and will remain here throughout the procedure," Strawbridge said. His usually tanned face, with its bristly white mustache, seemed to grow ruddier as his frustration grew, due to this resistance from his chief cardiologist.

Prima donnas, Strawbridge thought, *I have assembled a collection of medical prima donnas. I expect temperament from heart surgeons, it goes with the speciality. But when cardiologists start fighting me . . .*

"You doctors are all alike! You come to me asking for money for ingenious expensive protocols for research or experimentation. As when you and Slade decided we should abandon our bubbler-type oxygenator for the new and more expensive membrane type—"

McCandless interrupted, "The membrane type is safer and more efficient."

"I'm not saying it isn't! All I'm saying is, things like that cost money. And where do I get most of that money? Government. Yet when it comes to cooperating with the government, you have nothing but questions, questions, questions! If not outright obstruction."

Lean, wiry, looking older than his forty-one years due to the slight steaks of gray in his dark hair, Allen McCandless was too concerned with his other thoughts to refute the Administrator's charges.

"Richmond," McCandless said. "What about Richmond?"

"Richmond?" Strawbridge responded impatiently, resenting what he took to be a deliberate distraction.

"Richmond. UNOS. The United Network for Organ Sharing. The heart would have to be cleared through them," McCandless said.

"I'm well aware of that!" Strawbridge replied with considerable annoyance.

"I just hope Washington doesn't ask us to take any 'shortcuts,' if you know what I mean," McCandless said.

"I know what you mean," Strawbridge snapped. "I'm sure no one is going to tamper with your cherished ethics."

McCandless was about to respond angrily to the Administrator's sarcasm when the phone on Strawbridge's desk interrupted.

"Damn!" Strawbridge said, then spoke into the phone. "Miss Costain, when I say no calls, I mean no calls at all! Dr. McCandless and I are conferring on a matter of great importance to this institution . . . " But a few words from his secretary changed his attitude at once. More softly, he said, "Of course. In that case you were right." He handed the phone to McCandless.

"McCandless here. What is it? Oh. Of course. O.R. Seven? Be right up." He hung up the phone. "Slade's having trouble with a balky heart. Got to go!"

There was no need to await Strawbridge's response. Both men knew that in the usual routine heart-transplant procedure there was no need for a cardiologist in the operating room. But when the new heart failed, or when it refused to respond correctly, then the special knowledge of the cardiologist was vital and his presence was mandatory.

As McCandless was going out the door, he heard the Administrator call after him, "Washington is insistent. Call me the moment you're free!"

Now attired in surgical greens, Allen McCandless entered O.R. 7 hurriedly and went straight to Slade's side at the operating table. Angstrom was busy repairing two sutures that had begun to seep slight traces of blood. Slade himself was concentrating on the action of the erratic heart.

As McCandless leaned over the patient's open chest to

study the implanted heart, he asked, "What's happened so far?"

"Started well enough. Then became lazy. I performed some hand massage. Then shot some epinephrine. As you can see, not with any encouraging effect."

McCandless studied the erratic action of the heart as it struggled to attain a regular rhythm.

"Adrenaline and nitroprusside," McCandless ordered.

"If epinephrine didn't work—" Slade started to say.

"Try it and see," McCandless said. "If that doesn't work, we may not have any choice but to go back on bypass."

"Adrenaline, nitro," Slade demanded of the scrub nurse.

From the wide array of drugs that were always in readiness for just such cardiac emergencies during the transplant procedure, the nurse selected and prepared the hypo of nitroprusside and adrenaline, passed it to Slade. He inserted the needle into the failing heart and injected the fluid.

The heart picked up in strength and pumping action. Both doctors watched it for many minutes until it began to flag once more. Reluctantly, Slade ordered, "Let's go back on bypass!"

The cannulas that had been inserted into the patient's vena cava and his aorta to permit the blood from the heart-lung machine to bypass the heart were still in place. Slade opened the clamps, once again permitting the blood from the machine to flow into the cannulas and through the rest of the arterial system, bringing life-sustaining oxygen to all the other organs. Thus, the laboring heart was now temporarily relieved of the burden of pumping.

While the heart was at rest and, McCandless and Slade hoped, regaining its ability to pump effectively, the surgeon and the cardiologist caught up with events relating to other cases.

"Examined that patient—what's her name—that young pretty woman . . ." Slade said.

"The postpartum cardiomyopathy," McCandless reminded him—reverting, as physicians often do, to identifying the patient by her disease. Then he recalled, "Brock . . . Sally Brock."

"Right," Slade said. "She's going to be a tough fit. Small chest cavity. We don't often get a heart that small."

"Want to bet that they buried a hundred healthy hearts exactly that size in this country this week alone?" McCandless replied.

"Don't get me started on that," Slade said, staring down at the new heart, which, relieved of its burden, appeared to be recovering, and resuming a more normal beat. It was encouraging, but both doctors knew that much more evidence of normalcy was required before taking the patient off bypass a second time.

"I heard they located you in good old Strawbridge's office."

"Yes," McCandless admitted, as he considered what the next step might be if this heart failed to take up its function when it came off bypass again.

"What now?" Slade asked sarcastically. "Does he have some suggestions about how to put transplants on a profit-making basis?"

"Damn near," McCandless replied. "We are going to be receiving a VIP."

"What kind of VIP?"

"A Washington-type VIP."

"Here?" was all that Slade said.

"Here. They want to keep the patient away from the hordes of media people in the capital. They figure, out of sight, out of mind."

"How high up a VIP, did Harve say?"

"Never said. But he did indicate it could have a powerful effect on getting research money. So whoever it is, must be very important," McCandless observed.

While they talked, both men kept their eyes fixed on the heart which was pulsing more convincingly.

"Think we should risk taking him off bypass now?" Slade asked.

'Let's give it a little more rest first.''

Half an hour later, which was seven hours and fifty-three minutes since the first incision had been made in the patient's chest, McCandless said, "Okay. Let's start taking him off."

Slade looked in the direction of the two perfusionists at the heart-lung machine. He nodded. It was the signal for them to begin weaning the patient off the machine by gradually cutting down the blood flow from four liters to three.

When Slade was satisfied with the heart action at three liters, he signaled once more to reduce it down to two liters.

McCandless and Slade studied the action of the heart to see if this time it was assuming its function more strongly than before. It seemed to be.

But the ultimate test would be how it functioned once it was completely on its own. They would know that soon enough. From three liters they had cut the flow down to two. And now, slowly, they cut it down to one liter of blood flow. The heart continued to perform well.

"Okay, let's take him off altogether," Slade said.

The perfusionist complied with his order. Soon there was no blood flowing from the machine through the transparent plastic tubes into the patient's body. The burden now rested solely and totally on the new heart.

Both McCandless and Slade, and Angstrom from across the table, as well as the entire transplant team, watched, aware that the option of going back on bypass again was too risky. This heart had better resume its normal function, because the conceivable alternatives were few and not particularly promising. A mechanical heart. Or another transplant, with only the rarest of chances that another heart might be available on such short notice. And this patient had been open for almost eight hours now.

At first their fears seemed groundless. The heart was pink, healthy and beat with force and regular rhythm. But

Slade and McCandless had been through more than a hundred such transplant procedures, and while not discouraged, they remained extremely cautious. They were intent on watching that heart until the last vestige of doubt was removed.

One of the team nurses brought Slade a glass of orange juice. Without diverting his gaze from the heart, he sipped the juice through the glass straw she had slipped up under his surgical mask. To surgeons who performed surgery that extended over many many hours, orange juice was like blood transfusions.

By now the heart had begun to slow somewhat. It appeared to grow lazy, almost arrhythmic. Slade reached in, slipped his hand under it and began to assist it in its pumping action.

While he did so, McCandless could not resist thinking, *Transplant surgeons are an aggressive, impulsive clan. Faced with crisis or uncertainty, they go for action. Why can't they be just a bit slower and more contemplative, like cardiologists?* Which caused him to wonder, *Is it possible that each speciality in this complicated business of heart transplantation has its own sense of pride? Do each of us believe that our own speciality is the crucial one, as well as the one temperamentally best-suited to this new medical art, so intimately and immediately responsible for life and death?*

Slade had withdrawn his gloved hand from the chest cavity and watched to see if his intervention had assisted the heart to achieve a more regular function. It had become even weaker.

"Let's go for dopamine," McCandless urged.

The nurse was ready with a hypo, which she passed to Slade. He injected it directly into the heart.

By now the atmosphere in the operating room was becoming heavy with that sense of defeat that usually precedes final admission that surgery has failed. The perfusionists stood at their highly technical, intricate mechanism which for all practical purposes was now useless, since it was too risky to go back on bypass. The anesthetists kept watching their monitors and carefully, very carefully, maintaining the patient on the anesthetic. The various nurses performed their appointed duties, but without their previous degree of confidence. There was no one in that operating room who had not seen at least one patient die on the table because a new heart failed to perform as it should.

But McCandless and Slade persevered, watching, assessing the action of the heart, while racking their brains for the next step, if one was recquired.

"Go for a balloon assist?" Slade suggested.

Because it involved a complicated procedure, McCandless resisted the idea. It would have meant inserting a balloon-tipped catheter into the patient's jugular vein, threading it down into the heart and then inflating the balloon in rhythm with the heart. Thus assisting the heart in its function and aiding it to gain strength.

It might yet come to that, McCandless realized, *but there are still some steps to take first.*

"Let's try another shot of dopamine."

The injection was administered. McCandless and Slade watched. The whole crew watched. All waiting, and silently urging the heart to act like a heart, damn it!

The initial response to the dopamine was encouraging. But they had been optimistic before. It was now a matter of wait and see. And hope, a little, too.

Strange, McCandless thought, *how this entire procedure can be carried out with utmost skill, and Slade is one of the most skillful. But all that doesn't mean a thing if that heart refuses to perform. The time and talent of so many specialists, the cost, which runs into the hundreds of thousands, all is of no avail if that handful of complicated human tissue and muscle does not assume the function for which it has been created.*

All eyes were fixed on the heart as it contracted, received fresh blood, then expanded as it pumped that blood through the rest of the body.

McCandless felt himself pumping with it, as if to encourage and assist it. He thought, but was suspicious of his own observation, that the pumping action was growing stronger. He exchanged glances with Slade. Their eyes, which peered out above their surgical masks, met and seemed to agree. Both physicians had reached the same conclusion. This heart was finally responding, thank God.

It would bear more watching before anyone could assume it would continue to gain in strength and regularity.

After more than half an hour of continuous observation, Slade finally said, "Okay. Let's close."

Since Slade was exhausted, Angstrom took over the job of suturing up the pericardium, the sac that envelops and protects the heart. He then proceeded to close the chest cavity and suture up the long vertical incision that Slade had made nine and a half hours ago, when surgery had begun.

Two hours later, Patient Malcolm Peters, age forty-four, with a new heart beating vigorously in his chest, was removed to Cardiac Post Operative Recovery.

Surgeon Chris Slade sat on the bench in front of his locker, too exhausted even to remove his green surgical gown and pants. He breathed slowly and deeply, trying to resolve the tense knot of pain that always afflicted his left shoulder after intensive, stressful surgery, particularly when a new heart proved dangerously balky and uncooperative.

Allen McCandless had shed his O.R. greens and was wearing his shirt, tying his tie, when he asked, "Chris, free for dinner?"

"Sorry. Got to go home. Claudia's birthday. I'll be late. But as they say, better late than never."

The silence that followed remarked on the difference in status between men with familial obligations and those who, for one reason or another, were loners.

"Just as well," McCandless said. "I have early hours tomorrow. Some new admissions—if they qualify."

"Like your VIP from Washington?" Slade asked, starting to button his shirt.

"Strawbridge's VIP," McCandless corrected, then

smiled. "Wouldn't that be something? If, whoever he is, he doesn't qualify for the program and we have to turn him down?"

"What do you think old Harve would say?" Slade asked.

McCandless laughed. "He'd probably say, give him a new heart anyhow. Like chicken soup, can't do him any harm."

Minutes later, Allen McCandless, lonely and with no one depending on him, and Chris Slade, with his daughter and his wife waiting for him at home, both met at the bedside of Patient Malcolm Peters. While they checked him out, reviewed his chart, watched the screen of the oscilloscope to follow his heart action, McCandless said, "Thought you said you have to get home."

"I do."

"Well, get going. And give my love to Claudia and Anita."

Slade would not leave until he was satisfied with the patient's vital signs and condition.

"Chris, get going!" McCandless said.

"Yeah. Sure."

As he started for the door, McCandless called, "Chris, you should have told me it was Claudia's birthday. I would have sent her something."

"That's okay. If I know Anita, Claudia's got more gifts than any eight-year-old is entitled to. See you in the morning."

McCandless resumed observing the patient. Until he realized, *This patient no longer needs my attention. He's doing okay. I am simply hanging around because there's no other place I have to go. Or want to go. How long does it take a man to become accustomed to having dinner alone again?*

2

... since it is my considered opinion that the
patient is cardiac functional Class IV (NYHA)
and has a poor six months prognosis for survival
I present him to your transplant unit for your
consideration.   Benjamin Kaplan, M.D.

Dr. Allen McCandless studied the familiar plea, much
like those he received only too often. Since University
Medical Center was the only hospital in that part of the
country authorized by the state to perform heart transplants,
such pleas came to him from cardiologists and internists who
practiced in cities and towns within a radius of hundreds of
miles, and sometimes even farther away. The only difference
in this case was that the request was signed by Ben Kaplan, an
old physician whom McCandless knew and respected. Perhaps
because Ben reminded him of his own father. Ben had phoned
him about this case only a week ago.

McCandless picked up the voluminous file that Kaplan
had sent along with his request. He flipped through it, seeking
those lab and test reports most crucial to his determination.

X rays. By merely holding them up to the light of his
desk lamp, he could see the enlargement of the heart. He
scanned the results of blood tests, which revealed the effects of
the faulty heart on the patient's other organs. Not too grave,

fortunately. All in all, the file confirmed Kaplan's original diagnosis: Ideopathic cardiomyopathy.

Meaning, fancy medical language for heart disease of unknown origin, McCandless observed silently, *and we wish to hell we knew the cause so maybe one day we could find a cure and not have to depend on heart transplants.*

He picked up the patient's cineangiogram and threaded it into the projector on the rolling table alongside his desk. He ran it through once, studying the actual action of the heart as revealed by the film. Then he ran it through a second time. He had seen sufficient medical evidence to interest him in this proposed candidate.

He turned back to the file to find the patient's Social Information Form.

> *Name: Campbell, James*
> *Address: 1615 Oak Street, Redmont*

McCandless glanced down the page past PERSON TO NOTIFY IN EMERGENCY, RELATIONSHIP. FIRST NAME OF FATHER, FIRST NAME OF MOTHER, EVEN IF BOTH DECEASED.

His eyes stopped when they reached:

> *Date of Birth: Nov. 25, 1956*
> *Age: Thirty-two*
> *Status: Married. Two children*

His mind supplied the very sobering conclusion, Campbell had six months to live unless he received, and could accept, a compatible heart from some unknown donor, now alive and unsuspecting of the fate that would accidentally overtake him in the next few months.

He did not even dwell on the other possibilities that confronted potential candidate Campbell, James. Rejection. Infection. Pneumonia. These were only a few of the dangers to which a suppressed immune system exposed the patient. If he were lucky enough to receive a new heart.

McCandless resumed his study of the file, his lean face intense, his gray eyes narrowing slightly. He insisted this was due to his sensitivity to light, but his ophthalmologist kept urging that he really should begin to wear reading glasses.

He discovered that Patient Campbell, James had a son of eleven, named James Campbell, Junior, and a daughter of nine, Dorothy.

The phone rang. That was against McCandless's orders when he was involved in making a determination as to whether the Transplant Unit could take on another proposed candidate.

With considerable annoyance, he answered, "Claire, how many times have I told you that unless it involves some medical emergency in the O.R. or ICU I do not want to be interrupted—" Before he completed the word "interrupted," he indeed was, causing him to ask, "Did you say the White House?"

"Yes, Doctor," Claire Fielding responded.

"Well, in that case, sorry I was so abrupt. Put him on."

After a moment, instead of the official male voice he had expected, he heard a feminine voice, which, though quite subdued, spoke with considerable authority.

"Doctor, this is Katherine Breed. I am calling on behalf of the President. First, I must caution you that this matter is to be treated with extreme confidentiality. Surely until you come to some decision."

"Yes, I understand. Mr. Strawbridge told me—"

Backed by White House clout, Katherine Breed did not brook interruptions or questions. She was determined to tell her story her way. McCandless could envision her now, tall, dark-haired, imposing. Wagnerian in size and stature. Yet there was a hint of sexuality in her voice.

Ms. Breed continued, "I know that you have not yet been told who your patient is to be. We deliberately withheld his identity from Mr. Strawbridge. No sense leaking a prominent name unless we were sure he would be accepted into your program."

"Before I can do that, I need a great deal of medical

information. Age. History. Condition. So if you will just tell me—"

Again Ms. Breed interrupted briskly, "I suppose I must. But this is highly confidential. The name is highly confidential. The name Winston Forrest, is it familiar to you?"

"Of course," McCandless replied. "Undersecretary of State."

"He was Undersecretary of State for Middle Eastern Affairs until the President appointed him his National Security Adviser," Ms. Breed informed him. "Need I tell you how important he is to the President and the nation?"

"Didn't I read somewhere that he had had a slight heart attack some months ago?" McCandless recalled.

"Heart attack? Yes. Slight? Only for publicity purposes," the woman replied in her crisp fashion. "The cardiologists at Bethesda say that his heart has been so damaged that unless he receives a transplant he must be considered terminal."

"And you want *us* to take on his case?"

"The feeling here is that it would be better for all concerned if this were done away from the Washington area. The overwhelming presence of the media here, the intrusive reporters, print and electronic, might create too much stress and endanger his life. The President feels that Mr. Forrest's treatment and recovery requires privacy, and his importance to the country demands it."

"I understand," McCandless said. "Send me his file, his complete medical history, CBC's, cineangiogram—"

Breed interrupted to ask, "CBC's? Cineangiograms?"

"Complete Blood Count. And a cineangiogram. An actual film of his heart at work. His doctors will know. Also his X rays, scans, everything."

"Suppose we do better than that, Doctor. We'll fly the patient in. Test him any way you wish. But do it yourself. No associates. No residents. No other physicians. Just *you!*"

A mixture of curiosity and resentment at being given such circumscribing instructions compelled McCandless to ask, "If you don't mind, of all the cardiologists in this part of the country, why me?''

"The White House physician went to medical school with you. Admiral Crider?''

"Of course. Fritz Crider. We shared a cadaver in our first year,'' McCandless recalled. "But that was a long time ago.''

"Evidently the admiral has followed your work in heart transplantation closely. He has the highest regard for you.''

"Well, that's nice to know,'' McCandless said. "When can we expect Mr. Forrest?''

"I wish to stress once more, Doctor, not 'we.' 'You.' The request from the Oval Office is that you personally handle this case in all its aspects, and that you do so on a highly confidential basis. Bearing in mind at all times how important to the nation this man is.''

"I understand,'' McCandless said, thinking, *In discussing this case I must make sure never to use plural pronouns or inclusive terms. No more "we" or "the team" or "the unit." Just "I," "me" and "my." Don't they realize that a transplant, particularly a heart transplant, can't succeed without a whole team involving cardiologists, surgeons, anesthetists, perfusionists, a transplant coordinator, psychiatrists, even dentists, a social service worker and a host of highly trained transplant nurses?*

But why take the time to explain? he consoled himself. *If Forrest doesn't qualify for transplant, all explanations become unnecessary.*

He rephrased the question. "How soon can I expect Mr. Forrest?''

"He will be flown out in an Air Force jet tomorrow,'' Ms. Breed informed him. "Of course, his medical history and all test results will accompany him.''

"Good,'' McCandless said. He was about to hang up when he could no longer resist asking, "Tell me, Ms. Breed, if it's not classified information, are you five feet eleven, black-haired, statuesque, and when you're not in the White

House, do you pump iron? Say, two hundred pounds or more?''

There was a moment of frosty silence before Ms. Breed replied in a much more relaxed and confidential tone, "For your information, Dr. McCandless, I am five feet three, blond, and damned good-looking. And I didn't always used to talk this way. It's amazing what being so close to the Oval Office can do for the ego.''

Intrigued and amused, Allen McCandless said, "I know you're not likely to get out this way. But I do get to Washington for an occasional seminar. If I called you, would you mind?''

"I wouldn't mind," Ms. Breed responded, "but my husband might."

"Yes, I can see how he might. Well, we . . . I mean I look forward to seeing Mr. Forrest tomorrow.''

He hung up.

Damn, he thought, *there was a woman I would have liked to know better. She sounded so interesting. Maybe my approach was too direct, too abrupt. Since Maggie left I've never quite recaptured the hang of it. I better practice. I feel more awkward now than when I was a freshman in college.*

The divorce . . . why did it have to happen? Maggie never did become accustomed to a doctor's lifestyle. And the demands on my time. But I must have failed in some other way. Some more personal way.

My dad. There was a doctor. A real old-time family physician. He was on call all hours of day and night, in all kinds of weather. Yet Mom hung in there, loyal to the very end, the day he died in his old car, from a heart attack, on his way to making a house call. Why was it so different with Maggie and me? Were those different times? Or different people?

To avoid thinking about the answers, he turned back to the file on Campbell, James, never suspecting any connection between this case and the case he had just agreed to consider by special request of the President of the United States.

He was studying the more relevant facts of potential transplant patient Campbell.

Surgical history: None
Asthma: None
Tuberculosis: None
Pneumonia: One previous episode
Last CXR results . . .

But Maggie's words kept intruding on his concentration.

"Allen, if I ever need a doctor, there's no one else in the world I'd go to. But as a husband, sorry, darling. You never quite made it. Just remembering every so often to send flowers to make up for some disappointment, or having Claire pick out some gift for me, even an expensive one, does not make up for the times I needed you and you weren't there. Especially during the miscarriage. I never felt so alone in all my life. I needed someone to cry with me. You weren't there. That was when it all became clear to me. I would always run second to your patients. You only have time for the sick. Well, I have too much to share, too much to give. I can't see myself living through a whole marriage so I can wind up a well-to-do widow taking world cruises, but still alone."

He forced himself to concentrate on the Campbell file.

History of Heart Murmur: Yes
History of Heart Gallop: No
History of Myocardial Infarction: No
History of Hypertension: Yes
History of Arrythmias: Yes
Hospital Admissions for Congestive Heart Fail-
ure: No

Patient James Campbell proved to be a man with strong, raw features that belied his fragile condition. His pale face and bluish lips were more accurate indicators of the weakened flabby heart muscle which could no longer pump sufficient blood to keep his large body functioning normally.

Alongside Campbell sat his wife Nancy. Despite her effort to appear calm and confident in Dr. McCandless's presence, her nervous hands and the tightness around her lips betrayed her highly emotional state. She was a slight young woman, brown-haired, pleasant-appearing, with intense brown eyes that bespoke not only her fear but her love for her young husband.

Aware of her anxiety, Allen McCandless decided to start his explanation on the most hopeful note. He smiled. Only a modest smile. It would be neither honest nor fair to project undue optimism.

"No matter what you've heard on the radio or seen on television, a heart transplant is no longer an unusual operation. So you're not going to be besieged by cameras and microphones when you enter the hospital or come out. You will just be one of the thousand men and women in this country who get new hearts every year."

"A thousand . . ." The words escaped the lips of a surprised Nancy Campbell.

"In fact, Mrs. Campbell, more than a thousand," McCandless said. "So I guess you could say that by now we know what we're doing."

"But, what if—" She leaned forward to ask.

McCandless anticipated her. "What if no heart turns up for Jim?"

"Yes," she admitted her fear, glancing at her husband to see if he disapproved of her being so aggressive.

Campbell said only, "Honey, give the doctor a chance."

"Sorry," she said softly.

Why do patients always feel that by asking questions they risk antagonizing the doctor? McCandless wondered. *And if they did antagonize him, what did they fear? That he might withhold his best efforts from them? This man is fighting for his life. His wife is fighting for the same thing. Yet they feel too timid, too afraid to ask.*

"About the matter of hearts turning up," McCandless resumed. "There are never enough, but somehow we manage in the majority of cases. It seems to work out."

"How long will we have to wait?" Campbell asked.

Interesting, McCandless observed. *Not, "how long will I have to wait?" But, "How long will we have to wait?" The whole family pulling together. That's good. Very good.*

"I can't predict how long before we get a heart that is your blood type and the proper size. It might happen next week. It may not happen for months. Some patients have had to wait as long as a year. You must remember that you will be only one patient on a list of more than thirty candidates here who are waiting for new hearts. Fortunately they are not all waiting for the same heart. Their blood types vary. Their weights and sizes vary. Their ages vary. Some candidates are as young as twelve. Some as old as sixty."

"A waiting list . . ." Nancy Campbell remarked. "Our own doctor said—"

"I know," McCandless replied. "I've read Dr. Kaplan's forwarding report. I've seen your husband's X rays, his test results. There has been some kidney and liver damage due to diminished circulation. Fortunately, not too much damage. So he has time to wait it out. However, if his condition becomes worse, that would make him an emergency. We'll admit him to the hospital. That would also move him up on the list. Quite a bit up on the list."

"Then it would become a race against time?" Nancy Campbell asked softly.

"Let's not make it sound so melodramatic," McCandless cautioned, smiling to put her at ease.

She apologized sheepishly, "I read that somewhere."

"You've been doing quite a lot of reading about heart transplants, haven't you?"

She nodded, glancing at her husband self-consciously.

"Nancy's quite a reader," Campbell said. "Magazines, books. She's up on things."

"Well," McCandless said, "Maybe we better *un*educate

her about certain things." He turned to her. "Mrs. Campbell
. . . may I call you Nancy? Or Nan?"

"Yes. Please," she responded.

"Nan, everyone who is part of this unit is expert at what
he or she is supposed to do. We have selected them like a
jeweler selects each gem to make a perfect piece of jewelry.
Should the time come when it is a race against the clock, Jim
will be in cool hands, steady hands. People who know what
they are doing."

He paused before continuing, then said, "Of course, I
can't say that the procedure always works perfectly. From
time to time we do lose a patient. But rarely."

"Exactly what *are* Jim's chances?" she blurted out.

"In the usual run of these things, he should get a healthy
heart and it should work well. But there are no ironclad
guarantees. Now, I think you ought to see Dr. Robbins. He's
the psychiatrist for the Transplant Unit."

"Psychiatrist?" Nancy Campbell asked, startled.

"Yes," McCandless said. "Before we risk a new heart
on a patient, we want to make sure he's the type who'll take
good care of it. Adeline—Miss Sawyer, the Transplant
Coordinator—will introduce you."

They started for the door. McCandless felt compelled to
remind them, "If Jim's condition deteriorates, we may have to
admit him to the hospital on a more permanent basis."

"Yes, yes, we know," Nancy Campbell said.

"Meantime, how far from the hospital is Redmont?"

"Eighteen miles," Campbell said.

"Driving time?"

"In rush-hour traffic, forty-five, fifty minutes. Otherwise
thirty, thirty-five."

"Good," McCandless said.

"Why did you ask?" Nancy Campbell wanted to know.

"Should word come that there is a heart for Jim, we have
to know how long it would take for you to get here."

"Look, Doctor, if it would help, he could stay in the

hospital right now. I mean, we could get a second mortgage on the house and the business.''

"No need for such steps at the moment," McCandless tried to reassure.

Though, familiar with all the facts of Campbell's condition, his deteriorating heart, McCandless knew hospitalizing Jim Campbell was a possibility he must bear in mind.

They were gone.

Allen McCandless sat back in his chair and reached for the next file he must evaluate. He tried to concentrate on it, but could not. The desperate look on that young woman's face, the way she leaned toward her husband, as if she were trying to breathe for him. It was more than the fear of losing the mainstay of her family. It was love, unselfish love. The kind of love that Maggie had tried to lavish on him, and which, under the pressure of his profession, he had treated as a burden.

Even their breakup was due to an unselfish action on her part. It was *his* sister who had called to invite them to the graduation party for *his* nephew. Maggie had accepted, feeling sure that he would want to attend. But late afternoon of the day of that party a donor heart became available suddenly. He could not risk being too far from the hospital in the event the new heart failed to function and they needed him urgently.

"Damn it, Maggie, how many times have I told you, never make any promises. Just say we'll come if we can."

"But it's your sister, your nephew," Maggie had tried to explain. "And we haven't seen them in months—"

He had never given her the chance. "That's no excuse! Families are supposed to understand such things! And if they don't, that's just too damn bad!"

Recently, during the lonely nights, he had relived that scene many times. Always he came to the same unhappy realization. *Why was it that he, who was so tolerant and understanding of patients, could have been so intolerant of his wife? There was something much stronger between Jim and*

Nan Campbell than there had been between him and Maggie. And it was not Maggie's fault, but his own.

He examined Campbell's file once more. The young man was a landscape artist and a tree surgeon. Good physical outdoor work. Which he was no longer able to do with any degree of safety. The physical demands were too great. While twenty or thirty feet up on some tree, he might pass out from lack of oxygen due to poor circulation. He could fall to his death.

For all practical purposes, Jim Campbell was out of business at a time when his financial needs would be greatest. McCandless flipped through the other papers in the Campbell file. He found evidence of some health insurance. There would be barely enough to see him through the operation, if that time came.

But what about his family and their needs? Allen Mc-Candless wondered. *What about the six thousand dollars each year for medication for the rest of his life? God, how do people manage in these times? It is tough enough to make ends meet when things are normal. But in times of prolonged emergencies . . .*

McCandless had to remind himself that he was a cardiologist, not a social service worker. First things first. He would have Patient Campbell brought into the hospital for a few days of evaluation. If his condition proved to be in the range between desperately needing a new heart and not so desperate that it would be wasting a good heart to give it to him, then all the other problems such as finances could be considered.

He would notify Ben Kaplan that he considered Campbell a potential transplant candidate, and have him advise Campbell to present himself here at the Medical Center for several days of evaluation.

3

AT MUNICIPAL AIRPORT the ambulance was cleared to drive out onto the tarmac. Airport security accompanied the vehicle to a far corner of the field.

When the ambulance came to a stop, the door on the passenger side opened and Harvey Strawbridge stepped out. In his trench coat, with its collar up, he looked more a military figure than a hospital administrator. He stood beside the ambulance eyeing the sky for the Air Force plane he was expecting.

Soon one of the uniformed security men, who had a handheld radio transmitter-receiver pressed to his ear, informed him, "They're making their approach from the northwest, sir."

Moments later a distant plane appeared. Strawbridge followed its approach and descent until it touched down. He watched it taxi along the runway, eventually turning off onto the strip, heading toward the ambulance. The roar of its jet engines was deafening, until the pilot cut the power. The plane braked to a gentle stop.

By the time the hatch had opened and the automatic steps unfolded to reach the ground, Strawbridge was waiting at the foot of the stairs. The first passenger to emerge was a tall, graceful woman, with a handsome face and ash-blond hair. Behind her was an even taller man. His face was thin from

obvious illness, his cheeks sunken, his lips a thin pale line.
Yet he carried himself with the dignity and bearing of a man
of importance.

Before either of them reached the tarmac, Strawbridge
greeted them, "Mrs. Forrest, Mr. Forrest, welcome. I've got
an ambulance standing by . . ." He turned to gesture impatiently to the driver to pull the vehicle up to the stairs.

Strawbridge extended his arm to shake hands with Mrs.
Forrest. She stared a him for an instant before complying.
When he held out his hand to Forrest, the man said, "Hell, I
don't need an ambulance! Why can't we use a taxi?"

Taken aback for a moment, Strawbridge recovered to
say, "We thought it was advisable. The medical men did."

"I'm not that sick," Forrest grumbled. "However . . ."
Shrugging off his wife's attempt to assist him, he started
toward the back of the ambulance.

While Forrest got in, Strawbridge asked Mrs. Forrest,
"You did bring his entire medical history, didn't you?"

"Yes, of course."

"Good. Then let's go."

She reached to tug at Strawbridge's sleeve.

"Winston does not like to be treated as an invalid," she
warned softly.

At the time the ambulance bearing Winston Forrest and his
wife was pulling swiftly out of the airport, James Campbell
and his wife Nan were starting down the corridor of the
Cardiac Wing of the hospital, following the efficient nurse
who led the way.

Both Campbell and his wife were aware of patients in
robes and pajamas who walked slowly up and down the
corridor with no apparent destination in mind. Some wore
surgical masks.

Just getting exercise, Jim Campbell assumed. *Do they
have their new hearts already, or are they only waiting . . .
hoping?*

He became aware suddenly, and self-consciously, that

his wife was carrying the small suitcase they had been told to bring. He was tall, over six feet, and big-boned. He looked healthy, having strived to get a good suntan in order to present his best appearance. Yet here was Nan, not quite five feet four and slender, carrying his suitcase for him. He tried to take it from her. She resisted, holding it more tightly. When he persisted, she grasped it with both hands, holding it against her body. He was not strong enough to wrest it from her.

A nurse was waiting to greet them outside Room 609.

"Mr. Campbell, there will be technicians in from time to time to take blood samples and other specimens."

Jim Campbell stood at the door, staring into the room. It seemed a pleasant place, not as institutional as he had expected. There was a hospital bed, of course. But the window draperies were colorful, and the walls were not the usual flat hospital white. Beyond the wide window was open countryside with tall buildings in the distance, quite similar, in fact, to the view from their own home. There was a television set, up high so that it could be viewed comfortably from the bed. A small armchair and a side table and lamp filled one corner of the room. Alongside the bed was a night table with a phone. On closer inspection the night table turned out to house a small refrigerator. Set in the wall behind the bed was a bank of instruments which made it possible to feed oxygen and other essentials needed in an emergency.

"Jim . . ." His young wife urged him to enter.

He stepped over the threshold. She followed. She placed the suitcase on the bed, started to unpack the essentials. Robe, pajamas, shaving equipment, then suddenly she stopped and said, "Good heavens, what's this?"

"Hon?" he asked, turning to discover that she had a small envelope in hand. "What's it say?"

"It's in Jimmy's handwriting. And it says, Dear Doctor."

"Let me see that," Jim Campbell said. She handed it to him. He opened it so hastily that he tore the envelope. Then he started to read, " 'Dear Doctor, Mom and Dad didn't tell us your name. But they said you are a very nice man. And a very good doctor. So please do your best for our dad. Because we love him so much. James Campbell, Junior. Dorothy.' '' To which Jimmy had appended, "She's my kid sister."

Campbell's eyes teared up and he said, "Those kids. God! What will we do with it?"

"Give it to the doctor, of course," Nancy said, smiling, and continued unpacking toothbrush, toothpaste, bedroom slippers, vitamin pills. Dr. Kaplan had advised that any other medication would be prescribed for him here at the Medical Center.

Jim moved to the window, looking out at the landscape. He spotted some trees that could stand pruning. Also a stand of dead cedars that should be cut down. A good week's work all in all.

"Jim . . ."

He turned from the window to discover that Nancy had unpacked and put away his things.

"What do I do now?" he asked. "Get into pajamas?"

"I don't know. Just wait, I guess," she said, thinking, *I've never seen him like this before. He usually knows what to do and does it. I've always waited for him to tell me. And now he's lost. God, this is even worse than the day Dr. Kaplan first told us that he had this . . . this cardiomyopathy. . . . I'm scared, because he's scared.*

They both remained standing, feeling awkward. There was only one chair. Finally Jim solved the problem by sitting on the bed. Nancy sank into the chair. Tense, uncomfortable, they stared at each other, silent.

Stop staring at me, she pleaded wordlessly, *else I'm going to cry. I'm scared, darling. Scared. And I can't tell anyone, most of all not you. All night I kept thinking, What's going to happen? To you? To the kids? To me? Jim, I've never been so scared. And I can't tell anyone. I can't even tell you that I went to see Dr. Kaplan yesterday morning after you left for the bank to cash in those bonds.*

He's such a nice old man. He tried to sound encouraging.

He said, "Nan, my dear, the miracles they can do these days were not even thought of when I was in medical school. And those doctors, McCandless, Slade, they're the best. I know them. They are great doctors, fine men. They'll do their best for Jim. He couldn't be in better hands."

But when I asked him, "Ben, will they be able to save Jim?" he couldn't answer. He only repeated, "He couldn't be in better hands." Then he kissed me on the cheek. Kaplan showed me more concern than my own father did when I decided to marry you, Jim. But he couldn't make any promises.

Jim Campbell sat on the side of the bed drumming his fingers against each other. To break the heavy silence, he asked, "What are you thinking, hon?"

"Thinking? Oh, nothing," she said, then added, "Just I hope the kids don't mind being left with Mrs. Noonan for the day."

"She'll cook and bake herself crazy for them. She loves those kids," he reassured her.

They were silent again.

He sat there, pretending to stare out the window but stealing glimpses of her as she sat looking so forlorn in that chair, which, small as it was, seemed too large for her.

She is actually a little girl, he thought. Small, slender. I remember when she was carrying little Jim, I used to think, That bulge is bigger than she is. How is she ever going to deliver a baby that size? I even asked Doc Kaplan to suggest to the obstetrician that he do a cesarean. But old Ben just laughed and said, "Jim, she is the strongest little woman I've ever seen. Don't worry about her." Well, she better be strong from now on. Very strong. I didn't tell her. I didn't know how. But yesterday after I went to the bank to cash in those savings bonds, I stopped by Kaplan's office. I asked him, "Doc, what are my chances? Really? Honestly?"

He said, "Jim, if my own son were in your condition, this is what I would recommend. And McCandless and Slade are the two men I'd entrust him to."

"But my chances, Doc, my chances!" I kept insisting.

He said, *"Jim, percentagewise, very good. They've got a fine record at that hospital. Almost eighty percent of their patients get hearts. Of those who do, more than half live longer than five years. Some a lot longer."*

"But some never get a heart, do they?" I asked.

"Jim, nothing in this life is guaranteed," the old man said. He patted me on the shoulder. I can still feel his hand there. At the end, he couldn't lie to me. He tried to put a good face on things, but he didn't lie. God, I hope she's strong enough now. I hope she really is the strongest little woman.

"Jim . . ."

Startled, he looked across at Nancy. "Yes?"

"What are you thinking?" she asked.

"Oh, I . . . I was just wondering, are heart patients here allowed to watch football on Sunday? Or is it considered too . . . too much for them?"

"Oh, I think football is all right," she said, managing a smile.

Football, he really isn't thinking about football. He's thinking about the kids, about me. God, it makes me want to cry to see him so afraid.

A young technician in a white lab coat, carrying a blood sample tray, knocked on the open door.

In their nervousness, they both called quickly and at once, "Come in."

The young man entered. He was short and slight, and smiled as he said, "I'm only the first. But by the time your evaluation is over, you'll hate us all." Then he added, "I don't mean that. We're a pretty friendly bunch around here. Though I have been accused of being Dracula in a white coat."

He realized that any attempt to lighten the atmosphere in this room would be futile. So he glanced at Nancy, saying, "Ma'am, if you don't mind . . ."

"Oh. Sure. Sorry." She rose at once and started for the door.

"There's a visitor's lounge down the hall," the young technician suggested.

She had almost reached the door when she turned back to Jim suddenly. She embraced him and kissed him. Then she turned to the technician. "Sorry. I hope that doesn't upset anything. I noticed some people wearing masks in the corridor."

"Those are patients who've already had transplants and are taking immunosuppressives. They have to be on guard against colds, infections of any kind. So when they come to the hospital for checkups, since hospitals are filled with sick people, they have to wear masks. It's a matter of protection. Until your husband gets his new heart, he doesn't have to worry about that."

"Until . . ." Nancy Campbell said.

"Most of them do," the technician assured her. "Most of them do."

On that encouraging note, Nancy Campbell went out to the visitor's lounge and was free to cry.

Allen McCandless was reviewing the current list of transplant candidates in the program. Those in hospital, those resident close by, those remaining at home awaiting the beeper summons or the phone call that would bring them racing to the hospital because a new heart had been secured for them.

His eyes moved down the list of thirty-six patients already processed and accepted for transplant. Alongside each name were the vital facts. Blood type. Weight. Priority on the list, determined by immediacy of need.

Allen McCandless was painfully aware that of the thirty-six, five or six would probably die before a suitable heart could be found. That very nice young mother, Mrs. Brock, she could be one of the fatalities. And at the age of only twenty.

His eyes had shifted to a second list which contained names of applicants for the transplant program whose evaluation and acceptance had not yet been completed and acted upon. His phone rang.

"Yes, Claire?"

"Doctor, Mr. Forrest has just arrived."

"Forrest?" For a moment he was puzzled by what was still an unfamiliar name. Then he remembered who Forrest was. "Yes, of course. Show him in."

The strange crisp manner in which Claire responded, "Yes, sir," made him know that she was trying to tell him more.

He soon discovered why. When the door opened, it was Harvey Strawbridge who ushered the Forrests into his office.

"Allen, I would like you to meet Mr. and Mrs. Winston Forrest," Strawbridge announced. "Mr. Forrest, Dr. McCandless, who'll be in personal charge of your case. He's one of the top cardiologists in the country."

"So Admiral Crider told me," Forrest said rather dryly, as if he preferred to make his own appraisal of McCandless.

"Half the hospitals in the East keep trying to steal him away from me." Strawbridge chuckled to lighten the moment. But Forrest's discomfort made him self-conscious enough to withdraw after saying, "Well, now that you've met . . ."

Once the door was closed, McCandless had an opportunity to take a good look at Winston Forrest. He recognized him from newspaper photographs and appearances on television newsreels when some important international event was going on. Some crisis. Or some treaty signing. Forrest was usually second or third from the President.

Because of his heart attack, Forrest appeared older and weaker than his fifty-four years, but he was still an imposing man. A man important enough in his area of expertise to make him vital to the President and the nation.

For medical purposes, as well as courtesy, McCandless extended his hand to greet Forrest. As they shook, he noted the weakness in Forrest's grip. That must have been quite a massive heart attack.

"Please, Mr. Forrest, be seated."

As Forrest settled into the chair alongside the desk, McCandless noted his pallor, the way his shirt collar seemed two sizes too large for him.

Having formed his preliminary professional opinion of Forrest's condition, he turned to Mrs. Forrest, who carried her husband's voluminous medical history in a leather portfolio. She appeared to be much younger than Forrest, no more than forty-three or -four. Blond, tall, she was a beautiful woman, smartly attired in a tweed traveling suit which McCandless recognized as being expensively tailored. In her own way, she was more impressive than Forrest himself.

She introduced herself. "Millicent Forrest."

She held out her hand. McCandless shook it, aware that her hand was stronger by far than her husband's. She was extremely self-possessed and positive.

The perfect government wife, McCandless thought. *Striking, self-assured, and beautiful. And the way she carries herself. If we ever have a woman President, this is what she should look like.*

Aloud, he asked, "You husband's file?"

As if reminded suddenly, Millicent Forrest said, "Oh. Yes. Yes, it is."

McCandless leafed through the file, searching only for the basic facts of Forrest's condition. All other detailed information could wait. He studied the tapes of Forrest's last EKG's. They revealed the extent of the damage the infarct had inflicted on his heart. Quite severe. Without a successful transplant, this man might die in the next three months.

If his own tests confirmed his suspicions, McCandless knew now that he would be tempted to admit Forrest to the hospital at once. On the other hand, with heart patients, attitude and emotional health had to be considered. For a man like Forrest, accustomed to an active life, too long a confinement in the hospital could be depressing. This could only increase his anxiety and stress while waiting for a new heart.

He would do much better housed in more homelike surround-
ings, yet close to the hospital in the event of an emergency.

Overall, at this moment, Allen McCandless rated Forrest's chances as only fair. On second thought, poor. This
patient needed a new heart, and he needed it soon. But need
itself does not produce suitable donor hearts. Chance, fate
alone, can provide that.

McCandless noted the intense, penetrating look in the
intelligent, knowing, hazel eyes of Millicent Forrest. She
seemed to have read his mind.

To put the brightest face on things, McCandless began,
"One fortunate thing about coming to a transplant by way of
a heart attack is that the other organs of the body haven't been
damaged by prolonged faulty circulation. Cases of cardiomyopathy, extending over long periods of time, usually damage
the liver and kidneys, leaving them in weakened condition. I
don't expect any such complications here."

Forrest appeared reassured. But McCandless detected a
hint of skepticism in Millicent Forrest's hazel eyes. McCandless could not account for it, but he sensed a strange unease
in Mrs. Forrest which troubled him. One of the important
factors in the transplant process, during the tension and
uncertainty of the waiting period and after the surgery, was the
patient's emotional and psychological condition, which depended greatly on the emotional support he received from
those closest to him, most especially his wife.

He decided, *I'll be very curious about Josh Robbins's
psychiatric evaluation of this particular case.*

"I think," McCandless said, "that to make sure of these
findings we better do our own EKG's, CBC's, and a new
cineangiogram. So I'll have to ask you to remain in the
hospital for a few days."

Forrest attempted to answer. His bluish lips moved but
produced no sound. His wife answered for him.

"We expected that. We brought the usual things. All the
necessities."

"And a bulging briefcase?" McCandless inquired.

Forrest pleaded guilty with a slight, tentative smile. "Not allowed, I suppose."

"Just don't overdo it," McCandless said, thinking, *If he's as weak as I suspect, he won't have the desire or the stamina to overdo.*

McCandless picked up his phone. "Claire, have someone show Mr. Forrest to his room. And have Clifford start him on the usual tests for evaluation."

He turned back to the patient. "Mr. Forrest, for the next few days you are going to feel like a guinea pig. You'll be tested in more ways than you've ever been tested before. Don't ascribe any other importance to it than that we want as complete a history of you as it is possible to obtain. Some patients suspect that the number of tests is an indication of how sick they are. All our patients are sick. Else they wouldn't be here. But don't start thinking that you are sicker than you actually are. Any questions?"

"Just one. When will I get my new heart?" Forrest asked breathily.

"Mr. Forrest, the truth is, I don't know. We can't tell when a heart becomes available. When one does, we give it to that patient who matches the donor in blood type and size."

"Size?" Forrest asked, puzzled.

"A heart used to pumping blood through a body one hundred twenty pounds will not sustain a body weighing one hundred eighty pounds," McCandless explained. "So size is important, too. The patient most compatible in blood type and size, *and* most in need, will get that heart. I can only promise you that if a heart becomes available and you are the best candidate for it, you will get it."

Claire Fielding opened the door. "They're ready for Mr. Forrest now."

Forrest and his wife had both started for the door when McCandless said, "Mrs. Forrest, if you don't mind, there are some routine matters to take care of. Please wait."

Forrest turned back, the patient's usual concerned look clear on his face. *What are they going to say about me that they couldn't say in my presence?*

"Just routine matters," McCandless assured him. "Insurance. Things like that."

Only slightly comforted, Forrest followed Claire Fielding.

As soon as the door was closed, Millicent Forrest said, "He's far worse than you expected, isn't he?"

"No. When another cardiologist recommends that a patient who's had a severe coronary would benefit from a transplant, I pretty much know what to expect. I doubt there'll be any surprises in your husband's case."

"What *are* his chances? I have to know so I know how to deal with him."

"I can't make any promises. Or predictions. The next time that phone rings, it may be UNOS with word of a donor heart."

"UNOS?" she asked, obviously puzzled.

"The United Network for Organ Sharing. All donated hearts have to be reported to UNOS, and are then assigned on the basis of need, geographic proximity and compatibility factors."

"I see," she said, though it was obvious that she had one other, urgent question.

Anticipating her, McCandless said, "Of course, it may take days, or weeks, sometimes longer, before we get one that matches your husband. All we can do is prepare him and hope for the best."

"Do you think he can last long enough, if it becomes a matter of months?"

"If his condition grows worse, I'll put him in Intensive Care. Rest assured, we'll do all we can."

"Is there anything *I* can do?" Millicent Forrest asked. For the first time McCandless detected a hint of tears in the woman's hazel eyes.

Finally, McCandless thought, *a show of emotion. She's been too much in control until now.*

"The first thing, after you've given the required information to our Transplant Coordinator, I would like you to see Dr. Robbins."

"Will he be Winston's surgeon?" she asked at once.

"No. He's our Unit psychiatrist."

"Psychiatrist?" she asked, suddenly alert and withdrawn. "Why? What's wrong?"

"Nothing wrong, Mrs. Forrest. All our patients undergo psychiatric evaluation. You see, the transplant itself is only the first major step in treatment. After that, the patient must observe an exacting routine for the rest of his life."

"The rest of his life?" she asked. "You mean he'll be an invalid? I hadn't expected that."

"An invalid? Definitely not. He should be able to not only resume his normal activities, but accomplish them even better from a physical point of view. The reason you see Dr. Robbins is so he can evaluate your husband psychiatrically to see if he is equipped, emotionally, to be a transplant recipient."

"Equipped emotionally?" Mrs. Forrest was evidently surprised and puzzled.

"Becoming a transplant candidate means adopting a whole new way of life," McCandless explained. "First stage, there is waiting for a heart. The days of depression, and the days of hope. Once there is a heart, there is the surgery itself—a major physical and emotional trauma. Once he survives the surgery, there is the post-operative care, which lasts a lifetime."

"A lifetime?" That concept seemed to create a new and strong concern in this attractive woman.

"A lifetime," McCandless repeated. "Every day for the rest of his life your husband will have to take his cyclosporine, that's an anti-rejection medication. And other medications. All at stated times. In prescribed amounts. At the start there will be post-op weekly checkups, then monthly checkups, then semiannual checkups, including heart biopsies. He will have to remain on a diet. He will have to control his weight.

He will have to take a prescribed course of exercise. We can't waste a precious heart on any patient who won't take care of it. But if he follows his routine, he will live a much more active life than he can now.''

McCandless could see that the woman was not as reassured as he had intended.

"Shall I call Dr. Robbins?" he asked.

"Yes. Please do," Mrs. Forrest said, still tense and somewhat apprehensive.

4

DR. JOSHUA ROBBINS, a man in his late thirties who had adopted a beard to add maturity to his slender face, sat at his desk, his fingers steepled, as he peered through his thick glasses at Mrs. Millicent Forrest.

She was concluding her straightforward response to one of his routine questions.

"Yes, I would say Winston is a man of regular habits. Punctual. And very precise. In his career there is always an agenda. Always a purpose. A plan to be carried out. Yes, very regular habits."

"About himself as well? I mean, such things as taking medication on time and whenever he should."

This time she hesitated before replying, "Yes. Yes, I would say so."

"Meaning, I take it, he is less conscientious about himself than about his work?"

"Look, I don't want anything I say to be held against Winston," she said quickly.

Robbins made a mental note of that while asking, "Men in government do so much entertaining and being entertained that a man might get to be, shall we say, a heavy drinker, perhaps an alcoholic?"

"He is not an alcoholic!" she said firmly.

51

"His sleeping habits . . . fairly regular? Or does he have difficulty?"

"There have been times, when he's been involved in extremely tense situations—well, for instance, during the hostage crisis in Iran . . . Winston was Undersecretary of Defense then . . . that was one of those long stretches when sleep was virtually impossible for him."

"Did he take anything?"

"Not that I recall—" she started to say, then admitted, "Yes. Our doctor prescribed something. Insisted. Said Winston would work himself into a breakdown if he didn't."

"Of course," Robbins agreed. "And after that? More recently?"

"Are you asking if he is a pill addict? As far as I know, he isn't."

"As far as you *know*?" Robbins asked, intrigued.

Millicent Forrest hesitated. She had to weigh carefully the effect of what she would say on her husband's acceptance into treatment.

"Winston and I . . . we have not been too close in the past two years."

" 'Not too close' can mean many things, Mrs. Forrest," the psychiatrist said. "It could mean he's been away on official duties. Or it could mean that there has been no sexual contact between you two. Or—"

To put an end to Robbins's speculations, she interrupted him. "We are separated, and I am considering a divorce."

"Yet you're here," he pointed out.

"After twenty-four years of marriage, I owe him this much."

"Any children?"

"There was a son. He was in the Marines."

"*Was?*"

"He was in the detachment that was sent to Beirut. As a 'peacekeeping' force," she said softly, trying to suppress her sense of anger and irony.

"He was in the building when the bomb-laden truck crashed through," Robbins realized.

"He had no reason to be there. No reason to be in the Marines. He was only nineteen. He'd already been accepted by two of the best universities in the East. But he wanted to see more of life before he went on with his education. More of life . . . he said. Some life. Myself, I think it was a way of his rebelling against his father!"

She fell silent, as if she had revealed more than she intended.

After giving her a moment to recover, Robbins asked, "And did your husband's difficulty sleeping increase after that?"

"Yes."

"And the difficulty in your marriage started at about the same time?"

She did not answer. But he noticed that her hands seemed to tighten one on the other.

"I assume Dr. McCandless explained to you the reason for all these questions," Robbins said.

"He did mention taking medication regularly and having some kind of treatment—biopsies, I think he said—for the rest of his life."

"Mrs. Forrest, a donated heart is a precious gift. There are never enough to satisfy the need that exists. Therefore we are dealing in something literally more precious than gold. We can always mine more gold. But a good healthy heart is quite something else. So, those of us entrusted with the disposition of such organs have a great responsibility. We can't waste them. Or misuse them. We must make sure that each patient who gets one will make the most of it. So we have to know the patient as well as we can. His habits. His sense of self-control and self-discipline. And equally important, his potential backup. Meaning, those people who by their relationship to him will encourage him, discipline him, help him through the periods of inevitable depression while waiting for a heart, the periods afterward when he grows fretful and rebellious at the daily, then weekly, then monthly examinations and procedures that go on forever.''

"I understand," Millicent Forrest said.

"I'm afraid 'understanding' may not be enough," Robbins said. "With your son gone, with your marriage possibly at an end, the people your husband would normally depend on seem to be missing from his psychiatric profile."

"Dr. Robbins, are you saying that you might recommend that Winston *not* be given a heart because our personal situation?"

"That will be one of many factors that go into our decision to accept him as a possible transplant candidate."

Millicent Forrest drew herself up in the chair. Robbins admired the carriage of this handsome woman. He could see what an asset she must have been to her husband in his official duties.

"Dr. Robbins, when you have your evaluation meeting, you may tell them that I am willing to put my own career on hold so I can remain here with Winston throughout the entire procedure."

"Your own career?" Robbins asked. "There was no mention of that in the file."

"We didn't think it necessary," she replied. "Ever since, well, after Paul died . . . was killed . . . I needed something to do. So I asked myself, What skills do I have to offer? And there turned out to be only one. My years as a diplomat's wife fitted me for one thing. I can entertain. A few visiting dignitaries. Or several hundred. I know how to handle them all. So I decided to go into business. I run one of the fastest growing catering businesses in Washington. But, as I said, I'm willing to put that on hold if it means giving Winston his chance at recovery."

Robbins nodded.

To her it was only an enigmatic gesture. She hastened to reassure him. "As for disciplining him, God knows I've done that for years. Else he wouldn't have survived this long. He is a compulsive worker in a career with never-ending problems. Men who devote their lives to government never receive the public credit they should. But they do the work. The hard work. And in recent times, as National Security Adviser to the President, Winston's work has become much greater in volume and intensity. So, assure your evaluation board I'll see him through this, no matter what the sacrifice,"

"And *after* the surgical procedure and recuperation?" Robbins asked, to bring her back to the point of his real concern. "What will you do then?"

"We . . . we will have to see," Millicent Forrest said.

"Thank you for an honest answer," Robbins said. "We will have to weigh that, too."

Believing she had jeopardized Winston's chances, she felt compelled to add, "I hope you will take into account his value to the nation."

"We take everything into account, Mrs. Forrest. But our main concern is the patient."

"I was told the White House had called . . ." she started to say.

"So I was told, too," Robbins said.

The way he slipped his notes into the file made her know that her part of the interview process was over. She rose, saying, "Thank you, Doctor."

She started for the door. He sat back in his chair, thinking, *A handsome woman, a very handsome woman.* He looked forward to meeting her husband.

Just outside the Cardiac Intensive Care Unit was a row of small private rooms for patients brought in for evaluation, or weak enough to require hospitalization yet not so critical as to require intensive care.

In Room 607 Winston Forrest was just getting out of his street clothes. He asked the nurse, "Do I have to wear one of those idiotic hospital gowns that lets my tail hang out?"

"No," she said, smiling. "You can wear your own pajamas."

"Good. The last time, right after my attack, I was in those damn gowns all the time. I have a theory; patients would recover a lost faster if they were not subjected to the indignity of being bare-assed all the time."

"I always thought embarrassment was an incentive for patients to get better faster and go home."

He turned on her sharply, to discover that she was smiling.

Instead of sharing her little joke, he asked, "Is that part of your job, too? To cheer up the patients? Are things that grim around here?"

The smile disappeared from her face. "Mr. Forrest, if I may suggest, part of *your* job will be to *keep* your sense of humor. Otherwise, waiting can become pretty depressing."

"Sorry," he said as Dr. Robbins entered the room accompanied by Adeline Sawyer, the Transplant Coordinator.

A small compact woman, Adeline Sawyer was an odd combination of warm friendliness and efficiency. Behind her pleasant smile one detected an active mind that was always balancing a thousand details. From her simple close-brown hairdo to her tweed skirt and blue cotton blouse, she was a model of practicality. She seemed to have no time for frills.

After the proper introductions, she said, "Mr. Forrest, if you will fill out these forms, I'll come by later and pick them up." And she was gone.

With a slight gesture of his head, Dr. Robbins indicated to the nurse that he wished to be alone with the patient. After she pointed out, "Mr. Forrest, if you need anything, just use that buzzer," she left the two men alone.

Forrest felt self-conscious until he had buttoned his pajama top. He had always been sensitive about being naked, even in the presence of men. Robbins noted that.

A private man, a very private man. Could that have been the trouble between him and his wife? The inability to share, to open up? What had it been like when their son was killed at so young an age? Was his failure to unbend then the beginning of the dissolution of their marriage?

"Do I have to get into bed?" Forrest asked.

"Not necessarily," Robbins said. "How do you feel?"

"Not bad," Forrest said quickly. Then admitted, "Not very good, either."

"A little frightened?" Robbins suggested.

"No," Forrest responded. "The day it happened, that day I was frightened. I knew it was a heart attack. I knew what it could mean. While I was waiting for help to be administered, I was afraid. I thought, Is this the way it ends? No chance to say a final word to anyone?"

"To your wife?"

Forrest glanced sharply at Robbins, to rebuke him for invading his privacy.

"Yes, to my wife," he admitted.

"Few of us are granted the opportunity to choose the time or the place. Or the opportunity to say those final words," Robbins remarked. "But I'll bet we've all made up heroic little speeches for the occasion. Words to be remembered."

"Do you wish to examine me now?" Forrest asked.

"I'm not a cardiologist or a surgeon. I'm the Unit psychiatrist," Robbins explained.

"I see. Seems I read a long time ago that when people have heart surgery they become psychotic for a day or two after," Forrest said. "Is that what you're here for? To see how nutty I will become when I get my heart?"

"Have you done a great deal of reading on heart transplants?"

"Just the usual. Magazines. Newspapers. Never made an intensive study of the subject."

"But that particular fact did stick in your mind," Robbins remarked.

"I collect odd facts. Don't mean to, but I do. It struck me as very strange that a purely physical procedure like a heart operation could have mental repercussions. Unless, of course, the heart actually possesses those emotional qualities that poets and romantic novelists have always endowed it with."

"It does more than pump blood," Robbins said. "But

I'm afraid that theory has been shaken a bit by newer methods.
In the early days of heart transplants, patients were kept in
much more severe isolation, due to the fear of infection while
under immunosuppression. Rooms were tightly sealed off. No
windows. More like prison cells than hospital rooms. So there
were cases of temporary post-operative dementia. We theo-
rized that the patient's fear of having his old heart removed,
and the dangers involved in getting a new one, so traumatized
him that psychosis was a natural development.''

"You said that was the *old* theory," Forrest remarked,
curious.

"Nowadays the patient recovers in a room with large
windows to the outside world. He has a television set. He's
allowed more frequent visitation from close relatives. As a
result the post-op psychosis has virtually disappeared. Thus
another highly ingenious intellectual theory has been shot
down."

Forrest stared at him. "Is that what you came in to tell
me? Or are you here to do a little professional poking
around?"

"Oh, I intend to poke around a little, as you phrase it,"
Robbins said, smiling.

"Well, shoot," Forrest said, anxious to get it over with.

"I've always been curious, professionally speaking,
about high government officials. How different are they from
the rest of us mortals?" Robbins asked.

"Not a hell of a lot. We have our job. We do it. After the
cocktail parties, the state dinners and the photo opportunities,
once we close the doors, it is business. Straight business.
Sometimes low-key, sometimes voices are raised. Sometimes
it takes a bit of acting to pretend more intensity than we
actually feel. But essentially it is arriving at a policy then
selling it, on a very high level, of course."

"But you don't always close the sale, as salesmen are
wont to say," Robbins suggested.

"We do have our days of 'complete' and 'frank' discus-

sions. That's like a Mayday call from a pilot. But somehow
the world staggers on. Or ends up in a war," he said grimly.

"It must be a difficult, nerve-wracking profession, to
know that your failure can lead to drastic consequences,"
Robbins said.

"Nerve-wracking? At times. Difficult, always. But we
manage," Forrest said.

"Tell me, aside from what you picked up about heart
transplants from magazines and newspapers, have you thought
much about it?" Robbins asked.

"Not until this damned heart attack."

"And after that?" Robbins pressed."

"When the doctors tell you you've had a pretty bad heart
attack, you start to look for alternatives. For me the only
alternative to dying is a transplant," Forrest admitted.

"Do you have confidence in the idea?" Robbins asked.

Forrest had been looking away, staring toward the
window. But that question made him face the young psychiatrist. He hesitated before answering.

Robbins could read his mind. He had encountered this
attitude many times before. "Mr. Forrest, you can speak
frankly. Your answers will not be held against you in the total
evaluation."

"In that case, no, I must admit I do not have total
confidence in it. You hear about new hearts being so scarce.
And those cases on television, where the man struggles along
with a mechanical heart while waiting for a transplant and then
finally dies anyway."

"Depressing, isn't it?" Robbins agreed.

Suddenly, Forrest said, "If Paul were here, it might be
different."

"Paul?"

"My son."

"Oh, yes," Robbins said.

Which made Forrest ask, "You spoke to my wife, did
you?"

"Yes. There is not much anyone can say to make up for the sorrow and pain of such a loss."

"Millie took it more bravely than I did. Maybe she had less guilt. I was in the thick of it. We had all been brought in to deal with the crisis in Lebanon. Civil war seemed perpetual there. Then after the Israeli incursion, there was the need to restore peace. There were two schools of thought in the White House. Send in the Marines as a show of support. Or just let the situation continue to boil and grow worse."

"Two very opposite schools of thought," Robbins commented. "Which side were you on?"

"Much as I knew about the Middle East, there was one man, a friend of mine, military attaché with the Israeli embassy in Washington, who knew even more. He'd been in on the rescue mission at Entebbe. When they flew in and rescued those people on that hijacked plane."

"Brought them all out safely, except for one woman, as I recall," Robbins said.

"Yes. Ben Yehuda had not only been in on the planning, he'd been on the mission itself. And other missions. All secret. All dangerous. So I went to him. I'll never forget his advice. 'Win,' he said, 'in the Middle East you apply overwhelming force. Or none at all. They do not respect a *show* of force. If you go in, be prepared to go all the way.'"

"What did you do?" Robbins asked.

"At the next meeting the entire staff was assembled. The Navy, the Army, the Commandant of Marines. They laid their plan before the President. The number of Marines to be sent in. Where they were to be quartered. To emphasize the peaceful nature of their mission they were not to be armed with live ammunition. The whole plan, charts, maps and all, worked out in detail. I reported what Ben Yehuda had said, how he'd warned against a mere show of force. How we must be prepared for the worst, not the best. But I was outbrassed. I was considered a mere civilian. So the military won the day. I don't know any feeling worse than failing when you know you're right."

"Unless it's feeling that your failure cost your son his life."

"I didn't know at the time that Paul would be on that mission. Or that he would never come back."

"But afterward?" Robbins asked.

"Not a day goes by that I haven't cursed myself for not being stronger in that meeting, louder, more insistent. If I had convinced the President to call Ben Yehuda and talk to him, one on one, it might have ended up differently."

"And you've been taking the blame for it ever since," Robbins pointed out. "Tell me, Mr. Forrest, did that have anything to do with the present situation between your wife and yourself?"

"Doctor, I'm here to be considered for a heart transplant. Not for psychiatric treatment."

"Psychiatric treatment, marriage counseling, we feel compelled to do whatever we have to to give each patient his best chance. Family support is one of the crucial factors."

"I think Millicent understands that. She's been at my side ever since the heart attack. She is quite a remarkable woman."

"Extremely attractive, too," Robbins said.

"Yes," Forrest admitted, with a feeling of regret. "She should have done better for herself. Could have, too. What she ever saw in me . . ."

"Tell me, Mr. Forrest, in the aftermath of the Lebanon disaster, were there harsh words? Recriminations?"

"God, how many times I wished there had been," Forrest said. "But, no, she never said one word of rebuke. Even after I told her how I had failed in that crucial meeting at the White House. All she did was put her arms around me. She kissed me on the cheek. But said not a word. To this day I don't know whether she blames me or not. She might, and still be too sensitive to say anything. Knowing how guilty I felt. That's why she's here now. Out of pity, I suppose. God knows, I don't deserve this kind of loyalty."

"Mr. Forrest, how much do you really want to live?" Robbins asked directly.

"How much do I . . . why else do you think I'm here?" Forrest demanded.

"Since Paul's death, have you ever entertained thoughts of suicide?" Robbins asked.

"Have I ever . . . of course not," Forrest said.

"Have you ever consulted a psychiatrist?"

"Well, I . . . once, after Paul's death. I felt I . . . I was losing my grip," Forrest hesitated. "And, yes, there were thoughts of . . . self-destruction." He looked into Robbins's eyes. "Does that bar me from the program here?"

"Not at all. We're used to periodic depression in our patients. Both before and after transplant. Constantly living with the fear of death, sudden death, will depress any normal human being."

Forrest appeared relieved. He seemed about to speak, but controlled the impulse. He toyed with a button on his pajama top, looking away from Robbins.

The psychiatrist could not avoid thinking, *No matter how important they are, when men are forced to accept their mortality, few of them are heroes. This man Forrest might benefit from the patient group sessions. I must mention that to Sawyer.*

He would urge that Mrs. Forrest attend as well.

5

AT THE INSISTENCE of his wife, Jim Campbell was dressed to make a good impression when he presented himself at Dr. Robbins's office for his interview. He was attired in his dark blue Sunday suit, white shirt with slightly overstarched collar, striped tie of two different shades of blue. His large frame seemed too big for the visitor's chair in the psychiatrist's office. And he appeared uncomfortable at forced rest. His right hand kept nervously stroking his cleanly shaven chin.

As did most patients in the introductory stages of the pre-transplant process, he was extremely eager to give what he thought would be the right answers to qualify him for the program.

"Well, Jim," Robbins proceeded with his inquiry, "tell me how you felt when Dr. Kaplan informed you about the seriousness of your condition."

"It wasn't exactly a surprise. I mean, first time I suspected was when I began to feel weak. I had this virus that laid me up for a week. That didn't matter too much. Since it was a rainy week and mine is outdoor work, I wouldn't have worked anyhow. Though I could have used the time to put my equipment in good repair. But I felt pretty down—lousy, I mean. So Nan said, Take the week off, rest. Which I did. Dr. Kaplan said it was probably a virus, so I could use the rest.

"But next week when I went back to work, I still didn't

feel right. Sort of weak. I said to myself, Christ, am I getting old? At thirty? That's not possible. Some day, sure, I'd get younger men to take over the hard work, climbing trees, felling them. But not at only thirty. My father worked until he was sixty-seven and did a good day's work even then.

"So Nan said, Go back to see Dr. Kaplan. This time he put me through a whole series of tests. Cardiograms and stuff. But he wasn't saying anything. Nan started getting worried. Me, too. But I didn't let on. Because she worries a lot, about everything. The kids. The house. Me. She reads magazines a lot, so she finds a lot to worry about. Myself, I think people would worry less if they knew less."

Robbins couldn't resist smiling. Campbell joined him. "That doesn't make much sense, does it?"

"Oh, I don't know," Robbins said. "Sometimes in the practice of my profession I come to exactly the same conclusion."

"Anyhow, I kept feeling weaker and weaker. Until that one Sunday about a year ago, almost two years, when I was out back . . . we have a big backyard with a vegetable garden and still room enough to throw a football around with my son. He was only nine then, but he was already good. Real good. One day he'll make the high school team. Wouldn't surprise me if he got a scholarship to one of the big universities. Do what his old man never did. Graduate from college."

Robbins coaxed, "That day out back when you were throwing the football around . . ."

"I began sweating almost from the start. Which was strange since it wasn't a warm day. Then I ran out for Jimmy to throw me a pass. I tripped and fell. Well, actually I realized I didn't trip. I just fell. And I had trouble breathing. I lay there thinking, Something is wrong. And I don't mean wrong like it could be fixed by a few days in bed. But wrong, like I could die from it."

"Is that what sent you back to Dr. Kaplan again?"

"Nan insisted. She is small, and soft-spoken. But when she makes up her mind, watch out. So I went. He didn't seem surprised. And this time old Kaplan said, 'Time to go to our local hospital for some more tests.' So I went. Then Kaplan got the results. He said they discovered what he'd been afraid of. This cardio . . . cardiomy . . . I never did get that word straight.''

"Cardiomyopathy," Robbins supplied.

"That's it. Kaplan said my heart was just deteriorating. They didn't know why. He didn't know why. I sure didn't know why. I always thought physical work was good for the heart. They're always telling you on television to keep your heart in shape with exercise. Well, hell, my kind of work *is* exercise. I just couldn't understand it.''

"Frankly, Jim, what you have the doctors don't understand, either. Tell me, you drink, Jim?"

"A beer with my supper.''

"Just one?''

"Never more than two. Nan doesn't like me to drink any more than that. Says it's not good for me. And not a good example for the kids.''

"Did you tell those doctors about that virus you had?" Robbins asked.

"They said that could have done it but no one would ever know for sure.'' Campbell said sadly, '' 'Course, it doesn't matter what caused it, does it? Not now.''

"No, it doesn't, Jim," Robbins agreed. "Now, what are your thoughts about the transplant?''

"I don't know for sure,'' Campbell said. His big rawboned face, his worried blue eyes, betrayed not fear but enormous concern. "If it was me alone, I wouldn't care. I mean, a lifetime of sitting in a chair or lying in bed, I'd rather be dead. I want to be like my dad. Work right up to the last day. But there are the kids. There's Nan. We're not at the point where I can leave them yet.

"We just moved into a new house three years ago. A house I built. One of those prefabs. But with improvements that Nan and I added to it. It's a pretty big house. Four bedrooms. Big kitchen. With all the latest equipment. I mean, it's really a house! Nobody could guess it was prefab. But there's a mortgage on the place. Had to, to pay off the package and to buy the furniture. When I think something can happen to me, then Nan and the kids would have to move out to God knows where . . . that's what drives me crazy. There's a little life insurance. But not enough to pay off the mortgage. Sure not enough to send either of the kids to college. When the thought of leaving them like that . . . Doctor, I'm scared for them, not for myself. As for me, to hell with it.''

He looked to Robbins, trying to read his response in his eyes. Robbins knew he would have to wait only a moment before he would hear the inevitable.

"I guess that disqualifies me, doesn't it? I mean, a patient should be desperate to survive in order to be worth a new heart. Right?''

"We don't care whether you want to live for yourself or for your loved ones. The point is, you want to live. So we want to help you live.''

"What are my chances, Doctor?''

"Jim, we never know when the next heart will become available. And, when it does, who will be the prime candidate. That depends on many things. Blood type. Physical size. Need. So we can make no promises.''

Dr. Joshua Robbins's interview with Nancy Campbell was fairly brief. He learned that she was a plain young woman, plainly dressed, plainly made-up, a little lipstick and not enough powder to conceal the gleam of perspiration on her cheeks. It was obvious to him that she felt under extremely close scrutiny, for she shifted in her chair in guarded ways which she tried to conceal, while her hands made small nervous movements as she tried to bury them in her lap.

She blurted out suddenly, "Whatever you want to know about Jim, just ask! He's a very good man. Honest in his work. Good to the kids—'' She began to cry. As she rooted in her purse, Robbins handed her a box of tissues he always kept ready.

"Thanks," she sniffled. When she had composed herself, she said, "I'm sorry. I don't want anything I do to reflect on Jim."

"It won't," Robbins assured her.

"He's so good about his condition. He doesn't complain . . . what I mean is, he doesn't let them know how sick he really is. He puts on a good show for them. He's out there playing with the kids like before. Even though I know it hurts. But he won't let it show. And I keep thinking—" She broke off and stared down at her nervous, active hands.

"Mrs. Campbell?" Robbins urged.

"I keep thinking maybe one time he'll overdo it with the kids and it'll kill him. Then what good will it have done, all this pretending?" She was weeping once more. Through her tears she said, "Will they hold that against him?"

Robbins reached for her hand. "Look at me." Once she was able to stare at him through wet eyes, he said, "I'm not trying to keep Jim from getting a new heart. I'm trying to find out how he'll care for it once he gets it. Is he a good, steady, reliable human being? With regular habits? If he is instructed to take certain medications at certain hours, will he take them?"

"Oh, I'll make him do it!" she declared.

"And if you're not around?" Robbins asked. "You see, we have to have confidence in the patient, as well as his support system."

"You can depend on Jim," she promised.

"Good," Robbins said. "Now, how is your life together? Do you get along? Is there much bickering? Is he irritable a good part of the time because he resents being sick? And when he is, how do you handle it?"

"We get along fine," she said, a bit too quickly to suit Robbins. He waited, knowing that she would come forth with the truth if he gave her enough time. "Lately, however—" She stopped once more.

"Lately?"

"He's a very affectionate man . . . I mean, he was

always very . . ." She was groping for the proper words. "He's always been a very . . . sexy man. Even when we first started going together. In fact . . . in fact, our son, our oldest child, he was conceived before we were married. Oh, we knew we were going to get married before it happened. It wasn't that we were part of that live-together-never-get-married group. But Jim was thinking of quitting his job and going out on his own in landscaping and tree trimming. He always said he wanted a business of his own, to have something to support his family then leave to his son when he was too old. So we put off getting married. But, as I said, he was always a man with strong feelings . . . sexual feelings. And I do love him. So . . . well, you know . . ."

"Of course," Robbins said.

"There wasn't any scandal or anything. I was only two months pregnant when we got married. In church. It was a lovely wedding. Yes, it was," she said softly as she recalled the day. "Even now, some nights, especially after Jim's condition became so bad, I stay up late in case he needs me. To pass the time I look at the pictures in our album. I study his face to see if I can discover any sign that one day he'd be as sick as he is. But he looks just terrific. He never looked better than on that day. Such good color in his face. He always had color. From working outdoors. Of course, lately—"

"That's the second time you've used that word 'lately' Mrs. Campbell," Robbins reminded.

"Well, lately," she began slowly, "I've been trying to avoid having . . . trying to avoid letting . . . I won't let him have sex with me," she managed to blurt out.

"Afraid, are you?" Robbins asked.

She nodded, her tears starting to flow more easily now.

"He thinks maybe I don't love him as much as I used to. But it isn't that at all. I want to make love with him. But I have this terrible fear that if I let it happen, it will kill him. You hear stories from time to time about some old man who dies having sex with some younger woman. So I think if Jim's heart is like an old man's, maybe the same thing could happen to him. So

I . . . I don't respond. What I mean is, my body won't respond. I am dry. It is painful. So I discourage it. After all, I don't want him to die. How could I ever face my kids and tell them their father is dead because of my sexual desires?" She was weeping freely. "This isn't the life I bargained for," she said suddenly. "Everything was going to be so wonderful. Jim in his own business. Our own house. The kids. And now I'll be taking care of an invalid for the rest of his life. If he even has that long."

"Mrs. Campbell, the picture is not as gloomy as you try to paint it."

"You don't understand. In Jim's business you can hire a man or two to help. But if the boss isn't strong and out there working every day, soon his helpers decide they can go into business themselves and take your customers away. In a year or two—Jim said it himself—we'd have no business at all. I'd have to go back to work. Which is not enough for us to live on. Especially with all the bills that'll be piling up. There's no way, no way. I feel so trapped. So helpless . . . sometimes I—"

She wiped the tears back from her eyes with the palms of her hands. He edged the box of tissues closer to her. That allowed her the opportunity to busy herself with them so she could avoid looking at him as she continued.

"Sometimes—mainly late at night, when he's sleeping and I'm still finishing the laundry or mending the kids' jeans—sometimes I think I'll just run away. I wouldn't ever do that. I couldn't leave the kids, couldn't leave Jim. But it seems like the only way out. What I'm trying to say is, I can't see the future. Not for Jim. Not for me. Not for the kids. We don't have family to fall back on. My mother barely gets along on Social Security now. In fact, we've been helping her out, till lately. I'm sick with worry. And even sicker for fear Jim'll detect it and it'll have a bad effect on him. I'm not good for him. Not the way I am now. I'm no good at all . . . at all. I wouldn't know how to cope with an invalid."

Robbins took her hand once more, made her look into his eyes.

"Mrs. Campbell, what in the world makes you think that if Jim gets a new heart he's going to be an invalid?"

"After he's been all through—" she started to protest.

"His new heart, when he gets one, is going to be better than the rest of his body. He's going to have to exercise to bring his body up to the level of that new heart. He's going to be able to go back to his work and be stronger at it than he's been in the last two years."

She stared into Robbins's eyes until she was sure he was being honest with her. Then he continued.

"Now, it isn't going to be all beer and skittles, as they say. There'll be waiting. The ups and downs that go with that. You'll see other patients get new hearts and leave here, and you'll keep thinking, That heart could have saved Jim. Not so. That other patient got that heart because it fitted his or her special requirements. Yet secretly you'll envy every patient who gets one and goes home in much better condition than when he came. But I feel pretty sure your turn, Jim's turn will come."

She appeared to breathe more easily now. She dabbed at her eyes until they were dry once again.

"I understand that since you live fairly close to the hospital, Dr. McCandless has decided it's okay for Jim to live at home."

"Yes."

"Good. That will make for a more stable family life until the time comes for his transplant. Of course, there will be frequent trips for checkups and such. But we'll try to keep your family together as much as possible."

"We'd both appreciate that. Jim's so close to the kids, loves them so . . ."

"I understand. Thanks for the interview, Mrs. Campbell. It's been very helpful."

"Nothing I said will hurt Jim's chances, will it?" she said before she rose from her chair.

"Not at all," Robbins reassured. "He has every reason to want to live. He has a wife and kids who want him to live.

So I will report that psychiatrically he is a good candidate for a new heart.''

When Nancy Campbell was gone, Dr. Joshua Robbins sat back in his swivel chair, rocking slowly, as he considered the notes from which he would dictate his report. He picked up the file on PATIENT CAMPBELL, JAMES. He skimmed through the medical detail and data.

Though his specialty was psychiatry, he was well enough versed in cardiology to make a reasonably accurate estimate of this patient's condition and his chances.

From the preliminary material in Campbell's file it was obvious that, due to more than two years of very poor circulation because of his failing heart, his kidney and liver function had been impaired. Which made it a race against time for him. If his bodily functions deteriorated much further, he could no longer be considered a fit candidate in whom to risk a new heart with confidence that he could survive long enough to make good use of it.

That poor young woman, Robbins thought, *her fears are no fantasy. She has good reason to be afraid.*

6

"DENTIST?" JIM CAMPBELL asked of Transplant Coordinator Adeline Sawyer. "I never had trouble with my teeth. Why do I have to see a dentist?"

Not wishing to arouse any antagonism, and thus endanger his chances, his wife interceded, "Jim, please—"

"No," Sawyer said, "we encourage patients to ask questions. The more the patient knows, the more secure he will feel. Now, Mrs. Campbell, about the dentist. He will examine your husband to find out if he has any hidden infections in his teeth or gums. They can exist without the patient ever being aware of them."

"What's that got to do with his heart?" Nancy asked.

"Once Jim gets a new heart, he will be on a strict regime of immunosuppressives to keep his body from rejecting it. Those drugs work by depressing his immune system, which keeps his body from fighting infections in the normal way. If he does have some hidden infection, it could break loose and become very dangerous. Possibly fatal. So it's important to make sure."

Nancy looked up into her husband's eyes, as if to plead, *It's all right, Jim. Let's get it over with.*

Jim Campbell nodded. "Where is the dentist? Let's go!"

*   *   *

They stepped into the stainless-steel elevator. It was so crowded Jim had difficulty reaching the button to push for the proper floor. The tall distinguished man, dressed in sedate clothes, seeming rather grim, his bluish lips pursed, was closest to the panel.

Jim Campbell asked, "Sir, would you please push nine?"

"I've already pushed nine," the man said.

The elevator continued its ascent, stopping frequently to discharge or take on young men and women in white lab coats or baggy green O.R. pants and shirts. Each had an identification badge pinned to coat or shirt. They greeted each other, exchanged personal bits of news, arranged lunch meetings or dinners.

Floor by floor they came on, they exited. The elevator seemed crowded all the while. When it finally arrived at the ninth floor, Jim and Nancy Campbell got off. The older man and the beautiful and sophisticated woman who was obviously his wife also got off. Both couples looked up at the direction arrows that pointed to various departments and clinics.

"It says Dental Clinic to the right," Nancy pointed out.

Jim and Nancy Campbell and Winston and Millicent Forrest started down the corridor toward the Dental Clinic.

The nurse in charge was expecting them. She requested both women take seats in the waiting area, then escorted both men down the narrow hallway to small private offices where the dentists attached to the Transplant Unit were waiting to examine them.

Self-conscious and afraid, Nancy Campbell tried to avoid the attractive woman's eyes. When she couldn't, she smiled in a timid, friendly manner. Millicent Forrest smiled back, outwardly more assured, inwardly as uncomfortable.

Each woman tried to assess the other without appearing too obvious.

God, to be so secure, Nancy Campbell thought. *She carries herself like a queen. And the way she's dressed. Like in the magazines. Not fancy, but good taste. Quality. And so calm. But then her husband can't be depending on someone else's heart to keep him alive. I don't know why he's here, but to judge from her calmness, it can't be too bad. Not as bad as Jim. God, I hope that dentist doesn't find anything wrong with his teeth. Would they turn a man down because of his teeth? They can always fix his teeth, but a heart . . . God, I hope they don't find anything . . .*

Millicent Forrest sat erect and rather stiff. From time to time she glanced across at the young woman opposite her.

Wonder why they're here? That strapping young man, obviously her husband, he can't be needing a new heart. At his age?

And she, my, but she is so young. She can't be more than twenty-three or -four. The same age I was when Paul was only five.

She seems plain. But actually she is quite pretty. Not movie-star pretty. Not television pretty. Not obvious. But clean, wholesome pretty. The way I must have looked when I left Iowa to go East to college. Of course, I was only seventeen then. Probably even more naive and self-conscious than this young woman appears to be.

Of all the things I was fit to be, a young diplomat's wife was surely not one. But I made up my mind I'd become the perfect government wife. I'd learn how to dress the part, look the part, be the part. It took more than twenty years, but I did it.

Yet now I'd trade it all to be her age again. Because this time I'd do it all differently. I would live my life, not Winston's. My son would still be alive. My husband would still be a healthy, young fifty-five. Not a man with a heart badly damaged from having to face one great governmental crisis too many. We could be just starting to live the best years of our lives, if things were different.

Damn, what's taking so long in there?

Patience, Millie, patience. No matter how you feel, this

is the time to be patient, supportive and understanding. Else what will people say? That you deserted Winston when he needed you most?

Not about me, they won't! she insisted.

Her thoughts were interrupted when Winston Forrest returned. Her look demanded an explanation.

"I'm fine," Forrest said. He chuckled as he continued, "Seems I'm going to die with a perfect set of teeth."

"Winston, that's not funny," she rebuked.

"What do we do next?"

"Miss Sawyer said we're to return to the room," his wife said.

"Then let's go."

As they left the Dental Clinic, Nancy Campbell heard Forrest say, "Look, Millie, I've been thinking it over. If this is too much for you . . ." But the door closed and she heard no more. Jim Campbell came out shortly after. He, too, had passed his dental exam with no dangerous or negative findings.

"Well, I guess my teeth qualified," he said to his wife.

When the Forrests returned to his room, the nurse in charge said, "Mrs. Forrest, there is going to be a stream of technicians in here to take all kinds of samples and specimens. You might feel in the way. So there's a nice, comfortable waiting room down the corridor."

It was phrased as a helpful suggestion, but Millicent Forrest had been a government wife long enough to recognize an order, no matter how judiciously it was couched.

She was trying to interest herself in an old, frayed magazine, of a type she would not have read even if it were new, when someone else entered the waiting room. She looked up. It was the woman whose youth she had envied while waiting in the Dental Clinic. She was surprised enough to abandon her usual reserve.

"Good heavens, don't tell me—" she began, then recovered sufficiently to become as proper as she had been trained to be. "Forgive me for asking, but is your husband a candidate for a new heart, too?"

"Yes," Nancy Campbell said.

"At his age?" Millicent couldn't resist commenting. "How old is he?"

"Thirty-two."

"What happened?"

"They don't know. His heart just started to give out. But the doctors here are very hopeful," Nancy said, trying to smile—a tentative, fragile smile that glimmered, then faded until her moist brown eyes became the most prominent feature of her face.

As if it were a rule of etiquette between visitors in hospitals, Nancy felt obliged to ask, "And your husband? He is your husband, isn't he?"

"Yes," Millicent replied, "Winston is my husband. He had a severe heart attack. They feel a transplant is his only hope."

"This hospital has a very good record," Nancy said, as much to take courage as bestow it. "I read that their percentage of successes is very high. Over seventy percent."

"Seventy-four percent," Millicent remarked.

"Right," Nancy Campbell agreed nervously. "Seventy-four percent." She tried to smile once more, but was as unsuccessful as before.

She's tense, too tense, Millicent Forrest decided. *I'd better keep her talking. It might relax her.*

So she asked, "Any children?"

"Two."

"Boys? Girls?"

"One boy. One girl. The boy is the older."

"Ah, that's nice. I think every girl should have an older brother. To look up to. And for protection."

They were interrupted when a slight, pale, blond young woman dressed in a pink robe and wearing furry scuffs of matching color came into the waiting room. She appeared surprised to find anyone else there.

"Oh, sorry. I hope I'm not intruding."

"Not at all," Millicent Forrest said. "If anything, we may be the intruders. Come join the party."

The younger woman felt obliged to explain, "It gets so . . . so claustrophobic being penned up in that room all the time. Even with television. In fact, those soap operas make things even worse. All day you see unreal people with unreal problems. Which is no comfort when you're a real person with a real problem."

"I know what you mean," Nancy Campbell said.

The young woman pulled her robe tighter around her and sat down opposite them.

"What are you doing in the Transplant Unit?" Millicent asked.

"Waiting," she said simply.

"For what?" Nan asked.

"What everyone else is waiting for. A new heart."

"At your age?"

The frail young woman smiled weakly, "Yes, at my age. I have a six-month-old infant at home, I should be there taking care of her. But I'm here. Waiting. Just waiting. For something that may never show up."

She began to weep, silently. She fumbled for some tissues, but could not find them in her pocket. Nancy Campbell leaned across to hand her some. The young woman tried to thank her but could not. She hid her face in the tissues, obviously ashamed of her display of weakness.

Finally she appeared to recover. She wiped her eyes, smiling a bigger, more positive smile as she said, "I've got to stop crying in front of strangers. Everyone who comes here, everyone I meet in this room, they have problems enough of their own. I don't have to bother them with mine."

Tentative, and quite shy, Nancy Campbell asked, "What happened? I mean, how did your heart suddenly go bad?"

"Seems I'm a very unusual case. Of all the things my obstetrician warned me about during my pregnancy, he never said there are some women, very very few, who get a postpartum heart effect. Cardiomy . . . something.''

"Cardiomyopathy," Nancy suggested.

"He said in a few cases that can be a postpartum effect. So, I'm a rare specimen. Not much comfort in that, I can tell you. Not when you want to be home with your baby, cuddling her, bathing her, changing her, feeding her, just loving her. Doing all the things you dreamed of during those nine long months. Now the grandmothers do that. Her mother. My mother. But she's my baby!''

She began to weep again. At that moment the nurse came to the door. "Mrs. Forrest, you can go in now. He'd like to see you.''

"Thank you," Millicent said. To the other two she added, "I have a feeling we're going to be meeting quite regularly from now on, so we might as well introduce ourselves. I'm Millicent Forrest. My husband is that very imposing-looking man in that room at the end of the corridor.''

Nancy rose and held out her hand. "I'm Nan Campbell. You've seen my husband.''

The slight, blond young woman came to her feet. Held out a hand to each of the others, saying, "I'm Sally Brock. I'm sorry I cried. I try not to. But today, somehow, I don't know. I guess I'm having one of my low days.''

Millicent looked at their hands, joined so that the three of them made a circle.

"We'll just help one another see this through," she said. "And it'll all work out. All we have to do is have faith. Chins up!''

As she turned to the door, Nancy Campbell said, "Your husband's name is Winston. And if your name is Forrest . . . well, Winston Forrest, that's a familiar name. He must be someone important.''

"My dear, *everyone* is someone important. Now, I've got to go. Win is waiting.''

The two younger women were left alone. Sally Brock

slipped into one of the easy chairs. She made an effort to inhale in regular measured breaths.

"Are you in trouble?" Nancy Campbell asked, a note of alarm in her voice. "In pain?"

"Oh, no, sometimes I just do that to see if it will strengthen my heart," she explained. Then she added, "I know it won't. But I keep trying. What I have doesn't get any better. Not with rest, not with exercise. It just keeps getting worse."

"I know," Nancy said. "Jim has the same thing."

"Are you going to the group tonight?"

"I didn't know there was a meeting tonight."

"There is. You should go. It makes you feel better. Seeing other patients. Hearing their experiences. It really does help."

"It'll be good for Jim," Nancy Campbell said. "He needs confidence."

"We all do. If you can't believe that it will work, you don't have anything left," Sally said. She confessed, "I cry a lot. At night. When I'm alone. I think about the baby. They won't give Bill permission to bring her here. Too many patients subject to too many infectious diseases. So I cry a lot."

She was fighting to hold back her tears. Nancy Campbell felt the impulse to reach out to her and lend her physical comfort, yet in the end restrained herself.

Sally Brock was finally able to regain control.

"When you have time to think, you try to imagine what the operation will be like. From what I've heard other patients say—the ones who've gotten new hearts—they start to put you under slowly. So you can feel you're gradually going off to sleep. Then, of course, you're totally out of it. That lasts for hours while they're taking out your old heart and putting the new one in. Then gradually you come back to consciousness. Well, I have this fear that they'll put me under but once I'm out I'll never come back. I won't have the chance to kiss my little daughter for the last time. To kiss Bill for the last time.

Tell him how much I love him. To tell my folks how much I appreciate what they've done these last months. I won't be ready to go, but I'll be gone. Gone.''

"Dr. McCandless said that very rarely happens,'' Nancy Campbell replied, trying to encourage her.

"What I have very rarely happens, too. But it did,'' Sally Brock said simply. "If I'm going, I want to say good-bye. At least to Bill and my baby.''

Suddenly she rose to her feet. "I'm sorry. You've got your own troubles. I shouldn't burden you with mine.''

She started for the door.

"See you at the meeting later?'' Nancy called.

"Yes. Sure.''

7

THE GROUP MEETING of transplant candidates, both outpatients and in-hospital, took place in a small conference room in the Cardiac Wing of the Medical Center. A long, bare rectangular table of dark wood dominated the room. Grouped around it were a nondescript collection of chairs. Armchairs, setup chairs, plain straight-backed chairs, some of wood, some of metal.

There was only a handful of patients and relatives in the room when Winston and Millicent Forrest entered. She opened the door for him. But when she tried to allow him entry, he indicated she go first.

"I'm not that sick," he protested.

She knew that attitude well. Always proper. Always with dignity and reserve. For the same reason, he had insisted he would not attend the meeting unless he could change back into his own clothes and not appear in pajamas and robe.

He looked about the room. She could read in his eyes and in his slow, familiar aloof gaze that he did not approve of his fellow patients or their families. She could imagine the thoughts that were going through his mind.

A far cry from the White House, from ornate meeting rooms in Geneva. From the green-baize-covered antique tables, from large luxurious armchairs with tufted backs. Most especially, a far cry from the sort of people with whom I am accustomed to convening.

Millicent hoped he would not say anything during the meeting to give the others any hint of his feelings. The essence of tact in his governmental activities, he could be difficult in personal matters. She was relieved to have her dour thoughts interrupted by the entry of the Campbells. She greeted Nancy warmly, was pleased to meet Jim. She took the opportunity to introduce them to Winston, hoping that at least he would appear interested. He barely managed that.

Several other patients, most dressed in street clothes, appeared, accompanied by either wives or husbands. Sally Brock arrived with an older woman.

She explained, "Bill had to work overtime tonight. This is my mother."

The introductions were cut short by the entrance of Elaine Duncan, a tall, slender black woman. Nancy recognized her as the woman who had first interviewed them and who took down all the details of their family circumstances, financial status, insurance, and whether it was sufficient so that, when it became necessary, they could afford the annual cost of six thousand dollars for Jim's medication for the rest of his life.

When Elaine Duncan smiled, her whole face lit up, bright black eyes, even white teeth, slight dimple in her right cheek. Even her strong chin seemed to turn joyful.

"We have some new patients with us this evening. I'm sure the rest of us will answer their questions. And they must have many. But first I suggest we listen to a report from Charlie Evans."

She turned to the small middle-aged man who sat at the far end of the table. He was nondescript in appearance, dressed in a worn blue-serge suit under which he wore a gray sleeveless sweater. His shirt collar was clean but wrinkled. His tie had been knotted carelessly.

He seemed reluctant to speak. So Elaine Duncan urged, "Charlie? Don't tell me, first day out with your new heart and nothing to report?"

"Yes, I do. It kinda surprised me. I mean, after they checked out my condition this morning, cyclosporin level, heart biopsy, and stuff, they said I didn't have to go to physical therapy. I didn't even have to go back to my furnished room. I could go out. Real outside out. On my own. For the first time. Take a walk. 'Explore the neighborhood,' Doc McCandless said. Up till now it's been show up here for my tests, my exercises. Then right back to the room. Sometimes, on my way back, I'd stop and pick up some groceries. I make my own meals, because these days even cafeterias are pretty expensive. So I beat a path from the room to the hospital to the market back to the room. But today Doc said, 'Get out, Charlie, get out and around. Give your new heart a trial run. Like it was a new car.'

"So I did. Instead of walking the two blocks north to my room, I decided to find out what's to the south of this hospital. So I started down Central Avenue. First thing I find out, this whole neighborhood is hills. Up and down. Of course, going down was easy. But on the way back trying to climb those hills, that was tough.''

One patient interrupted to ask, ''Was it anything like your old heart used to be?''

''That's the funny thing, George, it wasn't my heart that felt it. It was my legs. They were working hard. Real hard. I had to stop and rest them. More than once. I thought, 'Jeez, I expected I would feel like a new man once I got a new heart.' I mean, I felt so much better after the operation. But now this. So finally when I got back to the hospital I asked to see Dr. McCandless. Lucky he had a few moments between patients. I asked him, 'Did I get a good heart? Or are you going to have to replace this one, too?'

''Doc just laughed. He said, 'Charlie, the trouble is, your new heart is better than the rest of your body. Because of your old heart, the rest of you hasn't been able to be as active as you should have been. Your leg muscles got weak and flabby. Other parts of your body, other organs, have been deprived of a proper blood supply. Now, with a new heart you have to start building up your body to the capabilities of that new heart. Six months from now you'll be in great shape. Legs, arms, everything. You'll be the old Charlie Evans again. Or the new one.'

"Imagine, my new heart is in better shape than I am."

Many of the patients and their relatives joined Evans in laughter.

Elaine Duncan used the moment to ask, "Does anyone want to ask Charlie how it felt just *before* the surgery, and just *after*?"

Nancy Campbell raised her hand, assuming permission was required before she could speak.

"Yes, Mrs. Campbell?" Elaine asked.

"The waiting, that's what I'd like to hear about. How do you handle the waiting?"

One of the patients joked, "That's the reason they call us patients. Get it? Patience. That's how you handle the waiting." He laughed at his little joke.

Not many joined him.

Charlie Evans addressed this question with more gravity. "Yeah, the waiting. It's tough. You're up one minute and down the next. A hundred times a day. Some days you feel it'll never happen. Some days you're so damn sure that you pick up your phone to find out if it's working. You think, 'There's a heart and they're trying to reach me, but my phone doesn't work.' Or your beeper doesn't work. Being only two blocks from the hospital, they gave me a beeper to reach me if a heart turned up. Four different times I brought that beeper back to the hospital because I was sure it stopped working. Else they would have called me. There must be a heart for me. Must be.

"Of course, the reason the phone didn't ring, the beeper didn't beep, because there was no heart. God, if people only knew how desperate we get for a heart, they wouldn't bury so many good ones. Of course, there are the other times. You come to the hospital. The doctors are satisfied with your condition. You get a good report, and you feel, I've still got time. As long as I have time, a heart will show up."

He paused for a moment to wipe the sweat from his cheeks.

"Waiting is something you just have to get used to. Good and bad, up and down, you just have to get used to it. Thing that carried me through was the thought that back home my wife was waiting, my two daughters were waiting. They couldn't come visit me often. My wife works. The girls are in school. And . . . well, frankly, we can't afford a lot of trips. We're lucky the insurance covered my surgery and maintenance. But I know they're waiting. And it's only a matter of time before I can be with them again. It's kind of like when I was in Nam. I knew if I could live through it, she'd be waiting for me. Same here. If you stay alive long enough, it'll happen."

Elaine Duncan used the silence that followed to remark, "Of course, the most hopeful part of waiting is that we know that more than seventy percent of our patients do get new hearts. It's almost four to one that each of you are going to get one. Those are pretty good odds."

Nancy Campbell reached across to take Jim's hand and squeeze it, a gesture intended to say, *See, I told you. You've got every chance of it working out.*

But Jim had other questions in mind. He leaned in Charlie Evans's direction to ask, "What's it like?"

Evans looked in his direction, "You're new, ain't you? I never saw you before. First day?"

"Yes, first day," Jim Campbell admitted.

"Man, do I know that feeling!" Evans continued. "First day here my wife was with me, too." He chuckled, "She didn't trust the doctors and nurses to take as good care of me as she used to. Didn't take her but one day to find out otherwise. Took me a little longer. You see, what bothered me was, here's this big medical institution, this whole group of people, Elaine, and Adeline—the Coordinator—and doctors, lots of doctors. Not just Dr. McCandless or Dr. Slade or the psychiatrist Dr. Robbins, but a whole host of doctors, men and women, and their assistants, and the physical therapy men and women, and I am thinking to myself, Are all those people going to put their time and their skill into taking care of me? Who am I to deserve so much care and treatment? I'm just a guy who used to run a little diner right off the Interstate that goes by our town. Till I had to sell it 'cause I couldn't handle it no more because of my condition. That's when Tess had to take a job as a waitress. I tell you, that day I felt like the worst failure in the world. So when I came here I thought, Why should they bother with a failure like me?

"But let me tell you, a Rockefeller couldn't get better treatment. You're all very lucky to be taken into this program. You're important. Every one of you. Just do what they say. Keep the faith. And one day soon you'll be feeling like I feel. Like a new man."

Jim Campbell had listened patiently but at the end he said, "I didn't mean that. I meant, what is it like when you know they're going to take your heart out and if the new one doesn't work, there's nothing . . . you're nothing . . . I have this picture in my mind. I'm lying there on the operating table and my body is wide open, and where there should be my heart, there's just a big empty hole."

Evans half looked to Elaine Duncan, then said, "It doesn't happen that way . . . uh . . ." He was groping for Campbell's name.

"Campbell. Jim Campbell," he volunteered.

"It doesn't happen that way, Jim. Elaine, tell him. Or maybe Dr. McCandless should tell him," Evans said.

"You know the routine, Charlie, you tell him," the Social Services director said.

"Well, Jim, the way it was explained to me, they don't operate on you unless they know there is a good heart ready and waiting for you."

Elaine Duncan added, "They won't even start to operate on you until they know the new heart is only an hour away, by whatever kind of transportation it's coming. So there's no possibility that your fear could actually take place, Jim."

"It's timed so fine?" he asked.

"It's timed not to the hour but to the minute," the black woman said.

"It feels a little better, knowing that," Jim Campbell said. He turned to Charlie Evans once more. "And after, how does it feel after?"

Charlie Evans smiled, "You wake up and you're looking into the face of your wife, and you know you made it."

"I mean does it feel different to have a strange heart beating in your chest? Do you know it's a different heart, not your own?"

"You know that you feel better, lots better. Right away. Why, Tess said to me, 'Charlie, you ought to see the change in your color. You're not so pale anymore.' She asked the nurse for a mirror so I could see my face. By golly, even I could see there was color in my face. In my lips. Seems that new heart didn't have to get used to me. It just started pumping away like it had always belonged there. Suddenly you have to get used to not being an invalid anymore. Like I said before, your heart is better than the rest of you. The rest of you has to catch up."

"Man, if that could only happen to me . . ." Jim Campbell said softly.

"Give it a chance, kid, give it a chance," Charlie Evans said.

"What will you do now?" Millicent Forrest asked, despite the fact that she was aware of Winston's reluctance at her becoming involved in the general discussion.

"Now?" Charlie Evans considered. "Well, I got to be close by for a short time, for my checkups. But when that's over I'm going back home and reopen Charlie's Diner. Doctors here say I'll be able to work as well as I ever did. And a lot better than the last few years. So I am going to become the man of the house again. My wife is never going to wait on another table as long as I live."

Elaine Duncan's warm brown face broke into a big grin. Which made Charlie Evans ask, "Why? Don't you think I can do that?"

"Oh, you can. And you will," the Social Services director said. "But you better remember one thing. During the last few years your wife and your two daughters have been taking care of you. Now you are going to come home and try to be head of the household again. They may not like being run by you instead of running you. I've seen too many cases like that. The wife and kids say, We liked it better when we were the boss and taking care of him."

"Tess? Amy? Florence? No, they'd never feel that way about me," Evans disputed, then added a somewhat less assured, "Would they?"

"I've seen it happen," Elaine Duncan said. "So don't you come running back to me with any complaints."

They both laughed. They were interrupted by the sudden intrusion of a beeper. Elaine Duncan's laugh turned to a look of serious concern.

" 'Scuse me," she said, and hastily departed the room.

During her absence, one of the other patients, a man in his mid forties, rather small and timid in appearance asked, "Mr. Evans, time is coming when they are going to want me close to the hospital. When you get ready to give up your furnished room, will you let me know? We haven't been able to find anything close by at a decent rent."

"Sure thing," Charlie Evans said. "But talk to Elaine. The hospital is very helpful finding economical places for outpatients to live in."

"I'll do that," the timid man said.

"Look, folks," Charlie Evans said, "I don't know if I'll be seeing all of you again. Any day now they might say it's okay for me to go back home, because I'll be on a schedule of monthly checkups. So I want to say now, if ever you're on the Interstate, get off at Exit twenty-seven, that's the Huntsford Exit. There'll be a meal waiting for you at Charlie's Diner. On the house. Stop in. Even if it's only for a cup of coffee. Or just to freshen up. Stop in. I'll be delighted to see you. It'll be like old army buddies getting together. After all, we've been through the same war together. Right?"

With the exception of Winston Forrest, they all responded, "Right!"

Elaine Duncan returned shortly thereafter to announce, "We'll have to call this session to a close. There's word of a possible donor heart in Milwaukee. So the whole team's been alerted. I'll be seeing each of you during the day tomorrow."

8

MILLICENT FORREST HAD escorted her husband back to his room. He begrudged her attempt to lend him physical assistance, though he needed it. From his demeanor it was obvious to her that he regarded the group session a waste of his valuable time. Until the moment of his heart attack on Air Force One, he had been a man who dealt only in important international matters with important people.

He had said nothing, until Millicent closed the door to his room. Then he remarked dryly, "You must remind me to take a nice long drive on the Interstate and get off at Exit twenty-seven. The Huntsman exit."

Softly she corrected him, "Huntsman is your tailor in London. It's the Huntsford exit."

"Okay, Huntsford!" he admitted, irritated at being corrected. "Shall we order the truck drivers' blue-plate special? Why not? It's on the house."

She knew him well enough to know that to respond would only offer him further opportunity for sarcasm. He settled down on the bed. She tried to excuse his testiness, thinking, *He's not angry with Charlie Evans. He's angry at his own predicament, and Evans is only bearing the brunt of it.*

"Shall I turn on the television?" she asked after a time. "We'll at least get some news."

"News?" he responded angrily. "You call that gossip mongering news?"

He had never been an advocate of television news. Not since they had exposed his efforts on behalf of the President to obtain the freedom of some hostages being held in Lebanon. His attempt had failed, and he always blamed the media for having blown the operation.

He reached for one of the files he had insisted on bringing with him. The mere effort of reaching seemed to tire him, so he abandoned it. He lay on his back, staring up at the ceiling.

"Seventy percent, they said, even more than seventy percent," he said.

"What?"

"Didn't that woman, that black woman, say that seventy percent get new hearts?" he asked.

"Miss Duncan," Millicent said. "Yes, she said seventy percent. Or more."

"Well, at least those are good odds," he said, then fell silent once more.

After a long pause, Millicent said, "You may never go to Charlie's Diner off the Interstate. But what's important, that man is going back to work. Taking up his life again. That's something to look forward to."

"Stop trying to cheer me up!" he protested. "Things are going on right now. Important things. Negotiations with the Soviets. And I am stuck in this cubbyhole of a room, cut off from the world. Haven't you noticed? There hasn't been a single phone call all day? Not one!"

"They don't want to impose on you at a time like this," she suggested.

"Hell, no! They want to work around me, gradually work me out of the White House altogether."

"That's why the President arranged for you to come here? Flew you out in an Air Force plane? Arranged that Dr. McCandless handle your case himself?" Millicent said, "Winston, don't let your anxiety to get that new heart make you angry or suspicious. You'll do what the others do. Wait. And like the others, you'll get a heart. But it will take time. So have patience."

As always, his sarcasm put an end to all conversation. And, as always, in a very short time he began to suffer a twinge of guilt and sought to reestablish a more amicable feeling between them. At home Millicent might be working on the problems of her newly established catering business, seeking ways to keep prices down by varying menus, or pursuing new recipes to avoid the sameness that afflicts most Washington receptions.

Now she was studying the figures her accountant had prepared for her to indicate how well her enterprise had done and how much better it could do with certain personnel changes.

Seeking to provoke a reaction from her, Winston said, "Very ironic." She continued to study the figures. This annoyed him even more. "It seems you're not interested in irony today."

"Or any other day," she said. She knew his moods well. Especially when he was feeling like a naughty child who was seeking forgiveness. If she ignored him, she knew that he would work his way around to being less grouchy and more the warm human being he could be.

Forced to carry on the conversation by himself, he began once more.

"When I said very ironic, what I meant was, for years, now, you've been complaining that I never have enough time for you. I'm either packing a bag to go to some foreign country or unpacking a bag from just having come back. Once you said, 'Winston, it's a good thing you ran out of clean laundry. Else you'd never come home.' "

She looked up from her figures.

"Yes," he continued, "I remember that. I'm not the insensitive man you've always considered me. I'm just busier than most men, that's all."

She went back to her accountant's report. Provoked, he pleaded, "Millicent, I'm trying to talk to you. You could at least listen."

"I'm listening, Winston."

"You only call me Winston when you're angry," he pointed out.

"Do I?" she asked, without looking at him.

"Will you please put down those damn figures!" he asked. Then, in response to her sharp reproving glance, he said, more softly, "It's difficult to talk to a woman who's got her nose in a bunch of figures."

With an exaggerated gesture she put aside the report. "Yes, Winston? You were saying?"

"What I was trying to say, Millie," he began quietly, "is that for years you've been complaining that we never have time to talk, really talk. That I'm always too busy. Well, here we are, with nothing but time, and we have nothing to talk about. At least, *you* seem to have nothing to talk about. I think that's ironic."

"All right, Winston, let's talk. Where shall we begin?"

"I'd like to hear all this pent-up conversation you've been holding back over the years."

"Are you interested, really interested, Winston?"

"If I weren't, would I ask?"

"As long as you're interested, let me begin. How shall I count the ways of my discontent? The trips, the sudden trips, to every damned corner of the world—I don't like them. But I understand them. And, after all these years, I've learned to put up with them. The receptions, when I'm supposed to play the gracious hostess, the interested listener, I've even put up with those. I've made a career out of being a government wife, though it's a career I never chose or was trained for."

"Nobody does it as well," he protested. "You should hear what the President says about you. He never fails to ask when there's a state dinner, 'Winston, your charming wife will be here, of course, won't she?' You're very important, Millie. Very important. I thought you knew that."

"Winston, I never wanted to be 'important.' I wanted to be loved."

"Loved . . ." he repeated. The word was a rebuke and a challenge. "Millie, if I'm not much for sweet talk and fancy declarations, there's a reason. A man who deals in words, especially words that are often used to mean the opposite of what they seem to say, such a man loses respect for words after a while. I am so used to lying in the most flattering ways that if I were to make those declarations of love that women are so eager to hear, I myself wouldn't know if I were telling the truth. Words are counterfeit coin as far as I'm concerned. Feelings are all that count. And I always thought you were aware of my feelings. You used to be."

" 'Used to be,' " she said sadly. "I think that sums it up, Winston. Our marriage, our lives together, are composed of *what used to be*. But there's so little of *now*. I think it all became apparent when Paul—" She could get no further. Her eyes filled up. She turned away, determined not to let him see her cry.

Softly, Winston Forrest said, "Millie, I think of him more often than you know. At the oddest times. Whenever I see a young officer in uniform—and I see many of them, too many of them—I think of Paul. One day, it was Frankfurt, or else Weisbaden, we were met by a reception detail of the military. There was a young Marine, I swear to God I thought he was Paul. And he'd already been dead for a year. I wanted to talk to him, find out who he was, where he was from. But the President was in a hurry and I had to keep up with him. So I never got the chance. But I've thought of that young man often."

"You never told me."

"To what purpose? To start you crying again?" he asked.

"It would have been nice to know, nice to share. I have times like that, too. But whenever I want to talk to you, either you're not there or else you're too busy. With important matters. I have lost my respect for important matters," she said.

"Millie, what if I told you that when this is over, when
I get this new heart, I'll resign. Quit. I've had it. The years of
travel. The constant concern. Being at the beck and call of the
President. I want to know what I will be doing next week, next
month. I want the luxury of getting up late on Sunday.
Reading the *Times* or the *Post* with my coffee without having
to worry about what every item on the front page means to the
nation and the President. I want the rest and the freedom I
think I've earned. That we've both earned."

It was phrased as a statement, but delivered as a plea that
begged for a response. She did not reply. After a time he
continued.

"When that attack hit me, first thing I thought was,
'Millie, if Millie were only here. There's so much I'd like to
say to her!' You see, the pain was so bad I really thought it
was the end. I even thought, 'She's always saying we have no
time to talk, and now she's right.' No time to talk. But once
they started doing things, the pain started easing. I felt that I
was in good hands, and fairly safe. So I thought, 'This is a
warning. Time to quit. I'll resign. We can get along on my
pension. We'll buy one of those condos in a nice suburb of
Washington. We'll have lots of time together. I'll make it up
to Millie for all the times away. Now when I travel, we'll
travel together. I'll go back to all those places I've been to in
the past. Then, all I knew was the airport, some military
installation or state building or palace with an ornate meeting
room. Then it was back to the airport again and out. This time
we'll just be tourists. Drive a lot. Off the autobahns, the
autostrada, the other main highways, and onto little back roads
to see the villages. Meet the people of the area. Eat in little
inns and restaurants. No more formal dinners with gilt-crested
menus. From now on, tables for two. Not twelve. Wine of the
countryside, not those distinguished vintages.

" 'Greece. We'll go to Greece. Somehow in all my trips
that was one country I never got to. Luck of the draw, I
suppose. I'd like to go there. We'll drive through the country.

On our own. No fancy limousine. No official guide. Just the two of us. We'll do the islands. Of course, for that we'll need to take one of those cruises. But we'll pick a small vessel. Not too many people.'

"Yes, I did a lot of thinking in those first two days. We'll do it, Millie, we'll do it all."

He was sounding more and more desperate. To avoid any promises that might turn out to be false, she said, "We don't even know when you'd be allowed to travel. Dr. McCandless did say something about daily medication. For the rest of your life."

"That's no problem," he was quick to rebut. "I'll take along a month's supply, two months. The main thing, as I understand it, is to take the medication every day and on time. Hell, I can do that no matter where we are."

"There are the monthly checkups. Things like that," she said.

"You don't want to go," he concluded sadly.

"Win, we really can't make any plans without consulting the doctors. They'll tell you what you can do and what you can't."

"You don't want to go," he repeated softly. "Well, maybe you'll change your mind. We have time. I did some reading up. They say most people who get a new heart live five years and more. Lots more. Why, they're giving new hearts to infants now, and to very young people. They wouldn't do that unless there was a chance for long-time survival. So, we'll have time."

The conversation was brought to an abrupt end when an Air Force captain, in uniform, with an attaché case of confidential papers chained to his wrist, eased the door open.

"Mr. Forrest?"

"Yes, Captain," he replied.

"If we can be alone for a minute, sir," the captain asked, indicating the need for privacy.

"This is Mrs. Forrest. It's quite all right."

"Sorry, sir. But I have my orders," the young officer said.

"Yes, of course. I understand. Millie, please?"

As soon as she slipped out of the room, the captain started to unlock the chain that bound the case to his left arm. As he was doing so, he reported, "Sir, the President and the Chief of Staff would like your opinion on the enclosed plan."

Forrest reached for the thin folder as the captain continued, "The material's been reduced to a minimum to avoid any undue strain on you."

"Hell, son! I'm not dying. I'm just a little . . . a little sick, that's all!" Forrest said grumpily.

Forrest had not read beyond the first paragraph of the memo when he realized his opinion was being sought on a matter of grave international consequence. The President and Chief of Staff were debating broadening American action in the Persian Gulf, possibly to include an attack on the Iranian oil installations on Kharg Island. The question was, what would the effect on the international oil situation be?

He had just finished the first page when the door opened briskly. McCandless, in white lab coat, entered the room to demand, "Captain, who gave you permission to intrude on Mr. Forrest?"

"Doctor, this is urgent defense business," Forrest explained.

"Exactly my point, Mr. Forrest," McCandless replied. "This is the kind of 'urgent business' that put you in the hospital in the first place."

"I'm sorry, Doctor," the young captain explained. "But I was following orders. White House orders."

"Well, next time you tell whoever gives the orders to check with me before disturbing Mr. Forrest."

"Yes, sir!" the captain said crisply.

"What do I do now?" Forrest asked.

"Now that you're into it, see it through," McCandless

said. "It'll be less stressful than if you're up all night worrying about what was in that file."

"I'll have to relay my advice to the White House when I'm through," Forrest said.

"Okay. One phone call. Make it brief," McCandless said.

9

TWO ROOMS DOWN from Winston Forrest's room, Jim Campbell lay on his back atop the bed. He rested his arm over his eyes. Nancy Campbell sat in the armchair in the corner staring at him, wanting to say something cheerful, at a loss for the words. Jim spoke first.

"Sal Candeleria . . ." he said. He was silent for a time. "Or maybe Al Shekata. Either one."

"Either one what?" Nancy asked.

"Sal would be best. He has a real feel for the work. I mean, there is a man who loves growing things. If you could get Sal, that would be perfect."

"Get him? To do what?" she asked.

"I got the deal all figured out. Got it written down here. With my list of customers, satisfied customers, you could set it up so that Sal services them. The deal you make is, you take Sal in as a partner. You supply the customers, plus the accounting—you know, billing and collecting. Like you do for me. He does the servicing. Then after two years you sell out to him on a basis where he pays you out of the proceeds of the business. But you still do the billing and collecting so he can't fool around with the figures. That way you and the kids should be taken care of for at least eight or nine years."

"Eight or nine years?" she asked, confused.

"That means you don't have to touch the insurance money. Or the kids' education fund," Jim said.

"In order for us to get the insurance money you would have to . . . Jim, what are you saying?"

She rose swiftly to his side. She stared down at him. He did not remove his arm from over his eyes.

"Jim?" There was a hint of tears in her voice. "Look at me, Jim!"

Slowly he moved his arm so that he could stare up into her eyes.

"Jim?" She paused. "What are you trying to say?"

"Plans. I have to make plans. After all, I have to think of the kids."

"But you're planning for the worst," she protested.

"It's only when things go bad that a man has to have plans. Good times take care of themselves."

He turned toward the window, not to seek the light but to avoid her gaze.

"Jim?" she persisted.

He reached out. She took his hand. But he did not turn to face her.

"I have this feeling, hon. I'm not going to make it," he confessed.

"No, darling, don't say that. . . ." She was already weeping.

"Nan, honey, please don't cry."

"You're giving up and you tell me not to cry? What do you expect me to do?"

"What I expect is for you to think of the kids. Live your life for them. Make plans. Do what I told you. Get hold of Sal Candeleria."

"Jim, you wouldn't be here if the doctors didn't think you had a good chance. Remember what Dr. Kaplan said when he sent us here. He said, 'Jim, if they accept you, that's half the battle.' So let's wait and see if they do."

"And if they do? They have more patients here than hearts. They always have more patients."

"But most patients do get them," she replied. "That man—that Charlie—he got one, and he said he's even better now than he ever was. His new heart is the best part of him. It works. And it'll work for you."

"But if I don't get one—"

"I don't want to hear that!" she protested through her tears.

"Nan, baby, you *have* to think about it. We both do."

"I won't listen! I won't! If you keep talking that way—"

Her tears had overwhelmed her. She fled the room.

"Nan! Honey!" he called after her.

In a moment one of the nurses came to the door. "If you need anything, Mr. Campbell, don't shout. All you have to do is buzz," she said. "What did you want?"

"Nothing, really."

"I thought I heard you call out."

"Nothing, thanks. I'm okay . . . really okay."

"Well, next time, use your buzzer."

Nancy Campbell fled down the hall toward the visitors' lounge. She was relieved to find it empty. She went to the farthest corner, slipped into a chair and continued to weep. In moments she realized that the handkerchief she needed so desperately now was in the purse she had left in Jim's room. She was wiping away tears with her fingers when someone handed her a tissue. She looked up. Through her tears she made out the warm, beautiful face of Millicent Forrest.

"Here, this might help."

"Thanks." Nancy Campbell tried to suppress her tears. She did not succeed.

"Go ahead," Millicent said. "I know the feeling. Trying to maintain a stiff upper lip. Trying to be brave. When my son died, I was supposed to be the brave mother. A symbol for the nation. I will never forget. They were folding the flag that covered his coffin. You know the way they do. God knows we've seen it on television often enough. You never see the mother or the wife cry when they hand it to her. Somehow tears are not allowed at such times. Maybe it diminishes the sacrifice of the dead husband or son. Whoever dies bravely should be mourned bravely, I suppose.

"Well, I didn't want to accept that flag dry-eyed. I *wanted* to cry. If only in protest. But all those years of being a government wife, of being in the right place at the right time, saying the right thing at the right time, wouldn't permit me. So I was as dry-eyed as all the others. Afterward I realized it wasn't courage that kept me from crying, but the opposite. Cowardice. Fear of what they would say about me. So I did my crying in private. A great deal of crying. But Paul was dead. Gone. Your husband is still alive."

"He's given up. He's making plans to die," Nancy explained.

"Strange," Millicent Forrest said. "He's so young, and giving up. Winston is middle-aged, but he's making plans for the future. Retirement. Travel. The two of us together again."

Nancy could not resist glancing at her, a look of surprise in her damp eyes.

"I just assume everyone knows. Of course they don't. Winston and I are separated. May be getting a divorce. I'm here to see him through what will probably be a very rough time. The doctors said, especially the psychiatrist said, that a heart transplant patient needs family backup, emotional backup."

Seeking to change the subject, Millicent Forrest said, "I wonder if you should talk to Dr. Robbins about your husband's feelings."

"I thought of that, too. Then I thought, Robbins could decide if Jim is that depressed he shouldn't be in the program."

"I don't think it works that way. Robbins even offered to find marriage counseling for us, to help out. I think he would work with your husband to change his attitude," Millicent advised.

"I'll . . . I'll think about it," Nancy said, still fearful of seeking Dr. Robbins's intercession.

"Of course, your husband could be having a down day. After all, being admitted to a hospital is never fun. A new room. Among strangers. People you never knew invading your privacy. Taking specimens. Having whispered conversations outside your door. They might only be making a dinner date. But you're always sure they're discussing you. And never optimistically. All that can be depressing. I'm sure once he's accepted he'll feel much more affirmative about his chances."

Millicent Forrest had intended to encourage the young woman. She realized that she had failed. She handed her more tissues from her purse.

"I came prepared to cry. But I guess it isn't my time yet," she explained. "So you might as well have them."

She smiled. Nancy Campbell finally managed a smile of her own.

"Thank you. You're being very kind. Too kind," she said.

"There's never such a thing as 'too' kind. Now, you go back and see if you can't change your husband's attitude."

Nancy nodded. Smiled once more. And started out.

She approached the door to Jim's room. It was slightly ajar. She heard voices inside. She recognized Dr. McCandless's voice.

"I've been over all your preliminary results, Jim. Not bad."

"What does that mean, Doctor, not bad?"

"The damage to your liver and kidneys is not as serious as I had feared. There's been some, of course, but not enough to disqualify you from the program," McCandless said.

"Does that mean I'm accepted?" Jim asked.

"That's a staff decision. The whole Unit votes on that. Dr. Slade, his surgical team, my staff cardiologists, Dr. Robbins, all of us. We hold that meeting Monday afternoon. But it looks good, Jim, real good."

"You're not just saying that, Doctor, are you?" Jim was hungry for more definitive reassurance.

"Jim, around here we don't 'just' say anything we don't mean. You're here. You're in the running. And that means a hell of a lot."

There was a moment of silence before Nancy heard McCandless ask, "What are these? Doodles? Or figures?"

"Figures," Jim Campbell replied. "I was just making some financial plans." But he did not elaborate.

"That's the ticket, Jim. Plans. Plans for the future," McCandless encouraged.

"Right," Jim pretended to agree. "Plans for the future."

McCandless almost collided with Nancy Campbell as he came out into the corridor. He smiled pleasantly and started toward the nurses' station. Nancy wiped her eyes before she entered the room. Pretending that she had not eavesdropped, she asked, "I noticed Dr. McCandless was in here. What did he say?"

"He said I have a chance. A good chance," Jim Campbell said as he slowly tore his sheet of figures into halves, then quarters.

"She's a very sweet young woman," Millicent Forrest said suddenly.

Looking up from the file in which he had tried to maintain some interest, Winston Forrest asked, "Who?"

"That young couple. Those Campbells. I spent some time with her in the waiting room. She's really nice. Terribly frightened, of course. And who can blame her."

"Must be hell, at their age," he agreed.

"Talking to her, I couldn't help thinking she's the kind of girl Paul would have fallen in love with," she said.

"Millie . . ." Forrest intoned with the rising inflection to which he usually resorted to rebuke her for dwelling on the unhappy past.

"You can't stop me from thinking about it," she insisted.

"It doesn't do any good. And it only leads to more tears."

"Or does it lead to you having bitter second thoughts?"

"I don't know what you mean," he said, trying to avoid her question.

"You know why he volunteered."

"That's only *your* idea," he replied. "Paul never said anything."

"He didn't have to. He spent his life trying to make you proud of him. But he had to strive to be noticed by you. You were always too busy with 'important' people. I think joining the Marines was his way of rebelling. His way of saying—"

Before she could continue, there was sudden activity in the corridor outside their door. She rushed to see the cause. Forrest pulled his robe about him and tried to rise from the bed. But the sudden effort was too taxing, so he leaned back and lay there breathing with great effort.

Millicent Forrest burst into the corridor, almost colliding with several medical assistants and nurses who were racing in the direction of the ICU. Other hospital personnel converged on the area, two of them pushing the emergency wagon before them. Millicent started down the corridor, somewhat hesitantly now, for she sensed that she did not belong there.

She reached the glass-walled ICU room, where a patient in distress was completely shielded from her view by the number of medical personnel who surrounded him. She was aware of intense activity and an air of desperation. Moments later someone brushed by her almost violently. Once he was past, she realized it was Dr. McCandless. He entered the room. Immediately all the others gave way to him. She could not see what steps he took with the patient, but she knew the activity level, furious as it had been, was now increased.

As she stood there straining to see, someone came alongside her. She heard what had become a familiar voice.

"What happened?" Nancy Campbell asked.

Without taking her eyes from the desperate scene, Millicent Forrest said, "A patient. In trouble. Very bad trouble. I hope they can help him."

They continued to watch in silence. After a time the feverish activity began to subside. An air of defeat pervaded the room. McCandless reappeared from the midst of the white-coated personnel of the emergency squad. From the set of his tall body and the look on his lean face, it was obvious that they had failed. His medical assistant caught up with him as they emerged from the glass-walled cubicle. They passed Millicent Forrest and Nancy Campbell without any sign of recognition and the two women overheard their conversation.

"Damn it," McCandless said. "Top of the list. Any AB heart from a normal-sized man would have done it for him. And to lose him now . . . damn it, damn it, damn it!"

"There was that call from Milwaukee. We thought we had one," his assistant replied, "but at the last moment the man's wife said no."

"So they buried another good heart. How can people be so shortsighted?" McCandless protested angrily.

Both women looked at each other. Neither spoke a word. But each knew what the other was thinking. *When my husband's time comes, will there be a heart?*

10

SURGEON CHRISTOPHER SLADE was writing up his report on his most recent case, in which the heart of a young man of twenty-one, who had been crushed in an accident while drag racing on a deserted strip of road in the industrial part of the city, had been transplanted into Patient Michael Boyko,a forty-one-year-old construction worker.

Though unexpected difficulties had been encountered in the course of surgery, the procedure had been successful and the patient was on his way to recovery. If Slade's expectations were realized, Boyko might be discharged from the hospital and become an outpatient within three weeks.

Because of the unusual problems presented during surgery, Slade was considering writing up the case for the medical journal *Circulation*.

He was in the midst of considering that when his phone rang and his secretary announced that Senator Bridgeman was in his waiting room.

Senator Bridgeman? Slade thought. *Why would he want to see me? If he's got a heart problem, or if one of his relatives has, he shouldn't be starting here. I'm the last one he should see.*

Yet he was out there, and Slade's secretary was insisting, "Shall I send him in, Doctor?"

"Yes. Sure. I guess so," Slade said, pushing aside his yellow pad and rising to his feet.

The door opened. Senator Bridgeman, a large man, a shock of white hair adding to his impressiveness, entered. Slade recognized him as one of those senators whose main claim to fame was his appearance on television during recent Senate hearings. Bridgeman moved with great vigor as he crossed the room, smiled, and held out his hand, greeting, "Dr. Slade, what a pleasure to meet you!"

Slade's instinctive reaction was, *He can't have come for a campaign contribution, yet he's giving me that sort of overly warm greeting.*

"Doctor, I've been following your career for some time," Bridgeman began. "Marvelous work you do! And the pressure you must be under. With human life literally in your hands every moment!"

"Thank you," a cautious Slade replied.

"That's why, when I decided to intervene for one of my constituents, I knew *you* were the man!" Bridgeman said.

The man speaks only in exclamations, Slade thought, *but I guess that's what it takes to be a successful politician. To pretend that nothing you have to say is ever casual or unimportant.*

Aloud, Slade said, "Senator, if you refer to a patient on our transplant list, I'm not the man to talk to."

"But whenever there's an unusual transplant operation here, you're the one whose name is in the newspapers or on television news."

"It's only when the patient gets to the operating table that I take over. But the program itself is run by a cardiologist. Dr. McCandless."

"Oh, I see," the senator said, less exclamatory and friendly now. "This . . . this Dr. McCandless . . . he's here, I assume."

"Two floors down."

"Ah, yes," Bridgeman said. "Two floors down. And McCandless is in charge of all patients who are awaiting transplants?"

"He's your man," Slade said, curious as to the senator's mission.

"Do you suppose he's in now?" Bridgeman asked.

Slade was quick to pick up the hint. He reached for his phone. "Irma, get Dr. McCandless on the phone."

After a wait of some seconds, Slade heard the familiar voice, "Yeah, Chris? What's up?"

"Doctor McCandless, I have a gentleman here in my office who would like to see you. At once, I assume." Bridgeman nodded vigorously affirmative to stress the urgency of the mission. "Send him right down? Thank you, Doctor."

To Allen McCandless, Chris Slade's use of the formal "Doctor" twice in such a brief conversation was a code alert to expect a rather unusual and possibly unwelcome visitor.

So as not to waste any valuable time, McCandless called to his secretary, "Claire, could you pick me up a turkey on rye, light on the mayonnaise. And a pot of tea, please. Might as well save time. Especially if Chris's hunch is right."

Within several minutes the door to Allen McCandless's office was thrust open. As if he had rehearsed it, Senator Bridgeman made his entrance into the office with exactly the same degree of vigor and enthusiasm as he had exerted on Chris Slade.

"Dr. McCandless, I can't tell you how delighted I am to meet you. I've been following the life-saving work of your unit very closely. Fine work. Excellent! Brings great credit to our state. Puts us right up there with New York, California and Pennsylvania when it comes to transplant expertise. You have no idea how your name gets around in important places."

"It's a total team effort, Mister . . . uh . . ." McCandless fumbled, at a loss.

"Bridgeman! Senator Arthur Bridgeman," the man explained, secretly offended that he had not been recognized.

"Ah, yes, Senator Bridgeman," McCandless said, thinking, *Why's he buttering me up? What's he want? With such a buildup, something's coming. I can smell that.* Aloud, he said, "As I was saying, this is a total team effort. It takes a group of many talented men and women, of whom I'm only one."

"Modesty becomes you, Doctor. Fits you like a well-made glove. But it's what I expected, from all I've heard about you," Bridgeman said.

For his own personal amusement, McCandless decided to encourage the senator. "Heard about me?"

As if imparting a confidence, Bridgeman leaned a bit closer to McCandless. "I guess I don't have to tell you, jealousy among senators is as nothing compared to the competition among doctors. So when all other doctors have nothing but praise for a man, then I know he's exceptional."

Almost as a preamble, Bridgeman continued, "Doctor, I'm sure you know that I have voted for every appropriation bill that benefits medical research, Medicare and the other needs of the scientific community."

"Yes, I know," McCandless agreed, trying to recall if indeed this was true.

At that moment, Claire knocked and entered without invitation. She carried a small tray with a turkey sandwich wrapped in transparent plastic and a short stubby pot of steaming tea.

"Excuse me," McCandless said.

"Go right ahead, Doctor. I know how busy you men are. And the stress you're under. Dealing in life and death every day. Must take a terrible toll," Bridgeman said.

He glanced at the sandwich McCandless had unwrapped. He chuckled. "Nice to see a doctor who eats the way he orders his patients to eat. Most doctors, they put you on a diet, give you all kinds of restrictions. While they themselves eat like hogs. I see them at the country club buffets on Sunday. And at those functions in Washington. So it's nice to run into a doctor who practices what he preaches. Or should I say, who practices what he practices?" He laughed at his own joke.

McCandless interrupted chewing to attempt a smile, but

failed. Instead, he poured himself some tea, thinking, *Why doesn't he get to it?*

"Doctor . . ." Bridgeman said suddenly, as if prepared to make an announcement of great consequence.

McCandless thought, *finally*.

"Doctor, you have a patient here who is a most unusual case. Oh, I know that *all* your cases are of life-and-death significance. But there are certain human values involved in this case that cannot be denied. And I refer now not only to a single patient, but to an entire family."

"We look on all our cases as involving entire families," McCandless pointed out.

"Including an infant?" Bridgeman asked.

McCandless did not have to run through his entire list of candidates to realize that the senator referred to Sally Brock. McCandless ceased eating at once. If this involved young Sally, McCandless was prepared to give the senator his total concentration.

"Imagine, Doctor, what it must be like. To go through nine months of pregnancy, finally give birth to a child, and then not be able to nurse her, fondle her, care for her. Bonding, that's what child experts are always talking about. No chance at all for bonding with her own baby. Can you think of any worse deprivation for a young woman?"

"No," McCandless admitted. "May I ask how you became involved in her case?"

"Tears, Doctor, a mother's tears," the senator said with as much dramatic emphasis as he could summon.

"Sally called you?" McCandless said, quite dubious.

"Not Sally. *Her* mother. Doctor, I can't tell you how it affects a man in my position. That mother on the phone. Four different times. Weeping pathetically. 'Save my daughter,' she pleads. 'Her life is just beginning. She's too young to die. She hasn't even started to live yet.' I tell you, Doctor, a plea like that haunts a man. Makes him determined to do something for that poor child. Whatever I can do."

"And *is* there something you can do?" McCandless

asked. "I mean, do you know where we can procure a Type AB heart for her from a donor roughly between a hundred and a hundred twenty pounds in weight? If you do, please tell me. I'm as anxious as she is, as her mother is, to see her recover and be back home with her baby."

"Well," the senator began, with the assurance of a man who felt that he now had the situation well in hand. "Remember some years ago when that father made an appeal to a convention of kidney specialists for a donor for his young daughter? And got one? And then President Reagan made an appeal from the White House for a little boy who needed a heart. And he got one? Remember?"

"Yes, indeed I do remember," McCandless said.

"What I am willing to do is use the total influence of my office to launch a public appeal on behalf of Sally Brock. My public relations people tell me that I could hit the nightly network news, reach the entire country. After all, how could anyone resist that fragile young woman, kept from her first baby by this unfortunate condition. I bet you we'd have a heart for her in a matter of days, hours maybe."

"That's what you'd like to do," McCandless considered.

"Just give me the information. All the medical details, what I appeal for, and authorize me to use your name and the name of this medical center," Bridgeman insisted. "I'm sure we could have that brave little girl—I mean woman—on her way to recovery in no time."

McCandless did not respond at once, which afforded the senator the opportunity to add, "This entire nation would get a tremendous lift out of such a warm human interest story. And we need it! Too much bad news of late. The scandals in Washington. The recent presidential campaign. Trouble with presidential campaigns, the candidates get to attacking each other, criticizing the party in power, until the people begin to feel that nothing's right with the country. The people need a restoration of faith and good cheer. Pride! Old-fashioned American pride! That's what they need!"

"And you intend to give it to them," McCandless observed.

"With your help, yes!" Senator Bridgeman declared. "I've got the machinery all set up. How we break the appeal. How we follow up. A toll-free number to call. Tie-ins with local TV stations. I'm dedicating myself to this, Doctor, dedicating myself. And my staff. We are determined to see poor Sally Brock well, healthy, and back home with her baby." After a moment of pause Bridgeman asked confidently, "Can I count on your cooperation, Doctor?"

"Senator, I'm afraid not," McCandless said.

The man's face flushed as if in anger and shock.

"I can't believe what I'm hearing! Doctor, are you telling me that you refuse to do everything you can on behalf of a patient whose very life rests in your hands? Depends on your decision? If you could have heard the appeals of Sally's mother—"

McCandless tried to interrupt, "Senator, I have heard such appeals. Many times in my career. But there is a limit to what we can do."

His pretense at shock having failed, Bridgeman resorted to the second of his prepared lines of attack. "Doctor, perhaps you don't appreciate the full implications of what I'm proposing. Think what this can do for the reputation of this medical institution. For your own reputation! We would feature your name in every television appeal. Of course, if you'd be willing, I'd love to have you appear with me. These days it's not unusual for doctors to appear on television. Everytime some important person, like the President or the First Lady— or some ex-President—gets sick, right away some doctor is on television explaining to the public exactly what happened. The public has a right to know. That's in the Constitution. First Amendment."

"I don't know too much about the Constitution, Senator. But for myself, I do not like doctors on television discussing their patients. Medical situations should remain confidential."

"In that case, you don't have to go on television. I'll handle that part of it. All you have to do is give me the information on which I will make my appeal."

McCandless noticed that the man was beginning to perspire just a little, betraying that he had not anticipated resistance.

"Senator, it isn't a matter of my going on television. It's a question of making such a public appeal at all," McCandless explained.

"Are you telling me you don't *care* if that young woman gets a heart?" the senator demanded, becoming belligerent.

"Senator, nothing would delight me more than to have that phone ring, with word that somewhere within a thousand miles of here there is a heart that would solve Sally's problem. We would mobilize our team of transplant specialists so quickly they would astound you with their speed and professionalism."

"Hell, man, I'm trying to help you do that!" the senator insisted.

"You don't understand, Senator."

"You're damn right I don't understand! Turning down the kind of public attention I could bring to bear on that poor woman's problems." Bridgeman shook his head in such disbelief that it almost set his carefully arranged white hair into disarray.

"What I'm trying to say, Senator, is that there is a regular, legal procedure by which hearts, and other organs, are distributed through the country, in a fair and equitable manner."

"Too damn slow, evidently," the senator interjected.

"Because there are never enough organs donated," McCandless pointed out. "Now, somewhere in this country at right this moment, there are young women, or children, who need a Type AB heart from a donor who weighs around one hundred pounds. I don't know how many. Some of them may have been waiting even longer than Sally Brock. Or they may be in worse shape than she is. In other words, by virtue of greater need they may be more deserving. We, and Sally, have to wait our turn.''

"But she doesn't have to wait! We can get that heart before it goes to one of the others,'' Bridgeman protested.

"If we try to do that, if all other transplant teams tried to do that, we'd be turning this into a medical jungle. Where power and money take precedence over human life,'' McCandless said. "I can't be part of any such process.''

"This is your hospital, she is your patient, you're responsible for her life, and you refuse . . .'' Bridgeman did not complete his accusation.

"Senator, I am *forced* to refuse your offer. It is neither fair nor professional,'' McCandless said.

"God damn, I never expected . . .'' Then in a final effort, he said, "I'll tell you one thing, you can't stop me!''

"I can only advise against it. You're free to do whatever you like,'' McCandless said.

"Well, I'll . . . I'll think about it. Confer with my P.R. people.''

"Tell them what I said,'' McCandless cautioned.

"Oh, of course,'' Bridgeman said, never intending to. "You disappoint me, Doctor, Very much.''

Once Bridgeman had left, a flicker of suspicion and curiosity began to tease McCandless. He reached for his phone.

"Claire, get me Lawrence Greene.''

"At this hour? He's likely to be in court.''

"Try him anyway.''

In moments his phone rang. "Mr. Greene's on the line.''

"Larry,'' McCandless began, "as a lawyer, you're up on such things. I'm not. When is Senator Bridgeman due to run for reelection?''

"Next November, Mac. Why?'' the attorney asked. "Has he hit you up for a campaign contribution?''

"Not exactly," McCandless said. "But it's interesting. Very interesting."

"What happened?" Greene asked.

"It certainly explains his sudden interest in 'deserving' cases," McCandless said.

"Mac, what the hell are you talking about?"

"You would have had to be here, Larry," McCandless said. "Oh, by the way, heard anything further yet?"

"Maggie's lawyer says he's having trouble convincing her that you don't own the Bank of America. Seems she has her mind set on going into business. Junk jewelry. And she needs the money. But don't worry. It'll work out somehow," the attorney advised.

"Larry, there's no . . . I mean, is there any indication that she might change her mind?" McCandless asked.

"Reconciliation?" Greene replied. "No. No hint at all, Mac. She means it."

"Sure. Of course. Considering the way she left," McCandless felt forced to agree.

He hung up the phone knowing two things. Though Maggie had not yet agreed to the divorce settlement, she was insisting on going through with the final decree. And the eminent Senator Bridgeman, having discovered what television exposure had done for him during the Senate hearings, was determined to capitalize on that by a wide TV appeal on behalf of Sally Brock. Much as Allen McCandless wanted to secure a heart for that young woman, the ethics of his profession forbade interference with the fair and established practice of organ procurement.

Waiting one's turn was still the rule of the game.

The senator's visit had stirred up feelings that tormented McCandless each time one of the candidates on his waiting list died for lack of a suitable heart.

Damn it, he thought, *if I ever did go on television, it wouldn't be to appeal for any one patient, but for all heart patients! I'd make the public aware. The most precious thing in this world, human life, is being buried every day in every corner of this nation. Out of mistaken devotion, religious beliefs or sheer sentimentality, perfectly good hearts are being denied to people whose lives depend on them. Who lives, who dies, who gets a heart, who doesn't, has become a game. A gamble. If we didn't bury so many healthy hearts, this wouldn't be a game at all. Or a gamble.*

11

THE WEEKLY EVALUATION meeting of the Transplant Unit took place every Monday afternoon. Unless, of course, a new heart had suddenly become available. Then all scheduled activities were off. The entire unit was galvanized into action. One surgical team was dispatched to secure the donor heart. The other team stood by in the operating room to prepare the recipient for the transplant and to await the new heart.

On this Monday afternoon, no heart having become available, McCandless, three other cardiologists, Slade, two surgeons, Psychiatrist Robbins, Transplant Coordinator Adeline Sawyer, Social Services Administrator Elaine Duncan, and all the other staff personnel met in the small auditorium to assess those applicants for admission to the program on whom all the tests and examinations had been completed. There would also be a review of those candidates already on the list, to determine if deteriorating conditions warranted a change in status for any of them.

In all respects this was the usual assemblage of the entire Unit, engaged in its normal weekly pursuit.

However, on this Monday one thing was different. As Allen McCandless called the meeting to order, Hospital Administrator Harvey Strawbridge entered the room to make an unprecedented appearance. McCandless being visibly annoyed by his presence at a meeting of purely medical importance, Strawbridge felt obliged to explain.

Smiling in an attempt to defuse the situation, he said, "Hardly a time I'm interviewed by the media when the question doesn't come up. How do we choose our patients? People suspect this is some secret ritual, clouded in mystery. I thought I'd sit in so I can explain more fully."

As a silent protest against Strawbridge's intrusion, Allen McCandless deftly slipped the Forrest file to the bottom of the pile. He then proceeded to present the cases of the applicants, one by one.

The first case presented was that of Patient Brevoort, Andrea. Cardiomyopathy. Age: forty-one. After all her test results and reports were evaluated, and once the opinion of Urologist Carl Wycliff was read aloud, it became apparent that the damage to Mrs. Brevoort's kidneys and other organs was so far advanced that it disqualified her from the program.

"It would be wasting a good heart," was the urologist's reluctant but final word on the case.

The files of several other patients were assessed. In two cases the psychiatric evaluations proved critical.

Robbins reported on one of them, "I simply have no confidence that he has licked his alcoholism, as he claims. I suspect he'd be off medication and into rejection in six months. Much as I sympathize with his family, I'm forced to vote no."

So it went through eleven cases. Eight were rejected. Three were selected to be added to the list of candidates.

The file of Patient Campbell, James came up in its turn. All agreed that by virtue of age, general condition, family backup and emotional support, he would be a welcome candidate. However, Social Services chief Elaine Duncan pointed out, "There may be a slight financial problem. But I think we can find the money from other sources."

"In that case," McCandless said, "we'll add James Campbell to the list. From my knowledge of his condition, I think it is safe to have him live at home until it is time to call him in for surgery. That will lighten their financial burden somewhat."

That left only one case remaining. McCandless pretended to be surprised when he identified the file. "Ah, and this last one. A patient named . . . Forrest . . . Winston Forrest." He cast a subtle glance in Strawbridge's direction.

The Administrator sat up in his chair, his hands clasped, his thumbs tapping against each other in nervous anticipation. Used to making horseback diagnoses, McCandless thought, *We've got him sweating already, so let's have a little fun.*

"This case does present a problem, I'm afraid."

McCandless noticed the flush of anger rising into Strawbridge's usually tanned face.

The cardiologist continued, "It would seem at first glance that Forrest is a likely candidate for a new heart. God knows, he needs it. And being the victim of a coronary infarct, he does not suffer severe residual damage such as Mrs. Brevoort. However, when one takes into account his personal situation—as adduced by Dr. Robbins, his marriage seemed to be in trouble right before his heart attack—we have to question his ability to stay the course. The will to persist in treatment might be lacking. He could become one of those patients who gets so fed up with the routine that he finally says, 'If this is the way I have to live, it's not worth it.' He seems a rather brusque, impatient man. So the question becomes, If we do give him a new heart, what are the odds of getting a long-term result?"

Equally annoyed by Strawbridge's unaccustomed presence in this meeting, Chris Slade decided to add a little fuel to the Administrator's developing case of heartburn.

"You know, Mac, we had a case very much like Forrest two years ago, or was it three? I can't recall the name. But a man in his early fifties, like Forrest. With some marital troubles. And a mistress. One day when I went to check him out in ICU—it couldn't have been more than two days after surgery—both women were arguing outside his room. And he could hear every word. Not a very pretty picture. Since then I've been even more wary than Robbins about patients with unstable home lives. I'm dubious about Forrest, very dubious."

Strawbridge could no longer control himself. Rising, he protested, "I've had quite a briefing on Mr. Forrest from the White House and the FBI. True, his marriage did seem to be undergoing a bit of . . . stress, shall we say. But there is absolutely nothing in his background that suggests a mistress. So I think the case Slade brought up has no relevance here. Is there anyone else here who has a valid, substantial, professional reason that would militate against his inclusion?"

They all pretended to consider the matter gravely. Then, since everyone familiar with the case knew that Forrest was a very good risk with a history that would qualify him, they assented, one by one, to his admission.

Swallowing his irritation, and with a feeling of accomplishment, Harvey Strawbridge said, "That's better." He strode out of the room.

After which, those who were in on the joke were free to laugh openly.

The meeting concluded, Allen McCandless and Transplant Coordinator Adeline Sawyer visited the room of James Campbell.

Jim and Nancy were overjoyed at word that he had been admitted to the program.

"Go home," McCandless advised. "Take it easy. Follow the instructions in the patient's manual Addie Sawyer will give you. And take this," he continued, as he drew out of the pocket of his white lab coat a small black object about the size of a pack of cigarettes. "This is your beeper. As soon as it sounds, call us at once. And keep this with you at all times. Awake or sleep. At home or out. It's our way of reaching you when necessary."

"You mean when you find a heart for him," Nancy assumed, hopeful.

"Yes. And at any other time we feel it necessary to reach him," McCandless said.

"Dr. McCandless, what do you think my chances are?" Jim asked.

"Jim, we've got to search for a Blood Type O heart from a man between one hundred fifty pounds and one hundred eighty pounds. Type O's like you can only accept a heart from another Type O. That may limit your chances somewhat. But I'm optimistic. And you should be, too."

McCandless knew that Campbell and his wife were anxious for stronger reassurance, but he made it a policy not to encourage false hopes in patients or their families.

Privately, if forced to evaluate Campbell's chances, he would have said , at best, fair. There were too many Type O's waiting for too few Type O hearts. To lengthen the odds against Jim Campbell, a Type O heart could be safely implanted not only into a Type O recipient, but into Type A, Type B, and Type AB as well, putting Type O hearts at a premium.

"Now, Jim," McCandless said, "go home. Take it easy. Check in with Ben Kaplan regularly. And have him stay in touch with me. "Okay?"

"Okay," Jim Campbell said.

"Miss Sawyer will give you a copy of the manual for transplant patients. It explains everything. How hearts are matched to recipients. How the heart functions. What you have to do after the transplant. The diet to follow. The various medications you take. The routine of tests you'll undergo afterward. Weekly, then biweekly, then monthly, then every six months. Everything you have to know before you get a new heart and after. Take it home. Study it. Both of you. Because, young woman, I am depending on you to make sure this man follows the regime precisely. Got it?"

"Got it," Nancy Campbell responded firmly.

McCandless's next call was in the room two doors down. He found the Forrests in that state of nervous unease that betrays itself by a startled response to the sound of even a door being opened quietly.

"Well, Mr. Forrest, good news. You've been accepted into the program," McCandless announced at once to reassure them.

Conditioned by his career in diplomacy and government, Forrest did not react with an outward show of emotion. But his wife brightened considerably.

In quite a matter-of-fact fashion Forrest asked, "What do we do now?"

"Your residence is in the Washington area. That won't do for our purposes. Talk to Addie Sawyer when she brings you your patient's manual. She'll help you find quarters close to the hospital. So you'll be handy when the moment comes."

"*Will* the moment come?" Forrest asked.

"It usually does, Mr. Forrest," McCandless said. "More than seventy percent of our cases—"

Forrest interrupted, "I know, Doctor, more than seventy percent of your candidates get new hearts. But a man in my condition doesn't have much time to wait out the odds."

"I understand how a man feels at a time like this—" McCandless began.

"Do you really?" Forrest interrupted. "How can you? You have to be there. You have to feel your life slipping through your fingers. Telling you it's time to go. But you don't want to go. There's so much yet to do. So much yet to make up for . . ."

McCandless noted that this last was subtly directed toward his wife. Before the conversation could become too intimate or embarrassing, McCandless knew he should withdraw as gracefully as possible.

"You're taking too pessimistic a view of things, Mr. Forrest. Nobody's saying it's your time to go. Certainly we are not saying that. The odds are in your favor. A good, healthy Type O heart can add ten years to your life. Even more."

"Type O? Is that what I am?" Forrest asked.

"Yes," McCandless informed him.

"Should have remembered from my dog tags back in the war," Forrest said.

"Korea?" McCandless asked.

"Yes," Forrest said. The question had provoked him sufficiently to admit, "Before I arrived here I was worried about . . . about my age. I wondered how young a man had to be to get a new heart."

"Years ago it would have been a problem. Now we do them on infants and men and women up to age sixty-five. So you are well within the limits. We look for a good result." And, because he knew that Forrest needed something to bolster his spirits, he added, "A very good result."

As McCandless turned to head for the door, his eyes made contact with the hazel eyes of Millicent Forrest. She was thanking him for his reassurance.

He was headed down the corridor, away from Forrest's room, when he thought, *Stunning woman, handsome in a majestic way. Good figure, too. A man would be very lucky to have a wife like her. What the hell is wrong with Forrest that their marriage is in trouble? Or, based on Robbins's report, was on the verge of breaking up. But she's here, back to see him through what can be a most difficult time. Remarkable woman.*

If this were happening to me, would Maggie come back? Remarkable woman, that Mrs. Forrest.

Allen McCandless sat in his office, rocking slowly in the swivel chair at his desk. He was studying the list of all patients who had been admitted to the Hospital Cardiac Transplant Service. There were thirty-eight names currently on the list.

Each was listed and identified by more than name. First and foremost, by blood group. A, B, AB or O. Each name had a number alongside it. A priority number, indicating their standing on the list based on need for a new heart. Those designated 1 were the most emergent cases. The others ranged from 2 down to 10. In another column was listed the date the patient had been accepted into the program. Then the number of weeks that had elapsed. Some patients had been on the list as little as two weeks, some as many as sixty-three weeks.

The other columns listed the diagnosis of the patient's heart condition which required a transplant, his or her weight, and the weight range of potential donors who would be deemed acceptable.

Thirty-eight names, each a line on a list. Thirty-eight lives, McCandless was well aware. As the patients did, he found refuge in statistics, too. More than two thirds of them would eventually get new hearts. The rest . . . would die.

From the two files he had before him, he penciled in the following information concerning two new approved names he was adding to the list. Following nine blood group O candidates, he added:

Blood Group	Priority	Name	Date on List	Diagnosis	Acceptable Donor Weight
O	5	Forrest	4/17/89	CAD	150–180
O	5	Campbell	4/17/89	ICM	150–180

He would give the new list to Claire to type up, make copies and distribute them to all members of the transplant team.

12

IT WAS EIGHTEEN miles from the Medical Center to the town of Redmont, eleven of it through city and town streets. Nancy insisted on driving, reminding Jim, "Dr. McCandless said take it easy. Don't overdo!"

"Driving a light van with power steering is not overdoing!" Jim protested.

"I'll drive!" she insisted.

During the journey, without a word to one another, both of them kept glancing at the clock on the dashboard. Each trying to estimate, *When the call comes, if it comes, how long would it take? Suppose the call comes early in the morning when the traffic rush is at its worst? The traffic near that new plant is impossible, and there's no way around it.*

Their eyes fixed on the clock at the same instant and they met in the rearview mirror. Both knew, both understood.

To allay his fear, Nancy said, "Didn't they say we would have an hour to get there?"

"Someone said that. I don't remember who," he concurred, clutching the small black object that had now become his lifeline and was damp with the perspiration from his tense hand.

"Don't you worry, hon. When the time comes, we'll manage," she said.

"The kids . . . what do we tell the kids?" Jim asked.

131

"We tell them the truth. Daddy needs an operation. When the time comes, we just have to go. Mrs. Noonan will be glad to take care of them."

She turned the van onto Oak Street. Halfway down the block she pulled into the driveway of their modest two-story home. Tasteful and expert landscaping made it appear more costly and imposing than it actually was.

As he stepped out of the van, Jim said, "We should call Dr. Kaplan and tell him how it went."

"Soon as I get you settled," she agreed.

He reached for the small suitcase behind the passenger seat. She said quickly, "I'll do that."

"For God's sakes, honey, it's just a light suitcase," he protested.

"Jim!" she rebuked, a single syllable which she used with great effectiveness at those rare times when she insisted on having her own way.

"Okay, okay," he surrendered grudgingly.

He started along the stone path that cut across the lawn to the front door. He heard the cry, "Dad!" James Campbell, Junior, age eleven, came bounding across the lawn, heedless of the way he trampled the grass underfoot. Jim had knelt to embrace his son, who flung himself into his father's arms.

Impulsively, Nancy cried, "Jimmy! No!"

The boy's joy and enthusiasm turned to a look of puzzled disappointment. To compound her sense of guilt, her husband stared at her, as if asking, *Can't a man greet his own son? Has it come to that?*

She explained gently, "Darling, for a little while Dad is going to have to take things easy."

"All I did was—" the boy tried to explain.

"Jimmy!" she interrupted sharply, before she could control herself. "Don't argue! Just do as I say!"

Since she was not usually so firm, or angry with him, the boy did not argue. He picked up his backpack where he had dropped it and started around to the kitchen door.

"You shouldn't speak to him that way," Jim said. "He's a good kid. A simple explanation would have done it."

"I know. I'm sorry." She picked up the suitcase and started for the door.

Before he followed her into the house, he looked around at the lawn, at the trees, at the street.

How much longer am I going to be able to do this? See this street, these trees, this house, Jimmy's face? And Dorothy's. What happens when I'm gone? Everything else will still be here. Except me. Sure, they'll miss me. Miss waiting for me to come home from work. Who will they wait for after I'm gone? I've been thinking of talking to Nan. If I thought she'd listen without crying. I think it would be a good thing if . . . well, she's young and nice-looking. There'd be lots of men—at least some—who would fall in love with her. Want to marry her. I would like to tell her, make sure, whoever he is, he loves the kids. They need someone to wait for. To look forward to when he comes home at night. So he's got to love kids.

His thoughts were interrupted. "Jim?" He turned to find Nancy standing in the open doorway, her look beckoning him to come in. He tried to take a deep breath, then started for the door.

Once inside, he headed for the stairs, but she stepped in front of him. "No, hon."

He turned to her, puzzled.

"Dr. McCandless said stairs might be too much, up and down a dozen times a day."

"I'm not an invalid. Yet!" he protested.

"Jim, please . . ." The surge of tears to her eyes was more convincing than her spoken plea.

"Okay. Sure," he replied. He went into the living room, relieved to drop into his chair. He felt winded, and damp.

Nancy sat down beside him, took his hand, felt the dampness of it. "Hon, until we get that call, you will sleep on the couch in the den. You will use the guest bathroom. No more climbing those stairs."

He nodded, acquiescing, "We should have bought the house that you liked. The ranch-style job. One floor, no stairs, no basement. It would be perfect right now."

"We couldn't afford it then," she said. Trying to relieve him of either guilt or regret, she added, "This house has done well by us till now. And it will again."

He nodded. She was conscious of his labored breathing.

They heard the back door being flung open as Dorothy cried out, "Dad! Mom! I saw the van out in the drive-way . . ."

She burst into the living room, bounded into her father's outstretched arms. This time Nancy restrained her impulse to intervene. Little Dorothy seized her father by the hand and started pulling toward the stairs, calling, "Jimmy! Jimmy!" As her brother came bounding down the stairs, she turned to her father. "Well? Did he read it?"

"Read what, baby?" Jim asked, puzzled.

"Our note! Our note to the doctor!"

Glancing over the child's head at his wife, he said, "First thing we did when we got to the hospital, we showed it to Dr. McCandless."

"What'd he say, Dad? What'd he say?" the girl persisted.

Jim seated his daughter to one side of him on the bottom step, gesturing Jimmy to sit on his other side. With his arms around both of them he started to explain.

"When that doctor read your note, he said it was the finest letter he'd ever read. And because it is, he's going to give your dad the best heart there is."

"It worked!" little Dorothy said to her brother. "Our note worked!"

"It sure did," her father said. He looked to his wife before continuing. "And that means that now, some day soon we hope, we are going to get a call to come to the hospital. It might come early in the morning, or when you're at school, or late at night. When it does, Mom and I have to leave for the hospital at once. Mrs. Noonan will come to stay with you until

Mom gets back. And when she does, you two are going to be the best behaved kids in Redmont. Promise?''

"Ah, Mrs. Noonan's easy," Jimmy said. "She never says no to anything we do."

"Then don't take advantage. Just do what she says. And all the time keep thinking, Dad's getting his new heart. And when he comes home it'll be like the time before he got sick. Remember that, kids, Dad's getting better. Of course, it might help a little if you prayed."

"Sure, Dad," Jimmy said. Then, a bit hesitant, he asked, "That operation, is it dangerous, Dad?"

With half a glance to Nancy, Jim was quick to assure, "Not anymore. Why . . . why, they do them every day now. Every day."

"That's good," little Dorothy said. "Real good." But she pressed her father's hand tighter to her shoulder.

Heritage Acres was a name that announced itself, as subtly as possible, to be a development of upper-middle-class condominiums for the aging, though the advertisements dubbed them "the mature." No children were allowed as permanent residents. If they came to visit their grandparents, it was understood their stay would be of short, and quiet, duration.

For the Forrests there was one other complicating limitation. No resident was permitted who was younger than fifty. This posed no problem for Winston Forrest. But since Millicent was only forty-four, and looked considerably younger, there was an objection. This was overcome when Coordinator Sawyer pointed out that their stay would be temporary, four or five months at most. Besides, it would lend a degree of prestige to Heritage Acres to have a resident as distinguished as the National Security Adviser to the President.

When the long black official limousine pulled up before their temporary home, one of a long cluster of Tudor-type attached houses, neighbors peeked out their windows to get a glimpse of the couple.

They saw Winston Forrest try to shrug off the assistance

of his wife as he stepped out of the car and started up the
fieldstone walk toward the front door. In the end he felt
compelled to reach for her arm just before the two of them
disappeared into the house, while the driver began to unload
their suitcases.

Inside the house, Millicent led her husband to the living
room couch, which was covered with flowered linen uphol-
stery of deep tan, interwoven with figures of rich blue and
modest brown.

Not bad, she thought. *I was dreading the place. But
whoever owns it seems to have good taste. Wonder why
they're no longer here? Did he die? Or did she? Or are they
on a cruise around the world?*

Her thoughts were interrupted by the driver asking
instructions with a simple, "Ma'am?" and a glance at the four
large suitcases he had carried in.

"This way, I guess," she said, starting for what she
assumed was the master bedroom. He followed. She passed
the smaller guest room, stopped. "Put the red suitcases in
here. And the gray ones in there."

She continued into the master bedroom and discovered it,
too, was tastefully furnished. She tried the huge double bed. It
was firm enough to ward off any back problems. One thing
Winston usually complained about when he came back from
those long overseas conferences were the beds. Too soft. They
gave him tormenting back pain. This bed would do him
nicely, for as long as he had to be here. She removed the
bedspread and uncovered fresh clean-smelling linen, color
coordinated with the drapes and the thick carpeting.

She went out into the living room, where Winston sat in
the same position as when she had left him, leaning forward,
breathing with some difficulty.

"Win, would you like to rest . . . maybe take a nap?"
she asked. "Get into your pajamas?"

"I do not wish to be treated as an invalid!" he declared.

"Then just lie down awhile," she suggested.

He did not resist that suggestion. But when she tried to

help him up, he very carefully put aside her hands. She watched him start for the bedroom, listening carefully in the event he needed help.

She could not resist admiring the way he insisted on carrying himself in the same posture he adopted when he was in white tie and tails, or morning coat and striped trousers. He seemed to have been born to be an important person. And, evidently, was determined to die the same way.

She followed to find him struggling to get his shoes off. She dropped by the side of the bed, unloosed the laces, slipped off his shoes. But when she tried to lift his legs onto the bed, he resisted. He had his own strict rules as to how much assistance he would permit.

In minutes he was dozing. When she was sure his breathing was regular, if not strong, she withdrew to her own room to unpack.

On the very top of her largest suitcase, carefully wrapped in bubbled plastic for protection, she found her silver-framed photograph of her son Paul, in Marine uniform. She was never able to look at that photograph without something within her protesting, *So young, he was so young and so handsome, such a handsome boy.*

She set the silver frame down on the night table. Now unpacking could begin.

When she inquired about where to shop, eager cooperative neighbors offered to drive her to the nearest supermarket. By the time Winston woke, she had been shopping and was already in the well-equipped kitchen preparing dinner. He found her dotting the chicken cutlets with margarine—low salt, no cholesterol, diet margarine.

He took her by surprise. "Chicken again?"

She half turned to him. "Your days of foie gras, caviar and Scotch salmon are over, I'm afraid." She started to laugh.

"What's funny about that?" he asked dourly.

"I was just remembering the old days. When we would eat like royalty at those diplomatic receptions but scrounge at home on hamburger and spaghetti because your government salary was so low."

"We had fun in those days, though."

"Yes, yes, we did," she agreed, a distinct touch of sadness in her voice. There was also the unspoken declaration that for them all that was past and done. To change the mood, she said, "Chicken, broiled. Green salad with lemon dressing. Green beans. And sugar-free Jell-O. That's the menu."

"Great," he said sarcastically. "I'll go look at the television news and see what lies they're peddling tonight."

He shuffled out of the kitchen slowly. She had time to turn and watch him retreat, marking how his trousers hung loosely in the seat. He had lost weight, too much weight.

God, they better hurry with that new heart if they want him alive when it gets here, she thought.

It was long past midnight.

In the upstairs bedroom in the Campbell house on Oak Street in Redmont, Nancy Campbell turned from her usual right-side sleeping position onto her back. She had not been able to fall asleep. It was so still in the house that she could hear the normally imperceptible whirring of the electric clock in the radio on the night table. She lifted her head to glance at it. Seventeen minutes after three.

Tired as she was, she had no desire for sleep. She stared up at the ceiling. One phrase kept throbbing in her head. *End-stage . . . end-stage . . . end-stage . . .*

That was the phrase Dr. Kaplan used when he sat both of them down to explain the results of all the tests he had ordered at the local hospital.

There lay spread before him on his desk long, glossy gray strips of Jim's cardiograms. There were lab reports with figures she could not distinguish. And a roll of film that looked like the kind that Jim had taken of the kids last Christmas.

But when Kaplan threaded it into the machine on his side

table and asked her to look in, she had seen unreeling before her the erratic action of a diseased human heart.

"I'll be sending all this down to the Medical Center," Kaplan explained. "There's no doubt, Jim is end-stage."

"What does that mean, 'end-stage'?" she had asked.

Kaplan's eyes revealed that he would rather not answer that question. But both Campbells were staring at him, waiting.

"Nan, my dear, Jim, to cardiologists 'end-stage' means there is nothing more they can do except a heart transplant."

"What if Jim gives up all work, what if he rests in bed?" she had asked.

"I'm afraid that wouldn't improve things," Kaplan replied. Because he was so conscious of Jim's stunned state of mind, he turned to this man who was young enough to be his son. "Jim, we have to face it. There is no medication, no amount of treatment or rest that can help. Your heart is simply deteriorating. And will continue to do so, no matter what we do. So, all that is left is a transplant."

Before they could react, before Nancy could break into tears, Kaplan tried to put a more optimistic face on things. "Fortunately, we are only eighteen, twenty miles, from one of the best medical facilities in this country. With an excellent heart unit, under a fine doctor. A friend of mine. Allen McCandless. I'll call him. I'll arrange for him to personally take care of you."

"And he can help?" Nancy asked.

"When he sees these results and this cineangiogram you just saw, I have no doubt he'll admit Jim to the transplant program."

"A transplant . . ." Jim said softly. "I never thought that I . . . I mean, I always thought transplants are for the kind of people you see on the television news. Not someone like me."

Kaplan patted the young man on the shoulder in fatherly fashion. "Jim, most of the transplants you never even hear about. In this country alone, twenty of them a week. Every week. A thousand a year. These days it's done so often it's no longer news. And that's good. The technique is refined. The drugs you have to take are much better, more effective. Those cases on television were in the experimental stage. Now it's routine, Jim, routine."

As subtly as he could, Kaplan tried to study Jim's eyes, and Nancy's, to see if he had been able to reassure them. Not really, unfortunately.

"Well, I'll get these down to McCandless. And we'll know soon enough."

"What if they don't accept Jim?" Nancy asked.

"Nan, my dear, let's not jump to conclusions," Kaplan said. "Tell you what, I'll call McCandless tonight. I'll explain the case even before I send Jim's results down. Okay?"

"Okay," Nancy had said.

Kaplan had patted her on the cheek. He was a kindly, sensitive old man, but he hadn't been as reassuring as he had tried to be.

Now she lay awake in this quiet house, listening. It had been only days ago, twelve to be exact, since she had first heard the phrase "end-stage," but it seemed as if it had been years. Everything that had preceded that day seemed long ago, ancient history, from another time, another life. Even those days when Jim had first begun to evidence symptoms seemed long ago.

She stirred in response to a sound she heard, or thought she heard. The kids. She had better go see about the kids. Lately, ever since Jim's condition had deteriorated so badly that he had to cut down on his work, then cut it out altogether, the kids had not been sleeping well. Young as they were, silent as they were, they had been affected by these changes in the family's routine. Their security had been badly shaken.

She slipped out of bed. She peeked into Jimmy's room. He was curled up on his side, asleep but uncovered. She straightened his blanket, tucked it in, kissed him on the forehead.

Dorothy was on her back, legs straight, arms stretched close beside her body, golden hair spread across her pillow. She was asleep, breathing shallowly but regularly. Nancy stared down at her daughter. Even in the darkness she was a beautiful child, beautiful. *Not plain like me,* Nancy thought.

She started down the stairs very cautiously. As she drew close to the den, she listened. She stood in the doorway and watched. Jim was breathing in those small gasps, which she had grown used to by now. But at least he was asleep and breathing.

She went out into the living room, sank into the big easy chair, which was Jim's chair when he watched football on television. She reached around to grasp her arms. She clutched them to her breasts, determined not to cry. Terrified, without hope, wondering how long this house would be their house, how long they could survive if Jim died, she was determined not to weep any longer.

The private night-patrol car that protected Heritage Acres from burglars and prowlers was making its way slowly along the meandering streets of the development. Its headlights on bright, it swept the streets and the homes like the strong beams of a lighthouse.

Those lights played across the ceiling of the second bedroom of the condominium now inhabited by the Forrests.

The unexpected light startled Millicent Forrest, who had wakened only a short time earlier. Her first impulsive reaction was, *It's the flashlight of an intruder.* She experienced a moment of indecision. *The police always say, in the event of an intrusion, lie still and pretend to be asleep.* But her anxiety compelled her to slip out of bed. She went to the window, cautiously parted the draperies in time to see the red taillights of the patrol car disappear around a curve in the street.

Once up, she went to see how Winston was doing. He

was asleep, but had slid off the high double pillows that had been recommended. He lay on his side, one arm under his head, the other alongside his body. His breathing was slightly labored. In all, he appeared in better condition than she had expected.

She went out to the kitchen, boiled some water for instant coffee, decaffeinated, of course. She took the steaming mug out into the living room. There she tuned in a late-late-night movie, turning the sound down so low that she could hardly hear the dialogue. But since she had no interest in the film, the dialogue didn't matter.

Too many years of television had addicted her, and most of the nation, to needing images, no matter how meaningless, to engage the eye like some drug.

In the house on Oak Street Nancy Campbell was startled when she became aware that her husband was standing in the archway to the living room.

"Jim?" she called softly, fearful that pain or some other sign of danger had wakened him.

"I thought I heard someone . . ." he said. He came into the room, slipped down on the ottoman before her.

"I'm sorry if I woke you, hon," she said.

"That's okay. Gave me time to think. Earlier, when the kids came in to say good night, I said to myself, Damn it, I'm going to lick this thing. That doctor . . . McCandless . . . he's everything Kaplan said he was. Knows his stuff. Everybody there knows their stuff. It's going to work."

She was comforted to see the change in his attitude.

"When we first left there, I thought, We're just going through the motions," he confessed. "They won't be able to help me. But tonight, seeing Dottie and Jimmy, I said, God is not going to let their father die. He won't permit it. He won't. My kids are not going to grow up without a father. I am going to make it!"

She leaned forward, took him in her arms and hugged him tightly.

"Damn right you're going to make it!" she said.

But she could not banish from her mind the statistic someone had used in the last few days, *Almost one fourth of them die while waiting for a new heart.*

13

NANCY CAMPBELL STOOD in the doorway of their home, watching as young Jimmy Campbell and his sister Dorothy trudged off to school in their raincoats, hats and boots, to protect them from a spring rainstorm. She took pride that, young as he was, her son was aware of his father's condition and had responded by being unusually well-behaved for an eleven-year-old boy with great energy. He was extremely solicitous of his younger sister, quick to volunteer to do errands or chores around the house, and in some ways tried to assume the role of his father.

In all, young Jimmy Campbell had made the weeks of waiting less of a trial to both his mother and father than Nan had feared they were going to be. Still, those weeks had gone by without that call. Yes, there had been calls to check up on Jim's condition. To make sure that he had not deteriorated. And twice Transplant Coordinator Adeline Sawyer had called to request their attendance at the patients' group. Both trips had been rewarding. Jim returned each time more confident about the program, more encouraged at the possibility of his getting that new heart.

But between those group meetings there had been the inevitable letdown of waiting, just waiting. Yesterday had been one of those days. Last night before she left him in the den to go up to be alone, he had asked, "Nine weeks. How much longer can it be?"

Meaning, *How much longer can I hold out?*

"I know now," he continued, "what that fellow Charlie said . . . what was his name?"

"The man in the patients' group meeting?" Nancy responded. "Charlie Evans."

"Yes. Right. Charlie Evans. Remember when he said, 'Some days you think, They're trying to reach me, but my beeper isn't working.' Well, I have days like that. Lots of days," he admitted.

Nancy watched both her children trudge off to school through the light rain, until they had turned the corner at the far end of the street and were out of sight. She was about to close the door and go back into the kitchen to make Jim's breakfast when she was interrupted by the sight of a car coming around the corner and pulling up in front of the house. She knew that car well. It had pulled up before their house many times, in broad daylight, in the middle of the night, at any hour when concern or panic had forced her to call.

It was Dr. Kaplan's car, and seemed almost as old as he was. But it was well-kept, always clean, with the white walls of the fat old tires spick-and-span. It was better cared for than the doctor himself, who tended to be quite careless about his own appearance. He climbed out of the car, hauling his black bag with him.

"Nan, my dear . . ." he called as he hurried up the walk, "I was making a house call in the neighborhood, so I thought I would stop in. Can you spare a cup of coffee for a tired old man?"

He had made a well-intended effort to conceal his concern about Jim, but Nancy was not deceived. Nevertheless, she allowed the old man to think he had succeeded at his ruse.

"Anytime you're in the neighborhood, Ben," she said.

"And you wouldn't have one of those honey buns you bake from time to time, would you?"

"I would," she said.

"Well, then, we're wasting time out here. Let's go."

He was not halfway through his coffee and that honey bun when he said, "Look, long as I'm here, maybe I'll take a look at Jim."

He tried to make his suggestion sound as casual as he had when he invited himself in. But Nancy was beyond pretenses now. Her face turned somber. She could no longer resist asking, "Dr. McCandless called you, didn't he?"

"No," Kaplan said. "He did not call me. I am not here at his behest. I am here on my own. So what if I wasn't in the neighborhood? Jim is my patient and I have a right to be curious—"

"Curious? Or worried?" Nancy interrupted.

"Worried, shmorried, what difference does it make? Jim is my patient, my friend. I am concerned. I would like to see how he's getting along. May I?"

"Of course. I'm sorry, Ben."

He rose to his feet. Since he was not much taller than she, he looked her in the eye as he took her hand and said, "We have to stick together, Nan, dear. Because I have a feeling that he is going to make it. Our job is to convince *him* that he's going to make it. Okay?"

Her eyes tearing up, she said, "Okay."

"Now let's go have a look."

Kaplan had performed his routine examination of Jim Campbell's heart and lungs. To his experienced ears the patient's condition had changed, and not for the better. But he pretended to be satisfied.

"Well, not bad, Jim, not bad at all," the old man said. "I am so confident you're going to get that new heart that I have sent off a note to McCandless and Slade. I would like to be in the operating room when you get it."

"Will they let you?" Nancy asked.

"They wouldn't dare stop me!" Kaplan defied. Then he smiled. "Of course they'll let me. So I'll be there."

Throughout the examination Jim had said nothing. Merely

surrendered himself to the doctor's probing. When it was over and he was buttoning his shirt, he asked, "How long, Doc?"

"As soon as the next heart shows up that's right for you, that beeper will begin making the most wonderful sound in the world," Kaplan said, sounding as enthusiastic as the situation would permit.

"I meant, if there's no heart, how long do I have?"

"Jim, you said you didn't feel that way any longer," Nancy protested.

"After all, I have a right to ask . . . to know . . ."

"Of course you do," Kaplan intervened. "You're doing well. You've got time, Jim. They'll find you a heart, I'm sure of it." He hoped he had allayed Jim's fears.

On his way out he stopped at the front door to whisper, "Nan, has he said anything lately? About new pains? Or new difficulty breathing?"

"No. Why?"

"Nothing. Just thought if he was feeling worse, that might have led to his new depression," Kaplan said. "Look, if anything happens, if he needs anything, you call me. No matter what hour of day or night. Right?"

"What do you expect to happen?" she asked forthrightly.

"Expect? Nothing. But we can't always be sure . . ." he said. He kissed her on the cheek, then said, "If you need me, don't hesitate to call."

Nancy watched as his old car started down the street. *He found something, something he didn't want to tell me about. It must be bad, if he wouldn't say.*

She mustered a smile and a hopeful look and went in to prepare Jim's breakfast.

Millicent Forrest came out of the kitchen of their condominium in Heritage Acres to announce, "Breakfast is ready." When she received no reply, she stiffened, then hurried to the master bedroom. There she found her husband slumped in the armchair, eyes closed. Beside him on the floor she saw a yellow pad and the gold pen that had been a gift from the President, as the engraved inscription attested.

Almost breathless, she called out, "Win! Winston!" She rushed to his side, dropped to her knees to take him in her arms.

He came awake, asking resentfully, "What's wrong? What's the matter?"

"I thought . . ." But she chose not to say what she had feared.

"I was starting to write my memoirs." He indicated the pad and pen on the floor. "I've been thinking, since we don't know how much time I have left, this is the last good thing I can do for the country. I guess I dozed off. Somehow I don't seem to have the energy I once had. Somehow . . ."

Greatly relieved, Millicent Forrest said, "Breakfast."

"Yes. Of course. Breakfast."

He rose from the chair, gently easing aside her attempt to assist him. He straightened up. With his usual dignity he started for the dinette. The way he walked reassured her somewhat. He was no better, but he seemed no worse.

After breakfast he dressed in khaki pants, plaid wool shirt, rugged shoes, and declared that he was going for a walk. She did not forbid him. She knew that very soon his flagging strength would do that. It did. Soon he changed his mind and decided to sit out on the patio and catch some late morning sun. She watched him furtively from behind the draperies in the den window. He breathed shallowly but regularly. Though each breath seemed an effort.

Her household chores done, she went out to join him. Neither had said anything beyond her asking what he might like for dinner.

"They don't give me much choice, do they? White meat of skinless chicken, I suppose. Dry, of course, Something green. Anything green. Also dry. No salt. No butter. What a feast to look forward to. Not exactly a White House State dinner, is it?"

They were both silent for a time. Until he said, "I am going to dedicate it to Paul."

"Dedicate? What?" she asked, surprised.

"My memoirs. To Paul and to all the young men who die because we fail. That's why I have to get that heart, so I can write my book."

"And you will. McCandless said the odds are in your favor," she encouraged.

"The way I figure, during the time I'm waiting, I can lay out the whole thing. I got started on the foreword this morning before I dozed off. Then I'll do a chapter or two on the early part of my life. Our life, too. Starting out in government. Working my way up the ladder. My first overseas assignment. Remember? Those were great years, the Kennedy years. Only two and a half years really. Remember where we were that day?"

"I'll never forget it. The party at the French ambassador's villa in Berne. A pre-Thanksgiving party in honor of the American contingent."

"Yes. Trying to shore up relations after De Gaulle gave NATO the back of his hand, militarily speaking. God, when you look back you have to wonder, with all the mistakes that were made, how have we come this far?" he asked grimly. "Until now I never realized how much I have to say. And how little time I have to say it."

"Dr. McCandless said once you get that heart, you can have a good ten to fifteen years, maybe more," she encouraged.

"McCandless. Nice young man," he said, then smiled wryly. "Nice *young* man? He is forty, maybe a little more. And I look on him as a young man. I'm only fifty-one. But I feel so much older."

They were silent once more. After a time he said, "Millie, would you get me my pad and pen?"

"Do you think you should?" she asked.

"I'm just going to sit here and make some notes," he replied. "That can't be overdoing, can it?"

She left him with his pad and pen, to make notes in what she recognized as handwriting quite shaky and less precise than his usual firm clean script.

Millicent Forrest was balancing a bag of groceries with one hand while trying to unlock the front door with her other. She finally succeeded and called, "Winston?" There was no reply. She set the groceries down on the kitchen counter, started out to the terrace, but could see through the patio doors that he was no longer there. She started for the bedroom. She could hear him coughing. *God,* she thought, *I hope he didn't catch cold out there. That's all he needs in his condition.* She raced into the bedroom to find him lying across the foot of the bed breathing in short desperate gasps.

"Winston!"

She rushed to his side, reached for his hand, found his pulse. For a moment she could not distinguish whether it was his pulse that was erratic or her own. She recovered and applied herself to concentrating on his pulse. It was fast. And irregular.

Through his labored breathing he managed to say, "It . . . hurts." He pointed out the area of his chest where the trouble lay. He continued to struggle for breath so desperately she was terrified he might die.

For a moment she hesitated, then, assessing the dangers, she decided the lesser risk was to leave him for just long enough to call McCandless.

"Mrs. Forrest, please. Get control of yourself and answer my questions," McCandless said.

"Yes, of course. Sorry."

"He said pain? Chest pain?"

"Yes, Doctor."

"And he has a fast, irregular pulse?"

"It feels that way to me," Millicent Forrest responded.

"He's coughing? And is he short of breath?"

"Yes."

"We'd better bring him in," McCandless said. "I'll get an ambulance out there at once."

"What is it, Doctor, another heart attack?" she asked.

"It doesn't sound that way to me. But we can't take any chances. Get him ready to go. An ambulance will be there in minutes."

McCandless leaned over the examining table, the diaphragm of his stethoscope moving across the bare hairy chest of Winston Forrest, who continued breathing in short gasps which were interrupted by a series of coughs. When McCandless was sure of his diagnosis, he ordered his assistant, "Get him into a room. Put him on oxygen. Do an EKG. I'll check him out again in an hour."

Millicent Forrest sat across the desk in Allen McCandless's consultation room.

"What is it, Doctor?"

"One of the complications that can follow a severe coronary."

"But not another heart attack?" she asked.

"We'll see what the EKG shows. But I don't think so."

"What can we do now?" she asked.

"Stabilize him. Draw off the fluid in his chest which is creating that cough and his breathiness."

"Will it—" she started to ask, but appeared to change her mind.

McCandless anticipated her. "Will it affect his standing on the list?"

"Will it make him ineligible now? Is he too far gone?"

"No," McCandless said. "Of course, we'll watch him closely. To make sure he doesn't deteriorate further."

"Am I permitted to see him now?"

"They're draining his chest. It would be better to wait," he said."

"Yes. Of course. I'll wait," she said.

"There's some reading matter out in the visitors' lounge. Or did you bring some?"

"I was so intent on getting him into good hands, I never thought about what I'd be doing," she said.

"Well," McCandless said, "you had better get used to waiting." She looked across at him, puzzled. "I'll have to keep him here. Until that heart shows up."

"I'll bring something to read," she said.

"Or needlepoint," he suggested. "I see women do it there in the visitors' lounge all the time. I have this fantasy that somewhere there's an Interstate highway paved with all the needlepoint of patients' wives and mothers. As far as the eye can see, a whole crazy quilt of different colors, like Joseph's coat. Do you do needlepoint?"

"No," she said, beginning to study him more closely, for she had the feeling he was engaging in idle conversation just to keep her there.

"Well, then reading will have to do for you. But I did once have a patient whose husband brought one of those portable word processors with him every day. Seems he wrote travel books. Yet here he was marooned at his wife's bedside, writing away about travels in strange and distant lands." He smiled at the memory.

She noted, *Once he smiles, he seems less tired, less the famous cardiologist, more the man.* She looked at him more closely and realized, *His shirts, done by some commercial laundry. Too much starch. Winston would never wear a shirt like that.*

McCandless sensed that he was under scrutiny. It made him uncomfortable.

"I'd better go see if they're finished in there," he said.

She had been waiting in the visitors' lounge when she recognized one of the women she had seen in the patients' group one evening. Their attempts at conversation were awkward, self-conscious, and dwindled down finally to trading the symptoms and conditions of their respective husbands. They had little else in common.

Millicent Forrest picked up a magazine from the side table. It was months old, battered, and someone had torn out several pages. Still, she made an effort to interest herself in it. Soon she was looking at photographs and reading captions, none of which made any impression on her. She put the magazine aside. When she looked up, the other woman was gone. She felt somewhat guilty at being relieved to be alone.

It seemed like hours. Actually less than two hours had elapsed before McCandless came to find her in the waiting room. She rose at once.

"How is he?"

"We've emptied his chest. He's resting comfortably. I did a second cardiogram. There was no attack. Just the expected complications."

"Can I see him now?"

"Yes. He asked for you."

"How is he . . . I mean, his attitude?"

"Scared, I'd say. Once a man's had a severe coronary, any symptoms after that are bound to terrify him."

"But he's all right?" she asked, trying to extract a hopeful prognosis from him.

"He's well enough to wait it out, if a heart comes his way fairly soon," McCandless said.

" 'Fairly soon?' "

"It would have to be only a few weeks," he said. "Go in and see him now. He wanted to be sure you're here."

She found Winston propped up in a half-sitting position in his hospital bed. He had oxygen tubes in his nose and he was tethered to an oscilloscope which monitored his heart action. The light danced across the green screen, making an erratic pattern which kept repeating itself. His face glowed with a sheen of sweat, but his eyes were as active as ever. He reached out. She took his hand. It was cold.

"Scared you, did I?" he asked. "Sorry."

"S'okay," she said. "Good thing we're so close to the hospital."

"That doctor . . . McCann . . ."

"McCandless," she corrected.

"Yes. McCandless. Seems I've lost my agility with names. He said I'd be staying here from now on, till I get my new heart."

"He thinks it's safer."

"I guess I've become some sort of national treasure. To be kept safe. I've had other honors I've appreciated more," he remarked bitterly.

She realized, *He is trying to joke, and not doing well at it. He was always good with a witty line. Now the intention is there but that's about all. Poor man. Poor man, hell, he's still my husband. Strange, but in my mind, once we separated, I had to force myself to think of us as finished, done. I thought I'd succeeded. But evidently I haven't. He's still my husband. And I want him to live! I want him to live!*

She patted his hand. Still cold.

I wonder, is he frightened, as the doctor said?

The orderly was knocking gently at the door.

"Mr. Forrest, how about a little dinner?"

"Is it that late?" he asked. "I'm not even hungry."

"Don't force it. Just eat what you can," the young man said pleasantly. He placed a tray on the cart, rolled it up until it was almost to Forrest's chest. Then he pressed the button that raised the bed, until Forrest was in sitting position. That done, the young man started to remove the stainless-steel covers from each dish on the tray.

Forrest stared down at his evening meal. A small piece of a white fish, obviously poached in water. Dry toast. Apple sauce. And a custardy pudding that seemed nondescript and would turn out to be tasteless for lack of sugar and rich cream.

"Well," Forrest said sarcastically, "all for me?"

The young man smiled. "The food gets better as your condition improves."

"That's something to look forward to," Forrest said, making no attempt to begin eating.

Once the young man withdrew, Millicent asked, "Need any help?"

"Hell, no!" he protested. He took up his fork and made a shaky attack on the flakes of white fish. His hand proved unsteady and the flakes slipped off. He gave up, dropping his fork onto the plate with a loud sound.

Without a word, she made an attempt to feed him. He turned his face away.

"Win . . ." she coaxed.

"Damn it, if I can't feed myself, maybe it's too late, too late."

"Winston!" she insisted.

"I'm not hungry," he protested.

"You did as much for me," she reminded him, thinking it might assuage his pride and soften his resistance.

"That time was different," he said.

"How?"

"Because Dr. Flood said if you didn't start eating, you could go into a severe depression," he said. "I'm not in any such danger. I'm not depressed. I'm just plain miserable. All the things going on in the world, and here I am, shut up in a hospital a thousand miles from Washington. No access to the news, the real news. Decisions being made, and me with no input."

"They'll just have to run the country without you for a while," she said.

"The President said . . . the last thing he said . . . 'Winston, get well. I need you. More important, I trust you. So get well and get back here.' "

"And you will. Now eat!" she insisted, holding a forkful of white fish to his mouth.

He finally relented, chewed his fish mechanically and deliberately to make clear his rebellion.

"Did Dr. Flood really say that?" she asked.

"Yes."

"I thought it was your idea to feed me."

"I was at my wits' end. I didn't know what to do. When the news came about Paul . . . I didn't want to come home. I didn't know how I would tell you. And once I did . . . well, I didn't expect you to react as you did. You'd always been so strong. Nothing ever defeated you. Till then."

"You forget, Winston, all the times you were away, it was just Paul and me. He was my life. But I had never thought of it that way, till it happened."

She had lost her impulse to feed him, and he had lost all tolerance for food.

The door opened. They expected the young orderly to come fetch the tray. It was Dr. McCandless. He made an effort to appear hearty and cheerful.

"Well, how are we doing?" he asked as he examined the tray, where only a few mouthfuls of fish were gone. "No appetite? Well, don't worry about it. Excitement will do that sometimes. By morning you'll be famished for a hearty breakfast."

"Kippers? Eggs fried in rich butter? Croissants and jam? Coffee? Real coffee with rich cream?" Forrest said, making sure to include most of the foods that had been forbidden him since his heart attack.

"Not quite," McCandless said, smiling. "But you'll be hungry enough to think that what we do feed you tastes like that."

McCandless pretended to be casual as he glanced at the screen of the oscilloscope. Millicent Forrest studied his lean strong face for some indication of his reaction. He did not appear to react. No sign of either optimism or concern. He started to take Forrest's blood pressure.

"Fine . . . fine . . . fine . . ." he said in a routine manner. "We'll be doing a few tests in the morning. CBC. Things like that. Nothing invasive." He glanced at the tray once more. "I'll have that removed. No sense forcing your-self." He turned to Millicent. "Nothing more will happen tonight. And he does need the rest."

She felt relieved of command, free to go. She gathered up her purse and coat, kissed her husband on the cheek and started out. Once outside the room, she did not depart but waited. In moments, McCandless came out.

Before she could ask, he spoke.

"I know. Every relative of every patient always lingers to find out if the doctor was lying to the patient and had some secrets he would impart to them. Well, there are no secrets, Mrs. Forrest. He had a usual complication that we expect in the weeks or months after a massive coronary. If he remains stable, the odds are he'll still be here and ready for that heart, when one becomes available."

Reassured, she started down the corridor. The only sound seemed to be the light clatter of supper trays being collected. She was halfway down the corridor, near the elevators, when she heard McCandless call.

"Mrs. Forrest . . ."

She turned. She waited. She expected that now he would impart the information that he had withheld from her.

"I assume you're here alone. So I wonder, would you like to have dinner with me?"

She was quite surprised. "Dinner? I hadn't even thought about dinner," she confessed.

"Then think about it. And say yes."

"If you're asking because you feel sorry for me . . ." she began to resist.

"I'm asking because I feel sorry for me."

She did not reply, but simply nodded.

"Good," he said, obviously relieved and pleased. "I'll check out some patients' charts, then we'll be free to go. Unless, of course, I find some problem."

14

THE RESTAURANT WAS a short drive from the Medical Center.

The name *Chez Raimond* on the canopy prepared Millicent Forrest for what she expected to find. A maitre d' who spoke in a questionable French accent. Drinks served in stemmed glasses that pretended to be crystal. A large ornate menu in French, with English translation in parentheses.

The meal began awkwardly. When the maitre d' asked if they preferred cocktails or wine, McCandless responded for both of them, "Drinks first. A Rob Roy straight up for my—" He interrupted himself. But not soon enough to prevent Millicent Forrest's notice. He turned to her. "What would you like, Mrs. Forrest?"

"Vodka. Ice," she said.

He repeated, "Vodka on ice for the lady. And I'll have a Scotch and soda with a twist, please."

Once the maitre d' was gone, Millicent said, "You haven't been divorced very long, have you?"

"Not long enough for the old habits to die, evidently," he admitted.

"Not long enough to be accustomed to eating alone, either."

He felt compelled to explain. "It wasn't one of those bitter divorces. No infidelity. No charges and countercharges. Just two mature people deciding to let go."

Her eyes betrayed her thoughts.

"Actually," he continued, "she was the mature person deciding to let go. As for me, I couldn't blame her. After all, it had been a solitary life for her. No children. Not after the miscarriage. And she didn't want to adopt."

Their drinks were served. They touched glasses and drank. She said nothing. With the instinct of a woman of discernment and insight, she knew he needed to talk. And that he would, without prodding.

"For a time Maggie went back to teaching. But somehow that wasn't enough. Whenever I mentioned adopting, she would say, 'I want a child of my own. It wouldn't be the same otherwise.' I suppose if I'd been more aware . . . more attuned—I guess the proper word is more *attentive*—to her needs, I would have suspected. But that day in the lawyer's office, it finally came out.

" 'Allen,' she said—she always called me Allen when she was being formal—'Allen,' she said, 'the real reason I would never adopt, I didn't want any child to have to live the way I've lived. With a husband who wasn't there. Or a father who wasn't there.' She had never said that before. If she had, I would have changed . . . would have done anything. . . ."

Millicent Forrest studied him as he studied his frosty glass, his eyes averted. There was more to come, she suspected.

"No, that's not quite true. I would have had to change specialties to live the way she wanted me to live. But I happen to love the work I do. With all its uncertainties. And sometimes, with its heart-breaking disappointments. Maybe she knew that if put to the test, I would have chosen my work over my marriage. So she relieved me of that decision and made her own."

Obviously he has never told anyone about his breakup before. Why me? Why now?

He seemed relieved when the maitre d' returned to ask, "Have you decided yet?" McCandless hid behind the large burgundy-colored menu. From his safe vantage point he asked, "Find anything you like?"

*   *   *

Once they were served, he said, "Sorry. Forgot. Some wine."

"Not for me, thanks."

"Good. Not for me, either. Frankly, I don't like being victimized by 'It's the thing to do.' In fact, I don't like being regimented by anything."

"Especially marriage?" she asked, without lifting her eyes from her food as she continued to eat.

He glanced at her, almost resentful. She was an especially beautiful woman. Ash-blond hair. Fine, precise features. And a sophistication that reflected years of mingling with the most important personages of the age.

"I will say one thing," he tried to explain, "she entered this marriage with her eyes wide open. A young doctor, specializing in cardiology in the early days, his practice would consist of nothing but covering emergencies for older men. Later on a man could become a consultant. But in the early days you covered for the top men. You were at their beck and call, day and night. She knew all that."

Feeling that he had absolved himself of blame, he resumed eating until she said, "That was the early days. Then what?"

Involuntarily, his eyes flicked upward to engage hers. She was not only asking for an explanation. She was making a comment.

"Once I became involved with the Transplant Unit, time lost all meaning. Who could foretell that if it was sleeting in the Black Hills of South Dakota one night, that would mean there would be an accident and that hours later there would be a healthy heart available for transplant. So the emergencies multiplied. You had life and death in your hands. And always you were dealing in hours, minutes. You could be called away from dinner, from a party, from home in the middle of the night, in the middle of . . . even in the middle of making love."

He looked into her eyes as he reiterated, "Yes. Even in

the middle of making love. That damned beeper sounds, and like a fireman, you're out of bed and on your way. Well, Maggie couldn't take it. The uncertainty. The long times alone. I always kept a change of clothes in my office at the hospital, in case I couldn't get home for a day or more.''

She knew he was seeking absolution from her, but she had suffered the same fate as his wife and had little sympathy to spare.

"The strange thing," he continued, "now that she's gone, all I seem to have is time. Time alone. In a very odd way, I'm beginning to understand and appreciate how she felt.''

"Have you told her how you feel now?" Millicent Forrest asked.

"I've tried. She doesn't seem to believe me, somehow." He stopped eating. "I don't know why I'm telling you all this.''

"I do. You want forgiveness," she said. "Unfortunately, I know exactly how she felt.

"I thought that's why you'd understand.''

Their eyes met. In that instant she realized that he had studied Dr. Robbins's report about her own marriage.

"I had to know about it," he explained. "It was part of your husband's total profile, which we had to consider before he could be accepted as a candidate.''

"Of course," she said, no more comfortable with the situation, feeling somewhat naked in his knowledge.

"Is there anything . . . was there anything I could have done? To hold things together, I mean," he said.

"I assume you did the usual," she said.

"The usual." He was puzzled.

"Made very sincere promises. And never kept them," she explained. "Like 'When this emergency is over, I'll take time off. We'll get away somewhere. Have time to ourselves.' ''

He anticipated her, and in his own defense, he said, "Four years ago we did go on a cruise of the QE-Two. Eleven days.''

"Eleven whole days, four years ago," Millicent repeated, a tinge of sarcasm in her voice. "At that, you did better than Winston. We never had eleven whole days ourselves. Not even when Paul died. The way he died, by itself, created an emergency in the White House."

"I read about that, too, in your husband's file. Did you know your son had been sent to Beirut?"

"Not until I got a letter from him. From that moment on I had a premonition. A restless feeling. I'd prowl the house like a cat. No hint of why, just something kept gnawing at me. Then early that morning, Winston came back to the house. It was before seven. He wanted to tell me before the news came on the air. He looked haggard and pale. He stared at me, but didn't see me. He dropped into one of the big easy chairs in the living room, his hands clasped between his thighs, shaking his head.

"I will never forget the way he told me. 'Paul,' he said. 'It's Paul.' 'What about Paul? Tell me!' He didn't answer. Just sat there, shaking his head and whispering, 'He was there. One of the ones . . .' 'One of *what* ones?' I pleaded. 'There was this truck, loaded with explosives. It ran the barrier. Crashed into the Marine headquarters. Blew it to bits. Hundreds of them . . . hundreds . . .' he kept repeating. 'Hundreds of what?' I asked. 'Marines . . . hundreds of marines . . . they didn't have a chance . . . and Paul was one of them . . . Paul.'

"I couldn't absorb it at first. Couldn't believe it. I'd just gotten a second letter from Paul the day before. He couldn't be dead. Couldn't. But he was. He was."

She had revealed more than she had intended. She tried to resume eating. Her food was too cold. Or else she'd lost her appetite.

Finally, she said, "Sorry. I didn't mean to burden you this way."

"It's quite all right," he was quick to reassure, then added, "It's been a long time since anyone's opened up to me in this way. Of course, there are patients' families. But they're always pleading their cause. Why their father, or wife, or husband is more deserving of a heart than any other patient. Always the same plea, 'Move my loved one up to the head of the list.'

"Once, one father said to me, 'Doc, you move my son up to number one and I'll make it worth your while.' As if new hearts are merchandise for sale to those who can afford them."

Allen realized he had deviated from what he intended to say. She reminded him.

"You said it's been a long time since anyone opened up to you."

"What I meant was someone opening up without some self-seeking purpose in mind. Lately I've had things I would have loved to share with Maggie. But suddenly she isn't there."

Gently, Millicent Forrest asked, "When she *was* there, did you share those things with her?"

He was forced to admit, "It's only lately that I've felt this need to talk to her, to tell her, to share with her. But you're right, not before."

"I find that Winston and I talk more now than we used to. Of course, he did have his heart attack. That slowed him down."

"Was that what brought you two back together? His heart attack?"

"I don't know yet what it will lead to. But right now he needs me. Any chance that you and Maggie will get back together again?"

"Not likely. There's another man now. From what I hear, it's quite serious. He's vice president of a bank. Regular hours. Home on time every evening. I hear he's also a hell of a squash player. I hope he appreciates what he's got in Maggie. She deserves it."

Neither of them had eaten very much, but it was plain to the waiter that they had finished. A busboy appeared to clear away the dishes. The maitre d' was back suggesting desserts, coffee, after-dinner drinks. They had no desire for any.

"I'll drive you back to the hospital," he offered, "so you can get your car."

"I didn't come by car," she said. "Ambulance."

"Of course. I'll drive you home."

Driving back, they were silent for a time. Until he said, "I hope I haven't imposed too much."

"One less solitary meal for me, too. It was a relief."

They were silent once more.

"It's ironic," she said suddenly. "Maggie complained of loneliness. I've had the other side of the coin. And that's no fun, either. Being a diplomat's wife is a full-time job. Our government gets quite a bargain. Two for the price of one. The husband has the title and the salary and the perks. The wife just goes along as an unpaid employee.

"The social side of politics and government, that's the wife's job. Night after night, it's either entertain or be entertained. Mostly with people you'd hardly associate with otherwise. Arrange this party or tea or reception.

"A foreign diplomat's wife is stuck in Washington during some conference, take her out, show her the sights you've seen a thousand times, have her to tea, take her shopping. And in the evening entertain them both.

"It all takes time and thought and concentration. You have to study up on their local customs so you don't offend your guests. You have to know enough about the situation involved so you don't make any diplomatic blunders. You are a diplomat in every way but one. You don't get paid.

"But the worst of it is, the time it takes away from your own life, your family's life. That's the reason why I never had a second child."

It was a confession that came unexpectedly, almost involuntarily. Only McCandless's understanding silence encouraged her to continue.

"All that time, the time I was giving to the government for free, was being taken away from Paul. If Winston wasn't the father he should have been, I'm afraid I didn't help.

"In the days after . . . what happened in Beirut . . . I would ask myself, When he enlisted, was he rebelling against me, too? I still don't know the answer.

"So when you say, Maggie never had enough of you, what am I to say? I had too much of Winston? No. Because actually his first loyalty was to the State Department, the White House, the President."

McCandless said softly, reflectively, "Maybe in the times in which we live there's no good way. No proper balance between a career and a private life. Life today may be too hectic for mere human beings. Maybe it takes some new species to contend with this new age."

"Maybe," she agreed. "Here we are. Two fairly intelligent people. With, I assume, decent motivations and desires. Yet both of us are confessing failed marriages. Mine, at least, still has a chance. I feel sorry for you, Doctor. In recent months I've had just enough solitude to know what you're going through."

The sudden sound of his beeper became a welcome intrusion. He responded on his car phone. He was being summoned back to the hospital. As he hung up he said, "An emergency. I've got to get back. I'll get you that cab. Do you mind?"

"Not at all."

He turned the car around and increased his speed.

"I was just thinking . . ." she started to say, but changed her mind.

"You were thinking," he coaxed.

"Wondering, actually, how many times this must have happened while your wife was in the car. A very enjoyable evening, a fine meal, and on the way home, when she might be anticipating more of you, suddenly you're called away and she winds up at home. Alone."

"You certainly know the routine."

"I've had my share. Winston was always at the beck and call of the President, the Secretary of State, and the next news bulletin on the radio," she explained.

"I'm glad you and Maggie never met," he said. "What horror stories you'd have to tell each other."

They drove on in silence.

*   *   *

As he raced from the parking lot to the Emergency entrance, she had trouble keeping up with him.

"I'll have one of the guards see you to a cab," he apologized.

They entered the Emergency door. McCandless was surprised to almost collide with Harvey Strawbridge. The Administrator had obviously been waiting for him.

Quickly, McCandless said, "Harve, I've got an emergency. I'll see you later."

"I'm your emergency," Strawbridge said. McCandless's puzzled reaction made him explain, "I have to talk to you. Now!"

Simultaneously, Strawbridge's instinctive eye reaction from McCandless to Millicent Forrest and back to McCandless made an obvious comment. McCandless felt himself accused of some breach of professional conduct. Strawbridge felt compelled to explain his own presence.

"I received word that Mr. Forrest was brought back into the hospital. I rushed down to see what had gone wrong. But you'd already left. For dinner, I presume." This last with a hint of rebuke. "So I decided to wait." He might as well have read McCandless an indictment.

"Forrest is out of danger and fairly comfortable," McCandless explained. "He suffered a slight setback, not unusual for his condition. Since he was out of danger and Mrs. Forrest was alone and had had quite a shock, I took her to dinner. I thought she needed it."

"Of course. Total family care," Strawbridge said, with no hint of a smile.

To avoid an open confrontation with Strawbridge in the presence of Millicent Forrest, McCandless said to her, "I'll drive you home now."

Strawbridge intervened, "Mac, I'd like to talk to you. Now, if you don't mind."

"I was going to drive Mrs. Forrest home," McCandless said.

"No need," she volunteered, for she sensed the conflict brewing between the two men and resented being the cause of Strawbridge's suspicions. "Besides, I'd like to look in on Winston before I go."

As Strawbridge started away, he called, "See you in my office, Mac?"

When the Administrator had walked down the corridor, Millicent Forrest said, "I hope I didn't cause you any embarrassment."

"On the contrary," McCandless replied. "Thanks for turning what could have been another dull, solitary evening into a very interesting one. And it seems it isn't over yet."

"I'm sorry about that. I'll find a cab," she said.

"No, this can't take long. Wait, and I'll drive you home," he said, then started down the corridor.

15

MILLICENT FORREST EASED open the door of her husband's room. He lay in bed, turned away from the door and avoiding the dim glow of his night light. She listened carefully. The rhythm of his breathing was irregular and labored. But he was asleep. Peacefully asleep, she realized with some relief. She watched for a time, then felt free to leave.

As she was closing the door silently, she heard the whispered voice of the floor night nurse, asking in surprise, "Mrs. Forrest?"

She turned to confront the young woman.

"Something wrong, Mrs. Forrest? Visitors are not allowed after eight-thirty."

"I just happened to come back with Dr. McCandless, so I thought I'd look in on my husband."

From the nurse's reaction, she realized at once that the young woman had made the same assumption as Harvey Strawbridge.

She was quick to explain, "Since we came here by ambulance, Dr. McCandless was driving me home when we got this emergency call. So we . . . ."

Her explanation only compounded the misunderstanding.

"Dr. McCandless had to take care of an emergency. When he's free, tell him I've taken a cab."

"Yes, of course," the nurse said. But her expression and the critical look in her eyes had not changed.

Feeling self-conscious, Millicent Forrest started down the corridor toward the elevators. She had the feeling she was being stared at and was tempted to turn back and see if, indeed, she was.

She wondered, Was it that young nurse's reaction? Or was it Strawbridge's response to the situation that made her feel self-conscious? Or was it more? Was it guilt? And if guilt, why? Could it be that she loved Winston more than she realized? That what she had considered an act of loyalty was really love? The kind of love in which their lives were so intertwined that no decision of hers could disunite them?

These days people talked very freely and glibly about separation and divorce. But did they take into account the emotional surgery necessary to give effect to those words?

How does one even begin to remove the memories, some memories as fresh tonight as they were the day they happened.

The first time she saw Winston Forrest. Her instructor in Government had ordered the entire class to attend a lecture in the auditorium of the main hall. Some official from Washington was delivering a talk on Southeast Asia. She had gone, expecting to hear some middle-aged government spokesman expounding the official line on United States participation in an unpopular war.

She had been surprised to discover the speaker was far from middle-aged. He was in his late twenties, tall, quite good-looking, all in all an imposing, attractive man. Obviously a man destined for a successful career in government. An important career. He had borne that stamp the first time she had seen him. It was less her interest in his speech than in him that had stimulated her to ask several questions. And to linger in the group that gathered around him when his speech was over.

The attraction between them was instantaneous, so undeniable that they were in love even before they realized it.

She was barely eighteen when she left college in her sophomore year to marry him.

The first years, the early years in Washington, were exciting. The receptions and the parties never seemed to end. Except for the late months of her early pregnancy, there was hardly an evening when there was no function they felt forced to attend. The array of brilliant personalities with whom she had contact provided a far better education than two more years of college could hope to equal.

The time came when the receptions, the parties, even the menus, were so much the same they became boring. What had been excitement turned into unavoidable obligation. Just as Winston's long absences for endless series of conferences abroad became career obligations which she eventually began to resent. More and more she turned her time and attention to little Paul. He became the bigger part of her life.

Eventually Paul became the tie between them. When he died their life together seemed over. Possibly because she could never completely dispel the feeling that Winston was, at least in part, the cause of Paul's death.

Yet now, alone once more, in the dead of night, on her way home from the hospital, she could not deny that she might still have deep, strong feelings for Winston.

When she accepted Allen McCandless's invitation to dinner, it was in hopes that she would learn more about Winston's condition, his chances for recovery. As the evening had worn on, she realized that it was an occasion for reciprocal pity.

She knew, as well as he knew, the forlorn sense of being alone after years of shared existence with another human being. The sense of coming home knowing that person was either there or would be there or was expected to return after a day, or a week, or even a month. The knowledge that Winston would be coming back made him real even in those times when he was not there. That feeling rounded out one's life. Without it there was loneliness, long stretches of loneliness.

Evidently Allen McCandless, too, knew that feeling well. The little tricks and artifices to which one resorted to fight loneliness. Things to read when eating alone in restaurants, or even at home. Not newspapers—they were too large and unwieldy to handle while dining. Small compact magazines were best. Though they did not completely solve the problem.

During dinner McCandless had mentioned that he did a good deal of his professional reading while eating, keeping up with the latest developments in his specialty. It not only saved time, it filled the emptiness. Besides, professional journals were a good size to handle while eating. Except for those printed on slick paper, which tended to be unmanageable.

When she had pointed out that she found herself eating far less when she dined alone than she used to with Winston, McCandless picked up on that.

"Yes," he had said, "eating with someone else is an experience. Eating alone is a necessity, to sustain life and health. Something to be done as quickly and efficiently as possible."

They had found a good deal in common, sharing their new and still strange solitary status.

But as the cab drew up at the door of their rented condominium, she realized it was more than that. Allen McCandless was closer in age to her than Winston. He was good-looking, too, she had to concede, in his lean, Lincolnesque way. When he talked about his youth, his early days in medicine, his eyes took on an intensity and his face revealed such a look of conviction that it made him seem . . . there must be a right word for it, she decided, yes, there was. *Dedicated*. He had a sense of noble dedication about the work he did.

And why not, she had thought as she listened to him, *he has the gift of life in his hands. I have never attended a funeral where the clergyman, no matter his faith, did not intone, "The Lord giveth and the Lord taketh away." Yet now there were men like Allen McCandless, who could reach out and stay the hand of God and say, "This one You shall not take away."*

Then why my strange, if vague, sense of guilt? she wondered. *Because*, she realized, *Winston, too, has that same quality, that same dedication. He, too, is dedicated and devoted—and yes, noble—about the work he does. How many times has he said to me, especially after he's been away for weeks on those interminable sessions with the Soviets in Geneva, and other places, "Never forget, my darling, if we fail, the bombs begin to fall."*

This was no self-serving pretension on Winston's part. He was an important man, engaged in work vital to the nation. And if the bombs could be prevented from falling, vital to the whole human race.

She was sitting before her dressing-table mirror, removing the last of her light makeup, when she thought, *Winston devoted himself to saving life by avoiding war. Allen McCandless is engaged in restoring—no, giving—life to those so close to dying. They are not so very different.*

She was turning out her bedside light when she was forced to ask herself, *Why am I so intent on comparing the two?*

The toll of the long day and evening had tired her, so she could avoid answering that question by slipping into much needed sleep.

The Administrator was sitting in his oversized desk chair, his feet up on the desk. Only his desk lamp was lit, leaving most of the office in shadow. The moment McCandless opened the door, the Administrator swung his legs off the desk and rose to his feet. He began to pace, as if he were delivering a lecture.

"You should have called me, Mac!" he rebuked.

"To ask permission to go to dinner?" McCandless asked sarcastically.

Strawbridge turned on him. "I hadn't intended to say anything about that. You're a divorced man. She is an attractive woman. Whatever you do about that is your own business. The important thing is, you should have called me the moment Forrest had to be brought back into the hospital!"

"That was a purely medical emergency, and I took care of it. The man is resting comfortably. We can only await developments."

"Developments, hell!" Strawbridge exploded. "This is our chance! A perfect chance to move him up on the list!"

"What do you know about the list?" McCandless challenged.

Pretending to make it seem a happenstance, Strawbridge said, "I like to keep my hand in. From time to time I glance at the list. Count the number of candidates. Count the number of possibles. The past few weeks I've noticed that Winston Forrest has been rather far down on the list."

"He's moved up, as have all the candidates, each time we've done a transplant."

"But not fast enough!" Strawbridge said. "This is our chance to move him right to the top of the list of Type O candidates."

"I can't do that. Not without more medical evidence," McCandless replied.

"Evidence?" Strawbridge scoffed. "Medical evidence? When you get right down to it, that's a matter of opinion. Two cardiologists looking at the same set of data can come to two different conclusions. They do it all the time. Else why even have such a practice as a second opinion?"

"Right now, right here, my opinion is the only one that counts!" McCandless pointed out. "Unless you want a different head of the Transplant Unit!"

"Now, now, Mac, I didn't suggest any such thing. There's no one I'd rather have as chief. But we do have to be practical."

"Yes, yes, I know," McCandless anticipated him. "Research grants, money to build a new wing—"

Strawbridge interrupted, "Imaging equipment! Right now I have on my desk your request for a new piece of imaging equipment."

"An Imatron. That would give us more exact diagnostic

abilities than our CAT scan or our present imaging equipment,'' McCandless replied.

"Yes. An Imatron. A mere million and a half dollars!''
Strawbridge pointed out sarcastically. "Trouble with good
doctors, they can never see beyond the next patient. Didn't
you ever stop to think what it would mean to this hospital if it
became public that we carried out a successful heart transplant
on a man as important as the President's National Security
Adviser?''

"I thought they sent Forrest here to keep this *out* of the
media,'' McCandless replied.

"For the time being,'' the Administrator agreed. "But
once the operation is done, once it's succeeded, then I can
invite the whole world in. Let them all know that when a key
man in the White House needed a transplant, they sent him
here. Not to Stanford, not to Pittsburgh, not to New York, but
here!''

Sarcastically, McCandless shot back, "Have you decided
yet which auditorium to hold the press conference in? The
small one? Or the large one?''

"Damn it, Mac, listen to reason!'' Strawbridge said.
"I'm not asking you to do anything unprofessional. All I'm
saying is, Forrest's relapse demands that he be moved up to
the top of the list.''

"If and when his condition dictates, I will move him up.
But not one moment sooner!'' McCandless said.

He started toward the door, until Strawbridge interdicted
him with a curt, "I have another way!''

McCandless turned to confront the Administrator.

"A designated heart,'' Strawbridge said.

The term had special significance to any cardiologist or
transplant surgeon. It meant a donated organ sought out and
intended for a specific recipient and that recipient only. That
Strawbridge should even suggest the idea outraged McCandless. But he kept his temper in check to discover the
Administrator's plan.

"What would be wrong if the President, during his press conference, made an appeal for Forrest?" Strawbridge asked. "Or happened to mention it in passing during an interview?"

"Have you suggested that to the White House?"

"No," Strawbridge said. "Not yet."

"Then don't!" McCandless insisted. "We are practicing medicine here. Not public relations. Winston Forrest will take his turn like all the rest. If his condition deteriorates, as it might, he will move up on the list. If not, he will remain another patient, taking his chances."

"How long do you give him, if he *doesn't* get a new heart?"

"Originally I said six months. Right now, pending new developments and test results, I'd say three," McCandless admitted.

"Then he will move up some, if not to the top?" Strawbridge pressed.

"I'll know better in forty-eight hours," was the only concession McCandless would make.

Strawbridge refused to accept that. "What if the President only made a general appeal for donors? I mean, if he merely stressed that there is now a federal law making it mandatory for hospitals to ask for donors where medically indicated? And let the media make the connection with Forrest."

"There isn't a hospital in this country that needs to be reminded of the new law," McCandless pointed out.

"Is there no basis on which I can get your cooperation in what may be the biggest bonanza for this hospital in its entire history?" the frustrated Administrator demanded.

"You want a bonanza?" McCandless demanded, "I can show you how to buy not one Imatron, or build not one new wing, but two, three! Just find yourself an oil-rich Arab whose kid needs a healthy kidney or heart. They'll build you a medical Taj Mahal, if you'd like. But that's exactly why we don't do things that way. The child of a migrant worker and that Arabian prince stand in exactly the same position, as far as I'm concerned. *Need*, and *only* need, is what determines who gets the next healthy heart, as long as I'm chief of the Unit!''

"Damn it, Mac—'' Strawbridge started to say.

But McCandless overrode him. ''You're not any different than Senator Bridgeman! Well, don't forget he isn't the only senator. There are ninety-nine more. And hundreds of congressmen. What if each of them started to throw his political weight around?''

"I'm only talking about one man. Forrest!'' Strawbridge protested.

"It starts with only one patient. Then the next thing you know, other patients, other families, other VIPs are saying, 'Remember that father who made that appeal for his daughter . . .' and so it goes. Sorry, Harve. I appreciate your ambitions for this hospital, but I know only one test. Need!''

"Okay, okay,'' Strawbridge said, apparently conceding to McCandless's policy. But then, adopting a softer tone of voice, he continued, ''I never wanted to mention this, Mac. The trouble I had protecting this hospital after that AIDS case.''

"That was an anomaly, a medical anomaly. No one in the field of transplants had become aware of it,'' McCandless protested.

"I'm not blaming you, Mac,'' Strawbridge said, in that special way intended to place blame, and guilt.

McCandless felt the need to justify himself and his team. ''Before we agreed to accept that heart, the donor was tested for cancer and AIDS. The results came back negative. We had every reason to believe he was free of both diseases. In those days no one thought to ask how many transfusions he'd had before he went brain dead. No one suspected that transfusions can so dilute a man's blood that even though he did have AIDS, the test results would always be negative. We know that now. We've all learned from that very unfortunate mistake. That's the way medicine progresses.''

"And what about the lawsuit that followed?'' Strawbridge challenged. "All that bad publicity! That's the way medical centers learn. Unfortunately. *And* expensively."

"We never claimed to be perfect. I know one thing, that kind of error will never occur again!" McCandless declared.

"I wouldn't have brought it up," Strawbridge said, "I just thought this was our chance—Forrest is our chance—to make up for that bad publicity of a few years ago."

"Sorry, Harve, very sorry. But he will have to move up as his condition dictates. Let's hope his time will come before it's too late."

16

THE NEXT AFTERNOON Allen McCandless was at his desk, viewing the cineangiogram that only hours before had been done on Winston Forrest. It clearly revealed the sluggish action of a damaged and deteriorating heart. The phone rang. With his eyes still focused on the disturbing film in his projector, McCandless groped for the phone. Before he could locate it, it rang twice more, adding to his annoyance.

"Yes, Claire?"

"The White House, Doctor," Claire informed.

"Dr. McCandless," came the brisk, imposing, but nevertheless tantalizing voice of Katherine Breed. "We understand that you have recently done an entire series of new tests on Mr. Forrest. Including an angiogram—"

"Cineangiogram," McCandless corrected, suppressing his anger that news only hours old had already reached the White House. Strawbridge must have a mole planted right in the Cardiac Service.

"Have you arrived at any fresh prognosis in Mr. Forrest's case?" the persistent young woman asked.

"I am almost on the verge of doing just that."

"Can you clue me in on any advance intelligence of your projected plans for him?"

"Would you like it directly from me, or can you wait ten

minutes and get it from that 'usually authoritative source,' Harvey Strawbridge?''

She ignored his sarcasm to say, "The President is interested in the most authentic source, which would be you."

"You may tell the President that, based on the results before me now, I am considering moving Mr. Forrest up on the list to a priority position. However, before I do, I must hold a consult with the entire Transplant Unit."

"I am sure you realize the President would appreciate anything you can do to ensure Mr. Forrest's early recovery. His value to the President and the nation cannot be overestimated."

"I'm very aware of that, Ms. Breed," McCandless said. "And should I ever forget it, Mr. Strawbridge is very quick to remind me."

Undeterred, Breed continued, "May I tell the President there is a strong likelihood that Mr. Forrest will be advanced to the top of the list soon?"

"You may tell the President that I have such a move under consideration this very moment. But without the concurrence of my staff, I can make no promises at this time," McCandless said. Then he added, "Ms. Breed, does it strike you that we are conversing as if we were issuing bulletins to the press instead of talking like two normal, intelligent human beings?"

Her sudden silence was in itself a disapproving comment.

"Ms. Breed, assure the President we are doing our damnedest for Mr. Forrest. And we'll continue to do so."

"Yes, yes, of course," the young woman replied curtly.

He could not resist asking, "Tell me, honestly now, *is* there a Mr. Breed? And do you talk to him like you just talked to me? Or is he an invention? A convenient way to discourage men who have become absolutely intrigued by your voice and your diction?"

She laughed, but with reserve, as if it were a luxury she permitted herself in only rare moments.

"There is no Mr. Breed, Doctor," she admitted. "But it

is certainly the shortest, least troublesome and embarrassing way of turning off unwanted passes.''

''Then do you think the fictitious Mr. Breed would object if, the next time I'm in Washington, I were to call you?''

''I don't see how he could.''

''And would you have dinner with me?''

''I would be delighted,'' she said, ''provided there is no sudden deterioration in the situation in the Persian Gulf, or in Nicaragua, or in the Philippines, or in South Africa, or in the national economy.''

''Perhaps I'd better bring sandwiches and we'll brown bag it at your desk,'' McCandless suggested.

She laughed again, more easily this time.

''Doctor, based on the way you sound, I suggest you come as you are. We'll manage somehow.''

The first semblance of a date since Maggie left me, he thought. *Maybe I haven't lost the touch, after all. Of course, there was dinner two nights ago with Mrs. Forrest. But that was sheer happenstance. No matter what old Harve thought. No, not thought, suspected is the right word. And, as usual, he was wrong. What better proof than that I think of her as Mrs. Forrest? It never dawned on me to ask her first name.*

But she is surely a most attractive woman.

He turned his thoughts back to Forrest's distressing cineangiogram. After another long, concentrated viewing, he decided he must meet with Slade and the Unit to discuss moving Forrest up, possibly to the top of the list. The man was now clearly in the highest-risk, least-time-of-survival category.

He reached for his phone to instruct Claire to set up a meeting. The phone anticipated him, ringing before he could pick it up.

''Yes, Claire?''

Instead of Claire's voice, McCandless was greeted by the anxious voice of Ben Kaplan.

''Mac? Ben. I'm down in Emergency. Can you join me here at once?''

''Sure, Ben. What happened?''

"Jim Campbell. I just brought him in. Please, Mac. Hurry!"

"Have him moved up to a room in ICU. Stat! I'll join you up there!"

Allen McCandless was leaning over Jim Campbell. Naked to the waist, Campbell sat up in bed, to make himself available to the cardiologist's stethoscope and percussion. Ben Kaplan stood at the foot of the bed, his arm around Nancy Campbell to comfort her. She had not ceased to tremble.

As McCandless listened to Campbell's heart, he asked, "Exactly what happened?"

"Tell him, dear," Kaplan urged.

"I was in the kitchen warming up some milk. I couldn't sleep. I thought warm milk might help. Dr. Kaplan doesn't like me to take pills if it can be avoided—"

"Nan, darling, just tell Dr. McCandless what happened to Jim," the old man urged softly.

"I was in the kitchen. I heard this sound. Like Jim was fighting for air. It was almost like . . . it sounded like this." She imitated the frightening gasps of a man struggling for air, in fear that he would die for want of it. "Desperate like that. And fighting hard. I rushed into the den. Held him in my arms. Then I started to give him CPR, calling up to Jimmy, 'Come down at once! Dad needs you.' Then, between CPR, I told Jimmy, 'Look up Dr. Kaplan. Get him on the phone.' I kept up the CPR until Dr. Kaplan got there."

McCandless had finished his examination. As he was rolling up his blood-pressure cuff, he asked, "Ben?"

"She said it all. Difficulty breathing. Shortness of breath. Chest filling up with fluid. So we rushed him here."

What the old doctor had said was for patient consumption only. The look exchanged between the two doctors was more grave.

Nancy detected that and said, "Dr. McCandless?"

"He's perfectly all right for now," McCandless assured

her. "Blood pressure's somewhat elevated. To be expected. But on oxygen he'll do fine, fine."

Nancy Campbell had been dealing with doctors long enough, and recently, often enough, to be suspicious of the word "fine." Especially if it was repeated. A double "fine" was no longer as reassuring to her as it was intended to be. But she had also learned not to ask too many questions in the presence of her husband.

She knew what was expected of her now. She kissed Jim and started out to the visitors' lounge, leaving Kaplan and McCandless free to confer. After that, the old man would tell her the truth.

As both doctors watched her go down the corridor, they talked.

"Well, Mac?"

"Ben, I was afraid of this."

"What does it do to his chances?" Kaplan asked.

"Depends on his PVR."

"It was only four Woods before," Kaplan pointed out, like a lawyer pleading his client's case.

"Probably higher now. Maybe much higher," McCandless said.

"What's the cutoff point?"

"If it gets up to seven Woods, I will have to take him off the eligible list."

"Take him off . . ." Kaplan tried to protest, stunned at having heard what amounted to a death sentence.

"Have to, Ben. Even if we did find a heart for him, and that's always a gamble, a Pulmonary Vascular Resistance measuring seven Woods creates enough resistance from the lungs to stop any new heart cold. And we can't risk wasting a good heart."

"On the other hand," Kaplan argued, "his PVR may not be seven. Or even six. Let's find out."

"Exactly. Let's find out."

*   *   *

When Patient James Campbell was wheeled into the small treatment room, McCandless's assistant was preparing the Swan-Ganz catheter required to measure his Pulmonary Vascular Resistance. It was an extremely thin, flexible, yellow plastic tube with a firm, equally thin, head. In the head was a tiny, invisible, colorless plastic balloon which could be inflated when necessary.

McCandless and Kaplan approached the table. McCandless felt Campbell's neck with practiced, sensitive fingers. He located his jugular artery, then pressed beyond it to find his jugular vein.

"Needle," McCandless ordered.

His assistant passed a large-bore plastic needle to him. He inserted it carefully into Campbell's neck and finally into his jugular vein. Then he passed the catheter through the needle into the vein. Now, slowly, following the progress of the catheter on the monitor screen, he began to direct the catheter down toward the right side of Campbell's ailing heart.

In the visitors' lounge Nancy Campbell awaited the outcome of the procedure, tense, holding back her tears, yet fully aware that if the result was disappointing, her husband would be removed from the only list that held any hope for him. She sat on the couch at the far end of the lounge, staring toward the window, seeing nothing.

Millicent Forrest came in, taking a break from the vigil she kept at her estranged husband's bedside. It was apparent to her at once that her new friend was in need of comforting.

"Nancy . . ." Millicent began.

Unaware of Millicent Forrest's entry into the empty lounge, Nancy Campbell looked up, startled. Whatever control the young woman clung to was shattered by surprise. Tears started down her cheeks. Millicent took her in her arms. Nancy tried to stifle her weeping.

"No, Nancy. Don't even try. First cry. Then tell me what happened."

In a while Nancy regained her composure. Millicent handed her her handkerchief. Still wiping her eyes, Nancy related the terrifying episode that had brought Jim back to the hospital. She told of her almost paralyzing fear, at home, that Jim was dying. That he would die before Dr. Kaplan could get there. Now the latest fear, that his condition had so deteriorated that they might be forced to remove him from the list.

Millicent consoled her. "First we fight to get him on the list. Then we're afraid he'll be taken off. And all the while we keep tormenting ourselves, what if he stays on the list but no heart appears? We just have to keep remembering, seventy to eighty percent *do* get new hearts."

"I kept telling myself that. Until last night. If they take him off the list, his chances become zero. Zero."

"I went through the same thing with Winston. They haven't taken him off the list. And they won't take your husband off, either."

She hoped that her well-intended assurance had accomplished its purpose. She could not avoid thinking, What will there be left to say if her husband is rejected?

17

UP IN THE SMALL treatment room Allen McCandless and Ben Kaplan followed closely on the monitor screen the progress of the catheter as it snaked down through Jim Campbell's jugular vein and into the right atrium of his heart. Carefully, McCandless maneuvered the probe of the catheter through the right atrium to the tricuspid valve that separated it from the right ventricle. He passed it through the valve into the ventricle until it reached the pulmonary valve.

Then McCandless gently eased it through that valve into the pulmonary artery itself, the artery that carries blood from the heart into the lungs to be enriched with fresh oxygen so it can be pumped back into the left side of the heart to feed the rest of the body.

When the left side of the heart becomes diseased and weakened, the lungs develop a high resistance to the flow of blood from the heart. When that resistance becomes too great, then the right ventricle of a new, normal heart will not be able to pump effectively and will fail.

The steps that McCandless had taken thus far were all prelude to making that crucial determination. If the resistance from Jim Campbell's lungs exceeded 7 on the Woods Scale, he would have to be eliminated from the program.

Aware of all that, Ben Kaplan watched with great concern.

He could recall only too well the first time Jim had appeared in his modest office in the Redmont Professional Building. Jim had presented vague symptoms. Lack of energy. General tiredness.

He recalled Jim's very words, "I don't know, Ben. I just don't have the same get-up-and-go. So Nan said, 'Get a checkup. It's probably nothing. But get a checkup anyhow.' So here I am."

During conversation about Jim's new business, about the kids, about Nancy, about conditions in Redmont now that the steel-fabricating mill had closed down, Ben Kaplan had given the young man a routine physical. Blood pressure. Pulse. Chest. Heart. Lungs. Disturbed by what he heard, he prescribed more conclusive tests. An EKG. And a stress test. Despite his eventual grim diagnosis, he consoled himself with the promise that, at worst, a new heart would restore Jim Campbell to a good productive life.

But he had not envisioned that Jim's condition would so deteriorate that he would now be pleading with the medical fates to keep him on that list of candidates. Jim Campbell's life, the future of his family, hung on what that yellow plastic snake now venturing through his pulmonary artery to his lungs would reveal.

Kaplan found himself urging, *Damn it, just for once, come up with the right answer! Not the accurate answer! The right answer! Give this young man a chance! Give his family a chance!*

Kaplan watched the screen as McCandless guided the catheter through Campbell's pulmonary artery until it lodged in the distal branch. He transferred his gaze from the monitor to Allen McCandless's eyes to detect the cardiologist's reaction to what he would discover.

In the visitors' lounge Nancy Campbell was telling Millicent Forrest about her children, especially little James, Junior, who so resembled his father.

"They even walk alike," Nancy said.

"Oh, I know," Millicent Forrest agreed, "Paul was the same way. In fact, when he first went off to nursery school, we had quite a time trying to convince him that he didn't need an attaché case, because Winston never left the house without one."

Nancy tried to laugh along with Millicent, but it was hollow, forced, and for a moment it seemed that she might begin to weep once more.

"The thing I worry about," she confessed, "is lately I notice that Jimmy imitates him in other ways, too. He doesn't want to go out to play. He likes to stay in his room. Lie on his bed much of the time. Like Jim's been doing these last weeks. He's acting like a very sick man. I'm scared. What if . . . if something terrible happens to Jim, what will his son do?"

"I don't think a young boy would carry a fantasy that far," Millicent said, more troubled than she dared reveal. She could recall her own son's concerns with death and dying when he was in his early years. "Did you discuss this with your doctor?"

"Dr. Kaplan says we may never have to face that problem. So why worry about it? Of course, that was before last night. Who knows what he'll say now? Or what they'll find."

They were alerted by the sound of Kaplan's voice approaching along the corridor.

"Mac, they are both intelligent young people. I've always been very open with them. Tell her what you found. Everything."

Instinctively, Nancy Campbell rose to her feet, reaching out to Millicent's hand for support and reassurance. The two physicians came into view to find her awaiting their verdict.

"Nan, my dear, Mac—Dr. McCandless—wants to give you the whole picture as it stands now. There is, as they say, good news and some . . . some not so good news. I'll let him tell you."

"Nancy, I've just done a cardiac catheterization on Jim. To test his PVR—Pulmonary Vascular Resistance. That means the pressure by which his lungs push against his heart. When that is too strong, a new heart would do no good.''

Millicent Forrest felt Nancy's hand tighten on her own. McCandless continued.

"Fortunately, Jim's PVR is within the limits that make him eligible to remain on the list."

Softly, as if to herself, Nancy Campbell breathed a simple, "Thank God."

"However, based on the episode of last night, and the possibility of it recurring, I think it would be advisable to keep him here in the hospital until a new heart shows up."

" 'Advisable,' " Nancy Campbell evaluated. "You mean safer."

"Safer," McCandless agreed.

"If it does happen again, what would . . . I mean- . . . the next time . . ." She was unable to ask the question.

But McCandless answered nevertheless, "He'll be in the best hands, with the best equipment right here."

When the young woman did not respond, Kaplan said gently, "Nan, dear, look in on Jim. Tell him. Then kiss him and I'll drive you home."

"Yes. Sure," she agreed, still numb from having heard the truth, gently as it had been presented. She walked to the door, where she stopped to turn back to McCandless. "How long, Doctor? How long can he wait?"

Kaplan tried to ease the moment for McCandless. "Nan, dear, you're asking for a sheer guess."

McCandless did not hesitate. "I can tell you this. His PVR keeps him eligible. His hepatic and renal function keeps him eligible. So does his psychiatric history. He has no history of a pulmonary infarct. No bleeding ulcers. None of the things that would disqualify him. And one big asset. A wife who loves him. And a family that needs him. I count those very significant factors. With half a break, he'll make it long enough to get that heart. When he does, he'll do fine. Just fine! Now you go in there and give him that kiss. And when you leave, leave believing that it's going to happen. It is going to happen!''

The young woman drew herself up, stronger now, with more purpose. Kaplan followed her out, but not without glancing back at McCandless to nod and silently thank him.

Once they were out of earshot, Millicent Forrest said, "That was very nice, Doctor."

"Also truthful," he pointed out. "I don't believe in buying a family's gratitude with false promises. Unless Campbell's heart weakens a great deal, he'll make it. Provided, of course, a heart shows up in time."

"So he doesn't become one of the unfortunate twenty-five percent," Millicent Forrest added.

"We can't promise to save them all. One day when people stop burying good hearts we will. Till then we are all gamblers at this game."

"Winston, too," she said softly.

"Mrs. Forrest, I want you to know I appreciate your having dinner with me last night. Even though it reminded me of how lonely I really am. I can no longer console myself with the thought that I'm free. Master of my own time. That I can do all the reading that doctors have to do to keep up. That I no longer have to think about Maggie, and is she waiting with dinner for me. Or wonder if I've forgotten some appointment she's made for us.

"Truth is, I think about her more now than I did when we were married. Maybe that's the saddest commentary of all."

"Tell me, Doctor, when you were trying to reassure Nan Campbell, were you also trying to tell me something?"

There was a look of surprise and puzzlement on his lean face.

"You said, 'One big advantage. He has a wife who truly and deeply loves him,' " she reminded him. "Was that your way of telling me that because of our problems, I am depriving Winston of his chance?"

"Depriving Winston . . ." McCandless said, puzzled.

"That his life depends on me. Unless I can recapture the feeling I once had for him—" She broke off, saying, "This is coming out all wrong."

He sensed that this woman, who until now he had considered to be stalwart and strong, was now herself on the verge of tears.

"When I spoke to Nancy Campbell, I was speaking only to her. But if you want my appraisal of your situation, I will give it to you."

"Straightforward and totally honest?"

"Straightforward. And totally honest," he said. "His condition is quite grave. But should a heart appear in a matter of a month, he's got a good chance. As for emotional support, it's always better if the patient has strong support. But it has to be real. It can't be faked. In his case, perhaps loyalty might take the place of love. And you've surely given him that."

She listened, then asked softly, "Then why do I feel guilty?"

"I'm afraid you have to answer that for yourself," he replied.

He watched as she started down the corridor toward Winston Forrest's room.

McCandless returned to his office to resume his consideration of the file of a proposed candidate-for-transplant sent to him by a colleague from out of state. He had turned off the lights and was studying the cineangiogram when he heard the door slip open softly.

"I know, Claire," he said. "I'm late for that consult. But I'm right in the middle—"

He was interrupted by a tearful but suppressed apology. "Please, don't hold it against Jim, but before I left I had to see you. Had to—" Nancy Campbell's apology dissolved into tears.

McCandless turned from the projector, snapped on the light over his desk to discover her standing across the room, quivering. He went to her, put his arm around her, led her to a chair across from his desk.

"Please, no, don't bother," she kept trying to protest,

still weeping. "I don't want to make things worse. I don't. I'm . . . I'm just scared . . . scared."

He considered offering her a sedative, decided against it. This was a painful, strong, honest emotion. To hide it or suppress it with the aid of drugs would only delay its impact.

He took her cold hand in his. "Nan, just take your time. And ask anything you want to know."

"First . . . will my coming here hurt Jim's chances?"

"We don't stand on ceremony around here. Didn't Miss Duncan or Adeline Sawyer tell you to ask anytime you have a question?"

"But they also said that we have to be strong, dependable. Help the patient to endure the waiting period. Keep up his courage."

"Because the uncertainty in these cases is different from most other medical situations. With other medical problems we can generally tell within a certain time if the medication will take effect and will cure. Or that surgery will take so long, recuperation will take so much longer, and then there will be a cure. But here, we just wait. All of us. For the sudden unpredictable availability of that heart. It may come tonight at midnight. Or tomorrow. Or next week."

"Or," she interjected, "never?"

"No one knows. Meanwhile the patient has to endure all that waiting, all that uncertainty."

"Jim can do it. I know he can," she insisted, "It's me I'm afraid of. I don't know if I'm up to it."

She half turned to cast a fleeting glance at McCandless, to assess the judgment of her confession.

"Other wives," she continued, "how do they stand it? I mean, I'd like to be like the ones who've seen their husbands through it. Jim deserves it. He's such a good man. And a good father. Hardworking. Until this got to be too much for him. To look at him, people think he's a big strong, rough man. He's very gentle. Around the house he's soft as a kitten. And with the kids, there's never been a better father. If anything happens to him—"

She stopped for fear she would give way to tears once more. McCandless reached out, lifted her chin so that she had to look up into his gray eyes.

"Nan, I've been at this specialty for nine years now. During that time I've learned a great deal that's not in the medical books. About people. Nobody comes here who isn't in great trouble."

"I know," she said. "End-stage."

"Right. End-stage. And those who come with the patient—be they wives, or husbands, or children—are aware of all the problems. Financial worries. Fear of the future. Fear of what can happen if anything happens to the patient."

"I can't sleep nights for fear of that," she confessed. "We had such dreams for the kids. College and all. But now . . ."

"I know," McCandless said. "Let me tell you what I've discovered during the last nine years. Those women who love their husbands all go through the same stages. At first they doubt themselves and their ability to see it through. Then, as time demands, or as emergencies demand, they discover they *are* up to it. Somehow they overcome all their doubts, all their fears. I've never yet seen a wife cut and run under the strain, or a husband, either. And neither will you. So you can go home feeling secure about yourself."

"My coming here won't affect Jim's standing . . ." She had to know.

"It'll help him for us to know that he has a wife who loves him so," McCandless assured her.

It took a moment for his words to have effect. Finally she nodded, even tried to muster a smile.

"Thank you, Doctor," she said softly.

"Anytime you have a question, just ask. Adeline, Elaine Duncan, Dr. Robbins, we'll all be glad to answer," he said. "Tell you what, next time bring the kids. We won't let them into ICU, of course. Or let them have contact with any patients. But it'll help answer all their fears and uncertainties about Dad, where he is, what he's doing. Kids have the most active imaginations. Especially when they suspect their security is threatened. So bring them.''

"You mean it would be all right . . .'' she dared to ask.

"Absolutely!'' he confirmed.

"I'd thought about it. But I was . . .''

Smiling, he anticipated her, "Afraid to ask. Well, not anymore. You bring them. I'll answer all their questions. Now, go back to Jim. And tell him for me what a lucky guy he is to have a wife like you. I wish I did.''

She had gone. He was free to resume his study of the newly proposed case. As he studied the cineangiogram, he thought, *How many women I've seen like her, who start out tremulous and afraid that they are not up to the challenge. Then I see them grow in strength and stature, until it comes time for their husbands to return home, well and ready to resume their lives once more. But the strength of the wife has changed their relationship, in some cases creating two dominant personalities who must now readjust to each other and start what is in effect a new marriage.*

As fascinating as were the medical and surgical aspects of his chosen field, the human dramas were sometimes even more so.

All of which seemed to mock his own solitary personal life of the last twenty months.

18

BILL BROCK, TWENTY-SIX-YEARS-OLD and looking older, waited anxiously outside the hospital room of his wife Sally. Dr. McCandless had suggested he wait in the visitors' lounge. But he was too tense and worried. So he paced before the door, alert to the first indication that McCandless had completed the most recent examination of his ailing young wife.

At the sign of the door opening, Brock darted toward it to seize the doctor by the arm and pull him away just far enough to be out of earshot of his wife. "How'd it go, Doctor?" he inquired in an anxious whisper. "Was I right?"

"She is a little worse," McCandless conceded.

Grimly, Bill Brock had to agree. "I mean, like she was having more trouble breathing than last night. That's why I had to bother you," he apologized.

"No bother at all, Bill, no bother," McCandless said, at the same time assessing the probabilities. None of which were encouraging, unless there was a new heart, which seemed a remote possibility at this time.

"What do we do now?" young Brock asked. "I mean, what's the next step?"

"The next step, like the last step, is just wait. And hope," McCandless said.

"Doc," Bill Brock began hesitantly, "I've been reading, and talking to people . . ." Suddenly, deciding to abandon all pretense he blurted, "I talked to our own doctor. He said this might be the time for one of those mechanical hearts. I mean, if no human heart shows up, can't she have a mechanical one to tide her over. You know?"

McCandless felt great sympathy for the young man, who, like so many of his generation, depended in times of stress on little crutch phrases like "you know" and "I mean" to ease him over his inability to express himself.

"Bill, let's go down to my office," McCandless suggested. For he was deeply concerned about the effect his opinion would have on this young husband and father.

Even before sitting down in the chair McCandless had pointed out, Bill Brock asked, "Can you do this mechanical heart, Doc?"

McCandless eased into his desk chair, leaned forward to look into the anxious eyes of the young man.

"Son, let me explain about mechanical hearts. True, we might use one on Sally. But it's a last resort. And not a very desirable one."

"It might at least keep her going until a new heart shows up," the desperate young man pleaded. "Another few weeks or a month. Because . . . because from the way she looks today, she don't have that much time. She don't—" The effort to control his tears prevented him from continuing.

"She is deteriorating faster than I expected," McCandless continued. "Despite everything we can do for her. That's the nature of her disease."

"Then at least give her more time, even another month," Brock pleaded.

"We can remove her heart and install a mechanical pump. But after she suffers the difficulty, the discomfort, the danger and other problems, then even if a heart shows up, it might not work out. Experience shows us that patients who come off a mechanical and get a transplant don't do well. She'll have a much better chance going right to a transplant. . . . "

"*If* a heart shows up," Bill Brock pointed out. "But if it doesn't . . . I mean, I don't know . . . I don't know what to do, what to think . . . there's the baby and all . . . you know? What I mean . . . if I knew what having the baby was going to do to Sally, I would have said, I don't want the baby. I mean, I'd be willing to live the rest of our lives without any children. If I'da known what it would do to her, I wouldn'a touched her, you know what I mean?"

He was weeping freely.

"Son, you can't blame yourself. No one could have predicted what would happen to Sally as a result of giving birth," McCandless consoled.

The young man gasped, trying to recover.

"I keep thinking, what's going to happen? I mean, it's no home without her. I wander around the place like a stranger. I can't find a comfortable place to sit, or sleep. And there's the baby. My mom comes to sit during the day, and Sally's mom. They got a daytime schedule worked out between them, you know? But when I get home from the hospital in the evening, they got to go back home. Make supper for their own families. And I'm left with the baby. She's a cute little thing. I mean, there's no baby in the world cuter. And she knows me now. She smiles at me. She kinda expects the bottle when I give it to her. While she's feeding I hold her in my arms and tell her all kinds of things. Like how I love her. I mean, you're supposed to say that to kids, even if they can't understand it.

"And I also keep telling her, 'Don't you worry, honey, your mama is coming back soon. And she's going to be just as strong and healthy as she used to be.' Things like that. But when I look into her little blue eyes, I keep wondering, Can she tell? Can little babies only a few months old know if someone is lying to them?"

"I don't think so, Bill. Besides, with a little luck it might turn out not to be a lie at all. Any minute my phone might ring—"

"It didn't ring so far," the young man pointed out.

McCandless had no adequate response to that.

"Doc, you know the worst thing?" Brock blurted out, then hesitated before continuing. "Sometimes—mainly in the middle of the night, when I reach out across the bed where Sally used to be—I say to myself, 'What if the worst happens? What if Sally dies? What do we do, me and the baby? Move in with my mom? Or with Sally's mom? Then live like that for the rest of my life?' And I think, 'I know myself. I know if that happens, I am going to be thinking, If it wasn't for the baby . . .' You know?" He found it too difficult to continue.

"Bill, it might help if you had a talk with Dr. Robbins."

"What's he going to tell me? Not to hate the baby—"

The ugly word had escaped his lips. He turned away to avoid McCandless.

"Doc, there are times—like I said—middle of the night, you know? When I say to myself, the rest of my life I am going to blame that baby. If not for her . . . you know? That would be terrible. To feel that way. Terrible for me. Terrible for her. But I can't promise it won't happen. That's what scares me most. I don't want to hate her. Don't want to blame her . . ."

"You won't, Bill. No matter what you feel now, or think you feel, you'll love that child. Because it's part of Sally. Meantime, we can't give up. You go back to Sally's room and give her courage, hope. No matter how *you* feel, think of *her*."

"Yeah. Okay, Doc," the young man said, wiping his face of his tears. "I didn't mean to unload on you. You got problems enough. But every once in a while it gets to be too much, you know?"

"Bill, anytime you feel the need to talk, I'm here," McCandless said.

Allen McCandless examined the charts at the nurses' station. The nurse waited respectfully for his instructions.

BERGMAN, WILLIAM. CLYMER, ANNA. FORREST, WINSTON. BROCK, SALLY. CAMPBELL, JAMES.

"Get Brock, Forrest and Campbell out of bed. I want them more active. Don't overstress them, just keep them active. Good for them. Physically and psychologically."

"Yes, Doctor."

He started toward the elevator, but had a change of mind. He went down the corridor to a room with a half-open door. The room was dark except for the bright flickers from a television screen. Though the door was half open, he knocked.

"Mr. Forrest?"

"Come in, Doctor, come in."

He found Winston Forrest propped up in bed, the reflections of the television images playing across his pale but distinguished face.

He must have been extremely handsome as a young man, McCandless thought. *Yes, most women would have fallen in love with a young man like him. Why am I so concerned about why she fell in love with him, or fell out of love?*

"Yes, Doctor?" Forrest asked.

"Just thought I'd have a look-in," McCandless said. "How do you feel?"

"Okay, I guess. Weak. A little breathy," Forrest admitted. "And sick . . . of television," he added, trying to make a little joke. "God, is this what the American housewife is subjected to all day long?"

"Afraid so," McCandless said as he took Forrest's pulse, merely to cover his true concern. The patient appeared listless, disinterested, dispirited.

Other patients, when the doctor appeared, either were, or pretended to be, bright and eager, as if begging to be told that there was a heart, a new heart. Forrest seemed not to care. Or if he did care, he had spent too many years hiding his intentions for negotiating purposes to evidence any eagerness. Or it could be sheer physical debility. That weak damaged muscle his heart had become affected his mental attitude as well as his body.

"Mr. Forrest, I want you out of bed every day. Walk up and down the corridor. Perhaps go out to the solarium."

"Yes, I understand. Wards off hypostatic pneumonia," Forrest said.

"Been doing some medical reading?" McCandless asked.

"No. My mother. Confined to bed the last year of her life. She died that way," Forrest informed him.

"At what age?" McCandless asked.

"Eighty-six."

"And your dad?"

"Seventy-two," Forrest said. "Flu."

"You have good genetic lines," McCandless commented.

"Then how come?" Forrest asked. "I'm only fifty-four."

"I could give you all kinds of reasons. Job stress. Dietary habits. Too much alcohol. Truth is, we really don't know. We're just guessing. And some days we change the guesses. Last dozen years it's been cholesterol. Now we're only sure of one thing: We just don't know."

"Same in my business," Forrest said. "When something goes wrong, some negotiation blows, or even if some treaty is finally arrived at, we always hold a postmortem. If we had done something differently, would we have secured a more favorable outcome? Or if we had phrased some clause differently, would the negotiation have succeeded? Or at least avoided some embarrassing incident that makes the television news? We just never know."

"How well I know the feeling," McCandless commiserated.

"This solarium you mentioned, where is it?"

"Turn right at your door. Down the corridor to the end, then turn left."

"Can I make it on my own?" Forrest asked. "I hate being trailed by some nurse or orderly as if I were about to collapse. A little dignity, is all I ask."

"You can make it on your own. If you feel faint, there

are metal railings along the walls. Just hold on and call for help. Even if it offends your dignity."

This last made Forrest glare at McCandless for an instant. Then he relented, permitting himself a slight smile.

"Hell, man," McCandless said, "you're in a hospital. Fighting for your life. What good is dignity at a time like this?"

"You're right. I'll give it a try," Forrest said. McCandless started for the door. Forrest called to him, "Doctor?" McCandless half turned to him. "Just how much have you told my wife?"

The question startled McCandless. *Is Forrest alluding to the dinner we had? Had she told him about that? Why not, there was nothing to conceal,* he realized. *But then, why my first instinctive reaction?*

"I told her exactly what I've told you," McCandless said. "Your condition. Your odds for getting a new heart are roughly three to one. But no guarantees, of course."

"And after?" Forrest persisted.

"After?" McCandless was puzzled.

"My condition after that?"

"You'll be good as new. Certainly better than you are right now."

"Time!" Forrest insisted. "Can you estimate how much time?"

"Given the state of the art as it exists now, you could live as long as your father, possibly even longer," McCandless said.

"That's enough time," Forrest said thoughtfully. "She'll stay. She will. And this time I'll do it differently. Differently."

McCandless felt uneasy enough to conclude the conversation with a simple, "Up and out. Get moving."

The solarium did not exactly conform to what its name implied. It was a large room, with all three walls of glass exposed to east, north and west. But it offered no direct

open-air access to the sun. Bright plaid fabrics on the several
sofas, maroon tops on the card tables, and racks of colorful
magazines united to give the room an inviting homelike
appearance, in contrast to the more institutional appearance of
the rest of the hospital.

Slowly Forrest entered the archway of the solarium,
surveyed the room and selected a card table as far from the
television set as possible. When he reached the table he found
a young man scribbling notes on a little white pad. Forrest
debated sitting down.

"Mind?" he asked.

The young man looked up. "Mind what?"

"If I sit down."

"No. Of course not." He resumed jotting down figures
in small neat digits.

Priding himself on reading human character from little
clues, Forrest decided this was a careful, meticulous man,
despite his large muscular frame. But he seemed quite young
to be a patient here. Thirty. Possibly even younger. Curiosity
overruled Forrest's usual reserve.

"Sorry. But just how old are you?"

Taken by surprise, the young man was a touch late in
replying. "Thirty-two. Why?"

"Just wondered, that's all," Forrest said. Then, having
initiated the conversation, he felt compelled to introduce
himself.

"Forrest, Winston Forrest."

The look of recognition in the young man's eyes made
Forrest conclude, *Seen me in the newspapers or on television,
no doubt. I hate that look. I'm always the man people think
they know but really don't. I'm surprised he even recognized
the name. Once some woman said to me I look so familiar, she
was sure I was on some television series. Seems I'm familiar,
but never familiar enough. I'd better put his mind at ease.*

"Yes. You've seen me. Often. On the television news.
Sometimes too often, I think," Forrest said, trying to be light
and appear amused.

But the young man replied, "You've seen me, too."

"Oh? Have I?"

"That day up in the dentist's office. We were examined the same day."

Embarrassed, Forrest pretended recognition. "Yes, of course. I should have remembered."

"Jim. Jim Campbell."

"Jim Campbell. Of course. Now I remember."

"Seems my wife and your wife spend time together out there in the visitors' lounge. That's how I know about you."

"Oh," Forrest said, suffering a twinge of disappointment at this totally unexpected and unflattering identification. Forrest picked up a deck of worn cards someone had left on the table. He began to shuffle them, almost absentmindedly.

"Care to play a hand or two?" Campbell asked.

"Play?" Forrest asked, puzzled until he became conscious of the cards in his hands. "Oh. Why not? Anything to pass the time. What's your game?"

"Gin rummy?" Campbell suggested.

Forrest chuckled. "Young man, you don't know what you're letting yourself in for. I've spent half my life on Air Force planes playing gin rummy."

He offered the cards for a cut, which Campbell refused.

Forrest warned, "You'll be sorry," and he started to deal. "When you travel as much as I do to important conferences, summit meetings—after you've done all the preparing you can do, you know your facts cold, have your arguments all set, your opening gambit, your cheerful lies, and you want to unwind—there's nothing like a game of gin and a good stiff drink. Which, believe me, I could use right now. But I guess that's against the rules here."

"Guess so," Jim Campbell said, assembling his cards one by one as Forrest dealt them.

They began to play, alternately picking up a card from the deck, then discarding one.

"Government's my profession. What's yours?"

"Surgery," Jim Campbell said.

"You're a doctor?" Forrest asked, surprised.

"*Tree* surgery," Campbell explained, as he usually did after he'd had his little joke.

"No wonder you've got that outdoor look about you." Forrest picked a card and kept it, discarding a different one. "Like the work?"

"Sure do. Keeps a man out in the fresh air. Active. Alive. Believe me, being cooped up in a place like this gives me the willies."

"I feel like a prisoner myself," Forrest said.

"Not only that—" Jim started to say, but interrupted himself to lay down his hand. "Eight."

"Caught me," Forrest said, counting up his hand, "Ten, thirteen, seventeen, twenty-one, twenty-three."

They both looked around for something to keep score on. Jim became aware of the pad on which he'd been making notes.

"Here. Use this," he said, tearing off the top sheet with his own figures on it. He folded it quickly and slipped it into the pocket of his robe.

As Forrest was drawing the columns and writing down the score, he asked, "Not only *what*?"

Puzzled, Jim Campbell asked, "What what?"

"Just before you knocked you said, 'Not only that . . .' then didn't finish the thought," Forrest reminded him. "In my line of work what's left *un*said is sometimes more significant than what actually is said."

"Oh. That," Jim said. He hesitated before he continued, and then only after he had begun to pick up the cards that Forrest was dealing. "All my life I've not been very good at talking but not too bad at doing. When I was a kid in shop class, Mr. Higgins used to say, 'Jim, you got good hands, you got a feel for wood. Some day you're going to do well at it.' Of course, he never expected I would end up working with living things. Trees, shrubs. Neither did I. But my last year in high school I got part-time work helping out Abner Burnside. He used to do the trees and things in our part of town. But he was getting old. Wasn't as spry as he used to be. Years before he'd fallen out of a tree, twenty feet, almost. Broke his hip. Age was beginning to make it worse. So he had to get a new hip or else give up all that climbing. That's where I came in.

"I loved the work so much, I never went on to college. Helping growing things grow beats anything I know. I mean, you have this tree that it took nature fifty years, or even a hundred to grow, and it starts dying. But you can save it by lopping of the dead branches, cutting back, infusing it with new growth, new life. Then you watch it, like a doctor watches a patient. To see, is it recovering like you hoped? Or is it doomed, no matter what you do? Man, you hate to see one of them come down when they fail. Nothing so sad or mournful as the crack of a big tree as it crashes to earth. I haven't had many of those. But each one is a sad memory. They're old friends that you hate to see die."

"I know," Forrest said. He had lost interest in his cards. "I lost one when I was a boy."

"A tree?" Jim Campbell asked, surprised.

"Yes," Forrest replied. "When I was young we lived in a small town outside of Detroit. The way towns used to be. Quiet. Big elms that seemed to join branches and form arches over the streets. Drugstore. Not one of the chains. But owned by Doc Wetherall. He wasn't a doctor, of course, but we called him that. People used to consult him for remedies for common ailments. Ran a great soda fountain, too. And we had one movie house. One was enough in those days. Nowadays I suppose they'd split it up and make ten out of the one.

"We lived on Fremont Street. Corner lot. That was considered real high class. Actually, we weren't rich. Just a little better off than average. Our house was back from the street. About fifteen feet from the house was this big maple. When I was about seven, after I'd annoyed my dad almost to death to build it, he made me a swing. Suspended it from a thick branch that jutted out from the maple. I loved that swing. Summer, fall, even winter, I'd be out there swinging away. The older I got, the bolder I got. Higher and higher I'd swing.

My goal was to swing so high that I could look into our second-story window. Never made it.

"Because the third summer we got hit by this god-awful thunderstorm. Lightning flashed about the house, so that even my mother was terrified. Then there was this loud crack and the smell of something burning. Later that evening, when my dad came home, we went out to survey the damage. There it was, the maple, practically split down the middle, torn virtually in half by lightning. And my swing hanging at a crazy angle because the part of the tree with the branch had split away from the rest."

Forrest became aware of their game once more. He reached to pick a card from the deck, hesitated and changed his mind.

"My father said, 'Win'—he called me Win. He never liked Winston. Thought it was a pretentious name for a kid in a family like ours. But my mother had insisted.—'Win,' he said, 'you know it'll have to come down, don't you?' I felt a rush of tears to my eyes. I was determined not to cry. But he'd seen it. He tried to explain. 'Son, that's a badly wounded tree. And it is never going to recover. If we leave it there, it'll come down on its own. And, to judge from the angle, it could crash into the house. We wouldn't want that, would we?' 'No, sir' I said. 'We wouldn't want that.'

"Three days later the crew my father had hired rolled up in a big truck. A couple of men got out with saws and axes. I started to watch. But couldn't take it. I ran away. Went to the high school to watch the bigger boys play pickup basketball in the schoolyard. I stayed away as long as I could. When I got back the tree was down and being cut up into firewood. Dad said, 'Might as well make use of it.' And where the tree had been, they'd pulled the stump and left a big brown hole in the earth.

"I took my swing, ropes and all, down into the basement and hid them there. Everytime we used some of that wood to build a fire, it was like burning part of my childhood. So I know what you mean . . ." He added, self-consciously, "I haven't thought of that in years . . . years."

"We live in a town like that," Jim Campbell said.

"Really? I didn't think they existed anymore."

"Small. Quiet. Oh, sure, we've got a big chain super-market. But aside from that it's pretty much small town. High school kids go to the big consolidated school over in Hights-town. But mainly it's like you describe. Street lined with trees. Except blight wiped out our elms. But we still got a small drugstore. Of course the movie house is gone. That's over in Hightstown, too." Jim Campbell smiled, a bit sheep-ish. "I guess now that I think about it, it isn't so much of a town as it used to be."

"Sometimes," Forrest said, "I wish we could go back to the time when I was a boy. The war just over. And we came out of it the strongest nation in history. Helping other nations to recover. It looked like the world was at peace and destined to remain that way forever. Of course, we here weren't that much concerned with what the Soviets were doing in Eastern Europe. We were just so glad to have our troops back home. It seemed like a perfect time. It was sure a great time to be a kid in America. There was hardly anything you wanted that you couldn't have. Or hardly anything a young man could aspire to that he couldn't achieve if he was willing to work for it.

"Then somehow it all started to come apart. Slowly. Quietly. Hardly without anyone noticing. Before you knew it, we were in a life and death struggle with another superpower. We were both armed to the teeth with nuclear bombs. Only the fear of mutual destruction was keeping the peace."

Drawn together by their exchange, Forrest felt a need to address the younger man by name.

"Sorry . . . did you say your name was Joe Campbell?"

"Jim. Jim Campbell."

"Jim," Forrest repeated. "Well, Jim, your generation didn't have that time of peace and quiet that we enjoyed after the war. I'd figure that by the time you were born, we were already in the Korean War. Pardon me. Police action. Too soon after that there was Viet Nam.''

"I missed that by a few years," Jim said.

"Point I'm making, Jim, your generation never had a chance to relax and enjoy life. And now . . .'' Realizing what he was about to say, Forrest cut short his declaration.

But Jim anticipated him. "I know. And now I'm here in this hospital, and who knows what's going to happen?"

"They say the odds are three to one for us," Forrest pointed out.

Jim shook his head.

"You don't believe them?" Forrest asked. "So far they've been very honest. McCandless. Sawyer. Slade. The whole Unit."

"Oh, I believe them. It's Jimmy," Jim said.

"Jimmy?"

"My son. Kids are curious. When all other dads leave the house every morning and go off to work but your dad has to stay home, it creates all kinds of feelings. 'Why is my dad home all the time? Why can't he play with me like he used to?' And I suspect there's also a feeling that I don't think kids can express. 'If my dad isn't working, what's going to happen to us?'

"So even before he asked, I tried to explain it to him. How doctors can now take out a bad heart and replace it with a new one. Seems he knew about that from watching television. So that part was easy. Until he started asking questions like, 'Dad, does it always work? I mean, all the time?' That's where I had to rely on the percentages. I told him about the odds of three to one, about seventy percent and all that. But it didn't seem to quiet his young mind.

"Especially one day, I overheard him trying to explain it to his little sister. I knew then I'd better explain it all over again in a way he could understand. I racked my brains. Until I finally found it. Jimmy loves baseball. Loves to play. Loves to watch. Come the Saturday afternoon games on TV, you can't tear him away from the set.

"So this one Saturday I sat down and watched with him. While the game was on, I asked him, 'Jimmy, bet you don't know Don Mattingly's batting average!' 'Oh, yes, I do,' he said proudly. 'Three fifty-four. Only Boggs is better, three seventy-one. He's the best in the world, Boggs is!' So I said, 'Son, do you realize that my chances of getting better are twice as good as Boggs's batting average? Twice as good as the best in the world!'

"He seemed impressed for a moment, and continued watching the game. Till he turned to me again. 'Dad, Boggs and Mattingly, they strike out every once in a while. What happens if your doctor strikes out?' "

Forrest nodded in commiseration, "No good answer to that question, is there?"

"That's why I'm not impressed by their percentages. I keep remembering what my son asked. 'Dad, what happens if the doctor strikes out?' "

"I know what you mean," Forrest said softly. "In a way, I feel relieved that there's no one depending on me."

"There's your wife . . ." Jim said.

Forrest chose not to discuss that subject.

"Sorry. I'm holding up the game," Forrest said, as he picked a card from the deck and discarded one from his hand. As he did so, his gaze hit the archway of the solarium.

From the look in Forrest's eyes, Jim Campbell knew that the man had spotted a familiar face. He appeared prepared to receive a visitor. Jim was about to throw in his hand, but Forrest said, "Don't. He's only making his usual courtesy call." As he started to rise, Jim heard a voice call out, "Please, Mr. Forrest, don't bother. Stay just as you are."

But Forrest rose and introduced the visitor, "Jim, I want you to meet Mr. Strawbridge, who runs this whole medical center. Strawbridge, meet my friend Jim. Jim Campbell."

"Mr. Campbell . . ." Strawbridge said perfunctorily, in his haste to get to the real purpose of his visit. "Forrest, I think you'll be delighted to know that this morning the Secretary of Defense called me. Seems he'd heard about your being admitted back to the hospital. I assured him it was completely precautionary. He was greatly relieved to hear it."

"Good . . . good," Forrest said. "Perhaps I ought to drop him a line. Or call him. Just to let him know how I feel."

"That would put his mind at ease. While you're at it, if you would stress the quality of the care you're getting . . ." Strawbridge suggested.

"Sure thing," Forrest said.

Mission accomplished, Strawbridge smiled and said, "Didn't mean to interrupt your game. Carry on, men."

He started out, turning back to smile and wave a cordial farewell. Forrest waved back, at the same time muttering so that Jim had difficulty understanding him, "I wish he wouldn't hover over me so. He makes me feel even sicker than I am.

"I guess that's what comes from being such an important man, Mr. Forrest," Jim said.

"Clout, is the word, Jim. Clout. Government funds is what he's looking for." Then, to change what he considered a distastful subject, he remembered, "We never did set the stakes for this game. How about a dollar a point?"

From the glint in Forrest's eyes, Jim Campbell knew the man was joking, so he said, "Let's make it two dollars a point!"

"You're on!" Forrest said, and applied himself to the game with added gusto.

By the time the lunch call reached the solarium, and after three full sets of gin rummy, Jim Campbell was ahead eleven thousand nine hundred sixty-four dollars.

"Wait till tomorrow," Forrest pretended to begrudge. "I'll win it all back and more!"

"Would you like to play again tomorrow?" Jim Campbell asked, feeling flattered.

"Meet you right here. At ten. Unless, of course, they decide to give me a heart tomorrow."

They both laughed.

"Tomorrow at ten," Jim Campbell said, as he started out of the room.

Winston Forrest watched him go, thinking, *Nice young man. See a young man like him with two kids and a young wife, you don't feel so sorry for yourself. God, I hope he makes it. Seventy percent. Got to keep thinking seventy percent. What was that he told his little boy? Twice Wade Boggs's batting average. Got to remember that.*

19

AS THE CITY HAD GROWN, as the Medical Center had expanded, more and more of the rich surrounding midwestern farmland had been sold off and converted from agriculture to real estate development. Clusters of houses had sprung up, as if overnight. Rich brown earth had been covered over with white concrete and black macadam. After almost two decades of an expanding economy, the closest cultivated farmland to the hospital was more than fifteen miles away. That land, too, was no longer given over to wide fields of wheat and soy beans. With the exception of some acreage devoted to growing eating corn, the rest was in vegetables for truck farming. Such produce fetched much better prices at the various farmers' markets that flourished in the suburbs surrounding the city.

Carl Digby, whose life as a child, and then as a man, had been spent in farming, ran one of the more successful truck farms in the area. With the help of two farmhands, his wife, and occasionally his young twelve-year-old son, Digby produced a rotation of crops that provided a steady flow of income during all but the coldest months of the year.

A prudent man with an eye to the future, and to his son's future, Carl Digby kept his farm in as neat order as his rows of lettuce, eggplant, romaine, cucumbers and other vegetables. His equipment was cared for with as much concern as a housewife would lavish on her prized furniture. When any truck or tractor reached the point of diminishing returns, he traded it for newer, more modern equipment. He was determined that when the time came to turn his farm over to his son, it would be a well-equipped, modern, smoothly operating, profitable agricultural enterprise. Neat, compact, and not so overextended that the bankers owned more of him than he did.

This day was one of the special days in the life of Carl Digby. He was taking delivery of a new tractor, larger and more powerful than any of its predecessors. Bright, new, shiny, and fire-engine red, it was unloaded from the back of the huge truck that had delivered it. His two helpers stood by watching as the machine, which smelled of its newness, was carefully backed down two broad thick planks which sagged under its weight. It touched the ground and its treads bit into the soft brown earth.

Carl himself mounted to the driver's seat, started the motor, engaged the lever in forward gear and slowly started toward the fields. He had gone about thirty yards when he turned the giant tractor about slowly and started back toward the house. The machine behaved well, was sensitive to his large hands on the steering wheel.A much more delicately responsive piece of equipment than the one he was trading in. Feather touch, the advertisement in the *Farm Journal* had labeled the steering. So it proved to be. Only half as much of a man's effort was required by this new tractor. Carl Digby considered it was an investment worth making. The notes would be paid off in thirty-six months, and it would be his for years to come. With proper care, perhaps even to be passed on to his son Bertram.

"Okay, boys, back to work," Digby called out. As the farmhands went back into the field, Digby signed the required acceptance. The huge delivery truck pulled out onto the state road and was gone.

Hannah Digby had watched the proceedings from the kitchen window, where she was preparing midday dinner for her husband and his two-man crew. She smiled at her husband's pride in his new acquisition. Every piece of new equipment he added to the farm was an achievement in which he took great satisfaction. When they had bought the new car, which meant they no longer had to drive to church in the pickup truck, that, too, was a mark of success. Other farmers might complain, some even lose their farms, but Carl Digby had demonstrated that he could change with the times and remain not only head above water, but successful beyond mere breaking even. She enjoyed his pride in his success. Which she did now, watching him from the window as he walked around his new tractor, admiring every facet of it.

Carl with his new toy, she thought as she smiled. *Just wait until Bert gets back from school and sees it.*

Dinner had been over for several hours when the school bus pulled up at the gate to the Digby farm. Twelve-year-old Bertram Digby swung off the bus, calling back to the boys who remained on board, "See yuh!" With his backpack over his shoulders he walked until he spied the new red tractor, then he broke into a run. He reached it and jumped up, trying to get a grip on the driver's seat. He barely reached it with both hands, and pulled himself up to slip into the seat that was too large for his slender young body. He sat there, monarch on a throne.

From the back porch where she was putting out the meal for their two dogs, Hannah Digby discovered her son. She smiled at his pride, as he seemed to dominate the shiny red tractor.

Like father, like son, she thought. Having set out two bowls of food, she retreated back into the house.

Ensconced in the driver's seat, Bert Digby stared at the shiny new controls, almost intoxicated by the smell of the new machine. He could not resist the temptation to start up the engine.

He reached for the key on the steering column. It was hard to turn, but with both hands he managed it. The engine roared into action. He found it impossible to resist putting it into gear. It started up. Being used to the old tractor, which was sluggish and slow, the boy pumped the pedal vigorously. The tractor took off more quickly than he anticipated. Instead of frightening him, it only encouraged him to try his hand at maneuvering it.

He aimed it toward the mound of earth that served as grading to divert the water away from the house in heavy rainstorms. The machine mounted the mound more quickly than young Bert expected. He turned the steering wheel sharply to veer away from it. His action would have suited the old tractor but was too sharp and abrupt for this new, more responsive, machine. It reared up to the crest of the mound and turned so swiftly that it rolled over onto its side, hurling young Bert Digby from his seat, imprisoning him underneath.

Hannah Digby turned from hemming new curtains for the living room to glance out of the window. She saw the new tractor roll over on its side. With her son no longer in view, she raced out onto the porch, crying, "Bert! Bertram! Son!" She directed her voice toward the fields, shouting as loudly as she could, "Carl! Carl! Our son . . ."

With the help of his two workers, and the use of the large produce truck, they were able to lift the fallen tractor. Hannah Digby fell upon her son's body, weeping, while trying to wipe the blood from his face.

Shocked as he was, Carl Digby ordered, in a hoarse whisper, "Jake, get the car!"

Gently he moved his wife aside. He lifted his unconscious bleeding son into his arms.

It took thirty-four minutes to bring young Bertram Digby to the Emergency Service of the small community medical installation. Fortunately it was one of those days when the visiting doctor was holding clinic hours.

Carl Digby tried to shield his wife from the action the doctor had to take to debride the boy's head wound and assess the extent of his injury. It took no more than a cursory examination for the young doctor to decide to put the boy on a respirator. Then he proceeded to perform a series of neurological tests to determine the extent of brain damage.

Carl Digby could tell from the doctor's silent responses that his son's condition was grave, quite grave. He pressed his wife's face against his chest to prevent her seeing. But in vain. She had seen. She had read the doctor's reaction as Carl had.

The doctor took only a few minutes to decide. The boy must be moved to the University Medical Center, for his own sake and, if what he feared was the boy's condition, for possible consideration as a donor of his heart or any other organs that could be harvested.

To save crucial time, in the event a transfusion was needed, he had the small lab determine the boy's blood type. The lab reported Type A.

With the comatose boy still on a respirator, the ambulance sped along the Interstate through flat farmland toward the city. The doctor continued to assess the vital signs of young Bertram Digby, while his mother and father sat in the ambulance, numb, staring, dry-eyed. It was too early to cry. The truth had not yet defeated hope.

Dr. Allen McCandless was in the midst of the weekly and monthly checkups of those outpatients who had received their hearts in the last dozen months. He had seen the first twelve and was examining William Crozier, a young construction worker who had received his heart four months ago. He had progressed so well that he was now on a biweekly examination schedule. This did not interfere with his work, since he was scheduled to present himself on one of his off days.

He had come, as had all the others, carrying his little airline travel bag which contained his medications. Since the prescribed medicines had to be taken in exact doses at very specific hours, each patient was instructed to carry his or her medications at all times. So that if they were stuck in a traffic jam or detained by some other unexpected event, they would still be able to take their medication at exactly the proper time.

Crozier had taken his cyclosporine blood-specimen tube to the lab as soon as he arrived, so that McCandless had the lab report available as he examined the young man. While he listened to Crozier's heart and lungs, McCandless said, "Take your temp today?"

"I take it every day," Crozier said, a film of sweat appearing on his upper lip as he wondered, *Has he detected some signs of rejection?*

McCandless put his mind at ease. "Your cyclosporine level is fine, just fine." Then he asked, "You know what to do if you do get a fever?"

"I know. Tylenol. Never aspirin," Crozier replied. "Thins the blood."

"Right," McCandless said, continuing his examination. "How are you doing on your diet?"

"Pretty good. Low fat, low salt, no alcohol," Crozier began to count off the restrictions.

Until McCandless interrupted, "No alcohol at all?"

Crozier did not respond at once, then admitted, "Some nights—I mean, when I'm watching the baseball game on TV—I might have a beer. But that's only some nights."

"Bill, I've told you, the nurses have told you, Adeline Sawyer has told you, no alcohol at all. You need your cyclosporine to avoid rejection of your new heart. Cyclosporine can cause liver toxicity, so any added liver damage from alcohol can be very dangerous, life-threatening. Now, this is the visit you're scheduled to have a biopsy, right?"

"Right."

"Okay, let's go," McCandless said, leading the way to a small operating room where Boyd Angstrom, Slade's surgical assistant, was waiting to perform the procedure, which consisted of inserting a plastic catheter into Crozier's jugular vein then watching it carefully on the monitor as it slowly made its way down toward his heart.

The tip of the catheter had entered the heart. Angstrom was about to snip off the infinitesimally small bit of tissue from the transplanted heart when the phone on the wall rang. Both Angstrom and McCandless reacted with great annoyance at this unwelcome intrusion at such a moment. The nurse answered the phone. Angstrom continued with the procedure, positioning the tiny scalpel in the head of the probe so it could snip off a sample of heart tissue.

If the rejection phenomenon were beginning, the first sign would appear in tissue from the foreign heart itself. The pathologist would have to make that determination; all Angstrom and McCandless could do was provide the sample.

Before Angstrom was able to secure that bit of tissue, the nurse intervened. "Dr. McCandless, a patient's just been brought into Emergency. They need you down there."

McCandless knew what that meant. The vast majority of hearts available for transplant were the result of emergencies. Swiftly, he was on his way.

On his way into the Emergency Room McCandless was confronted by a sight he had become familiar with very early in his career as an intern and a resident. The stunned relatives waiting outside the Emergency Room. Fear, hope, doubt on their faces. The woman usually in tears. The man, awkward and wordless, trying to reassure or console. This time it was Carl Digby and his wife.

McCandless made an automatic calculation. Judging from the age of the mother and father, the victim was a teenage girl or boy.

Kids, these days, McCandless concluded automatically. *Drugs, drag races . . .*

He entered to find the Emergency Room doctor bending over the inert body of young Bertram Digby, trying to stop the flow of blood from a head wound. McCandless took in the entire scene at one glance. Respirator pumping. Boy's body reacting to it. Otherwise no signs of vital activity.

The young resident said, "I figured you should be here. In case you wanted to talk to the parents yourself."

"Do all the tests?"

"Yes, sir. No reaction at all. I've sent for a neurologist to make sure. But I'd say brain dead."

McCandless was always uncomfortable in moments like this. Though his work was life-saving in the fullest sense of that term, unfortunately, death must always be a part of it.

He made a cold appraisal of the situation. The boy was small, twelve-years-old, thirteen at most. His weight, one hundred ten pounds, fifteen possibly.

Instinctively he made the connection. Sally Brock. Small-chested, weight one hundred three pounds. She could accommodate and use to best advantage the heart of such a young donor. Before he was free to use the heart, McCandless knew he must advise UNOS in Richmond, Virginia.

But first, the neurologist's assessment. It was the law, as well as the ethics of his specialty, that the physician who might use the potential heart was never allowed to make the determination of brain death. This, to avoid the temptation of overeager transplant doctors to reach that conclusion too quickly or in cases where it is not justified.

In the interest of saving time, McCandless asked, "Did you type him?"

"The report that came with him said Type A."

"We always have our lab cross-check."

"I know. The blood's on the way up now."

McCandless nodded, went to the wall phone and asked for Transplant Coordinator Sawyer.

"Addie, inform UNOS we have a possible donor here. Boy. Type A. About one hundred ten pounds—"

Adeline Sawyer could not resist interrupting. "One hundred and ten pounds—Sally Brock!"

McCandless continued his instruction. "Report that we also have a Type A recipient. It would make better sense, medically and surgically, to harvest the heart and implant it right here. Tell them that Brock is not only end-stage, but terminal. Let me know as soon as they run it through their computer. Meantime, get things rolling. Have them start prepping Sally for surgery. It'll take hours, if they start now."

"Yes, Doctor!" Adeline responded crisply.

"As soon as the neurologist gets here, I'll talk to the parents."

The neurologist repeated every test, not twice, but three times. When he signed that certificate he wanted to be absolutely sure that all brain activity had ceased. He finally nodded to McCandless. It was the signal, silent, grim, but final. Young Bertram Digby was brain dead. The moment they turned off that respirator, all his functions would cease.

McCandless now had to go out and inform the Digbys. Ask their permission to remove the kidneys, liver, lungs, and heart of their son, who only this morning had been a bright twelve-year-old boy who had recited well in social studies class.

Up on the ICU floor of the Cardiac Wing, word that Sally Brock was being prepped for surgery spread quickly. In the solarium, patients heard about it. In the visitors' lounge family members learned of it. Winston Forrest and his wife both learned of it when, curious about the excited conversation in the corridor, Millicent Forrest had gone out to discover why.

She came back. "Win, isn't it wonderful? The Brock girl. Sally Brock—she's going to get a heart!"

"Marvelous!" Winston Forrest exclaimed. "I tell you, it's been tragic watching a young girl like her, wasting from day to day. And wanting so desperately to be with her baby. Old bastards like me, who cares . . . but the young should have their chance."

"They'll find one for you, too," Millicent reassured.

"How do you know?"

"Dr. McCandless tells me your chances are good."

"Dr. McCandless," he scoffed. "I think his main job around here is being a cheerleader."

"He is not. He is a very practical, hard-nosed type. He

doesn't like to fool anyone. Especially not patients. Or the families of patients.''

"You seem to know him well," Forrest responded.

"We've talked a bit. In fact, we've had dinner together. Twice.''

"Oh?"

It was difficult to discern if Winston was expressing surprise or disapproval.

"He's recently divorced, and he hates eating alone all the time. I guess it's a case of mutual pity," she said. "I hate eating alone, too.''

"Tell me, Millie, if this thing works—I mean, if they get me a heart—what I really mean is, if I come out of surgery in pretty good shape, *I'm* going to hate eating alone all the time, too.''

"I'm willing to try, Win. I'm willing to try." It was as much of a promise as she could honestly make.

In the solarium, Jim Campbell was shuffling the cards, trying to decide whether to play solitaire. Whenever Millicent Forrest visited her husband, Jim was deprived of his usual opponent. He missed playing gin. But even more, he missed the exciting and fascinating stories Winston Forrest told. His adventures in government. The important men he had met. Presidents. Chiefs of Staff. Prime Ministers. Once you got past his gruffness, Forrest had a good sense of humor.

Forrest's gruffness, Jim had concluded, was due to his resentment at being sick, rather than his usual disposition. The man had things to do, important things, important to the nation. Yet here he was, cooped up in a hospital. Waiting. Just waiting. Waiting for a heart, or waiting to die.

To justify his own sense of anger, Jim thought, *At least Forrest's had his life. The man is fifty, maybe more. I'd settle for fifty right now! For twenty-five years with Nan. To see Jimmy live to be twenty-two. I'm the one has a right to be angry at the world. If only—that phrase keeps coming up all the time—if only I get my chance, like Sally Brock is getting hers . . . if only . . .*

In Sally Brock's room Allen McCandless was reviewing her latest lab figures, which had just reached him. The most important finding—there was no evidence that she had an infection. As important—no fever. For if there were, that would eliminate her as a possible transplant recipient until those conditions cleared up. And the heart, which was readily available, would have to be passed on to a patient with the physical condition to receive it.

Fortunately, Sally Brock was not suffering any such disqualification. He examined her once more, heart, lungs, pulse, blood pressure.

Meantime, the excited young mother kept asking, "Does Bill know? Did someone call my husband?"

"He knows, he knows," McCandless assured her. "He's on his way here."

"Is he . . . is he bringing the baby?" she hesitated to ask.

"No, I'm sorry, Sally. I thought it best not to complicate things. He said the baby has the sniffles."

"Sniffles? He never told me." She began to weep. "He keeps things from me. Doesn't want me to worry. The sniffles . . . she has the sniffles . . ."

"All babies get the sniffles. Maybe a hundred times before they're a year old," McCandless consoled. "I'm not a pediatrician, but I can guarantee your baby will recover."

"When I'm . . . I'm okay again . . . and after she's over her sniffles, will she be able to come see me?" Sally asked.

"Sally, the odds are that in three weeks, four, you'll be home, McCandless reminded her. "With a new heart."

"Home . . ." Sally repeated. The single syllable expressed all her longings, hopes and dreams.

*   *   *

Adeline Sawyer was on the phone, feeding the vital information to the National Organ Center. She responded to their
routine checklist, like a flight crew readying a plane for
takeoff.

"Donor age: twelve years seven months . . . Cause of brain
injury: trauma due to overturned tractor . . . Neurologist's
death status: death from injury to brain and brain stem."

She started to read off a set of lab figures that had just reached
her, when one of the lab technicians rushed to her side. He
tried to interrupt, but she waved him off impatiently until she
could conclude her report to the Organ Center.

Waving under her eyes a lab report, he insisted, "Addie!
Stop! Please!"

"Hold on a minute," she said, turning impatiently to the
young technician. "I'm talking to UNOS!"

"What blood type did you give them?" the technician
asked.

"A, of course. That's on the report they sent along."

"Addie, he isn't A. He's AB."

AB? Instinctively, Adeline Sawyer repeated to herself, as
if the fact was encoded in her mind, *Blood Type AB can only
donate to a Blood Type AB. Sally Brock is Type A.*

Somewhere in the lab at that small hospital, or in the
transmission of the information, someone had made an error,
reporting Type A instead of AB.

Slowly, Adeline Sawyer imparted the correction to the
Organ Center. The heart of Bertram Digby would now go to
whoever was first on the list of some transplant center within
a thousand miles, someone who needed a heart of proper size
to fit into a small chest cavity and whose blood type was AB.

Once she had imparted that information to the Organ
Center, she called Allen McCandless who was reviewing with
Surgeon Chris Slade the scans, X rays, and pertinent test
results of all the procedures that had been carried out on Sally
Brock. The anesthetists as well as the perfusionists were

making their notes in preparation for surgery. McCandless resented any intrusion at such a critical moment. He seized the phone, demanding gruffly, "Yes? What is it?"

"Doctor," Adeline Sawyer said, "there's been a mistake. An unfortunate mistake."

"Is there any other kind?" he shot back.

"The Digby boy . . . he's not Type A."

"What do you mean, not Type A?" McCandless demanded, while all the others in the consultation room stared at each other in puzzlement, then dismay, as they heard, "He's what? Type AB? Are you sure?"

"There was an error in the transcript that came with the donor. Our own lab caught it," Sawyer reported.

"Yes, sure. Good thing we double check," McCandless said, trying to conceal his disappointment.

"Shall I tell Brock?" Adeline Sawyer asked.

"No, Addie, that's my job," McCandless said. He hung up the phone. He faced his surgical staff. "Ladies and gentlemen, you heard. The boy is AB. There's nothing we can do for Sally Brock tonight."

He left the room, passing among his staff, who silently commiserated with the tragic young mother, for whom they had all formed an affection during her stay in the hospital.

Allen McCandless strode down the corridor of the ICU floor of the Cardiac Wing. He could recognize from the excitement and the expectation that seemed to emanate from the visitors' lounge, the solarium, and almost every room, that patients and visitors alike were delighted that Sally Brock was to get her new heart. It was on the faces of the patients and staff as he passed them in the corridor on the way to her room.

Even before he entered her room he could hear Bill Brock encouraging her through the open doorway, "And, honey, when I asked, the doctor said the change is immediate. Like one minute before the operation you're pale and weak and hardly able to breathe—"

"Like now," she said.

"Yeah, but right after the operation, even before you come out of Recovery, you're pink and healthy. It's like a miracle," he continued encouragingly.

"I wonder how it feels going under . . . I never had an operation before. Giving birth to Sarah was different. I mean, I didn't have any anesthetic . . . but this . . ."

"It's nothing, sweetie, nothing at all. I mean, that time when I was still in the service and had that appendectomy? They just gave me a shot and I was out, you know? It's like falling asleep. And next thing, you're waking up and it's all over. Except in your case instead of just taking something out, they're putting something in. A brand-new heart."

"Did they say who it was?" Sally asked.

"Gee, I don't know for sure. But I heard it was a boy. A twelve-year-old boy," Bill Brock said.

"A boy . . . and only twelve years old . . . what could have happened?" Sally asked.

"Some kind of accident, they said."

"Oh, God, that's sad," Sally said, then asked, "I wonder if it will feel any different?"

"Of course it will," her husband assured. "That's what it's all about. To make you feel different. Better."

"I mean, is there a difference between men's hearts and women's hearts? How will it feel having a boy's heart?"

"I don't think that matters," he said. "Main thing is for you to have a good heart, come home, and start getting to know our daughter. She's fantastic. Changes every day, you know. Gets brighter and smarter. And she knows me. I mean, she smiles and plays with me. And funny thing, the way she can get hold of her toes. You'll see. Believe me, darling, you've got a fantastic child waiting to greet you when you get home. And Dr. McCandless said you could be home in just three weeks. Three weeks, how about that!"

"Three weeks," she repeated, savoring it, as if it were the most wonderful phrase in the entire language. "Three weeks."

There was a knock on the open door.

"Come in. We're ready," Bill Brock greeted, expecting the attendants, the nurse and the gurney stretcher. He turned to see Dr. McCandless. "Hi, Doctor!" he said, all smiles.

Until he and his wife both became aware of the sober look on the cardiologist's face.

"Doctor?" Sally Brock asked.

"Sally, Bill, I have to talk to you," he began. "There has been a mistake—"

"Mistake?" she asked instantly. "What do you mean, mistake? It's my turn, isn't it? They started to give me the drugs, get me ready . . . there can't be a mistake, there can't be! I've waited this long . . ."

Her husband was less emotional. "What kind of mistake, Doctor?"

"The donor heart, it isn't Type A," McCandless said.

"Not Type A?" Bill Brock asked. "But they said—"

Sally interrupted. "It doesn't have to be Type A. The patient manual says Type O can give to anyone! Anyone!"

"Sally, this boy was Type AB. And AB's can only give to AB's" McCandless informed her as gently as he could. "The manual says that, too."

"Yes . . ." the young woman said, so softly that it could barely be heard. Then the tears started. Her husband took her up in his arms.

"Honey, honey," he consoled her gently. "So it isn't this time, it'll be next time."

"There won't be any next time," she protested through her tears, "There won't be any next time . . . there won't be any next time . . . there won't be any baby to hold . . ."

"Honey, please? Please?" her distraught husband kept entreating.

McCandless watched, unable to offer encouragement or help. He could only think, *If I could get my hands on the bastard in that lab who made that mistake, I'd strangle him. Strangle him!*

*   *   *

Later that day the AB heart of young Bert Digby had been harvested and flown to Denver, where it was implanted into the body of a fourteen-year-old girl who was also Type AB and who suffered from severe cardiomyopathy of no detectable origin.

The disappointment that Sally Brock and her husband experienced was silently echoed through the rooms, the corridor and the visitors' lounge of the Transplant Unit.

Patients and their families, through sharing experiences in the solarium, the lounge, or in patient-group meetings, were one large family. They rooted for one another, sympathized with one another, shared the excitement and joy each time a member received a new heart. Hope for one was hope for all. In Sally's case, disappointment for one became a shared burden.

The next morning, when they arrived for their usual visiting hours, both Millicent Forrest and Nancy Campbell visited Sally to encourage her.

Soon, very soon, there must be a heart for her, they were sure.

Despite her attempts at a cheerful smile, Sally Brock remained inconsolable.

Some days later, a floor nurse making a routine midmorning check of Sally Brock's condition detected a suddenly elevated pulse rate. She immediately phoned Dr. McCandless. He interrupted a consultation on a new patient to rush up to the sixth floor.

He performed a quick but thorough examination and detected several other unsettling signs. Not only was Sally's pulse rate above one hundred, but she was experiencing shortness of breath. He applied his stethoscope to her back and chest, and heard clearly discernible rales of the type that reflected accumulation of considerable fluid.

He had her lie back, and began to palpate the veins in her neck. As he suspected, there was noticeable distension.

He left orders for her to be given a diuretic and also some Slow-K to increase her potassium level. And he instructed the nurse to apprise him of Sally's condition every hour.

He had only been gone from her room for some fifty minutes before the emergent sound of his beeper summoned him from a class he was conducting for young cardiac residents. He reached the phone outside the lecture hall.

"Dr. McCandless, you'd better come up right away," the alarmed nurse requested.

"What is it?"

"Brock. I think she's started to fibrillate."

That one word was enough to cause McCandless to order, "Move her into ICU at once! I'll be right up!"

He started for the staircase. There was no time to wait for an elevator.

Up on the sixth floor things moved with great speed. Sally Brock was lifted onto a gurney and sped down the corridor to ICU. By the time she was being eased into bed and hooked up to an oscilloscope, McCandless came through the door.

One look into her terrified eyes told him that Sally Brock knew the danger she was in.

"Bill . . . I want Bill," she gasped.

"Easy now," McCandless said gently.

He began to examine her by stethoscope. What he heard told him. Tachycardia. Ventricular tachycardia. She was not yet fibrillating. But that could occur at any moment. Even as he listened, he heard the onset of that erratic, wild, out-of-control racing of her damaged heart.

"Defibrillator!" he ordered.

The ICU crew produced two round flat objects the size of Ping-Pong paddles. He applied one to her chest, one to her back, and ordered, "Juice!"

A jolt of electricity shot through her frail young body, causing her to rear up suddenly and then relax. McCandless applied his stethoscope. He listened for a long time, to make sure. Her heartbeat had been restored to under ninety beats a minute and was no longer erratic and uncontrolled.

"That's better," he said softly.

Those two words did not completely express his relief. For ventricular fibrillation of any duration was only one short step from death.

He patted Sally's damp cheek to reassure her. The look of terror in her eyes slowly gave way to one of peaceful exhaustion.

He waited, keeping watch on the oscilloscope screen. After the rhythm continued in a regular if somewhat swift pattern, he felt assured enough to leave.

But on his way past the nurses' station he stopped to order, "Get hold of Bill Brock. Tell him to get here as soon as he can."

The nurse's puzzled look deserved an explanation.

"We may not be so lucky the next time," he said.

Less than an hour later, Bill Brock entered the ICU room where Sally lay half asleep, eyes closed. He looked to the nurse. She nodded permission for him to approach the bed.

Very softly, in a tense whisper, he said, "Sally . . . darling . . ."

She opened her eyes. She tried to smile. She did not succeed. He took her hand. It felt cold. He held it between his two hands to warm it.

"You feel okay, darling?"

"Uh-huh," she managed in a voice that he barely heard, even though his ear was close to her mouth.

"You're going to be all right now," he assured her, then added a justified lie, "Dr. McCandless said you're going to be fine."

She closed her eyes. He thought she was drifting off to sleep. But her breathing became strange, and it frightened him. He glanced at the screen, across which raced a pattern of long irregular slashes of light. He raced out to find the nurse.

But she had already spotted the dangerous change on the screen at the nurses' station where all ICU patients were continually monitored. She was on the phone when Bill Brock hurried up to her.

"Dr. McCandless! It's Brock. She's fibrillating again!"

"Call a Code Blue. I'll be right there!"

By the time McCandless reached ICU, the Code Blue team had arrived and had the defibrillator paddles in place. McCandless pushed by Bill Brock to get to Sally's side. Making sure the paddles were properly applied to her back and chest, he ordered, "Defibrillate!"

The charge of electricity shot through the girl's body. Once. Twice. He glanced at the screen. The signs of fibrillation were only too apparent.

"Defibrillate!" he ordered a third time. And then a fourth.

Each time Sally's body rose up in sudden response to the electrical charge. But when she settled back, the screen revealed a straight flat line and emitted a single, continuous warning sound indicating that all cardiac activity had ceased.

McCandless began to pump her chest to restore some heart action. But after long minutes of desperate effort, he realized that the result was irreversible.

Bill Brock leaned over the bed, took his young wife in his arms and held her tightly.

"Sally . . . sweetheart . . . Sally . . ." he pleaded.

Guilty and defeated, Allen McCandless started out of the room.

He sat at his desk trying to complete dictating his notes on the case of Patient Brock, Sally into the recorder. The effect on him had been even worse than he had anticipated. He would complete dictating in the morning.

When he reached the parking lot he spied Millicent Forrest as she was getting into her car.

"Mrs. Forrest."

She stopped, turned from her car to identify the caller.

Once she recognized him, he asked, "Wait, won't you? Just a moment?"

She nodded.

As he reached her side, he asked, "Would you mind . . . I mean, do you have anything else . . . are you free for the evening?"

"I have no special plans," she said.

"I was wondering if you'd like to have dinner with me again?"

She recognized that more than an invitation, this was a plea. She had intended to have a simple dinner, a warm bath and an evening of relaxation from the strain of spending hours in the imprisoning environment of a hospital where life and death were constantly in the balance. And where, today, a young woman of twenty, a new mother, had died even before she had begun to live her life.

She suspected that the young woman's death had left its mark on the doctor. So she replied, "I'm not only free, I could stand some company."

"Good," he said, with great relief.

20

THEY ARRIVED AT the quaint Italian restaurant, where Millicent Forrest realized that the proprietor Romeo and his wife knew Dr. McCandless well. They greeted him warmly. Romeo, a short portly man, showed him to a table in a corner, which was secluded and quiet. Evidently, they knew the doctor's preference for privacy.

Romeo waited until the waiter arrived, then with a knowing wink to McCandless, started away. The significance of that wink would not dawn on the doctor until much later. The man assumed that the presence of a woman who wasn't Mrs. McCandless was a sign of courtship. Not only that, but the little man approved.

Despite the care Romeo had lavished on them, eating became a chore for McCandless. Watching him was a chore for Millicent Forrest. She said nothing. Years of living with a man like Winston had inured her to those times when he would finally return home from an international conference, or a long tough night at the White House, seething with feelings yet too disciplined to give vent to them. Eventually he would. And so, too, would McCandless when he was ready. The first sign of it came when he firmly put down his fork, making it clear he could not force himself to eat.

"My fault," he said.

He said no more. Nor did she ask, or comment. Eventually he resumed, "Nobody knows, but it *is* my fault."

The waiter cleared the table of their main meal and asked, "Coffee? Cappuccino?"

"Coffee, please," Millicent replied.

When McCandless did not respond, the waiter asked, *"Dottore?"*

"Hm? What?" McCandless asked, as if he had not heard the first time.

"Coffee," she ordered for him, "with skim milk instead of cream." She remembered from the two previous times they had dined together.

"Yes, yes," he confirmed. "Coffee. Skim milk." He realized Millicent Forrest had just done what Maggie used to do when he was too involved with his thoughts to pay attention to the simplest things going on around him.

An observant and thoughtful woman, he realized.

Once coffee was served, and he remained reluctant to reveal the nature of his torment, she asked softly, "Sally Brock?"

He looked at her, as much a glare as a glance. She had read his mind. Did she also know the reason for his guilt? She couldn't. No one knew. Or could know.

"I had a chance," he replied. "There might have been a good, healthy Type O or Type A heart for Sally Brock."

"But there wasn't. As I understand, it was Type AB," she pointed out.

"Not the Digby boy, not that heart. Another heart. Somewhere in this country during the past few weeks there must have been a heart of the right size and blood type for Sally. The only one who stood in the way was me! Who had been making promises to her all along. But when the time came to deviate from the routine, to bend the ethics a little, I said no! What the hell right did I have to say no? She wasn't my wife. She wasn't the mother of my child! What right did I have to be so goddamned righteous?"

The puzzlement on Millicent Forrest's face, combined

with the obvious sympathy that reached out to him from her hazel eyes, made him say, as if she should have understood all along, "The senator! Senator Bridgeman!"

Her look of increased bewilderment made him realize she had no idea what he was talking about.

"Senator Bridgeman came to my office. Several weeks ago. Offered to put on a special television campaign to find a designated heart for Sally Brock. A perfectly understandable act. After all, she was one of his constituents. As a conscientious senator, he would go on television and make an appeal for a heart for Sally Brock. What a touching story it would make, this young woman, twenty years old, a new mother, who wanted only to live so she could hold her infant in her arms.

"Of course, it was a cheap political stunt. Because he's facing a stiff fight for reelection. But I, proper go-by-the-book McCandless, I said, 'No! It wouldn't be fair. It would break the rules. It would help create anarchy in the transplant world. There's too much of that going on as it is.' I said no!"

"If those are the rules, if that's what all other transplant centers abide by—" Millicent tried to intercede.

In his guilt, he refused to be interrupted. "It wasn't my decision to make! It wasn't my life. I was risking nothing by saying no! She could have been alive today. She might have been home with her baby by now!"

She noticed that his hands were trembling in anger. He noticed, too, for he slid them off the table and out of sight. After a moment of silence, he said more softly, "Sorry. I shouldn't have made you a part of this. It's not your responsibility. But somehow I assumed you would understand."

"I've had some experience with a man forced to make important decisions and then live with the consequences," she said softly.

"I never asked for this kind of responsibility," McCandless said. "My father was a small-town practitioner, a man who instilled in me the desire to become a doctor. But he never had to make such decisions. He diagnosed. He prescribed. In more serious surgical cases, he referred. But no one ever said to him, 'Dr. McCandless, you have the right to choose who lives and who dies. *Choose!*' But now . . . now . . .'' He did not complete the thought. Abruptly he said, "It's late. I've kept you longer than I intended. Sorry."

"I'm not. Now, may I say something?"

"Of course."

"You take this too personally—" she started to say.

"Shouldn't I?" he interrupted. "Or should I be like some men I know in some medical centers, who blithely cut corners, cheat on the facts. Describe the patients' condition as worse than they really are so they can move them up on the list and thus receive more donated hearts than they're entitled to?"

She waited out his burst of anger, then said softly, "I was about to say, it's not your fault that we live in an age when our technology has advanced so far so fast that our ethics haven't been able to catch up."

He glanced at her, wondering if her words were calculated to ease his guilt over Sally Brock or were honestly intended as a statement of support and understanding. In either case he appreciated them, and was touched.

This woman would have understood what Maggie never did, he thought. *Why do so many things in life happen too late? Or not at all?*

On their way out of the restaurant, Romeo and his wife bade them a hearty good night. But not until after the portly restaurateur had pulled him aside to whisper, *"Dottore*, she is a beautiful woman. You are a very lucky man."

"Romeo, I'm afraid you're making a big mistake," he tried to explain.

But the little man smiled and said, *"Dottore*, in my business, like in yours, we study people. I know the signs."

As they started out the door, McCandless looked back to confirm what he suspected Romeo had intended to say. The man was smiling broadly, holding out his right hand, the thumb pointed upward to indicate his hearty endorsement of Millicent Forrest.

In the car on the way back he broke a long silence. "It was kind of you to take the trouble to listen."

"No trouble. I've had plenty of practice," she said.

They were silent for a time. This time it was she who broke the silence. "Something happen suddenly?"

"Happen?" he repeated, caught off guard.

"Back there in the restaurant you talked freely, and with such feeling. The moment we left, you seem to have withdrawn into your shell."

"Have I?" he asked, avoiding an answer. There was no way he could admit to her what Romeo had said, which had troubled him.

"Or is this one of those silences that Maggie used to resent?"

"No, not quite the same," he replied. "I was just thinking . . ." he began, but did not continue.

"Thinking? What?" she prodded.

"Twenty-four years ago, when you were a sophomore in college, what did you think of becoming?"

"Twenty-four years ago? That was the fervent, unsettled sixties. We thought we could take over the government, change the world, set everything right. Of course, that was also the time I met Winston. Everything changed for me. His ambitions became my ambitions. His reality became my reality. Running the world didn't seem so easy anymore."

He did not respond, but continued driving in silence.

"What made you ask about twenty-four years ago?" she finally inquired.

"I was curious."

"About what?"

"The mind plays little games. You wonder—actually I wondered—what would have happened if Winston hadn't come to your college on that particular day and made that speech? If you hadn't heard him? Met him? How different would your life have been? What would you have gone on to become? Who would you have met, fallen in love with, married?"

"I don't know," she confessed. "I'd been planning on studying psychiatry. After I set the world straight, of course." She laughed lightly. Then she said, "Yes, I think it would have been psychiatry. Mainly with children. Troubled children."

"You would have had to go to medical school for that," he pointed out.

"I had the grades for it," she replied proudly.

"I bet you did," he agreed. "But if you had gone on to medical school, met another young med student, married him . . ."

"Is that how you met Maggie?" she asked.

"No, I was resident on the Cardiac Service at a hospital. Covering for our chief when he was off at some seminar. He had a patient in difficulty. That patient was Maggie's father. One afternoon on my rounds I came by to check on him. And I met her. A chance meeting. She was there only on that one day. Then she had to go back East to her teaching job. But that meeting was enough. She was a lovely young woman. Beautiful. If her father hadn't been sick, if I hadn't dropped in at that particular time on that particular day . . . strange, despite all our great plans and ambitions, our lives are really determined by small accidents."

"What happened?"

"Oh, he recovered."

"I meant with you and Maggie."

"I found out where she lived. Wrote her to tell her how well her father was doing. She wrote back thanking me for saving his life. He would have recovered despite what I did for him. But I wasn't going to deny saving him. Then, between my heavy schedule at the hospital and the cost of air fares, we had a long-distance courtship. I figured it out once. Before we decided to get married, we had had only six dates. Spent a total of fifty-four hours together. When I look back on it now, fifty-four hours is not long enough to make a lifetime decision. In fact, when I think of it now, I've actually seen you more times on more days than I saw Maggie before we decided. I feel I know you better now than I knew her on the day we decided to—"

He stopped abruptly. To avoid pursuing the thought to its inevitable conclusion, he said, "Of course, that was under quite different circumstances."

"Yes, quite different," she agreed softly.

He had a strong feeling that she was as uncomfortable with his comparison as he was. There was a communion of shared attraction and guilt between them.

When he dropped her off at her car in the parking lot, he said, "I hope you didn't misinterpret what I was saying before . . ."

"No," she replied, but too quickly. "Of course not."

21

THE DEATH OF SALLY BROCK had a depressing effect not only on Allen McCandless, but on the entire Transplant Unit. But its impact was felt most profoundly by the other candidates on the Unit's list of eligibles.

Alone, or between them, they engaged in a grim game of cardiac roulette. If only that boy had been Type A or Type O, if only Sally had been Type AB . . . if only . . . the speculation went on endlessly.

Her death had heightened the sense of anxiety in all patients. Outpatients who appeared for their weekly checkups came hoping to show some change in their condition. Not so great or grave a change as to immediately endanger their lives, but just sufficient to move them up on the list from Priority Status 3 to Status 2. Or even Status 1.

Inpatients tended to keep their discussion of Sally Brock's passing to a minimum. There was the exchange of the expected and obligatory expressions of sadness and regret. There were words of pity for the bereaved husband and the infant who would have no mother. But then the need to turn from death to other matters took over. Those patients in the most immediate danger preferred not to dwell too much on death.

By the end of the second day after the event, patients ambulatory enough to make it to the solarium went about their usual preoccupations and hobbies. One man, in his mid-forties, who had been editor of a small magazine, clipped items out of the many publications to which he subscribed. He maintained voluminous files on a host of subjects. But no one ever learned what he intended to do with all the information if he survived.

There was a woman of middling years, fiftyish, who crocheted afghans. She spoke little to anyone else, but worked away industriously, as if she were racing against time. When her husband or her son came to visit, they brought not books, or magazines, or toilet water, but more wool. Throughout their visits she kept crocheting, still racing against time.

The effect on Winston Forrest and Jim Campbell was to dampen their spirits during their usual mid-morning gin game. Unless either or both of them were being taken to one of the testing rooms for reevaluation, they met mid-morning of every day in the solarium.

The card game itself had become a matter of amusement rather than a contest. The stakes had increased to ridiculous sums. Thousands of dollars were being won and lost every day, on paper, of course. But it served to draw the men closer together. It became not a game of chance or skill, but a pretext for personal conversation and intimacy.

The younger man was hungry to learn what went on in high places. Forrest was willing to share his remembrances, the moments of triumph, the bitter moments of defeat. The errors he had observed in the making. The opportunities he had seen swept aside for political or other shortsighted reasons.

"How does it feel," Jim Campbell once asked, "when you're there in the—what did you call it?—where all the information comes in . . ."

"The Situation Room," Forrest informed him.

"Right. There you all are. The President. The Chief of Staff. The heads of the Army, the Navy. And that information—"

"Intelligence," Forrest corrected.

"Yes. Intelligence keeps coming in. Decisions have to be made. Decisions that could mean war or peace. How does it feel?"

"Just about the way you think it would feel. Big problems being decided by small men. That's what scares me, Jim. The problems and the challenges keep getting bigger, but the men are still the same size. Smaller, if anything. I think back to when I was a kid. There was Roosevelt and Churchill and that bastard Stalin. But they were big men wrestling with a big war. We don't have giants anymore, Jim. Just giant problems."

Forrest was silent for a time, until he leaned close to his younger opponent and said, very quietly, "That's one of the reasons I want to stay alive so desperately. To see how it all comes out. I don't dare die, because I'd be leaving the President and the nation in the lurch. I have to be here to do what I can to work things out.

"Of course, I know if it's not me, it's going to be some other man. Maybe even a man better qualified for the job. But I still can't let go. I'm like a man racing to catch the last train out of the station. I've got a grip on the railing, but I don't know if I can pull myself aboard. I'm just running alongside, trying, trying to make it. I'm out of breath but I keep running. Can you understand that, son?" At once he apologized, "I didn't mean to call you son."

"That's okay, Mr. Forrest," Campbell said.

"It might sound like I'm talking down to you. I'm not. Not any more than I talked down to Paul when I called him son. It was a term . . . a term of affection. I hope you understand that."

"Yes, sir, I do," Campbell said. "I also understand what you mean about running alongside trying to catch that train. I feel that way, too. Of course, with me it's not important things like a war or a whole nation. It's Nan. It's the kids. Got to catch that train for them. I can't leave them. Not now. Not when the kids are so young. I figure if I have another ten years, or even seven or eight, just until they're old enough to cope without a dad, you know?

"I know," Forrest said sadly. "Trouble is, Jim, we're greedy. Greedy for life. Give a man seven or eight years and he's going to want seven or eight more. There's never enough. I've had twenty more years than you and it's still not enough."

"It isn't just for me . . . it's the kids . . . it's Nan . . ." Jim Campbell insisted.

"It's always for some higher, unselfish purpose," Forrest said. "For you, it's Nan and the kids. For me, it's Millie and service to the nation. Why are we ashamed to say it straight out, 'I want to live because I'm not ready to die.' Just like that. But we never do."

They were silent for a time, until Forrest laid down his cards because he had lost interest in them.

"There is one thing—one really unselfish thing— Millie . . . she deserved more out of our marriage than she ever got. I'd like to be here to see that she gets it. I'd like a second chance. To be the husband I should have been the first time. You're too young to have such regrets. And I hope as you grow older you never have reason to have them."

To cover his sensitivity at having revealed more about his failed marriage than he had intended, Forrest gathered up the cards and started to shuffle them.

Aware of Forrest's feelings, Jim Campbell made an effort to change the subject to one less personal. So he improvised, "You know, lying in bed here at night, those nights I can't sleep, I listen a lot. You ever listen to the night sounds here?"

"Yes," Forrest said, relieved to talk of other things. "The sounds of nurses' footsteps tell you so much. When they're very quick you wonder, Who's in trouble now? And how much trouble is he in?"

"I always listen to hear if there's a man's voice after that. That means it was bad enough to send for the doctor."

"I noticed the same thing. Sometimes I can even identify the voices. McCandless. He's got a distinctive voice. Never loud. But full of authority," Forrest said.

"Dr. Kaplan says he's the best. I sure feel better having him on my case," Jim replied.

"Yes. Indeed. Good man," Forrest agreed.

" 'Course, if I had a choice, there are other night sounds I'd rather hear," Jim said. "At home, especially those nights when we get a heavy rainstorm, or a windstorm, I lie awake wondering, How much damage this time? What'll I find tomorrow when I inspect my customers' property? There are certain trees you worry about. Shrubs, flower beds, hedges, you can replace those. But it takes a long time to grow a sturdy tree. When one of those goes down, it's sad. But I guess you know that, from when you were a boy."

"Yes, yes, I do," Forrest said.

"I wonder some nights, will I ever listen for those sounds again?"

"You will, Jim, you will," Forrest encouraged.

"I sure hope so. I've got lots of things to do. If I could just set it up so the kids have what they need to see them through. Not necessarily a big inheritance. Just enough to see them through college."

"You get that new heart and you'll be able to do everything you promised yourself, kid."

"You called me 'kid.' I'm no kid. Not anymore. Not after this," Jim protested.

"At your age you'll always be a kid to me."

"Mr. Forrest—" Jim began again.

Forrest sighed softly and asked, "Jim, do you think you could call me Winston instead of Mr. Forrest?"

"I don't know. Only two Winstons I ever heard of before. One was Churchill. And the other was a cigarette. I never thought I'd get to know a real person named Winston."

"Well, I'm a real person, so give it a try."

"Okay. Winston. Hi, Winston," Jim ventured.

"See? It works," Forrest said.

"Yeah."

"Now what were you going to say before I interrupted you?"

"What was I going . . . oh, we were talking about night sounds. I was going to say, at home, those nights I can't sleep,

I'd listen for the kids. We always let them fall asleep with their doors closed. But after they're asleep we open them just a crack to be able to listen. In case there's trouble during the night. I would lie there sometimes to hear the funny sounds kids make when they're asleep. They talk to themselves. Or they have a dream that makes them cry out suddenly. You go in to make sure they're okay. Cover them up again. Give them a pat on the fanny. Sometimes they look up at you, most times they don't. Either way, in seconds they're asleep again. And you go back to bed feeling better. I'd like to be able to do that again.''

"I know what you mean, Jim . . .'' Forrest said, considerable regret in his voice. "I didn't have too much time for that when Paul was young. There was Viet Nam, and other problems, so I was away much of the time. Or too busy. After, when Paul was gone, Millie never said it, but I'm sure she felt that I'd cheated him of so much. She always felt that Paul wasn't our child. But her child.''

As if he felt that once again he had revealed too much of their private life, Forrest cleared his throat and asked briskly, "Well, don't just sit there, tote up the score. How much did I lose today?''

Embarrassed, Jim Campbell proceeded to industriously add up the score and report, "Well . . . Winston . . . looks like you are down twenty-three-hundred points. That's twenty-three-thousand dollars.''

"Just put it on my account, I'm good for it!'' Forrest said.

"You bet, Mister. . . . Winston,'' Jim Campbell said.

"Jim, you've got to practice that name. So you can say it without hesitation or second thoughts. Winston. Winston. Just like that.''

"Winston . . . Winston . . . Winston. You're right, it gets easier the more you say it.''

"Back in school, the guys used to call me Winnie. Which I didn't like. On two counts. Winnie was a girl's name. From Winifred. It was also the sound that horses make. So I liked

Winston. Or Win. Millicent used to call me Win all the time. Lately, though, it's been Winston mostly," he said sadly. "Guess we'd better get back to the room. Lunchtime pretty soon."

"And Nan'll be here."

"Millie, too. Jim, ever notice that in hospitals time isn't told by hours. But by meals. It's either before lunch. Or after. Before dinner. Or after. They become the most important things that happen during a hospital day. Unless, of course, there are those emergencies."

"Yes," Jim said grimly, "those emergencies. There've been three of them since I got here. All three . . . died."

"Couldn't wait it out. I often wonder, maybe it's waiting that takes the toll. Maybe if there weren't hope, the chance of that new heart, we wouldn't stress ourselves so much. It would be easier, instead of thinking, 'Today, soon, now the word will come.' Waiting seems to take great effort. Some days I think it would be easier just to . . . to slip away peacefully, without the anxiety of waiting, or hoping."

"You don't mean that, Winston, you can't," Jim insisted. "We are going to make it. Both of us. You'll see."

"Of course, kid, this is just one of my down days. Let's go. Don't want lunch to get cold, do we?"

As they started toward the door to the corridor, Forrest said, "It was sad. About Sally. Nice young woman. A girl, really."

"Yeah," Jim Campbell commiserated. "Nan cried when I told her."

"She did? Millicent, too," Forrest confessed.

That was all that was said between them about the tragic event.

On the way back to their respective rooms to await lunch, Winston Forrest felt a stab of pain in the pit of his stomach. But since it was considerably less in intensity than his heart attack, he dismissed it as unimportant.

Later that afternoon, during a routine examination, Dr.

McCandless detected unsettling sounds. He ordered a new
EKG for Winston Forrest.

Even before the resulting tape was delivered to McCandless's office, there was a call from Harvey Strawbridge.

"Mac, quite by chance I discovered you ordered another
EKG for Forrest this afternoon—" the Administrator began.

McCandless cut him off sharply. "Yes, I did. But I
haven't got the tape yet, so I have no results."

"I was just curious, why another EKG? Is that routine?"

"I heard something I didn't like," McCandless admitted.
"So I thought I'd make sure."

"Good. With an important man like Forrest, we can't be
too sure," Strawbridge said. "Let me know what you find.
Okay?"

"Of course," McCandless said, as Claire brought the
tape into his office. The long strip had been cut and pasted to
stiff cardboard to make it more easily readable.

He scanned the tapes, then called his secretary, "Claire,
get me the Forrest history!"

Once he had laid down the three most recent of Forrest's
EKGs one beneath the other, so he could make comparisons,
he came to the conclusion that a consultation was necessary.

Along with Chris Slade and two other members of the
Unit—Assistant Surgeon Angstrom and Coopersmith, a
younger cardiologist—it was decided to reclassify Winston
Forrest from Priority Status 2 to Status 1, making him a prime
candidate for the next available Type O or Type A heart from
a donor who weighed between one hundred fifty and one
hundred eighty pounds.

McCandless informed Strawbridge of the change. The
Administrator was delighted to report to Ms. Breed in the
White House that Winston Forrest was now in the most
favored position to receive the first suitable heart the moment
it became available.

Within the hour, Allen McCandless received a call from
Ms. Katherine Breed, expressing the President's satisfaction
over the improvement in Winston Forrest's chances.

McCandless listened politely but in the end replied, "Ms. Breed, please bear in mind, and relay to the President as diplomatically as possible, that if Mr. Forrest's condition had not worsened, he would not have been moved up to Priority One. That means his condition is now more precarious than it was."

"Yes, of course," she replied in her usual clipped, efficient and domineering style.

He could not resist asking, "Five feet two? Blond? Are you sure?"

"Afraid so," she replied.

"Then why do I keep having these Wagnerian visions of you?" he asked. "Swords, spears and armored breastplates."

"Beats me," was all she said as she hung up. But not before he detected a slight chuckle.

Almost a week later, as the night nurse was passing Room 609 she heard a sound that caused her to stop and consider its source. It was a stifled cough, definitely from a male patient, and was followed by a gasping that indicated extreme shortness of breath.

She listened at the door and confirmed her suspicions. She pushed the door open and found Jim Campbell rising up in bed as he fought for breath. He was perspiring profusely and gasping as if fighting for life.

"Easy, Mr. Campbell, I'll have a doctor here in a moment." She pressed the buzzer that registered an emergency out at the central ICU station. She helped Campbell higher up on his damp pillow to ease the pressure on his chest. In moments the second nurse came racing into the room.

"Get the night resident!" the first nurse ordered. "Stat!"

An injection of digitalis from the female resident helped to restore Jim's heart action sufficiently to enable him to breathe more freely, and as important, allayed his fear of sudden death.

The nurse had toweled him dry and changed his gown.

The resident stood by, waiting to apply her stethoscope to his chest. As she expected, it was filled with fluid. Before attempting to drain it off, she should consult with Dr. McCandless. In the meantime she ordered Campbell put on oxygen and she prescribed a diuretic.

Once Jim Campbell was relieved of the acuteness of the attack, the resident felt free to take the time to phone McCandless at home.

"Is he resting comfortably now?" McCandless asked, still rubbing his eyes and trying to recover from being suddenly wakened.

"Yes, sir," she replied.

"I'll look in on him first thing in the morning," McCandless said, then glancing at the digital clock in his bedside radio, he continued, "Hell, it's already quarter to five. It *is* first thing in the morning. I'll be down there in twenty minutes. Make it forty minutes. Got to do my damn exercises."

He raced through his morning exercises, partly to ward off his lower back pain, partly for his own cardiovascular health. He did most of them ten times instead of his usual fifteen, conscious every moment that he was cheating himself, yet feeling the pressure of time.

Campbell had been a nagging presence ever since he had been admitted back into the hospital. Doctors, especially cardiologists, have hunches about certain patients. The tests, the statistics, the percentages, the cardiograms, the angiograms are reliable scientific indicators. But there are also instinctive suspicions that doctors cannot explain, subconscious warnings, random, unexpected, sometimes unwelcome thoughts that insinuate themselves from time to time, forecasting unfortunate developments. To Allen McCandless, Jim Campbell had been one of those patients.

Perhaps this latest development was the first sign, the forerunner, of events that might remove him from the list of candidates and doom him to an early death.

McCandless abandoned his sit-ups before he had completed the last of them. He went out to the kitchen of the small apartment he had taken after he moved out of their big house. At times like this, in the early hours before dawn, he missed Maggie most. During the years of their marriage, when such emergencies intruded on their lives, while he was exercising she would be out in the kitchen making a pot of fresh coffee and urging that he have something to eat before he left the house.

He would insist that she go back to sleep, that he didn't need any breakfast, that he would grab something at the hospital. She would bully him into having orange juice, fresh squeezed, toast and coffee. He resisted, complained, but in the end always obeyed. All the while feeling touched by her devotion.

He missed that now, and had ever since they parted. He consoled himself that he no longer felt guilty at having midnight emergencies intrude on Maggie. She never had developed an intern's ability to be wakened and then go back to sleep easily. Once up, she usually stayed up. Which made him feel even guiltier. Now, he was free of all such guilts, he told himself.

Until he realized that if he were really so free of past guilts, he would not be reliving those early mornings in such detail and with such feelings, which, instead of lessening, seemed to increase with every passing month of his unsought freedom.

To avoid such thoughts, he started to line up in his mind all the tests he must perform on Jim Campbell this morning. Not the least important was to get a new fix on his PVR. If that had changed for the worse since his last one, he might have no choice but to remove him from the eligible list.

By the end of the day, with all the lab reports and test results before him, Allen McCandless was forced to admit that Jim Campbell's condition had indeed deteriorated.

Fortunately, his PVR had not changed. Campbell would remain on the eligible list.

However, McCandless and Slade agreed that he must be moved up on the list as an emergent candidate. At his present weight of one hundred sixty-two pounds, he was a candidate for any heart from a male donor, thirty-five years or younger, of Blood Type A or O, weighing between one hundred fifty and one hundred eighty pounds.

By the end of the weekly staff meeting, the list of eligible candidates showed that in blood group A there were two men whose deteriorating condition caused them to be listed as Priority 1. Forrest, Winston. Campbell, James. Below them on the list were seven other Type A's, rated 2, 3, and 4. In blood group B there were four candidates. And among blood group O, being the longest list, there were twelve candidates rating from Priority 1 to 9.

The fact that in blood group A there were two candidates both rated Priority 1 did not unduly disturb Allen McCandless. If it came to a choice, the histocompatibility profiles in their charts, when matched against the HLA profile of the donor, would decide who would receive the heart. The candidate exhibiting the closest human-leukocyte-antigen compatibility with the donor would suffer the fewest possibilities of rejection.

Right now, more important to Allen McCandless than considering such a hypothetical choice, was keeping both men alive and in good enough condition to accept a new heart.

Allen McCandless had been in Transplant Clinic all afternoon, examining and testing previous recipients to determine how they were faring with their new hearts. Were they religiously following the regime, the medications, the diet, the proper exercise? As a group they were quite reliable. But occasionally one or two of them betrayed deviations. Undue weight gain. Elevated cholesterol. Low cyclosporine level.

Several times during the afternoon he had felt forced to lecture patients, "You must exercise to keep that new myocardium, that middle muscular layer of your heart wall, strong. You have to keep your entire body strong. Because when we gave you your new heart, we did not attach the nerves. So you have a denervated heart. That prevents you from feeling any warning angina pains, as you did with your old heart. The best way to tell us your heart is in good shape is by your increasing muscle strength.''

One of the patients pleaded, ''But Dr. McCandless, I'm afraid of overdoing.''

''Overdoing?'' He laughed. ''We have transplant patients who've run twenty-six miles in marathons. You've got a good heart. Use it! Keep it strong!''

He was making rounds at the end of the day. When he reached Room 607, he found Millicent Forrest there. She was sitting in the armchair in the corner, trying to read by the faint light. Forrest was in bed, propped up but dozing. He was breathing with some difficulty, but not so distressed as to create concern.

Millicent Forrest lowered the book she was reading. She made a signal that indicated she would like to speak to him without risk of being overheard by the patient.

He gestured toward the door. She followed. Once out in the corridor she asked in a whisper, ''That latest electrocardiogram, what does it say about his chances? I have to know, so I know how to conduct myself, what to say to him.''

''His condition has become slightly worse. Which in a way means his chances are better. He's top of the list. But one thing remains the same. We're still at the mercy of events.''

''Yes. It's a strange feeling for me,'' she admitted.

''Living with the uncertainty,'' he assumed.

''Not that. I've never had to wish for something, knowing all the time that for my wish to come true, someone, somewhere, some stranger will have to die first. I'm not that kind of person. Or at least I didn't think I was.''

''Why not? Or does it go with the job, with your husband's career? Do men like him and wives like you always have to be unselfish and totally given to the job and the public good? Believe me, if it were my wife in there, needing a new heart to live, I'd be praying that somewhere someone with the right heart would have that accident that would make her or him a donor. So don't be surprised to find out that you are not noble. None of us really is.''

A look of surprise at having been rebuked came into her hazel eyes. Her features, usually strong and almost perfect, became softer, and for the first time since he had known her, he suspected she was going to cry in his presence.

"I'm sorry," he said at once. "I shouldn't have gone on that way. And please, don't feel guilty. None of us can in any way affect the outcome."

22

THE SMALL CITY of Garden Grove, which lay just east of the Rockies, was experiencing a typical early spring weather pattern, showers, alternating with heavy rains. The wet weather had moved in that afternoon and grown worse during the night hours.

Despite the usual inconveniences that always accompanied rain, most residents of Garden Grove welcomed it. It had been too dry for too long. The snows of winter had melted and drained away long ago. Lawns were beginning to turn brown instead of green. The farmers in the surrounding countryside had been forced to resort to irrigation. So they, like most of the people of Garden Grove, looked on the rain as a blessing.

Only those men like Larry Clinton, who had to leave his snug, dry home and drive to his night job resented the rain. His wife Heather not only resented it, she feared it.

Larry kissed his young son Eric good night. He came downstairs, reached for his raincoat on the hall rack and called out, "Heather . . . darling . . . on my way! See you later. Unless you're asleep."

His wife came out of the kitchen, where she had just taken out of the oven the three layers for the birthday cake she was baking for her son's party tomorrow. With her came the sweet fresh smell of delicious things.

"Now remember—" she started to say.

257

He finished the warning for her. "Drive carefully. I know. It's only the tenth time since dinner that you've said that."

She smiled, and teased, "I wasn't going to say that at all."

"No?" he questioned dubiously.

"I was going to say . . ." She lowered her voice to a whisper. "Remember . . . when you get back, if I'm asleep, wake me."

Her smile, the look in her bright black eyes, drew him to her. He embraced her, whispered in her ear.

"I know. It's been a while. Days."

"Weeks," she corrected softly.

"That long?" he asked, truly surprised. "Sorry. Once I get my Master Plumber's License, no more night job. I'll have more time for Eric. And more time for us. These last two years . . ."

He kissed her. She clung to him. She needed him. He could feel it in the pressure of her young body. She was as hungry for him as he was for her. The sexual part of their lives together had always been important to both of them. But of late, lack of time and the sheer exhaustion of holding down two jobs had deprived them of the love and intimacy they had shared.

Many times during his work hours he thought of her, of having her, only to return in the early morning too tired to do more than slip into bed, put his arm around her and go off to sleep before she even became aware that he was back.

They consoled each other, reassured each other, with dreams of the future that lay ahead. True, they had overreached their budget, but they had not been able to resist the house they lived in. It was such a good buy that nothing approaching it would come on the market in the foreseeable future. The sacrifices they had to make were worth it.

They had had to borrow six thousand dollars from her father to be able to make the down payment. Though her father had never once even hinted that they return the money, they both felt a strong obligation to make their payments on time. Once he had protested, "Look, kids, you'll get my money in the end, anyhow. Why not accept it as a gift now?"

But Larry Clinton was a proud young man. He chose not to be beholden to anyone. Least of all his father-in-law. He had never got over the feeling that Malcolm Singletary was not pleased to have his only daughter marry a man who was not a college graduate. A young man who, though he did not speak with an accent, had been a refugee from Communist Poland as a child of six, and whose name had not always been Clinton, but Klinzinski.

A strong individualist, Mal Singletary had delivered a long lecture to Larry Clinton on the night when his daughter Heather announced their intention to marry.

"Young man . . ." Singletary had addressed Larry as "young man" for the first two years of their marriage. It was only afterward that he began to call him "Larry." And then, finally, "son."

"Young man," he had said that night, "the thing that made this country great was not the *chance* every man has to strike out on his own. But those men who took *advantage* of that chance. Men who said, 'I want to be my own boss. I want to run my own business. Make my own money. Set my own hours. I want independence.' That's what I did. And what I hoped any man that Heather picked would do. But, well . . . I've never been able to say no to her about anything. I guess I can't say no now. I just hope you'll be able to make her happy. And comfortable. She's used to the best. Remember that."

Larry Clinton had never forgotten that half-hearted welcome into the Singletary family. Out of sheer, if unexpressed, defiance, he swore he would outdo the old man. As much as anything, it was that defiance that drove him to pay back, and on time, every dollar that he had borrowed.

But it had taken its toll. On him. On his family. To keep up the mortgage payments and repay the loan, he had to hold down two jobs. In the time he spent on his night job, he had to study for his Master Plumber's exams. So he was a plumber's apprentice by day and ran a convenience chain store during the night shift, seven P.M. to two A.M. Then, with only a few hours sleep, he was up and back to work as an apprentice plumber.

Fortunately, he was a healthy young man, sturdy. Weight one eighty when he started double shifting, he was now down to a slim one hundred sixty-six. This, despite Heather's efforts to keep him well fed with hearty balanced meals. She was as much dedicated to his career as he was. If Larry had no college degree and had had to quit high school in his last year, he was as good, as able, as intelligent as the college men she used to date before she met him. She had secretly resolved that one day her father would be forced to admit that. Opening his own plumbing-contracting business would be the first giant step in that campaign.

She considered herself a very fortunate young woman. Some of the women with whom she had gone to college and with whom she still kept in contact, had confessed to her that they were somewhat less than happy in their marriages. They had fallen in love with men whom they did not admire nearly so much as they loved them. More than once she had heard the excuse, "Believe me, Heather, if it wasn't for the kids . . ." The rest of that inevitable declaration did not even have to be spoken. Or the other refrain, which she had begun to hear with more distressing frequency, "He says it's only recreational, but I think it's got a hold on him. He can't stop."

At night Heather went to sleep alone most times, but with the comfort of knowing that what possessed her Larry was a healthy ambition and the drive to succeed at it. Rather than resent it, she supported it. She, too, had something to prove to her father.

Now she watched from the window of the dining room that overlooked their driveway as Larry backed out their van. She saw the raindrops beat down on his windshield with such fury that even at top speed, the wipers couldn't keep it clean.

God, she thought fervently, *a night like this. I hope he doesn't drive too fast. Take care, darling, take care.*

He pulled out of the driveway and turned left. By the time she could reach the living room windows to get a last glimpse, he was out of sight, except for the gleam of his red taillights reflecting on the rain-soaked street as he turned the corner. Only the stiff slanting rain in the glow of the streetlight could be seen. She stared at it, wondering, was it turning to sleet? The sound of it against the windows made her fear that it had.

Her impulse was to rush to the phone and call the store. But she realized how foolish that was. It would take at least ten minutes, possibly fifteen on a night like this, for him to get to the store. She would call later. She had better go back to the kitchen and turn out the three layers of her cake, which should have cooled sufficiently by now.

It seemed the first layer might stick to the pan, but it finally came loose and rested, nicely browned, on the clean dish towel she had laid out. The second came loose with no effort, behaving as they always did on the television commercials. She was about to turn over the third when the phone rang.

Her heart jumped at the sound. Fear, fear of an accident. She calmed herself by thinking, *He always knows when I'm tense. He must be calling to say that he arrived okay.* She answered the phone.

"Heather . . ." she heard, pronounced as if it were spelled Hea*d*er. She recognized the voice of Larry's father, Wladyslaw. As if he had need to identify himself, he said, "Header, darling, this is your old Polish father-in-law. How are you, my dear?"

"Terrific, Dad, terrific," she said, sensing that the man had called for more than casual conversation.

"And Eric?"

"Excellent."

"In school, too?" The old man was always anxious that

his grandson have the education he had been forced to deny his own son.

"In school, too," Heather said, smiling to herself.

"And my son . . . did you warn him to drive carefully? It's not exactly the best night I've ever seen. In fact, I haven't seen a night so bad since we stole out of Poland. Did I ever tell you about that night?"

Though he had, and many times, Heather indulged him by saying, "I don't think so."

"First, did you warn him to drive carefully?"

"Yes, yes, I warned him," she said quickly, thinking, *If he doesn't get off the phone, Larry can't call me and I can't call Larry.*

"The night we smuggled out of Poland was a night like this. But worse. That's why they said, 'This is the night to go. The border guards will be keeping warm and dry in their barracks, and drunk as usual. So we can make it easily.' Well, it was not so easy. There were three families, sixteen of us altogether. In an old truck with a tarpaulin cover that leaked. The rain was coming down like a waterfall. So we were all huddled up there, the parents protecting the children from the rain, at the same time trying to look out to see if there was trouble. The closer we get to the border, the more nervous we became.

"And then . . . then . . . suddenly the truck grinds to a stop. Skidding a little. We don't know, has the truck broken down? Or was it stopped by police? We know soon enough. Because there are voices. You can always tell when a Communist policeman is talking. Somehow it sounds different from any other kind of policeman. There is more arrogance. Like he is speaking in the name of the entire government. I knew then we had to do what we planned. Quick, out of the back of the truck. Each adult grabs a child with each hand and we scatter. Don't give them one large target to shoot at. Spread out. Off the road. Into the brush. But keep your bearings. Remember, Gdansk is straight ahead. The same direction as the truck. We spread out. Lena takes Eric by the hand. I take little Larry in my arms. He's too young, too small even to run. And we spread out.

"It was a night of running, tripping, falling into puddles and holes. Lying there in the mud so they don't see you. Then start up again. All the while I keep telling Larry, Don't cry, don't cry. He was as good as gold. Not a single sound. All the while I'm thinking, Lena, Eric, where are they? Are they lost? Have they been captured? Will we ever see them again?

"We fall down this embankment and into a stream. I was just getting up when I heard shots. Rifle shots. My heart stopped. I put my hand to Larry's mouth. I didn't want him to cry out for his mother. Then more shots. And then quiet. Far away, men's voices. Angry voices. I knew it must be soldiers, or police. I wanted to turn back and see. But we had been warned, and warned each other, no matter what you hear or see, *keep going!* You cannot save the ones in trouble. Just *keep going!*

"It was the most difficult thing I ever had to do. Pick up my little Larry. And keep going. I went. Looking back half the time. Wondering. Fearing. Everytime I noticed Larry about to ask for his mama, I put my hand over his mouth. That way, we just kept going. Going.

"It was almost dawn. You could already see the light beginning to come up there . . . on the Russian side of the border. I knew we had only a little time. So through the mud and the rain we kept going. As we approached Gdansk, I saw ahead of us, men straddled across the road. God, I prayed, no, please, no, to come this far and have it end here. I started back into the woods. But they called to me. This time not arrogant angry voices, but friendly.

"I turned to them. They came to greet me. They had blankets to wrap around Larry and me. They spoke quickly, very few words. But enough. Some others reached there before me. It seems while the soldiers went searching for me and some of the other men, the driver started the truck. He had brought some half dozen through, and they were already at the port on the old fishing boat that would take us around East Germany to Hamburg.

" 'And Lena. My wife?' I asked.

" 'She's here. She's here.' I was assured. But I should have known from the tone of their voices.

"When I came on board I discovered. Those shots. They were aimed at that old truck. Just random shots. Fired at the truck as it was starting up again. One of them . . . one of them hit Eric. Hit him. Passed through him and lodged in Lena's breast. When I hear that, I want to turn Larry over to them and go back, find Lena, find Eric, at least give them a decent burial. Three men it took to keep me on that little fishing boat until it sailed. The rest of that night I sit there with my arms tight around little Larry. He is now all the family I have. Back there is Lena, and Eric, and I don't even have a chance to bury them. Who knows, if somewhere there is even a tombstone with their names on it?

"I could never go back to find out. They would throw me into jail for the rest of my life. But I have written to friends, to men who helped us that night. They searched. But somehow no one knows. Where they are buried. If they are buried. Larry and me have been half a family ever since that night. That's why rainy nights—

"Anyhow," the old man suddenly interrupted himself, "what did I start out to say? Oh, yes. I hope Larry drives very very carefully tonight. I also hope I didn't bore you, my dear. Give my love to little Eric, and to you also."

He had no sooner hung up than Heather pressed down to disconnect and started to dial a number she knew very well. She waited for one ring, then a second. By the third she had become quite tense. The fourth ring was interrupted by a pickup and the very welcome voice.

"Hello, 7-Eleven. Can I help you?" Larry Clinton answered.

"Oh, darling. What a relief!" Heather said. "When you didn't answer—"

"I had a customer."

"I was scared. Very scared. How was your drive?"

"A little slippery. But I took it easy."

"Good. Your dad called. He was worried, too."

"Rainy nights always get to him. Did he tell you why?"

"For the tenth time," she said. They both laughed. "I'll wait up for you, darling."

"Yeah. Right. Oh, here comes another customer looking like a fugitive out of the storm. See you later."

Larry Clinton hung up and turned to greet his new customer.

"Good evening, can I help—" He got no further. He realized he was staring into the muzzle of a black Magnum. "Okay. Take it easy. Whatever's in the register is yours. Just don't shoot."

"Move!" the thief said.

As Larry Clinton moved back from the counter, the man mistook his move for a hostile action. He fired. Once. Once was enough. The bullet lodged in Larry Clinton's brain.

Nine minutes after the thief had cleaned out the cash register, filled his pockets with cigarettes and candy bars, stepped over Larry Clinton's motionless body, a customer entered the store. Seeing no one, he called out, "Hey, anybody here?" Getting no answer, he edged toward the door to the stockroom, "Hey, nobody minding the store?" He intended it as a joke, until he came upon the body behind the counter with a trickle of blood from the head.

"Christ!"

His first impulse was to flee the place. But because he detected some slight shallow breathing, he picked up the phone and dialed 911.

"I want to report a . . . I don't know. But a man's been shot. And I noticed the cash register is open. Wait? Me? Wait here? Why? Okay, okay. I'll wait."

23

THE POLICE, THE PARAMEDICS, police forensics, and the media descended on the store. The victim was still breathing. But once they carried him into the ambulance, it was necessary to put him on a respirator to get him to the hospital alive.

The police followed the routine procedure in such cases but came up with no clues. It was an obvious holdup of a type similar to a rash of such crimes against all-night convenience stores.

At the hospital, after extensive testing by the Chief of Neurology, it was detemined that Larry Clinton was brain dead. Breathing could only be maintained by mechanical intervention.

At eight minutes after nine o'clock, Heather Clinton was startled by the telephone ringing. She reached for it, found it, said, "Hi, darling . . ." Then a stranger's voice brought her suddenly and sharply alert.

"Mrs. Clinton? This is Detective Boseman. Would you please get dressed? I am sending a squad car to pick you up in ten minutes."

"Squad car . . . pick me up . . ."

"Mrs. Clinton, your husband has been shot."

"Shot? How? What happened? Tell me!"

"Mrs. Clinton, please, just be ready when the car gets there."

"What hospital?"

"Garden Grove General. Please be ready in ten minutes."

"Is he—"

"Mrs. Clinton, be ready! Please?"

She lay there, the telephone still in her hand. Larry? Shot? Garden Grove General? It was a bad dream. It had to be. She'd had them before, ever since he had taken on that all-night job. She became aware of the phone in her hand, replaced it in its cradle. She darted out of bed, started to dress, until she remembered Eric. She couldn't leave Eric alone. She called her father-in-law.

"Papa, get dressed quick. Come over here. I can't leave Eric alone."

"Leave Eric alone . . . why?" the old man demanded.

"Larry—he's been shot. He's in the hospital. I have to go."

"Larry, shot? I want to be there!" the old man insisted. "I have to be there! What hospital?"

She hesitated for an instant, debating whether to tell him. The old man was so excitable. He might be difficult to deal with in a hospital.

"Header, what hospital?" he demanded.

"Garden Grove General," she finally said.

"I be there!" he said, and hung up before she could dispute him.

Twenty-two minutes later, having arranged with her neighbor to take Eric in for the rest of the night, Heather Clinton entered Garden Grove General Hospital under the guidance of a uniformed police officer. The corridor was unusually busy for this hour of the night. Most of the activity was being carried on at the far end, outside the last room on the floor. Instinctively Heather knew. She started to run. As she neared the room she began to cry and call out, "Larry! Larry!"

At the door she was met by a slender middle-aged man in a white lab coat. Behind his spectacles, his blue eyes were sympathetic, but firm. She tried to go around him. But he took her by the arms and said, "Not yet."

"Not yet?" she demanded through her tears. "What do you mean, not yet? He's my husband! I want to see him!"

"Please, Mrs. Clinton, first I have to talk to you. I'm Dr. Shapiro and—"

"I don't care who you are! I want to see my husband!" By now her voice was so loud and strident that night personnel came out of various rooms and offices to stare.

Shapiro put his arm around Heather Clinton. Softly, to calm her, he said, "Mrs. Clinton, I will let you see him. But first I have to talk to you. I have to explain . . ."

She shook her head. Her tears began to flow in greater profusion. She wrestled with the doctor to break free and enter the room. But he kept her in control, urging, "Mrs. Clinton, please . . . please?"

From down the corridor came the voice of an agitated man. "*Header!* Where is he? *Header!*"

As she turned, Shapiro asked, "Who is that? Your father?"

"His father."

"Good," Shapiro said.

The older Clinton reached them. He asked, "Is my son in there?"

"Yes," Shapiro said. "But before you go in, I have to talk to you, both of you."

"Is my son all right, that's all I want to know!" Wladyslaw Clinton demanded.

"Please!" Shapiro said, gesturing the old man toward an empty room across the corridor. At the same time he guided Heather to the room. Once inside, he closed the door.

"Mrs. Clinton, Mr. Clinton, your husband, your son, has been shot by a holdup man. A single bullet. It lodged in his brain."

"In his brain?" Heather asked in a terrified whisper. "Will he be paralyzed?"

"Mrs. Clinton, your husband is now what doctors call brain dead."

"Dead?" old Wladyslaw repeated. "I don't believe it. I want to see for myself!"

"Mr. Clinton, don't go in there yet!"

"Who the hell do you think you are to tell me not to see my own son?"

"I have to explain something—" Shapiro started to say.

But old Clinton was out of the room and across the corridor. He burst into the room where a young resident and a nurse were tending the body of Larry Clinton. Wladyslaw went to the foot of the bed and looked at his son, who seemed to be breathing regularly. The hissing sound of the respirator was so soft and regular as to be hardly noticeable. The old man stared down at his son. Aside from the almost imperceptible wound in the side of his head, Larry Clinton seemed to be sleeping peacefully. The old man moved to the side of the bed. He leaned close to his son. As he did, Dr. Shapiro and Heather entered the room.

Clinton turned on Shapiro. "You call yourself a doctor? Take a look at this young man! Look at his color. Look at the way he breathes! Then tell me he's dead!"

"Believe me, Mr. Clinton—"

"Believe you? I know what my own eyes tell me. I know dead when I see it. God knows, I've been through enough. Seen enough dead men to know. I saw men tortured to death in Polish prisons. I saw them before. I saw them after. Don't tell me what a dead man looks like. My boy is not dead!"

Heather Clinton approached the bed, leaned close to her husband.

"Larry . . . ." she whispered. "Larry," as if expecting him to reply. The suddenness of events had stunned her. She could not yet accept that Larry was dead. "Larry?"

The resident said softly, "Mrs. Clinton, he can't hear you."

She reached to touch her husband's face. It was colder than usual. But not lifeless. She reached for his hand and held it. She tried to warm it. She pressed it against her face. The nurse looked to the resident, who gestured to leave her alone.

Distracted from his dispute with Dr. Shapiro, old Wladyslaw Clinton put his arm around his daughter-in-law. "He'll open his eyes. You'll see, soon he'll open his eyes," the old man said. "He's just asleep, that's all. Asleep. I don't care what any doctor says."

"No, Papa, I think . . . I think the doctors are right," Heather Clinton said finally.

"You, too?" the old man demanded, as if confronted by treason.

"Papa, I know Larry. I know when he's asleep. And when he is not. This is no longer the Larry I know."

"Don't say that!" the old man persisted.

Her acceptance gave Dr. Shapiro the opportunity to ask, "Mrs. Clinton, would you come with me?"

She nodded. Very carefully and tenderly she placed Larry's hand alongside his body. Then she decided to cover it, to keep it warm. She turned away from the bed to join Shapiro at the door. As she did, old man Clinton said, "Wait! I must be there, too. He has been my son longer than he has been her husband!"

Shapiro led them back to the empty room across the corridor.

"I'm sorry I have to do this now. But there isn't much time."

"Time for what?" old Clinton asked, even more suspicious than he had been.

"Please, Mr. Clinton, don't interrupt. What I have to say is not easy, or pleasant. But both of you should be aware that due to the circumstances under which Larry died, only his brain died. The rest of his body is in excellent shape. Because he was in excellent shape."

"Excellent shape," the old man scoffed. "A hell of a lot of good that does him now!"

"That's my point. Those excellent parts of him, those healthy organs of his body, his heart, his kidneys, his liver, his corneas, which can't do *him* any good now, can do good for other people."

Heather Clinton looked up into Shapiro's blue eyes. "What are you saying?"

"Somewhere in the country, right this minute, there is someone on the verge of dying who could live a long life if he could have Larry's heart."

"You mean . . ." she started to ask, but could not bring herself to say the words.

"Yes. I mean if you give permission, Larry's heart can be beating in another man's chest hours from now. If you refuse permission, that good heart that could have saved another man's life will be buried in Larry's body and do nobody any good. Not that stranger. Not Larry."

Heather Clinton did not respond. She shook her head slowly, not in dispute or rejection, but trying to absorb what had happened to her and her young husband in a matter of just hours. Odd, disconnected thoughts flooded her mind. Her son Eric when she had to wake him and carry him through the rain to the neighbor. Larry. And the last time he had played with Eric just before he went off to work.

Larry. Larry alive. Larry laughing. Larry in bed, sleeping after they had made love, looking not much different than he did in that hospital bed in the room across the hall.

He can't be dead. Papa's right. He can't be dead and look so healthy. He can't be dead, he can't be dead! The thought screamed in her brain. *How can the doctor be sure? I've read stories in the papers about someone already sent to the undertakers and found to be alive. The fact that he doesn't move or open his eyes doesn't mean that he's dead. Coma. He could be in a coma. How do they know?*

"Doctor, how can you be sure he's dead?" she finally asked.

"There is absolutely no indication of brain activity," Shapiro said.

"How can you be *sure*?" Heather insisted.

"The electroencephalogram is never wrong," Shapiro replied. "If it would convince you, I'll redo it. But the result will be the same. Flat. No activity at all. Believe me, my dear woman, I would never mislead you about that."

When the doctor's statement appeared to impress Heather, Wladyslaw Clinton seized Shapiro by the lapels of his white lab coat.

"You! What right you got to ask such a thing?" he demanded.

Shapiro freed his coat from the old man's grasp. "Mr. Clinton, what I'm doing is not my right. It's my duty. There is now a federal law that makes it mandatory that I ask you to consider donating your son's heart and other organs for transplantation."

"What if I don't give a damn for your law? What about that?" the old man defied.

"Mr. Clinton, under the law, I believe that the wife is considered next of kin. She has the right, and the duty, to make the decision."

"My son . . . my boy who I carried out of Poland to freedom . . . and I don't have no right to say what happens to him?" the angry man demanded, his voice rising now so that Shapiro moved to close the door.

"Papa, please . . ." Heather said as she gripped his arm to calm him. He thrust her hand aside with unprecedented violence.

"Don't 'Papa please' me!" he said. "My son, my boy, my baby . . . he wants me to give him the heart out of his body?"

"Mr. Clinton, please try to understand," Shapiro said with especial calmness, hoping thereby to mollify the man. "Your son's heart is a perfectly good heart. But his brain, the part of him that kept him living, breathing, is dead. So if we let him keep it, his heart can only die. But somewhere there's another man with a good brain, a good body, who needs your son's heart to go on living."

The grim-faced old man was unmoved. "You can take my son's good heart and give it to some other man, but you can't take some other man's good brain and give it to my son. Is that what you're saying?"

"We can't transplant a human brain."

"But you can do it with a heart," Clinton scoffed. "My son's heart." He contemplated the idea, for a moment giving Shapiro his first glimpse of hope. "And there is this other man who wants it . . ."

"Needs it," Shapiro said.

"Yes, needs it. A lot?"

"Without it, he will most likely die," Shapiro said.

"Die, eh? Then it must be very valuable, my son's heart," Clinton said.

"Yes, it is," Shapiro agreed.

"So how do I know you're not planning to sell it to him? Answer me that!"

Shocked, Heather begged, "Papa, please . . ."

He turned on his tearful daughter-in-law. "These days you read how they sell babies to people who want them? Ten thousand dollars, twenty thousand dollars, more even! What must a heart be worth? How do we know this doctor . . . this Shapiro . . ." He stared at him. "You're a Jew, aren't you?"

With a sadness resulting from ages of prejudice, Shapiro said, "Yes. I'm a Jew. And you're thinking I would do anything for money. Well, if it means anything to you, by law and by ethical practice, since I am the doctor who declared your son brain dead I cannot be the doctor who would be involved in the use of your son's heart."

"But you could sell it to another doctor, couldn't you?" the anguished old man insisted.

"Papa, no . . ." Heather said. To Shapiro she said, "I'm sorry, Doctor. But he's not himself. He's had a lot of tragedy in his life. And this is the worst."

Suddenly the old man demanded, as if to the world at large, "Why me? Why must it always be me?" he cried out.

"One son who never lived to see his ninth year. My wife. I could not even bury her! But I promised, this one son I will carry him to safety. To freedom. The day we stepped off the plane here, I say to myself, whatever God has done to me, at least I have done this. My son grows up good. A fine young man. He marries a nice girl. They have a fine son. Named for my own son Eric. It is almost possible to forget the pain. But no, God has His eye on me. He says, 'I will let Wladyslaw Klinzinski have only so much joy in this life. Then just when he thinks he is free, I will strike him again!' So now, this! Not enough my son is dead, now they want to take the heart out of him and give it to another man! So another man's son will live while Wladyslaw Klinzinski's son is dead. Me! Always me who has to suffer. No. I say no!"

Heather turned to her father-in-law, down whose strong, angry face tears of grief had begun to flow freely.

"Papa, if the heart is no longer any good to Larry—"

"You're his wife, don't you feel any loyalty?" the man accused.

"Papa, I love him. But if what the doctor says—"

The old man turned away, spurning her.

"Papa?" she pleaded.

"I got a right to bury a whole son. Not part of a son, not a son without a heart. A whole son!" he insisted.

"What difference would it make?" she asked. "If he's dead, he's dead."

"They will cut him open. They will tear the heart out of him . . . no! I can't even stand to imagine it! To cut him to pieces . . . no!"

Shapiro looked to Heather Clinton. His eyes conveyed what needed saying; the decision was not the old man's but hers. Yet he could see that she would not agree unless the old man agreed. She could not hurt him any more than he had already been hurt.

She attempted one more plea. "Papa, suppose it was the other way?"

"What other way?"

"Suppose Larry needed a new heart, and some man like you, some father whose son was dead, said, 'No, not my son's heart'?"

The old man shook his head slowly, turning away from her. After a silence that seemed longer than it actually was, his body started to convulse as he broke into unrestrained weeping. His daughter-in-law embraced him. They wept together.

Shapiro stood mute. As chief in charge of the Emergency Service, this was not the first time he had been confronted by families who, in their grief, had to make such a painful and emotional decision. He hated asking. He hated the attempt to persuade. These were moments when he hated the idea of being a physician.

After their sobbing had subsided, Heather leaned back from her father-in-law, looked up into his face and said, "Papa, God would want us to give the gift of life to some other man. Let me say yes. Papa?"

The old man rocked back and forth, silent, wet-eyed. "That other man, whoever he is, he had better be a good man to deserve my Larry's heart."

Thus, the old man granted his permission. Heather Clinton took the pen that Dr. Shapiro held out to her. She pinned the document granting permission against the wall and signed, *Mrs. Lawrence Clinton.*

She handed the paper and pen back to Shapiro, who said softly, "Thank you."

"Will we know?" she asked.

"What?"

"Who gets his heart," she said.

"If you wish, I will find that out and let you know," Shapiro promised.

She nodded. She turned to her father-in-law. "Come, Papa, we have to go home. Little Eric needs us now."

Shapiro followed them out into the corridor. He watched the two of them walk slowly down the hall toward the doors at the end, through which the first early traces of dawn could be seen. He saw them stop. Saw the young woman turn back. He knew. One more look. She wanted one more look. He beckoned to her to return. She started toward him.

Half an hour later, with all the data before him, Dr. Arnold Shapiro sat at his desk, lifted the phone and instructed the hospital telephone operator, "Doris, get me the Organ Center."

"Yes, Doctor, of course." She dialed the number. When she got a response, she reported, "They're on the line, Doctor."

"This is Dr. Arnold Shapiro at the Garden Grove General Hospital. We have a donor of a heart and other organs. Declaration of brain death has been made in accordance with the law. Next of kin's consent has been obtained. And the coroner's consent has been obtained, since there was a homicide involved."

"May we have the particulars, Doctor?"

"The donor is a man of thirty. Blood Type O. Weight one hundred sixty-eight pounds. There is no history of cardiac irregularity. Systolic blood pressure is ninety-five Hg. Central venous pressure eight centimeters H20. Urine output sixty-eight milliliters per hour. Pulse rate eighty-four. Body temperature 98.9.

He continued to supply those factors that would identify the donor precisely enough to suit it to a possible recipient.

24

SINCE THE OFFICE of the Transplant Coordinator had to be manned twenty-four hours a day, seven days a week, in anticipation of a donated heart, Adeline Sawyer had to take her turns at night duty. This night she was using the quiet hours to struggle with a new application which Allen McCandless had sent to her earlier in the day.

Until eighteen months ago, the new candidate, a young girl of seventeen, had led an active life as an honor student and athlete, in a high school some eighty miles from the Medical Center.

She had become the victim of cardiomyopathy, which not only curtailed her numerous activities, but had virtually invalided her. McCandless, Slade, two other cardiologists and Robbins, the psychiatrist, had conferred on her case. Their verdict: end-stage, with a life expectancy of no more than six months. *Gomez, Nina* had been medically adjudged an eligible potential candidate for transplant.

Due to her precarious condition, it was deemed advisable for her and her mother to live close to the Medical Center. The cost of the transplant itself had been raised by fund drives carried on by her high school class. But there remained a problem that it now fell to Sawyer to solve: to find living accommodations suitable for Nina and her mother, close enough to the hospital, yet inexpensive enough to be affordable

for a family whose major source of income was Emilio
Gomez, Nina's father. He earned only thirty-five-thousand
dollars a year as assistant manager of a supermarket.

Adeline Sawyer was considering various possibilities.

*There's the low-rental sublet that will soon be vacated by
Sam Rissman when he's discharged to go back home. With
possible additional funds from some charitable or governmental source, that might do it. I'll have Elaine Duncan and
Social Services follow up on that. If only people realized . . .
but all they know about heart transplants is what they see on
television or read in the papers, the dramatic medical-rescue
stories that make news. They don't realize the day-to-day,
nuts-and-bolts problems behind the exciting surgical scenes.*

*When I saw the Gomez girl she was so pretty . . . and
bright. Unfortunately that's not going to solve her financial
problem. Maybe . . . just maybe, if I appealed to the super-
market chain, they would transfer her father to a store near
the hospital. The family living together would cut down on the
expense. The chain has a store here. I'll suggest that. Of
course, if that fails, I'll have to—*

The telephone interrupted her thoughts. With a half
uttered protest, "Oh hell," she picked up the phone.

"Cardiac Transplant. Sawyer."

What she heard made her sit up, reach for a pencil and
ask, "Donor? Where? Blood type? Weight? Details, give me
the details!"

At the same time she covered the mouthpiece with her
hand, called to her nurse assistant, "Charlotte! Get Dr.
McCandless on the other line!"

Speaking into the phone once more, Sawyer replied to the
question she had been asked, "Yes, yes, our candidate list
remains exactly the same as last week. We've had no
mortalities since the Brock woman. And no changes in order
of need. Now, details! Cause of brain injury? Current vital
signs? Degree and duration of inotropic support? Neurologic
death status? Details!"

As the information was supplied, Adeline Sawyer listed each important fact. Meanwhile, part of her mind was calculating, *Garden Grove . . . that's two states away, eight hundred miles . . . two and a half hours by chartered jet . . . better make that three hours, the weather being what it is . . . an hour to examine and remove the heart . . . at least forty minutes back to the airport, even under police escort . . . two and a half hours more in the air . . . thirty-seven minutes from our local airport to here . . . from moment of removal of that heart to insertion into our patient, that's three hours and roughly fifty minutes. Within the five-hour limit that a heart remains usable after removal from the donor. Safe enough, if all goes well. If all goes well? What was the weather forecast for tonight? Cloudy with a chance of rain . . . or was that the forecast for last night, when it was cloudy but didn't rain? Chance of rain tonight . . . how's that going to affect landing conditions at our airport . . .*

Allen McCandless was poring over the figures and the facts Adeline Sawyer had sent down to his office only minutes ago. Surgeon Chris Slade leaned over McCandless's shoulder to scan the information. Since he had not been scheduled for surgery tonight, Slade had rushed to the hospital from the squash court where he was working out when his beeper summoned him. He was dressed in the old corduroy pants and wool shirt he had worn to the gym. While both doctors studied the pertinent facts about the donor heart, they continued to exchange ideas and questions.

"Your donor team ready to go?" McCandless asked.

"Spangler is off for the week. I'll send Angstrom," Slade said.

"Who'll replace him on your team here?"

"Camerata," Slade said.

"Good man. It'll be excellent experience, assisting you."

"Camerata is a woman," Slade corrected.

"Of course. The dark-haired girl."

"Don't let her catch you call her a girl. Dirty word, these days."

"Right. Sorry," McCandless said. "I keep getting her mixed up with your other young surgical resident."

"Cameron."

"Yeah," McCandless said. "Angstrom ready to go?"

"I'll start him assembling his team right now. He'll take Cameron. Sawyer will go along, of course."

"Right!" McCandless said. "To judge from this data, this is a perfect heart for a Blood Type O between a hundred fifty and one hundred eighty pounds. And we've got two prime candidates."

"I'd better start calling in my own team. I want a word with the anesthetists and both perfusionists. That new heart-lung machine is more efficient, but it is still new, and they're getting used to it."

As Slade got going, the door was thrust open unexpectedly. Harvey Strawbridge entered briskly, a beaming man with great expectations. He smiled as he greeted the departing Slade with a wave and crossed quickly toward McCandless's desk.

"This couldn't have come at a better time!" Strawbridge exclaimed.

Curious, Slade turned from the door to listen.

"Mac, this is perfect! Absolutely perfect! I got this call from the White House, from—"

"Ms. Breed," McCandless anticipated.

"Right!" Strawbridge said. "The President was inquiring again today about Forrest's condition. Which means, of course, 'How much longer is it going to take?' He even went so far as to ask how much recuperation time is involved after transplant. He is extremely anxious to have Forrest back as soon as possible."

"We can't answer that right now," McCandless said.

"Of course not," Strawbridge agreed. "But it gave me

tremendous satisfaction to be able to call Ms. Breed back just now and say that we've got a heart for Forrest!''

"What do you know about a heart being available?'' McCandless asked while he and Slade exchanged looks of anger and alarm.

"In cases of unusual importance to this institution, I make it a point to stay well-informed,'' Strawbridge declared with a self-righteous air.

"Then, in the interest of keeping you 'well-informed,' I must tell you that there has been no decision yet as to who will receive this heart,'' McCandless said.

"Don't try to pull that on me!'' Strawbridge replied. "That heart is from a Blood Type O donor. His weight is one hundred sixty-six pounds. Forrest is Type O and one hundred seventy-four pounds! And Status One on the list.''

Slade could not resist being drawn into the argument. "Man, you sure *do* keep informed. Right down to the last detail.''

"It is my *business* to keep informed,'' Strawbridge maintained.

Slade responded angrily, "Look here, Harve, it is not your job as Administrator to take part in medical and surgical decisions!''

"Chris, I'll handle this!'' McCandless intervened.

"The hell you will! Nobody, no administrator, tells me who I operate on!'' Slade was shouting now.

"Chris!'' McCandless insisted, "just alert your team. I'll handle this!'' Slade seemed ready to give vent to another outburst, but McCandless prevented it. "Chris, please! You have your job. This is mine!''

Slade glared at Strawbridge before he turned and left the room.

"A very cheeky lot, heart surgeons,'' Strawbridge remarked.

"When every time you approach the operating table your work consists of handling human hearts and human lives, you had damn well better be confident and brash. And, yes, if you like the word better, cheeky. Now, let's get to our business.''

"About time,'' Strawbridge said. "Mac, one thing you are *not* going to do is disgrace this institution!''

"Disgrace this institution?'' McCandless asked, puzzled.

"Once I gave the White House assurance that the President's National Security Adviser is being given a heart transplant, we can't go back on our word.''

'' *'Our* word'?'' McCandless challenged. "Not the word of the Cardiac Service. Not my word. Not Slade's word.''

"Leave Slade out of this! Surgeons are nothing more than mechanics! Very skillful. Highly paid. Overpaid, if you ask me! But still mechanics! It's up to you to make the final decision. And there's only one decision you can make. Make it!''

"I will. In the next few hours,'' McCandless said.

"Why not now?'' Strawbridge demanded.

"Because we have not one candidate for that heart, but two.''

"Surely you're not considering Campbell.'' Strawbridge was outraged.

"Blood Type O, also Status One on the list based on his condition, and one hundred sixty-two pounds. That makes him a prime candidate. In fact, if Forrest weren't here, Campbell would be *the* prime candidate.''

"But Forrest *is* here!'' Strawbridge protested.

"I know,'' McCandless said grimly. The need to make the decision had begun to weigh heavily on him.

In the usual case, the cardiologist's greatest concern was that once the patient's heart had been removed, the new heart might fail. The patient might die on the operating table despite anything the surgeon or the cardiologist could do. But now, when choosing one man could mean dooming another, this was quite a different challenge.

"Well?'' Strawbridge insisted. When McCandless did not respond immediately, he continued, "How can there be any question? Forrest is important to the President, important to the nation. There can't be any comparison between the two men. If you can save only one life, it must be Forrest.''

''Harvey, I'm a doctor, not a politician.''

''Politician or not, you have an obligation to your country!'' Strawbridge exploded. ''Damn your generation! No sense of patriotism! Won't we ever see the end of Viet Nam? Were you one of those college kids who paraded in the streets condemning your country!''

''We are not talking war. Or politics. Or patriotism. This is a medical decision, and it will be made medically!'' McCandless declared.

''I will not leave this office without your word that Forrest will be the recipient of that heart. The reputation of this institution is on the line!'' Strawbridge appeared prepared to wait.

''*Your* reputation is on the line. Not mine. I have to study all the data on both patients. Then I will decide.''

''Would you like me to pick up that phone, call Ms. Breed and tell her to inform the President of the United States that Dr. Allen McCandless refuses to comply with what amounts to a presidential order?''

''I haven't refused anything,'' McCandless pointed out. ''I simply have not decided!''

''Perhaps you'd like to tell that to Mrs. Forrest?'' Strawbridge asked. ''And shatter all her expectations?''

''What do you mean?''

''As soon as I heard the good news, naturally I called her.''

''You've already told her?'' McCandless demanded, furious.

''She's on her way here. She wants to see Forrest before surgery.''

''You had no right!'' McCandless protested.

''I had every right to assume you would do the proper thing. The only intelligent thing.''

The phone rang. Claire Fielding announced, ''Dr. Slade is on the line.''

"Chris?"

"Well?" Slade asked, in essence asking the same question Strawbridge had asked. When McCandless did not respond at once, Slade continued, "Mac, I have to know. The anesthetists, the perfusionists, all have to know. Forrest? Or Campbell?"

"I'll let you know in enough time," McCandless said and hung up.

Strawbridge felt free to pursue his purpose with what he expected would be his clinching argument. "You might like to know that once I informed Ms. Breed, and she told the President, she called back in minutes—minutes, mind you—to say that if we needed an Air Force plane to transport the heart, the President would make one available. That's how important he thinks Winston Forrest is to this nation."

"We don't need an Air Force plane. We will use our regular charter service. It's never failed us in the past. Then we won't be indebted to the White House or anyone else. And we can keep this a purely medical matter. Now, if you don't mind, I need time alone!"

In face of such a direct invitation to leave, Strawbridge seemed to comply. He started toward the door, then pretended to be possessed of an idea he could not contain.

"I had hoped I wouldn't have to mention this. But I find that I must. I trust, while you are pondering your decision, you will limit yourself to the medical facts."

"Meaning?" McCandless demanded.

"Your recent attentions to Mrs. Forrest have been quite obvious."

"Meaning?" McCandless insisted once more.

"I trust you will not allow personal considerations to play a part in your decision."

"If I were to play favorites," McCandless pointed out, "that would only work to your benefit."

"Not necessarily," Strawbridge said, with such provocative overtones that McCandless responded angrily.

"Just what the hell are you hinting at?"

"Mrs. Forrest is an extremely attractive woman," Strawbridge pointed out. "And a man in your situation, so recently divorced—"

"Are you suggesting I would jeopardize Forrest's chances so that I could . . . so that she and I . . ."

"Me?" Strawbridge replied, pretending to be ingenuous. "Not me. But other people . . . no matter how innocent and professional your motives, if you deprive Forrest of that heart, there will always be some people who will suspect that you allowed personal feelings to make the decision for you."

"That's an outrageous lie!" McCandless shot back.

"I would hate to have to explain to the White House why you considered a nonentity like Jim Campbell more deserving of that heart than an important man like Winston Forrest."

"I did not choose Campbell. I haven't chosen either one yet. That's a decision still to be made!"

"The fact that you even hesitate is extremely significant," Strawbridge said. He softened his tone, leaned across McCandless's desk to urge more intimately, "Mac, you don't want such suspicions hovering over your career for the rest of your life. Look at it this way, the public will never know, or even care, if Jim Campbell gets this heart. But if Winston Forrest *doesn't* get it, if he were to die before another suitable heart becomes available, that *will* be national news. Which can't do this institution any good. Can't do you any good. Since you're the man who made the decision."

"I didn't ask to make this decision!" McCandless protested.

"Of course not," Strawbridge agreed too readily. "But that's the burden of command. The way I see it, comparing the medical histories of both men, there's little to choose between them."

"Evidently you've done more than a little comparing," McCandless realized.

"Having a strong interest in the outcome, I took that liberty. Both are close enough so no one could ever fault you for deciding in Forrest's favor. No one."

Strawbridge had left. McCandless sat at his desk staring at two medical histories. Both men were legitimate candidates for the heart that was now eight hundred miles away, sustained by mechanical means in the chest of a man who was, for all medical purposes, dead.

Forrest? Or Campbell? Campbell? Or Forrest? To choose one might virtually doom the other. No doctor should be forced to make such a decision, McCandless protested silently. *Neither of them have too much time left to await the possibility of another heart. Time could run out on either of them, as it did on Sally Brock, or the others who had died waiting.*

There was yet one more set of data that could take the decision out of his hands. He lifted the phone.

"Claire, get me Sawyer!" He waited until he heard the Coordinator's voice. "Addie, the data from Garden Grove, what was the HLA report?"

"They didn't give me any detail on that. They may not have done an HLA on the donor."

"Then have them do one! And report the results by fax machine. Stat!"

"This could take a little time," Sawyer replied.

"I know. Just do it!" McCandless ordered.

Since he had to await the outcome of that test, he decided to perform one more procedure of his own. It would not yield an answer in numbers or percentages, but it was a test his old chief cardiologist William Baldwin, who had taught him all he knew about heart transplants, used to depend upon.

It was a hearty and jovial Winston Forrest whom Allen McCandless found when he entered the room to make one final examination. Strawbridge having leaked the news that there was a heart, and virtually assuring Forrest that he would get it, had wrought a miraculous change in the man.

While McCandless probed with his stethoscope, Forrest joked, "Is this what it comes down to, Doctor? After all the gleaming, newfangled, electronic equipment? One doctor listening through a primitive stethoscope?''

"Sometimes I think we were better off in the old days," McCandless said, evading the question.

"And the President would be the first to agree with you. He once said to me, 'Win, this job could be fun if crises came by horseback instead of by hot line.' ''

As McCandless continued to examine Forrest's chest and back, the older man continued, "I'm glad there's finally a heart for me. I tell you, it is not dignified for a man to live out his days waiting for another man's misfortune. Praying for another sleet storm, another disaster. But I want to live, Doctor. I want to live.''

McCandless was applying his stethoscope to the chest and back of Jim Campbell. He could sense the tension in the young man's body.

"I know I shouldn't ask," Jim began, "but what are you looking for?''

"Just routine, Jim, routine checkup," McCandless said, and continued listening.

"What I mean is, I wonder if you know how it feels. To lie here with your life depending on the next time that door opens, each time? You think, The doctor, what's he here for? Whatever he's looking for, I'll do it. I'll say it. Anything. Breathe slow, breathe fast, breathe deep, breathe shallow, don't breathe, anything! Anything to convince him to say, 'Here, there's a new heart for you. You can go on living. For your wife, for your kids.' Who are so sure that Daddy is going to make it. Because when I talk to them on the phone I keep saying, 'Don't worry,Daddy's going to be all right!' Well, Doctor, what the hell do you expect Daddy to say?''

Fearful that his explosion of feeling had antagonized the doctor, Campbell said softly, "Sorry. But it's a big responsibility promising miracles to children. But maybe the most terrible promises are the ones we make to ourselves. 'The doctor will do it. I can see it in his eyes. He's sure, he's capable, he's confident.' Doctor, you have no idea the powers we bestow on you, all on behalf of children who believe, and wives who go on smiling. God, I wish Nan didn't feel she has to smile all the time.''

As McCandless folded his stethoscope, Campbell asked, ''Well, Doctor?''

''You're doing fine, Jim, just fine.''

''I'm sorry I let loose like that. But sometimes . . . sometimes the waiting gets to be too much. Too much.''

There was nothing McCandless could say to alleviate Jim Campbell's anxiety. Not yet. If at all.

25

ALLEN MCCANDLESS WAS pacing the confines of his private office, which suddenly seemed too small, much too small. Awaiting those HLA histocompatibility results from Garden Grove had given him more time to weigh the two candidates and to realize that he did not wish to make the decision. The sound at his door made him turn quickly. But instead of Claire reporting those results, he discovered Millicent Forrest.

His instant suspicion was that Strawbridge had sent her to plead Forrest's case. The Administrator was capable of such a tactic. McCandless prepared himself to defend his doubts.

She disarmed him by apologizing, "Sorry to intrude. But your secretary wasn't out there."

"She's down at the fax machine awaiting the results of some tests on the donor."

"It's been almost two hours," Millicent said. "I thought once the transplant procedure began, things moved very swiftly. Like clockwork, I think you once said."

"Yes. Once the procedure starts, it does move quickly and with great precision."

"But nothing's happened. They haven't done anything to Winston yet. No preparations. No preoperative procedures. *I* began to get worried, because *he* is worried."

McCandless realized that Millicent was not aware that the choice had not yet been made.

"He'd been so depressed. Until he got word about that new heart. He's been so excited that he isn't even considering the risks of surgery. He's confident that he'll make it. He's even making plans for after the surgery. Getting back to Washington. Resuming his duties for the President. I haven't seen him like this since his heart attack. He's so upbeat. So determined. But in the last two hours, nothing's happened. He's started to worry again. And so have I."

McCandless stared at her, debating how, or indeed if, he could explain to her the dilemma that confronted him. He took her hand, led her to a chair.

"Mrs. Forrest—"

"I thought we knew each other well enough for you to call me Millicent."

McCandless realized that the poisonous hint that Strawbridge had dropped had already begun to affect the way even he thought. What would others think?

She detected his uneasiness and concluded, "There's no heart! Something went wrong. They couldn't keep the donor going long enough!"

"No. Nothing like that," McCandless said.

"Allen . . . or do I have to call you Dr. McCandless now? Something *is* wrong."

He began to pace. As much to avoid looking into her hazel eyes as to dispel the tension mobilized by his conflict. "Look," he began suddenly, "I never asked for this!"

She was so startled and puzzled that he fell silent. After a brief pause he began once more, slowly, and more softly.

"When I chose cardiology, it was with the aim of prolonging people's lives by detecting their heart ailments. Anticipating them in time to treat them and assure them the longest possible painless, trouble-free existence. It seemed a worthy ambition, to delay disease and death for as long as medically possible. But then science and surgery conspired to actually bestow the gift of life on some patients who were doomed to die. That was too tempting a power to resist. So when my Chief of Cardiology said, 'Allen, how would you like to transfer from routine clinical practice to the Transplant Unit?' naturally I jumped at the chance."

He turned to catch the puzzled look on her face, and realized that he had taken a circuitous and confusing way to present his dilemma. But he felt compelled to explain to someone. And there was no one to whom he had felt closer in these recent weeks than this woman who seemed to understand him.

"I can't describe the feeling of satisfaction," he continued. "Desperate patients arrive, in their eyes the fear of death. Then weeks later or months later, after we give them a new heart, they leave to take up their lives, not as before. But much better than before. They go on to careers of their own. Lives of their own. To families that had all but given up on them. It justifies everything for which a man studies medicine. The first generation of physicians who truly have the gift of life in their hands."

"Allen, you're telling me what I already know. What are you avoiding?" she asked.

"Usually the use of that gift is clearly indicated. A patient is waiting. A heart for that particular patient becomes available. Two teams go to work. The donor team. The transplant team. They coordinate their work with great efficiency and precise timing, like a military operation. Then the question of life and death comes down to only one thing, Will the new heart do its job?"

"You've warned me. There are occasional failures," she admitted.

"Sometimes . . . the candidates—"

She interrupted to assume, "You're trying to tell me Winston is no longer well enough to be considered a candidate for this heart."

"He still *is* a good candidate."

"Then why this explanation that hints that he isn't?" she asked, even more puzzled than before.

"Because he isn't the *only* candidate," McCandless said finally. She failed to understand. "There is another candidate,

another man with equal medical qualifications, equal need for
this particular heart.''

Once the truth had been made clear to her, she said,
''Another man . . . another candidate . . . Mr. Strawbridge
never said . . . I never imagined . . . may I ask who he is?''

''I'm sorry. Professional ethics prevent me from revealing that.''

''Of course. I understand,'' she replied. ''What do
I . . . what do I do now? What do I say to Winston?''

''There is nothing to say. Yet. First, I have to make the
decision. I wish I didn't have to.''

''Is that what you meant before, 'I never asked for
this'?''

''I feel like Pontius Pilate when he said, 'Let this be taken
out of my hands.' Fortunately, there are some medical data yet
to compare that may make that possible. I'm waiting for them
now.''

His door opened hurriedly. Claire Fielding raced in,
carrying a single thin file. ''The HLA results on the donor.
Since you've already got the Forrest and the Campbell files, is
there anything else you need?''

''No. No, thank you, Claire.''

She left as swiftly as she had entered.

Millicent Forrest stared at Allen McCandless. She had no
need to ask. Her inquisitive hazel eyes did that for her.

He did not admit it. But neither could he deny that Jim
Campbell was the other candidate.

She acknowledged that fact with a soft, ''Oh,
God . . . no.''

Allen McCandless had placed before him three sets of HLA
tissue-typing results derived from studies of the blood of donor
Larry Clinton, Winston Forrest and Jim Campbell.

In the early days of heart transplantation, the drugs used
to fight rejection were not nearly as effective as cyclosporine.
Thus, the most exact match possible between donor and

recipient had to be obtained to avoid fatal rejection. Tissue typing assured the most compatible match.

Though in these times blood-type match was sufficient, McCandless hoped that the selection between these two equally qualified candidates might be scientifically determined by HLA comparisons, thus taking the burden of the decision out of his hands.

Chris Slade leaned over McCandless's shoulder, studying the same three sets of data. He felt forced to say what McCandless already knew but would rather not admit.

"They're too closely matched to dictate a choice."

The phone rang. Without taking his eyes off the three reports, McCandless reached for the phone vaguely, found it, responded, "Yes, Claire?"

"Him again," was all she needed to say.

"Put him on," McCandless said impatiently. Before Strawbridge could even inquire, McCandless announced, "There's been no decision yet."

"I simply wanted to report that I have had a second call from the White House. The President is quite anxious to mention at his news conference tomorrow morning that—"

McCandless interrupted, "Please tell the President that it is wrong to give the impression that heart transplants are media events. It is unfair to the public and to all other transplant candidates to make a special case of any one patient."

Strawbridge shot back sarcastically, "Perhaps you'd like to tell him that yourself!"

"I will if I have to," McCandless replied.

"Be my guest!" the exasperated Administrator retorted angrily, then modified his tone to urge, "Mac, be practical. No matter what you decide, you can only save one patient. Select the one who can do this institution, and you, the most good. Think of how much better you can serve all future patients if we get you that Imatron."

"Harvey, this isn't a practical decision. It's a medical decision."

"What do I tell the White House? They're waiting for my call back," Strawbridge demanded in his exasperation.

"Tell them the truth. There's been no decision yet. As soon as there is, they'll be the first to know."

"He won't like it—" Strawbridge started to warn.

McCandless cut him off with a curt, "We are in the process of making that decision right now!" He hung up. "Chris, speaking solely as a surgeon now, knowing the history and condition of both patients, which one has the best chance of giving you the optimum result?"

"Based on what I know of both of them, general condition, condition of cardiac arteries, I can get a good result with either."

"It would matter to you if there was a significant difference in the PVR's," McCandless pointed out.

"Naturally, I'd prefer the one with the lower PVR. Of course, if one of them is over six, you'd have to drop him from the program altogether," Slade said.

McCandless lifted the phone. "Claire, have them get O.R. Nine ready for a PVR procedure. Call the floor and have them send Forrest down. Tell them to stand by with Campbell."

The nurse knocked on the half-open door of Room 607, calling, "Mr. Forrest?" She pushed open the door. "Oh, sorry, I thought you were alone. Hi, Mrs. Forrest!"

Millicent Forrest responded with a smile that was not quite warm enough to conceal her conflicting emotions.

Forrest called back as heartily as he could, "Are they ready for me?"

"Dr. McCandless wants you down in O.R. Nine."

"O.R. Nine? Is that where they do it?"

"Yes," the nurse responded, to a question she had misinterpreted.

"I guess I'll be under by the time they take me in there, won't I?"

"I don't think so," the nurse replied.

"Good! I'd love to see the operating room where they do it. It must be a marvel of the electronic age."

"For a PVR?" the nurse asked, puzzled.

"PVR?" Forrest echoed, confused in his own way. "I thought . . . they said there's a heart for me. A new healthy heart."

"I was only instructed to get you down to Nine for a PVR."

Forrest looked to Millicent, who could only stare back and pretend surprise. After the height to which Forrest's expectations had been raised, it would have been cruel to deprive him of hope now. There was still a chance, a fifty-fifty chance, that the new heart would be his. She decided a little white lie was justified.

"It's probably one of the routine steps they have to take before surgery."

The nurse was about to correct her, but Millicent's eyes signaled, *No, please.*

"Well," Forrest said, "as they say, let's get the show on the road."

"An orderly will be in with a gurney any moment."

"Good," Forrest joked. "One thing you learn at the White House. Never walk if you can ride."

The nurse had been gone only a few moments. Winston Forrest sounded far less amused and happy as he began, "One thing, though . . ." He became silent again.

Surprised at the sudden change, and fearing he had realized that his chances were now in doubt, Millicent coaxed, "Win? What is it?"

"Once I'm okay again, it won't be the new beginning I've looked forward to, but the end. Well, Millie, I'll say this. You've done your part. And, as always, done it well. Very well. And I appreciate it."

"You sound as if you're going to give me a gold watch and send me into retirement."

"Shouldn't I? A few weeks from now I'll have recovered. And you . . . you'll be on your way again."

"Will I?" she asked softly.

He looked at her. Unsure, he finally said, "When you came back, you said it was only for long enough to see me through this. I remember your exact words. 'If you need me, Win, I'll see you through this. But after that . . .' And you never finished that sentence."

"Maybe because I never knew the ending," she said. "But I do now."

"And?"

"Win, remember when Paul was still little and he would ask you, 'How long you going to be away this time, Daddy?' And you'd say, 'For the duration, son.' And he would ask, 'What's a duration?' And you'd explain, 'It's a word diplomats and officials use when they don't know how long something will take.' Well, Win, these last few months have given me the chance to rethink my decision. I'm here, Win. For the duration."

He slid his hand along the bed, for it seemed he had not sufficient strength to lift it. She cradled it in hers to warm it, holding it close to her breasts and silently wishing, *Let him pass this one last test, give him his chance. Please?*

The door was pushed open by the arrival of the gurney under the command of a young black orderly, who greeted, "Up we go, Mr. Forrest!" He tried to lend Forrest a hand. But Forrest resisted.

"I can make it on my own, thank you." He climbed onto the stretcher. When he was comfortable, he joked, "Not exactly Air Force One, but it'll have to do. Ready for takeoff."

With a jaunty wave to Millicent, he signaled the orderly to push him out of the room.

The nurse lingered long enough to whisper to Millicent Forrest, "We haven't received any orders that he's to have a transplant tonight. But he seems so sure . . ."

"Yes, he's quite hopeful and chipper this evening. I

haven't seen him like this since we arrived here,'' Millicent said.

But she was thinking, *That test, that PVR, Allen explained that once, over dinner. I don't remember the exact term. But the P had to do with pulmonary. And the R had to do with resistance. Something about a defective heart causes resistance to build up in the lungs. If that resistance gets above a certain number on something called a Woods Scale, then the normal right ventricle of the new heart would not be able to pump against it and the heart would fail. "Stop cold," I think he said. So any patient with a high number on that Woods Scale would be ruled out of the program. Is that what he's trying to do now? Rule Winston out? No. Of course not. Poor man, still wrestling with that decision. I felt so sorry for him when he said, "I never asked for this!"*

In O.R. 9 Allen McCandless had begun to thread the yellow plastic catheter into Winston Forrest's jugular vein. Following its progress on the monitor, he directed it slowly into Forrest's heart, through the right atrium and the right ventricle into the pulmonary artery. The catheter finally in place, McCandless waited for the digital response of the Woods meter. The number turned up finally. A reading of 5.

Within the acceptable range for successful surgical intervention with a new heart. Winston Forrest was still a good candidate for the heart that was kept beating by mechanical means in the chest of brain-dead Larry Clinton.

Now to test Jim Campbell.

Nancy Campbell usually visited Jim during those daytime hours when the kids were both in school. This time, however, she arrived on the ICU floor of the Cardiac Wing at night.

After weeks of visiting, she knew most of the staff by name and most knew her well enough to greet her with a warm, ''Hi! How are the kids?'' Twice, on Sundays, she had brought the children to the hospital. Since children are carriers

of many infectious diseases that could imperil immuno-
depressed patients, they were below visiting age for the
Transplant Unit. All Nancy could do was have Jimmy and
Dorothy stand in the parking lot and wave up to their dad.

Being accustomed to Nancy Campbell's routine, the staff
was surprised to see her arrive so late this evening. Besides,
she hurried along the corridor even more quickly than usual,
for she had news. Good news for Jim. News that would cheer
him up. Perhaps it would lift him out of his recent depression,
caused by what seemed endless waiting.

The death of Sally Brock was still fresh in mind. Since it
was followed by the discharge of another patient whose
condition had deteriorated so badly as to make him ineligible
for a transplant, Jim had become discouraged to such a degree
that each time Nan came to visit during the last few days, he
would insist, "It won't happen . . . can't happen . . . not in
time . . ."

It did no good to remind him, "But sweetheart, Mr.
Biller, that nice young accountant, he got a heart only three
weeks ago, and already he's been sent home."

"It won't happen," Jim kept insisting. "Why me? Why
did God pick on me? Have I ever done anything so wrong?"

"I won't let you talk that way," she had said. "God
doesn't do things like that."

She had embraced him, trying as if by some process of
osmosis to infuse him with the hope she clung to. Secretly she
feared that if his defeated attitude were to reach Dr. Robbins,
he might disqualify Jim on psychiatric grounds.

Only three afternoons ago, when she had arrived, she saw
Robbins leaving Jim's room. Her fears had been so intensified
that she could not leave the hospital without seeking out the
psychiatrist.

As usual, Robbins's schedule had been tight with
appointments with prospective candidates, so Nancy had to
wait. When she was finally admitted to his office, she could
not resist blurting out, "It's only a mood. It'll pass! He's
really very encouraged. He talks all the time about how

things are going to be once he gets his heart and can go back home.''

Her last words were garbled because she had begun to weep.

"Now, now, Mrs. Campbell, what's wrong? Something Jim said during your visit?''

Between weeping and trying not to, she blurted out her fears about Jim's depression, how it might affect his status in the program, what it would mean to her and to her children. She ended up pleading, ''So no matter what you found when you saw him today, I'm sure it's only temporary. He'll get over it. His attitude will be fine. Great!'' She had endowed her assurance with as much enthusiasm as a frightened woman could.

"Mrs. Campbell—or if I may, Nancy—since I know Jim and you well enough . . .'' He took her cold hand in his. ''Nancy, the only reason I dropped by Jim's room today was to pay off a bet. He has an uncanny knack for picking winners in the Sunday football games. And I am delighted to lose to him. For the same reason you're here. To keep his spirits up. Of course, he becomes despondent from time to time. Any human being facing possible death who can't feel depressed from time to time is not exactly what I would call normal. So, Jim gets depressed. But he also has his good days. And he has formed a very fine relationship with Mr. Forrest, a more mature man, a more philosophical man.''

"Yes,'' Nancy said, ''I know his wife. She's a lovely woman. So nice. So friendly. And she's beautiful.''

"She is indeed,'' Robbins agreed. ''Forrest and Jim have become good friends, too. They play their gin game every day. They pretend they want to beat each others' brains out. But they have established a genuine affection for each other. Like father and son. And there's a reason . . .''

"I know,'' Nancy said. ''Mrs. Forrest told me once about their son who was killed.''

"Mr. Forrest, whether he knows it or not, has transferred his feelings for his son to your husband. So they are good for each other. Their moods fluctuate in compensating fashion. When one becomes depressed, the other man pumps up his own optimism to help him overcome his depression. At the moment Jim is down, so Forrest pretends to be up. When his turn comes, you can be sure Jim will do his own share of pretending. In that way both of them gain from the relationship. So I am not worried about Jim.''

''As long as he won't lose his place in the program,'' Nancy said.

''He won't lose his place,'' Robbins assured her.

That had been three days ago. She had slept better the last two nights. And now, bursting with her exciting news, she entered her husband's room, calling, ''Jim! The greatest news! Remember my cousin Irma, the blond bridesmaid at our wedding—'' She realized that he was not there. She hurried down to the solarium, thinking she might find him engaged in an evening game of gin with Mr. Forrest. But when she reached the open archway, she spied both Forrests seated in the corner near the windows. But there was no sign of Jim. She became suddenly fearful. She was about to race back to inquire at the nurses' station, but Millicent Forrest had already started toward her.

''You're looking for Jim.''

''He's not in his room, he's not here—''

''I understand he's being given some test.''

''Something's wrong, he's gotten worse,'' Nancy said, alarmed.

''Of course not. Nothing like that,'' Millicent Forrest replied, debating with herself whether it was wise to tell Nancy the reason for the test. She decided it was not fair to impose that burden on this trembling young woman. ''It's just one more test, that's all.''

''Are you sure?'' Nancy asked, searching Millicent's hazel eyes.

In a lifetime of being a government wife you've had to lie many times in a good cause. This may be the most important, she thought. Her hazel eyes concealing her true emotions, she tried to reassure her friend, "The test is only routine, Nan. Nothing to be concerned about."

"Thank God. I was so scared when I didn't find him . . . and I had just got a call with such good news—" she started to say.

"Good news?" Millicent Forrest interrupted. "They called you to come to the hospital?" she asked, as she thought, *Has the decision been made? Is it Jim, not Winston, who gets that heart? Allen . . . didn't tell me. He should have. So I wouldn't have to be playing games now with Nancy. With Winston. Who still goes on thinking he will get that heart. He keeps making plans. For the future. For both of us. It may not be both of us. But I can't tell him that. Now now. Not yet.*

In an instant the young woman who had been so distressed had been put at ease. The other woman, who had been determined to reassure her, now needed reassurance herself.

"I didn't get a call from the hospital," Nancy said, to Millicent's great relief. "It was from my cousin Irma. She just married this young man who studied forestry at a university in the Southwest. Irma said they talked it over. And Carl, that's her new husband, he is willing for them to move here and go into Jim's business, if there's the possibility of a partnership later. Jim'll be delighted. It's just what he needs to cheer him up."

"Isn't that marvelous," Millicent Forrest was quick to enthuse, now that her own fears had been allayed. "I've been telling you all along, things have a way of working out."

"You were so right," Nancy said. "I don't know what I would have done without your help and encouragement."

Impulsively, she embraced Millicent Forrest and kissed her on the cheek.

*   *   *

Up in O.R. 9, having carefully guided the PVR probe into and through Jim Campbell's heart to his lungs, Allen McCandless was awaiting the digital readout.

It appeared under the magnifying glass, coming to rest on the number 5. Without a word or a sign to Jim Campbell, McCandless realized, *Forrest 5, Campbell 5. The selection is not in their PVR readings.*

Tense, fearful, Jim Campbell asked, "How is it, Doc? Worse than last time?"

"No, Jim, not worse at all. You're doing fine . . . just fine," McCandless said.

At the same time, he was thinking, *Blood type, HLA, PVR, is there no test that will make this decision? Not much time to decide now. That heart, being kept alive eight hundred miles from here . . . the sooner it is harvested and on its way here, the better. For whoever the recipient will be.*

Jim Campbell was wheeled out of O.R. 9. McCandless lifted the phone. "Get me Sawyer!" Once he heard the Coordinator's voice, he instructed, "Addie, get the donor team on the way!"

"Who will the recipient be? Forrest? Or Campbell?"

"Just get the donor team on the way!" He hung up.

Back in his room, Jim Campbell listened as Nancy revealed her good news.

"Isn't that terrific, honey? The business will be in the family. We don't have to worry about it being stolen away."

Jim had not reacted with as much enthusiasm as she had expected.

"Jim?" she asked.

"Oh, it's . . . it's great. Terrific," he finally said.

"Honey, what's wrong?"

"That's what I'd like to know," he said. "That test before, McCandless said it came out fine. But I'm thinking, Why are they giving me a test all of a sudden unless they think something's gone wrong with me?"

After trying to reassure him, with little success, Nancy

Campbell acceded to the nurse's reminder that visiting hours were over.

She drove home in the rain, asking herself the same question. *Why did they suddenly decide to test him again? Has he shown signs of failing? Like Sally Brock? Oh, God, I hope not.*

26

A HEAVY MIST covered the airport. The revolving light from the tower swept through the fog but could not reach the end of the runway. The airport manager, Hank Stepanik, awaited the arrival of the ambulance from the Medical Center. He held out his hand to determine if it was mist he was feeling or rain. It was a light rain.

Through it came the probing high beams of the ambulance. It pulled up alongside the Lear 55 Jet that waited, door open, steps lowered. Out piled Boyd Angstrom, who would serve as surgeon on the donor team. Behind him came his assistant, two lab technicians—both women—and finally Coordinator Adeline Sawyer, in charge of the entire Unit.

The lab technicians hauled out all the materials necessary to carry out their mission. They were contained in what might appear to be the least likely piece of equipment for such a vital surgical venture, a large beer cooler. Inside it, carefully stowed, was a total complement of surgical instruments, containers, saline solution, potassium solution, all with one purpose, to bring that donor heart back in good, sound, healthy, viable condition.

As the others boarded the jet, Sawyer lingered at the bottom of the steps to ask Stepanik, "How's it look, Hank?"

"The tower in Garden Grove tells me it's all clear there now."

"I meant, how's it look for when we return?" Sawyer asked.

"They say this front should move through and be gone in another six or seven hours," the airport manager said.

"Six hours is a long time," Sawyer said.

"Yeah," Stepanik agreed. "But we've talked you in before. We can do it again."

"Hope so," Sawyer said, starting up the steps.

Once they were all strapped in, the pilot started up both engines, raced them. When he liked the feel of them, he asked the tower, "Okay? Cleared to take off?"

"Cleared to take off. Runway Three. Good luck!"

The pilot started the plane slowly away from the gate. He approached Runway 3 through the mist. When he was lined up, he gunned his engines. The plane started down the runway with a roar.

Hank Stepanik watched her go, aware that even before she lifted off, she was already lost in the mist. *This is going to be one long night*, he thought.

Once he was sure the Lear had safely lifted into the air and was on its way, he started up the steps of the tower. Inside he ordered, "Cut all lights! Nobody'll be touching down here for hours! Not on a night like this!"

Allen McCandless sat at his desk, making his final appraisal of every bit of medical evidence that had been accumulated concerning Winston Forrest and James Campbell. He had factored in all that could be learned about the donor, Larry Clinton.

He had consulted with Robbins, who reported that both men were in equally good psychiatric condition to assure that they would be dependable post-operative patients.

McCandless remembered only too well his professor at Stanford bidding him farewell, saying, "Allen, this is the ultimate in medicine. The gift of life is yours. Use it wisely and well, without fear or favor."

*But he never said the time would come when to give life
to one patient might mean condemning another patient to
death,* McCandless protested now. *Campbell, or Forrest,
whoever is denied this heart is so end-stage that he will have
very little chance of survival unless another heart were to
become available soon. Very soon. And that's asking for a
miracle.*

Still, the choice had to be made. And with the donor team
on its way, it had to be made now.

He reached for the phone. "Claire, ask Dr. Slade and
Mr. Strawbridge to come up here. Stat!"

Harvey Strawbridge arrived first. Chris Slade was only minutes behind. He could tell from the grim look on Allen
McCandless's lean face that he had come to his decision.

McCandless stood behind his desk, on which were laid
out all the pertinent lab reports, data, EKG's, scans, angiogram results, HLA's, PVR results of both Forrest and Campbell.

"Chris," McCandless began, "in the presence of the
Administrator I have to ask you once more, do you consider
these two patients equally good surgical risks? Equally good
candidates to accept a new heart?"

As gravely, Chris Slade replied, "From a surgeon's point
of view, I would approach either patient optimistic of achiev-
ing a good result. Bearing in mind always that no test, no
diagnostic device, no matter how modern and sensitive, can be
as revealing as what the surgeon will find at the site of the
surgery. We are always at the mercy of the unexpected."

"Aside from the unexpected?" McCandless persisted.

"I consider them equally good candidates for transplant
surgery," Slade said without equivocation.

"As do I," McCandless said. "Therefore, since all the
medical and surgical indications do not dictate a choice, it is
up to us. To me, actually."

Strawbridge could not resist intervening, "Mac, I know
we've had our differences in the past. But my ambition, like

yours, has been to protect this medical center. To ensure our ability to serve the public with the best and latest in medicine. And I have never done anything to depart from that ambition.

"Now, I know how you on the medical and surgical staffs feel about me. But I assure you I am not looking forward to a bronze plaque on the front entrance of this hospital with my name on it after I retire. I only wish to make it possible for you men and women to practice your specialities in the most efficient and constructive environment. That's why I ignore your behind-the-hand sarcastic remarks and carry on as I think best serves this medical institution."

McCandless and Slade exchanged extremely subtle eye contact. Strawbridge had delivered only his prelude. They were awaiting his message.

"However," Strawbridge continued, "that is all personal. What we face now has much broader implications. For this institution. For the nation. And mainly for your profession."

Neither McCandless nor Slade could suppress their curiosity and skepticism about Strawbridge's last statement.

"Yes, gentlemen, for your profession. We have become a nation in which the media thrives on disaster, scandal and failure. Muckraking has become the stock-in-trade of the most powerful medium of all time. Television. They can call themselves investigative reporters. But scandal mongers is what they are.

"A thousand patients can come to our doors seeking help. And receive it. But no camera is there to record that. Nor to interview the patient or his family, who have only glowing things to say about us. But let one patient get less than a perfect result, and there on that damned tube is the weeping widow or mother, telling her sad tale. Those of us who serve medicine in any capacity have become victims of the media and malpractice lawyers."

He turned on McCandless. "Mac, I hate to bring this up again. But the damaging publicity generated by that lawsuit—"

"Yes, I know," McCandless anticipated. "The patient

who got AIDS from a transplanted heart. The fault was not here, but in the donor hospital. If indeed there was any fault at all. AIDS is so new a plague that no one had yet discovered that transfusions given to trauma victims can so dilute their blood that all AIDS tests will come up negative.''

"You know that. I know that," Strawbridge argued. "The only thing the public learned was that this hospital gave AIDS to an innocent man who came here to be healed! It's that kind of unjustified scandal that gives medicine a bad reputation. If you men feel no loyalty to this institution, at least consider the benefit of this situation to your own profession."

"What are you getting at, Harve?" Slade asked.

"What is the best way to wipe out that blot on our record?" Strawbridge asked. "Television. Like it or not, gentlemen, there it is. National policy is influenced by it. Public opinion is formed by it. I say we now have the chance to use it."

"Exactly how?" McCandless asked.

"Picture this. Our auditorium—the large auditorium— filled with reporters, television cameras, microphones. Mac, as chief of the transplant service you get up and, to nationwide coverage, explain our work in heart transplantation. Then you introduce Chris. He explains the surgery. What he did. What he found. How he overcame unexpected difficulties he encountered. The media eats that stuff up."

"Harve, I hate to burst your bubble, but that is old hat," Slade pointed out. "The public has seen news conferences going way back to the master of the art, Christiaan Barnard. Forget about the networks. You won't get even a local TV crew out for that."

To McCandless's surprise, Strawbridge was quick to agree. "You're absolutely right, Chris." Then he added, "*If* the recipient is someone named Jim Campbell. However—"

Before he could continue, McCandless took over. "However, if the patient is someone important, someone newsworthy, like Winston Forrest—"

Whereupon Strawbridge interrupted, to add pointedly,

"The President's National Security Adviser! A man on whose behalf the President himself interceded, which makes it news. Big news. How many cases of breast-cancer surgery are done in this country every day? Thousands. How many have been covered by the media in the last year? One. The First Lady. If we do this transplant on Winston Forrest and he survives, which Chris feels sure he will, this center will receive the finest publicity in its history. We'll be up there with the best in heart surgery, along with Stanford, Pittsburgh, New York. You don't see them shying away from publicity!''

Having made his strongest argument, Strawbridge modulated his tone. ''Mac, you owe it to this institution and to the medical profession to put our best foot forward. I also happen to think that the President is entitled to Winston Forrest's advice and counsel on matters that may affect this nation far into the future.''

McCandless did not respond. Instead, he turned to Slade. ''Chris, anything you want to add?''

''I'm a surgeon. I will do my best with either candidate. My regret is, there's only one heart.''

''Okay, then,'' McCandless said. ''Frankly, I have tried in every way I know, by every test there is, to avoid making this decision. Once that proved impossible, I tried to add up the score for each man.''

He began to pace as he revealed his thoughts. ''Winston Forrest. A highly capable, intelligent man. Years of training in government that fit him for his job as advisor to the President. I respect that. More than you think, Harve. And also a man who's had enough suffering in his life. Saddest thing I know is for a parent to bury a child. Which he had to do, under most tragic circumstances. It cost him not only his son, but possibly his marriage and his wife as well. He is a man deserving of great sympathy. My sympathy.

''There is also a fellow named Jim Campbell. It could be John Smith. He has a wife, two kids, a small business, a modest home. In terms of national importance, he may never amount to much. He will never advise the President of the

United States. Probably the most advice he is ever going to give anyone is to say, 'Mrs. Jones, that oak in your front yard is suffering blight. I would advise that it come down before it causes damage to other trees or to your front porch.' If Jim Campbell survives, he'll raise two kids, feed them, clothe them, send them to school. He'll watch television. Root for his favorite team. Vote his own choice for mayor, governor, President. Maybe coach Little League baseball. Or serve on his church board of vestrymen. He will love his wife and his kids. When the kids are old enough he'll send them off to college. All in all, a rather uneventful life. Certainly not an 'important' life.''

As if interrupting his own line of thought, he stopped pacing and turned to Strawbridge. "They say, Harve, that the way to get the best medical care in this country is to be either very rich or very poor. The rich get it because they can afford it. The poor get it because the best doctors serve them in free clinics. It's the big, broad middle class that gets the leavings.''

"You can't accuse us of that!" Strawbridge protested. "We deliver the best cardiac care to all who come to us.''

"Yes, we do,'' McCandless agreed, then fed Strawbridge's words back to him, " 'We deliver the best cardiac care to all who come to us.' The question is, what *is* the best care? How do we best use the one heart that is at our command now? I have been wrestling with that ever since that phone call came. What is the best use of such a rare commodity as a living, pumping, healthy heart? The only fair, honest conclusion I can come to is this. That heart will serve better, *and longer*, a man as young as Jim Campbell.''

"I gave the White House my word,'' Strawbridge cried out. "What can I tell them now?''

"You won't have to. It's my decision to make. I am willing to call the President and explain.''

"I doubt very much he'll take kindly to your peculiar logic,'' Strawbridge warned.

McCandless picked up the phone. "Claire, locate Mrs. Campbell. Tell her to get back to the hospital as soon as she can. Jim Campbell is having a heart transplant in the next five hours. And when you've done that, call Ms. Katherine Breed at the White House number.''

He went up to the ICU floor. He approached Room 607. When he knocked, Millicent came to the door. She could tell that he had made his decision. Preferring to hear it first, she stepped outside.

"I have to tell him. It's not his turn this time," McCandless said.

"*This* time . . .'' she repeated, betraying that she believed there would not be another chance for Winston.

"I may be doing him a favor. No one can predict what happens once we turn off that heart-lung machine.''

"Yes, I know. You explained that once. Possible fibrillations. The new heart refusing to function.''

"There are no guarantees," McCandless said. "I'd better tell him now.''

"It will be easier for him coming from me," she said.

"Are you sure you can do it?" McCandless asked.

She attempted a smile and said, "Winston has a test for a government wife. You wake her in the middle of the night, tell her that World War Three has just broken out. If she smiles, starts putting on her basic black, orders finger sandwiches and coffee for two hundred guests, she's a good government wife. Nothing surprises her, nothing shakes her, nothing moves her.''

"She'd have a right to be moved now," McCandless suggested sympathetically.

"Don't worry about me. I'll do what I have to. I understand . . . No, No, I don't," she suddenly protested. "Right now I hate every noble word I've ever heard. 'Mature,' 'understanding,' 'unselfish,' I hate them all. No matter what our past differences have been, I want Winston to live. I want him to have his chance. . . .''

It seemed she was about to start weeping. He was

strongly tempted to put his arm around her to comfort her, but resisted.

"I'm sorry, Millicent, very sorry."

She sniffled back her tears and started to apologize, "I'm glad he isn't seeing me this way. 'Now, Millie,' he'd say. 'We don't do that sort of thing.' And the truth is, 'we' didn't. Together we were one thing. But it's not fair to ask me to act now as if it's 'us.' After this, it won't be 'us.' Ever again. Just me. There'll be no one to say, 'Now, Millie . . .' No one to tell me I'm brave, noble, good, all the things I never really was, except for him."

"Do you want me to tell him?" McCandless asked.

She shook her head and turned back to enter Room 607.

27

"MRS. NOONAN, SORRY to get you out of your own bed at this hour of the night," Nancy Campbell apologized.

"Now, don't you worry, darling. You just finish dressing and get going to that hospital."

"With Dorothy, please, be very gentle when you comb her hair in the morning. It tends to tangle overnight. And Jimmy, he'll ask for white toast with breakfast. Give him the whole wheat," Nancy instructed.

Mrs. Noonan, a plump gray-haired woman who had been the Campbells' neighbor since they moved in three years ago, smiled. "My dear, don't worry. I remember your instructions from last time. Just get yourself dressed and on the way. And don't worry about the children. You just make sure that man of yours is all right."

"He will be! He has to be!" Nancy insisted.

A bit too determined, Mrs. Noonan suspected. *Poor child*.

She embraced the young woman. "If you don't mind, I'll be saying a prayer for him in my own way." She pressed something into Nancy's hand.

Nancy stared down at it. It was a rosary.

"Mrs. Noonan, we're Methodists."

"Take it. During the waiting, it's a comfort just to have it in hand."

Nancy kissed the woman on the cheek and started for the door to the garage. She looked back. "When they wake up, please tell them—"

"I know, child, I know. Now you just go! And God be with you both!"

Nancy Campbell pressed the button that raised the garage door. She could see the hard-driven slanting rain that threatened a long, slow, treacherous drive to the city. She cautioned herself, *Drive carefully.* Based on what Dr. McCandless's secretary had said, the new heart wouldn't arrive for hours. She could be there in time even if it took more than an hour to reach the hospital.

As she turned the ignition key to start up the motor, a car appeared in her driveway, bright lights up full. If there was one thing she did not need now, it was delay. She sounded her horn to warn whoever it was to pull out and let her get under way. The door on the driver's side opened. A small but familiar figure emerged. Dr. Kaplan. He came toward her through the rain and into the protection of the garage.

"Nan! Out of your car, into mine!" he ordered.

"I have to get going—"

"I know. McCandless called me. I'll drive you! Come on! Quickly!" the old doctor insisted.

She sat in Kaplan's car staring through the windshield as the old man drove quite cautiously. Silently she kept urging, *Hurry, please, please, hurry. I have to be there. To kiss him before they take him up to the operating room.* Still, Kaplan drove in the right-hand lane of the Interstate, with cars passing them on his left.

"You know," he said, making an effort to seem calm and conversational, "just by chance I happened to be catching up on my *JAMA* reading." Then he realized she wouldn't understand. "*JAMA*, that's the *Journal of the American Medical Association*. There was an article in there. Happened to be about heart transplants. Did you know the success rate these days is phenomenal. And the survival rate? Ten years ago it would have been incredible!''

Why is he telling me this? Nancy asked herself. *Is it because the danger is actually so great? And why is he coming, too? So there'll be someone there to comfort me if it goes wrong? Can it be even more dangerous than I think?*

"I tell you," Kaplan continued, "the miracles I've seen in just my lifetime—beyond belief. If anyone had ever told me when I was in medical school that I would live to see an operation in which they take a sick heart out of a man and put in a healthy one, I would have said, *bubbah meinses*! That means nonsense, old wives' tales. But they are doing it. And tonight, for the first time, I am actually going to see them do it. McCandless got Slade's permission for me to scrub. After all, I promised Jim that I would be there. I couldn't go back on my word. Could I?''

His question caught her by surprise, so she was a moment late in responding, "No, no, of course not.''

"Then I figured, long as I'm going, no reason for Nancy to drive. She's got enough on her mind as it is.''

That's it, she thought. *He was afraid I'd be too nervous to drive carefully. Maybe he was right. Maybe.*

She stared ahead into the night. The rain beat against the windshield with such fury that even at top speed the wipers fought in vain to keep it clear.

Cloudy with possible rain, Kaplan kept thinking. *That's what that funny weatherman said on the television news. Why do they always keep making jokes when what people really want is an honest forecast? If this is 'possible' rain, I'd hate to see his idea of a real storm.*

As if she had been reading his mind, Nancy asked, "Do you think this'll let up soon?''

"By the time we get close to the city, it'll be just a drizzle,'' Kaplan assured her. Silently, he hoped, *Just don't ask that next question, because there's no good answer to it.*

But she did. "That new heart, they said sometimes it can

come from as far away as a thousand miles. How does it get here?''

"There's only one way. They fly it here.''

"On a night like this?''

"I've flown on worse nights,'' Kaplan said, to belittle the danger. ''Once, Anna and me, we'd been to Florida to visit our first grandchild. We leave Miami, the sun is shining, the air is balmy. Half an hour before we arrive here, there is a cloudburst like you wouldn't believe. Terrified, Anna is holding my hand. And I'm letting her, because frankly I'm more scared than she is. I, too, need someone to hold onto. But we made it. Landing smooth as silk. And only ten minutes late. These days weather is no real big problem.''

To see if he had eased her fears, he glanced in her direction, taking his eyes off the road for an instant. *Not from how tightly she is holding that rosary*, he realized. *More reassurance is needed.*

"You know, they have this procedure down to the split second. For instance, they won't even touch Jim's heart until Dr. Slade sees that container with that new heart come through the door of the operating room. So there's nothing to worry about. Even if the plane is delayed, all it means is just that. A little delay.''

He carefully refrained from mentioning that if there were an undue delay of not minutes, but several hours, the heart would become useless for transplant. It was the reason that only a heart within a thousand miles could be depended upon.

To know the truth could only distress the nervous young woman at his side. Five hours. Five hours was all the time that could be allowed to elapse between the time that heart was removed from the donor's chest and inserted into the chest of the recipient. If this storm did not let up, if the plane had to divert to another airport than the one closest to the hospital, there was no way that healthy heart could arrive in time, even with the police escort.

Old Kaplan drove on, peering through the rain and staying in the right lane of the Interstate.

* * *

At the Garden Grove airport, a hospital minibus awaited the arrival of the Lear 55. Even before it came to a halt, the bus was pulling alongside. The door of the Lear opened. As the steps touched the ground, the driver of the bus called out, "Dr. Sawyer?"

"Adeline Sawyer," she corrected from the top of the stairs. "I'm not the doctor, I'm the Coordinator."

"Okay, s'long as it's you and your team. Pile in, let's go!"

As the bus pulled out of the airport and onto the Interstate, Adeline Sawyer remarked to Angstrom, "At least the weather's good here."

"Yeah," was all that Angstrom said.

She noted that the young surgeon was tense. *And why not?* she thought. *First time on his own as head of the donor team. But he'll do fine. Slade doesn't make mistakes about his assistants. When he thinks a man is ready, he is ready.*

At Garden Grove General Dr. Arnold Shapiro was waiting to show them to the operating room where Larry Clinton's body was kept breathing with the aid of an efficient respirator.

On the way, Sawyer said, "I'd like to see the paperwork. Neurologists' statements on brain death. Family's permission."

"It's all waiting for you," Shapiro replied. "Right this way," he directed, as they reached the end of the corridor. He led them to the door of the operating room.

In the operating room, Boyd Angstrom, Adeline Sawyer and the rest of the donor team found the two other teams that had preceded them, one to harvest the kidneys, the other to harvest the liver of Larry Clinton, who was referred to by that impersonal word, *donor.*

Once Angstrom had introduced himself and established the duties and functions of the other teams, he and his crew scrubbed at the bank of washbasins alongside the wall. In

O.R. gown and cap and mask, Angstrom was ready to begin the procedure.

Taking the scalpel from his team scrub nurse, he made the first incision. A clean, straight midline incision from the donor's sternal notch down to the pubis. After cutting through the breastbone with an electric saw, he carefully cut through the pericardial sac to expose the heart.

It was a good, healthy, deep pink color, and beat with a steady rhythmic thrust. He reached into the chest cavity to assess the heart by hand contact. It was vital and strong. He nodded to Sawyer, who went to the wall phone and asked to be connected with University Medical Center Cardiac Wing. Once Chris Slade was on the line, she reported, "Everything is okay at this end. Two other organs, liver and kidneys, are to be harvested. But Angstrom says the heart is A-okay!"

"Good," Slade replied. "Keep us posted."

"Will do," Sawyer said.

At the Medical Center, Chris Slade phoned down to the ICU nurses' station.

"Okay. Bring Campbell up to the O.R.!"

On the ICU floor of the Cardiac Wing, Patient James Campbell was already several hours into the pre-op routine. He had been denied supper. His chest had been shaved and the nurse was now washing it down with antiseptic soap so that the surgical field was sterile.

She was interrupted when Dr. McCandless entered briskly. He was carrying a hypo, the needle of which was embedded in alcohol-soaked gauze.

"Hi, Doctor," Jim Campbell said, smiling, to give the impression that he was confident and at ease.

"Hi, Jim," McCandless responded in kind, watching as the nurse completed her chore. He held up the hypo. "Got to give you a shot, Jim. Azathioprine. Fights rejection. This is the first of many, Jim. There'll be prednisone and then cyclosporine."

"That stuff you told me I'll be taking for the rest of my life?"

"That's it," McCandless said as he completed the injection in Jim's bicep.

Campbell looked at the doctor. "Nancy? Does she know yet?"

"She's on her way now."

"I hope she didn't leave the kids alone."

"You know she wouldn't do that," McCandless said, taking Campbell's pulse and examining the puncture that he had made in his neck earlier, during the PVR catheterization. Sometimes, rarely—but it was good practice to make sure—routine procedures like entry into the jugular vein resulted in infections. He looked closely at the fairly fresh wound. No sign of any infection.

Nor could there be one so soon after the puncture, he reminded himself. *Then why look? Do I feel guilt toward Forrest, toward Millicent? Because I chose Campbell? Or am I trying to make sure I chose correctly? I won't know until it's over. Even then there'll be second thoughts. For instance, the way Forrest said, "Doctor, I have complete confidence in you." That's going to linger a long time, a long long time. What a way to repay his confidence.*

He did not realize how immersed he was in his own thoughts until Jim Campbell said, "Well, Doctor?

"Well, what?" McCandless asked, puzzled.

"The way you were examining my neck, I thought there was something wrong"

"Nothing wrong. You're fine. Fine!" McCandless assured heartily.

At that moment a gurney stretcher was pushed into the room by two orderlies. They lined it up alongside the bed.

"Can you make it on your own, Mr. Campbell?" one of the orderlies asked.

"Sure thing," Jim Campbell said, sliding from the bed onto the stretcher. As he did so, he said to McCandless, "I was hoping that Nan would get here before . . . well, I wanted to say something, kiss her, maybe, you know?"

"Sure, Jim, I know," McCandless said. "This weather must have delayed her."

Campbell lowered his voice. "Doc, when she gets here, will you tell her I was asking for her? That no matter what happens, I always loved her. And the kids. Be sure to mention the kids."

"Of course I will," McCandless promised, then added, "Jim, you're going to be fine. Great, in fact."

They wheeled Jim Campbell out of the room, wrapped in a large white blanket. McCandless smiled at him, waved and gave him a cheering thumbs-up signal. But the moment he was out of sight, McCandless breathed a sigh and lost his smile. Until, from down the corridor, he heard a voice he recognized as Nancy Campbell's.

"Jim!" she called. "Jim!"

McCandless heard running footsteps. He came out of the room to see her racing along the corridor to catch up with her husband. Behind her, puffing, but persistent, was old Dr. Kaplan, who passed McCandless, saying, "We just made it. Just!"

Nancy Campbell reached her husband's side. She started to feel under the blanket to find his hand, then stopped abruptly. She looked to the orderlies for permission. One of them nodded. She found Jim's hand and held it to her cheek.

Walking alongside the stretcher, she continued talking to him, "Jim, this is it. It's like a prayer come true. Which reminds me. Mrs. Noonan, she's staying with the kids. She gave me this." She held out the rosary by one of the beads so it swung gently as she walked. "I told her we weren't Catholic, but she said take it, anyhow."

"She's right," Jim said, trying to conceal his fear by joking, "It always seems to work in the movies and on TV."

"I'll be here, darling. When you wake up, I'll be right here," she promised.

"I know you will," he said as they reached the swinging doors beyond which no visitor was permitted.

She bent over him and kissed him on the lips, thinking, *God, dear God, don't let this be the last time. If only for the kids' sake . . . no, no, for my sake, too . . . for my sake . . .*

She became aware that the orderlies could no longer be indulgent and stood back. The stretcher passed through the double doors. Dr. Kaplan followed it, saying, "I'll be up there every moment, my dear."

Then he, too, was gone.

28

Nᴀɴᴄʏ Cᴀᴍᴘʙᴇʟʟ ᴡᴀᴛᴄʜᴇᴅ until the doors swung closed, blocking her last view of Jim, of the stretcher, of old Kaplan, who plodded determinedly alongside her husband.

She continued staring at the closed doors, asking, *Is this the way it ends? It can't. It mustn't.* But a sudden pain in her belly told her, *It can. It might.* She tightened her hands into fists and pressed them into her belly where the pain was. The pain grew more intense. She could not deny her fear.

Now, where to go, what to do? Dr. Kaplan said surgery would take hours. All night, possibly. Back to Jim's room, she decided. *Where else?*

She entered the room. Found the bed as Jim had left it. Out of habit, she straightened the bedclothes, tucked in the sheet. It was what she would have done if Jim had left their own bed at home. Except that for many weeks now he had not slept in their bed. To protect his failing heart, she insisted he sleep on the couch in the den.

She curled up in the easy chair in the corner, hoping to get some sleep. After half an hour, discovering that she could not become comfortable, she contemplated lying on the bed. That didn't seem proper. Somehow it meant that she didn't expect Jim back. Everything in the room seemed to warn her of his death. To escape her claustrophobia, she fled the room.

There was always the visitors' lounge. There were two

couches there. At midnight it would surely be deserted. She
could lie down and catch some sleep.

As she expected, the visitors' lounge was empty. Other times
when the doctors were in Jim's room, carrying out some
examination or test, she had looked on it as a place of refuge
from her worries.

Now she looked around, thinking, *This, too, may be for
the last time. No! I can't think that way. I'm being disloyal to
Jim. Deserting him. It's going to work. It has to work! It has
to! Eighty percent of the patients—or was it seventy percent?—
eventually get new hearts. That's what they said. Yes. But did
they ever give us a percentage for what happens to those who
do get hearts? Some die on the table when the heart refuses to
work. But how many? They never told me that. Or did they
and I don't remember? I can't remember. I should. It would
help now. When there is no other consolation, percentages
help. Percentages . . .*

In the operating room at Garden Grove General, two other
donor teams stood by until Boyd Angstrom had prepared the
donor's body for harvesting.

Though the initial steps in harvesting surgery were
carried out by the heart team, the heart was the last organ to be
removed, since its continued functioning was necessary to
keep the other organs supplied with fresh oxygenated blood.
The kidney team performed the first excision. The team sent to
harvest the liver followed.

Those two teams having finished and departed, Angstrom
was free to proceed with his ultimate function, to remove the
heart cleanly, empty it of blood, prepare it, and maintain it at
four degrees centigrade.

To prevent coagulation, he injected three milligrams of
heparin intravenously. Then he clamped off the vena cava,
careful to avoid the cardiac sinus. He allowed the heart to
empty, cross-clamped the aorta and injected a cold cardiopho-
bic solution into the aortic root to induce cardiac arrest. The

heart perfectly still, he proceeded to sever the pulmonary arteries and all connective tissue. He was able now to lift the cold still heart out of the cavity and remove it to the stainless-steel basin. He carried the basin to the sterile table for preparation.

He immersed the heart in the cold sterile solution the team had brought. He could now examine it thoroughly for any hidden malformations. Aortic valve, right atrium, tricuspid valve, left atrium, mitral valve—he examined them all with meticulous care. For he could not transmit word to proceed with Jim Campbell's surgery until he was absolutely sure this was, by all medical standards, a good healthy replacement.

Once sure, he nodded to Sawyer, who was on the phone.

She reported back to the O.R. at the Medical Center, "Angstrom has removed the heart. He reports it is A-okay."

After he had completed his examination, Angstrom removed the inert heart to a plastic bag containing cold sterile saline solution. He sealed the bag with umbilical tape. He then placed that bag into a second plastic bag also filled with cold saline. He passed the second bag to his lab technician, who carefully placed it in the ice-laden beer cooler where it should remain at four degrees centigrade to sustain it in excellent condition for the journey.

Angstrom had a final concern. Before the beer cooler was sealed, he peered into it to make sure of two important details. First, that the heart was being maintained in absolutely sterile condition. Second, that there was no direct contact between the heart and the ice in the cooler. Such contact would cause crystallization within the heart muscle and destroy its usefulness.

Both conditions having been met, this heart was now ready for its life-saving journey.

Sawyer reported on the phone, "It's in the cooler now. We're on our way to the airport!"

Their precious cargo in hand, they were under way.

Time began to count now. Five hours was all the time

they had to deliver this heart to the operating table where it could give new life to Jim Campbell.

Once Sawyer's message, "We're on our way to the airport," reached the O.R., Chris Slade glanced at the wall clock. It read twelve minutes past ten P.M.

He began to do his vital heart-transplant mathematics.

Donor team on the way to Garden Grove airport, thirty-five minutes. Flight time, three hours twelve minutes. Ground travel time from airport to Medical Center, even on a rainy night, forty minutes. New heart due to arrive a little after two o'clock. Patient in Campbell's condition, with end-stage cardiac deficiencies, has to be anesthetized very very slowly. Usually takes about two hours.

He passed the word to the anesthetists who had charge of Jim Campbell in the holding room outside the O.R. "Start putting him under at fifteen after midnight."

Though the visitors' lounge was empty and very quiet, Nancy Campbell could not fall asleep. She lay on the couch, aware of something in her pocket that pressed against her breast. The rosary Mrs. Noonan had placed in her hand. She gripped it tightly. It might not work, but it certainly could do no harm. Not now. She would lie there and pray. That would take the place of sleeping.

In an attempt to relieve her tension, she began to draw deep breaths, holding the air in each time before exhaling. It did nothing to relieve the pain in her belly. She could identify that pain now. Years ago, before Jimmy was born, she had menstrual cramps that felt like this. Since her two pregnancies and the births of Jimmy and Dorothy, those pains had ceased. Until now.

She became aware of soft footsteps outside the open door. *Some nurse on her way to answer a call button,* she thought. *One thing about the nurses on the Cardiac ICU floor, they are prompt in answering patients' calls.*

These steps did not pass by, but seemed to enter the

lounge. Guiltily, she sat up, assuming, *Visitors aren't allowed to sleep in the lounge. I wasn't sleeping,* she protested, *just lying down. Trying to get some rest. Surely there can't be a rule against that.*

She was prepared to explain about Jim, about the surgery, about—when she realized it was not a nurse. It was Millicent Forrest. Nancy was relieved to discover a familiar and friendly face. She rose quickly and went to her, speaking at the same time.

"It happened!" she said excitedly. "They found a heart for Jim! He's up there right now!"

Millicent Forrest pretended to be surprised and delighted, "Oh, how wonderful for you both!"

Nancy took Millicent's hand, led her to the couch, sat her down, eager to unburden herself.

"There I was, after taking the kids' things out of the dryer . . . I was mending Jimmy's jeans—he has a terrible way with jeans. You'd think he walks on his knees, the way he wears them out. I was putting in a patch when the phone rang. It was Dr. McCandless's secretary, Claire. She said that he said Jim was going to get his heart tonight and for me to come to the hospital right away."

"I'll bet that's the most exciting call you've ever gotten," Millicent Forrest said, patting Nancy Campbell's hand, which still clung to her arm.

"Exciting. But scary, too," Nancy admitted. "When Winston's turn comes, you'll know what I mean. We wait for weeks, then months, with only one thought in mind. A heart. Please, God, a heart for Jim. Somewhere, somehow, there's got to be a heart for Jim. You know the feeling."

"Indeed I do," Millicent agreed, giving no indication of what had preceded McCandless's decision.

"Let me warn you now," Nancy continued, "it's not exactly the relief you expect."

"No?"

"Sure, for maybe a minute or two, you think, 'Thank God! He's getting his heart. My prayers have been answered.'

But then, right after that, you begin to think, 'What if something goes wrong up in the operating room? What if the heart doesn't get here in time? What if the new heart doesn't work? Or something else goes wrong?' What was joy only minutes ago becomes fear. Terrible fear. Like right now, I've got pain in my belly. This terrible pain. So it isn't all joy and relief. You'll see.''

"Yes, yes, I'll see," Millicent agreed. "Now, tell me, where does it hurt?"

Nancy indicated the pit of her belly, the soft area just below her breastbone.

"Nan, stretch out," Millicent ordered. When Nancy hesitated, she insisted, "Just stretch out." She began to massage the site of Nancy's pain. Her gentle fingers massaging Nancy's belly gradually caused the tension to resolve.

Suddenly Nancy remembered, "Good God, here I've been going on about Jim, about myself, and never thought to ask about Winston."

"He's getting along, getting along," Millicent lied casually.

"Is he really?" Nancy asked.

"Yes, of course. Why do you ask?"

"If he's getting along well, why are you here so late? It's almost past midnight."

"Winston was feeling a little depressed tonight," Millicent improvised.

"Oh, don't I know how that is! Many's the time I'd visit and find Jim deep in depression. You know, 'I'll never get a heart. I'll be one of the thirty percent who die before they get one.' You know how it is."

"Yes, yes, indeed I do," Millicent said. "Win was having one of those nights. So I stayed on. Then I must have fallen asleep. When I woke up it was late. So here I am."

"Don't let him give up," Nancy encouraged. "I know what. Tomorrow morning, I'll go in there and talk to him. I'll tell him how it was with Jim. This morning he had no hope at all. Then suddenly there's a heart and he was on his

way up to surgery and a whole new life is starting for him.''
She could not resist adding, ''That's if everything goes well,
of course.''

''It will,'' Millicent assured. ''They say Slade is one of
the best heart surgeons in the country. Dr. McCandless said to
me once, 'When Slade takes that scalpel in hand he becomes
the perfect technician. If I ever need heart surgery, he's the
man I'd choose.' ''

''Dr. Kaplan feels the same way.''

''So you have nothing to worry about,'' Millicent said.
She continued to massage Nancy's belly. ''Feeling better
now?''

''Oh, yes. Much. thanks.''

''Good,'' Millicent Forrest said.

''I wonder how it's going up there,'' Nancy said softly.

''How long has it been? Since he was taken up?''
Millicent asked.

''Almost two hours.''

''I don't think much happens in the first two hours,''
Millicent said. ''Dr. McCandless told me once that it takes
two hours just to put a heart patient under anesthetic.''

''You've had some long talks with Dr. McCandless,''
Nancy remarked.

''Yes. I've been fortunate enough to have that opportunity.''

''Has he . . . has he ever said anything to you about Jim?
About his chances after he gets his heart?''

''We . . . we didn't talk about any other patient. Just
about Winston,'' Millicent said, carefully avoiding any further
disclosures.

''Of course. It would have been unethical to discuss
another patient, wouldn't it?''

''Yes. Yes, unethical,'' Millicent said. The situation
becoming too difficult for her, she excused herself. ''Now,
you just lie there and try to get some sleep. I'll go back and
have a look-in on Winston. I want to make sure he's
comfortable.''

She started to rise, but Nancy reached out to grasp her hand and hold it.

"I . . . I want to say something to you. I hope you don't mind."

"Mind?" Millicent said, puzzled. "Why should I?"

"Just before, when you were massaging me, it felt like I was a little girl again. And you were my mother. You're not really old enough. But you're such a . . . such a strong, confident, experienced woman . . . I mean the way you carry yourself . . . you could be a wonderful mother. My mother wasn't as pretty as you are. But she was like you in one way. Warm, loving."

"You talk about her in the past tense."

"She died when I was seventeen. One day she was pinning up my graduation dress, and the next day she was dead. A blood vessel burst in her brain."

"Oh, dear, how terrible that must have been for you."

"If she were here now, she would have done the same for me as you did."

Nancy drew Millicent's hand to her lips and kissed it. Millicent Forrest was free to go back to her husband's room.

She reached the door of Winston's room to hear soft voices inside. Allen McCandless's voice. And the voice of one of the floor nurses. She could not make out any words, so she pushed the door open gently in time to hear McCandless.

"That should hold him until morning. However, check him every hour. If there is any change for the worse, get me. I'll be here in the hospital until the Campbell transplant is completed."

He had noticed Millicent, but did not interrupt his instructions to take account of her presence until the nurse had left.

"She called me," he explained. "It seems Winston was having difficulty breathing. But he's fine now. And asleep."

"Good," Millicent said.

"I . . . I feel I owe you an explanation . . ." he began.

"No. I understand. One of those decisions doctors have to make," she said, trying her utmost to appear totally intellectual and unemotional about the situation.

"You have a right to know why," he told her.

"We didn't come here with any guarantee of 'rights.' The risks were carefully explained before we left Washington. Winston was to take his chances."

"The President did intercede," McCandless said. "But doctors can't be guided by politics. Especially in our field, where the need is so great and the supply of hearts so limited. Else, next thing you know, hearts would be sold to the highest bidder. In this case, between Jim and your husband, ultimately there was one deciding factor. Who could make the best and longest use of that heart?"

"I understand," she replied, hoping, *Please, please, don't keep explaining, don't keep trying to exorcise your guilt by justifying yourself to me.* "There is only one thing I would like to know. What are Winston's chances now?"

"If he can hold out for a few weeks, there is always a chance another Type O heart of the right size will turn up."

"*Can* he hold out?" she asked directly.

"I make no promises. But he is first on our list in terms of need. So there's a chance."

"A chance," she said, evaluating the word.

There was no more he could say. He felt that he had failed to justify his decision to her.

29

HANK STEPANIK STARED out of the windows of the airport tower. His gaze sweeping slowly around, he made a complete 360-degree appraisal of the night. Aside from the swirling mist, he could see little. The end of the runway was obscured from his view. Twice he ordered all landing lights turned on. They did little more than illuminate the mist.

On the desk before him lay the telephone, an open line to the operating room at the Medical Center. Above his head, the radio speaker that, for the moment, was transmitting only the crackle of static. There had not been word from the Lear 55 for fifteen minutes now.

A fresh burst of wind-driven rain against the windows behind him made him turn suddenly. Desperate for some vestige of encouragement, he thought, *A good hard rain driven by a stiff wind could sweep out this damn mist. I don't mind the rain. It's the mist can kill you on a night like this.* Then he had to admit, *The damn wind, wind shear could do it, too.*

Above the crackle of the radio he could hear a voice on the open telephone line demanding attention. He picked it up.

"I'm here, I'm here," he reported testily.

"Any word yet?" a nurse in the operating room asked.

"Nothing yet. They must have entered the storm system, and it's rough going. So just hang on. It's got to be soon,"

Stepanik replied, interrupting himself when the radio started to report.

"Lear 55 to Field. Having a little rough going. So I'm revising our ETA. Should be two ten."

"Got ya," Stepanik said. "Stay in touch." He picked up the telephone once more. "Just got word. Pilot says ETA is now two ten."

"Two ten?" the nurse replied. "Add forty minutes for ground travel time, they won't be here for another two hours."

"That's about right," Stepanik said.

He heard her transmit the information to Slade, who called back, "Bring the patient into the O.R.!"

Wrapped in a white blanket, and already under mild sedation, Jim Campbell was rolled into the O.R. Carefully, he was lifted and placed on the operating table. The bright lights caused him to blink and close his eyes. Then he opened them slowly. Barely conscious, he stared up into the masked faces of the surgical team. Slade. Second surgeon Aileen Camerata. Briscoe, Slade's surgical assistant. Scrub Nurse Colwell, Circulating Nurse Weiner. Two anesthetists, Kilmer and MacRee. The perfusionists at the heart-lung bypass machine, Ward and Gordon.

One masked face lingered over Campbell for an instant to whisper, "Jim, this is it. What we've all been hoping for. You're going to be fine. Great! Good luck!"

He recognized the paternal voice of Dr. Ben Kaplan. Reassured, he closed his eyes and surrendered himself to the procedure with a silent prayer, *God, not for me, but for Nan and the kids, let me wake up again. Please?*

The clock on the O.R. wall read one fifty-three. Slade took the phone from the nurse's hand to inquire, "Hank, what's the latest word?"

Hank Stepanik, on the other end of the line, reported,

"They've fallen a little farther behind. Due to arrive at two twenty-four now."

"Thanks," Slade said. Then proceeded to do his mathematics. *Thirty-one minutes to touchdown. With police escort, forty minutes ground travel time. One hour and eleven minutes until the heart arrives.* "Okay. Let's go!"

Slade took his place at the table. The scrub nurse handed him a scalpel. Slade made a long clean incision down the center of Jim Campbell's exposed chest, from just above his breast bone to below the rib cage.

"Retract," he ordered Assisting Surgeon Camerata. With the skin and flesh of Campbell's chest spread wide, Slade held out his hand. The nurse passed the shiny stainless-steel electrical saw. To the shrill high-speed sound of the saw, he proceeded to cut the breast bone down the middle.

The breast bone separated, exposing the chest cavity, Slade could see firsthand, through the pericardium that encased it, the weak erratic heart which until now had been seen only under X ray, scan, cineangiogram and other electronic devices. From its irregular, mushy action, it was clear that, without a transplant, Campbell could not survive more than a few weeks, if that.

To prepare the patient when the moment came to go on bypass, Slade carefully inserted a surgical cannula into the aorta, keeping the clamp closed. Then he did the same to the vena cava. When the proper time came, by opening both clamps he would divert the flow of Campbell's blood around his heart, into the heart-lung machine, where it would be mechanically aerated then pumped back into his body, thus sustaining a continuous flow of fresh oxygenated blood to the rest of his body while his heart was being removed and replaced.

Once both cannulas had been inserted, the next move could occur only when word arrived that the heart was within fifteen minutes ground travel time of the hospital.

Now it was wait and see.

*   *   *

Hank Stepanik had been through this tense procedure too
many times not to be aware of the crucial facts. Five hours was
all the time they had to get that heart here safely. Which meant
not only getting it here, but getting it into the ambulance that
had been waiting alongside the runway. Then, accompanied
by the two-car police escort, speeding it to the hospital and up
into that operating room. The ambulance was ready. The
police cars were ready.

The Lear 55 had been checking in every fifteen minutes.
To report that they were behind schedule, but trying to
catch up.

Catch up, Stepanik thought, *now that they're in this
storm pattern, fat chance. And down here, what a mess!*

The rain had not only failed to clear out the mist, it was
raining even harder. The wind now came up in such treacherous gusts it seemed to be beating against the windows of the
tower on all four sides.

*How do you advise a pilot to make his landing in crazy
winds like these? What direction? Which of the three runways?*

He picked up a container still half full of coffee which
had grown lukewarm. He took a mouthful and spat it out. It
tasted bitter to him. He recognized 'that as the first sign of
being overcoffeed. Food was what he needed. But the sandwich that had been waiting for him far too long now tasted
dry. The bread was stale. He tossed it toward the wastebasket.

He knew what was really bugging him. Not the stale
sandwich. Not too much coffee. It was the knowledge that if
this were any other incoming flight except one delivering a
heart for transplant, he would divert it to the nearest safe
landing area, as he had earlier in the evening. Bellville. Or
Salem. Or, if necessary, the Air Force base. But none of those
was closer than sixty miles away, which meant that even with
a police escort it would add another fifty minutes to the trip.
There simply was not that much time to spare.

Hank Stepanik had no choice. If that plane were to
complete its mission, it had to land here, had to do so safely,

had to do so within the next fifteen minutes. He got back on the radiophone.

"Lear five-five. Come in. Give me a reading."

Soon the pilot's voice came back over the speaker. "Due to touch down in twelve minutes. How are conditions?"

"Not too good," Stepanik reported, minimizing the risks in hope that they might improve slightly before actual landing. "Make your approach to Runway Two. Runway Two." He turned from the radio to the phone that lay on his desk, picked it up. "Twelve minutes to landing. Though there might be some delay in getting down," he reported to the operating room.

He studied the field before him. The end of the runway was misted over and invisible. He picked up his field mike, growled, "You guys sure we're up full on Runway Two?"

"Every light's on," the mechanic reported back by field phone.

"Damn it," Stepanik said as he watched the swirling mist which stubbornly refused to clear.

Minutes later his radio came to life once more. "Lear five-five. Hank, I think I got the field in view now. At least I can see a glow. I'd better make a pass to be sure. Over."

Stepanik held his hand mike close to his mouth, ready to give emergency instructions. He listened carefully. Aside from the crackle of the radio, he heard nothing. Then, out of the misty darkness, he began to detect the approach of a plane. His practiced ears followed it, beckoning it closer until he heard it pass overhead.

Close, he realized, *too damned close and too damned low. Climb! Climb!* With some relief he heard it climb.

"Lear five-five, can you hear me?"

"Got you, Hank. I tried to get a fix on Runway Two. But all I see is a dim glow."

"Give it another try."

Inside the cabin of the Lear, sitting in the window seat, Adeline Sawyer rubbed her hands alongside her thighs, partly to relieve the strain, partly to wipe the sweat from her palms. Alongside her, Angstrom noticed, said nothing, but silently shared her fears.

"Climbing again," Sawyer said.

"Feels like," Angstrom said. "See anything?"

"Sort of a glow, that's all."

"No lights?"

"Just a glow"

"Better than nothing," he said, offering small consolation.

In the tower, Hank Stepanik followed the sound of the descending plane, silently coaxing it in for landing. Once more the plane came in overhead, then started climbing suddenly as the radio crackled and reported, "Can't see the damn runway, Hank! I'll have to divert, after all."

"Divert? You can't!" Stepanik protested. "You can't waste that heart!"

"What do you think I'll be doing if I crack up?" the pilot shot back.

"Look, Lou, give it another shot," Stepanik pleaded.

He picked up his intercom mike to give instructions to his field mechanic. "Tell that ambulance and those two police cars to line up at the end of Runway Two. Then turn on their high beams. I want to flood that area with all the light we can!"

He watched from the tower and could make out three vehicles below. They started up slowly, wheeled out of the misty darkness, proceeded slowly to the end of the runway. Once in line, all three faced the runway, turned on their high beams.

Six strong headlights tried to pierce the stormy night. They appeared to be blunted by the heavy mist, as if it were a stone wall. However, diffused by the mist, they helped to create a stronger glow than the runway lights alone could project.

"Okay, Lou," Hank advised over the radio. "We've got extra lights on the runway. Give it a try!"

"Roger. See you on the ground. One way or another," the pilot said.

Hank Stepanik listened with practiced ear to the sound of the jet as it approached from the far end of the field. It sounded on course. He kept hoping to hear that touchdown, that reassuring scrape of the tires as they hit the runway, that sudden roar of the forward thrust of the engines to brake the plane and slow it to a stop.

Too long, he kept saying to himself, *it's taking too long. They could run the length of the runway and crash into the ambulance and those escort cars. Ah, thank God, there it is. Touchdown. Reverse thrust. Now, nice and easy. Slow, slow. Bring her to a halt.*

He stared out of the tower windows into the illuminated mist to see the white nose of the Lear 55 come into view and stop no more than a dozen feet from the ambulance.

Relieved, Hank Stepanik picked up the phone. "They just touched down!"

He saw the door of the jet open, the steps slide out and down. Sawyer emerged first, then Angstrom, then the two technicians carrying their cargo. They hurried to the back of the open ambulance, loaded the beer cooler aboard. Sawyer, Angstrom and the rest of the team climbed in. The doors were slammed shut. Swiftly, the ambulance started away into the rainy mist, one police car in front, the other bringing up the rear. Red and white lights rotating, sirens sounding, the caravan was under way.

30

IN THE O.R. the nurse who had been holding the phone for the last twenty-five minutes was brought alert by what she heard. She listened, then reported.

"Dr. Slade. The tower again! They've just touched down!"

"Finally!" Slade said. "Let's go!"

Aware that Slade was distressed by the delay, Ben Kaplan tried to encourage, "So it was a little late. But not too late."

"Forty-two minutes late," Slade pointed out.

"Still under the five-hour mark by the time they get here."

"Twenty-two minutes under five hours," Slade said. "I like a little more leeway than that."

He looked to his perfusionists, who were ready. Slade released the clamps on the cannulas he had inserted in the aorta and the vena cava, diverting the blood from Campbell's heart into the transparent tubes of the heart-lung machine. He watched the blood circulate through the intricate mechanism, be oxygenated and fed back into Campbell's arterial system to sustain all other organs of his body while Slade worked on his heart. The anesthetists in charge of the patient's vital signs had their eyes on the screens of the monitors that reported Campbell's condition moment by moment. After some minutes, the perfusionists and the anesthetists exchanged reassuring eye contact.

One of the perfusionists announced, "Stabilized on bypass."

It was the signal for which Slade was waiting. He was ready now. The moment the new heart appeared in the doorway, he was free to proceed with his next step. To cut through the pericardium surrounding Jim Campbell's heart.

At the same moment that Jim Campbell was pronounced stabilized on bypass, a caravan of three cars—two police cars and an ambulance—turned off the Interstate onto the boulevard that led to the hospital. Now in city traffic, on a rainy night, the police cars sped along, their sirens sounding. They followed an established and practiced route which took them around most traffic lights. When they were confronted by a red light, they slowed down, made sure they were safe and drove through it. The rain that pelted down, beating against their windshields, had one advantage. It kept late-night traffic to a minimum, permitting the caravan to arrive at the hospital Emergency entrance in six minutes less than had been anticipated.

Twenty-four minutes after Jim Campbell had been stabilized on bypass, Adeline Sawyer appeared in the doorway of the O.R. to give Slade the nod of assurance he had been awaiting. Behind her, carrying the beer cooler, came her two assistants. They set it down, opened it, removed the sterile plastic container that held the sterile bag in which the heart rested in the icy saline solution. Slade examined the heart carefully. He exchanged looks with Donor Team Surgeon Angstrom.

"As good a specimen as I've seen in a long time," Angstrom stated.

"Scrub!" Slade replied. "I may need you before this is over."

Back at the table, Slade held out his hand. The nurse slapped a scalpel into it. Carefully, he inserted the scalpel and cut open the pericardium, laying bare Jim Campbell's ailing heart. With deft definite strokes of the scalpel, he cut away the fore part of the diseased heart, leaving the back and most of both atria intact.

After he had removed both ventricles and only part of the atria, he held out his hands and the nurse laid the fresh inert heart into them. Cautiously, Slade placed it in the cavity of Jim Campbell's chest.

Angstrom and Kaplan exchanged eye reactions over their masks, relieved that the new heart fit comfortably into the area vacated by Campbell's diseased heart—as it should have, since the donor had been a man of equivalent size and weight. The first critical question had been answered to the doctors' satisfaction. But they all knew this surgical procedure had a long way to go and many crises still to confront.

Kaplan admired how skillfully Slade sutured the new heart into place to the back of the old one, trimming snips of tissue here and there to assure a more perfect fit. The connection of the heart to Campbell's aorta posed a greater problem. Slade was forced to carefully bevel Jim's aorta to make it join more exactly with Larry Clinton's heart. But when Slade had tied the last suture, the fit seemed perfect. There was no apparent seepage of blood from any of the stitches.

The implantation had taken thirty-nine minutes and appeared to be successful.

Slade was not nearly so relieved as was old Kaplan. For even the most skillfully executed surgery was no guarantee that the new heart would function as everyone hoped.

That test would now commence.

Slade reached out his hand to the scrub nurse. "Prednisone!" She handed him a hypo with a strong dose of the anti-rejection drug, which he proceeded to inject intravenously. Having done that, he opened the clamp on the aorta to allow Campbell's blood to begin circulating from the bypass machine into and through the coronary arteries, restoring circulation to the new heart.

The flow of fresh oxygenated blood should reinvigorate this heart, which had been bathed in saline and kept at just above freezing for almost five hours. Would it resume the normal functions of a healthy heart?

Slade, Angstrom and Kaplan stared down into Campbell's open chest to study this fresh heart in its new environment. At the first flush of blood through the coronary arteries, the heart seemed to leap into action. Erratic action. It fibrillated, out of control. Kaplan was alarmed. Slade and Angstrom were not. Fibrillation at this early stage in the procedure was not unexpected.

"Panels!" Slade demanded.

The scrub nurse passed two surgical panels, which Slade placed along each side of the erratic heart.

"Countershock!"

Camerata pressed the lever to feed a jolt of electric current to the panels. In response, the heart jumped, then beat more steadily. But in moments it began to limp along once more at a less than encouraging pace.

Kaplan looked to Slade, whose eyes could not conceal his concern.

"Countershock!" the surgeon ordered once more.

A second surge of power caused the heart to jump once again. The heart beat more steadily, only to settle into a slow, erratic rhythm. A third application of shock evoked a more regular response.

The doctors continued to watch the heart pump along, its rhythm more steady, though not yet normal. Kaplan felt somewhat relieved. Not so Slade, who knew from experience that if several jolts of countershock hadn't done it, this heart had not yet accepted its new burden. There was still another and possibly more dangerous test yet to come. After Slade had observed the heart beat with more convincing strength, he decided to risk that step.

"Let's wean him off bypass," he ordered the perfusionists.

While Slade continued to study the heart's action, the

perfusionists began to slowly reduce the amount of blood being fed from the heart-lung machine. Gradually they cut down the flow from the four liters it had been feeding to three.

The heart appeared to tolerate the change, responding well to its increased burden. Slade signaled the process to continue, keeping his gaze fixed on the open chest, intent on detecting any possible dimunition in the heart's action. Taking a patient off bypass was a slow process, during which things could go wrong. The heart might rebel and fail. With this balky heart,the next half hour should tell.

Millicent Forrest had been watching her sleeping husband, listening to his erratic breathing, punctuated by slight rasps and an occasional cough.

I wish I could breathe for him, she thought. *Until his heart attack, he was always the strong one. I only pretended to be. I had to appear to be ready for any emergency, prepared for any challenge. What did one of those Washington gossip columnists call me once? Yes, "the unflappable Mrs. Forrest." It's good she can't see me now, when he needs me and there's so little I can do. When I need him because I realize how much I love him, but it's too late. Too late. I'd better go get help for him.*

She hurried down the corridor toward the pool of light that illuminated the night nurses' station.

"Please, something for Mr. Forrest. He's having difficulty."

The charge nurse consulted his chart. "He received a sedative at midnight," she reported.

"He's asleep, but he's struggling," Millicent said.

"In that case, I'd better locate Dr. McCandless!"

"Do that. Please! And hurry!"

As the nurse picked up her phone, Millicent Forrest started back along the dimly lit, deserted corridor. Passing Jim Campbell's room, she heard the gasping sound of a woman in tears. She found Nancy Campbell curled up in the armchair in the corner, her face buried in a damp handkerchief, her slender body heaving with each gasp. Millicent slid down beside her, embraced her.

"What's wrong? Did you get word from the O.R.?"

Nancy continued to gasp until she could finally respond, "Nothing. But it's been so long . . . hours . . . hours."

"Nan, this operation *takes* hours. Allen—Dr. McCandless—told me it can sometimes take as long as twelve hours. Depending on how things go."

"Something's wrong. I can feel it!" She began to weep once more, burying her wet face in Millicent's bosom.

Torn between comforting the distraught young wife and tending her own husband, Millicent gently freed herself and started out of the room. As she reached the corridor, she spied McCandless hurrying toward Winston's room. They met at his door.

"What happened?" McCandless asked.

"His breathing, it's not . . . usual, even for him," she explained.

"Did he complain of pain, chest pain?"

"He's still asleep, so I assume if there's pain, it's not too bad."

"I'll have a look. Wait out here," McCandless said.

For an instant he felt the need once more to apologize for his choice of Campbell. The exchange of looks between them revealed his impulse.

Her response was as clear as if she had spoken. *We are past the time for explanations, just do what you can for him.*

"I will be in Campbell's room. She needs me," Millicent Forrest said.

Allen McCandless stood beside Winston Forrest's bed, studying his labored breathing, his gray face, his bluish lips, evidence of his cardiac deterioration. A damaged heart was trying its utmost to carry on functions for which it was no longer equipped. Mechanical assist was not indicated, not yet, but oxygen would surely help. McCandless lifted the phone to quietly give the order to the night nurse.

As he took Forrest's pulse, he thought, *If there is not a new heart for him, a month is as long as he can possibly go.*

Once the nurse had affixed the oxygen tubes in Forrest's nostrils, his labored breathing eased and he fell asleep again, more peacefully. McCandless was free to leave him and report to Millicent.

He found her in Campbell's room, and understood at once what she meant by "she needs me." Nancy was weeping uncontrollably despite Millicent Forrest's comforting embrace.

Millicent turned to him. "Well?"

"I've put him on oxygen. He's resting comfortably. He'll be fine."

"Fine," she repeated with a hint of irony which McCandless interpreted as a rebuke, though her eyes did not accuse him.

Conscience, he realized, *guilt. Not my fault*, he protested silently. *Doctors should not have to make such decisions.*

He addressed himself to Nancy Campbell. "There is no reason to cry. I keep in touch with the O.R. So far, aside from the heart arriving a little late, everything is going according to plan."

"He's all right?" the tearful young wife asked.

"His new heart is already sewn into place," McCandless assured.

"When can I see him?" Nancy asked.

"It takes quite a bit of time after the heart is implanted before the operation is over. Hours."

"Hours?" The manner in which she repeated the word summed up all her fears

"That doesn't mean anything has gone wrong," McCandless said, trying to encourage her. "It's a long involved procedure. And no two operations proceed exactly alike."

"Which means things *can* go wrong," she insisted.

"If something was wrong, they'd send for me. And they haven't," McCandless said. "So, there." He used his own handkerchief to wipe her eyes. "Now, next time I see tears, I want them to be tears of joy. Okay?"

"Okay," she finally managed, trying to smile.

He felt free to leave, but not before he cast a glance at Millicent Forrest, urging her to remain with Nancy.

"I'll take another look at Winston," he said as he slipped out of the room.

31

NINETEEN MINUTES HAD elapsed since Slade had ordered weaning Jim Campbell off the heart-lung machine. The flow of blood which had been reduced from four liters, down to three, then to two, was now being reduced to one. With some satisfaction the entire team was relieved to see that the heart continued to pump with encouraging regularity.

Slade was now ready to order complete shutdown, a crucial decision. Complete shutdown could cause the heart to falter, which might demand going back on bypass, in itself a procedure not without risk. No two hearts were exactly the same, or reacted in the same way. In his experience, Slade had seen hearts that seemed eager for the challenge. They continued pumping more strongly than when they were assisted by bypass. Others faltered. Some failed. The surgeon never knew. Not until he was faced with the result. This was one of those moments when he would make that discovery.

He nodded to the perfusionists to signal their final shutdown.

Slade, Angstrom and old Kaplan kept their eyes fixed on the heart. It bore up well under its new burden.

Slade's practiced eyes detected it first. The others seconds later. The heart was beginning to dwindle. Almost imperceptibly at the outset. Then it became more pronounced. Now there was no denying it. This heart was beginning to fail.

Slade half turned to his scrub nurse, "Hypo! Dopamine!"

While injecting the drug intravenously, Slade ordered, "Call McCandless! He's somewhere in the hospital!"

As he completed injecting the dopamine, Slade considered all the options in his armamentarium of drugs. *Isuprel, epinephrine, nitroprusside . . . but get McCandless's opinion first. He's the cardiologist. In extremes, go for a mechanical heart to keep the patient alive. Or even put out an emergency call for another heart while going back on bypass. But not too many patients come off bypass in good condition after too many hours. Mac, wherever you are, get here fast!*

Dr. McCandless had been gone for some minutes when Millicent Forrest and Nancy Campbell heard scurrying footsteps in the deserted corridor. The muffled warning sound of rubber soles whisking swiftly across the tiled floor alerted them both. They listened, heard the intense whisper of the night nurse as she called, "Dr. McCandless! Dr. Slade just called. He needs you up there! Stat!"

Nancy Campbell froze at those words, then whispered, "He said, 'If anything was wrong' . . . they just sent for him. Jim! Jim!"

Millicent Forrest placed both her hands on Nancy's shoulders, looked down into her stunned, terrified face. "Nancy Campbell, this is no time for tears. It's a time to be strong. We will be strong together. You are not to cry! Understand?"

Nancy finally nodded, leaned close and pressed her face against Millicent. At the same time, she reached into the pocket of her dress, found the rosary Mrs. Noonan had given her what seemed like days ago, but actually was only nine hours. The contact of her hand on the religious artifact did not move her to words of prayer, but reminded her, *Jimmy, Dorothy, I have to be strong for them, no matter what happens. I have to be strong for them.*

*　　.*　　*

Wearing O.R. greens and mask, Allen McCandless entered the operating room, to find Chris Slade peering into Campbell's open chest, studying the action of the heart that had once beat so strongly in the chest of Larry Clinton but was now flaccid and irregular. Fortunately it was not fibrillating, but it threatened to do so.

There was no need for any explanation beyond Slade informing him, "Dopamine. Full strength."

McCandless studied the heart action, considered all the options. "I'd go for nitroprusside right now. Directly into the heart."

There was no need for Slade to give the order. The scrub nurse was already filling a hypo with the drug. She passed it to Slade, who injected it into the struggling heart. While they watched the response, a circulating nurse held a glass to Slade's face. He lifted his mask and drank through the straw, orange juice to give him energy. The procedure, which had started with that first long clean incision the length of Campbell's chest, was past its sixth hour.

While they studied the heart's response to the nitroprusside, they discussed other possible modalities.

"Could go back on bypass," Slade suggested. "Wouldn't like to. It's a last resort."

"A balloon would be more advisable," McCandless suggested.

"Might," Slade conceded. "We'll see."

Angstrom asked, "Chris, want me to take over? You're bushed."

"No. Not yet," Slade replied. "Let's see what happens."

On the other side of the operating table, Ben Kaplan strained to look into the chest cavity, at the same time trying not to interfere with the team involved in carrying out the procedure. He caught glimpses of the heart as it struggled.

Silently the old physician kept urging, *Come on, damn it! Come on! Pick up that rhythm. A perfectly good heart, how can it go wrong now? There's Nancy and the kids. Four lives are hanging on this heart! Pump! Damn it, pump!* He realized the futility of raging against this organ which, for some unknown reason, was refusing to act as it should. He was forced to continue watching in frustrated silence.

Slade and McCandless, too, studied the recalcitrant heart. Time was now beginning to count heavily. If this heart dwindled any further, it might cease completely, despite any stimulants.

"It's either back on bypass or else go for the balloon," McCandless said finally.

Slade considered the suggestion for a moment, then agreed, "Balloon kit!" As he turned to accept the catheter from the scrub nurse, he noticed something that caused him to whisper, "Hell! That's all we need now!"

In an instant McCandless realized what had alarmed Slade. There was a slight ooze of blood seeping from the area where the sutures joined the new heart to Campbell's aorta.

Angstrom volunteered, "I'll handle that, Chris." He prepared to repair the sutures and shut off the seepage which now endangered the success of the entire process.

Slade pushed aside the surgical drape from Campbell's thigh to locate his femoral artery. He held out his hand. The scrub nurse passed the large-bore needle to him. He inserted it into the artery. Then he took the long, thin, yellow plastic catheter she passed to him. He inserted it through the needle into the artery.

Both Slade and McCandless followed the slow progress of the catheter up the artery that finally directed it toward the struggling heart, which now was pumping with even less force and regularity.

Once the monitor confirmed that the catheter was in place in the heart, Slade began to press the tiny plunger at the lower end of the slender tube, inflating the balloon at the tip end inside the heart. Picking up the rhythm of the heart, Slade worked the plunger, inflating the balloon then deflating it in consonance with the cardiac cycle. Thus he assisted the errant heart by decreasing the load on that struggling organ.

Pump. Release. Pump. Release. Pump. Release. The

entire team, including old Kaplan, studied the action of the balloon on the monitor. The anesthetists glanced from the monitor to their own instruments to check Campbell's vital signs.

The perfusionists watched, aware that any moment Slade might be forced to order, "Back on bypass!" With both cannulas still in place in Campbell's aorta and vena cava, they could comply quickly and efficiently. But that might only increase the hazard when the moment arrived to come off bypass a second time. After a certain number of hours on the machine, the patient could be at even greater risk.

Everyone in the O.R. watched the action of the balloon, each with his own hopes. And fears.

More than an hour of balloon-assisted cardiac action had gone by. Meantime Angstrom had repaired the sutures around the aorta and stopped the seepage of blood. McCandless had relieved Slade of the burden of rhythmic pumping.

Inflate. Deflate. Inflate. Deflate. Slade stood over the open chest cavity, diagnosing the action of the heart.

"Hold it, Mac!" Slade said. "Let's give it a chance on its own."

McCandless ceased pumping, moved up the table to stand alongside Slade. They both watched. For some minutes the heart seemed to be strong and regular, then it started to show signs of dwindling once more. Without a word, McCandless resumed his position at the pump. Inflate. Deflate. Inflate. Deflate.

After thirty more minutes of mechanical assistance, Slade decided to test the heart on its own once again.

Slade, Angstrom, McCandless, Kaplan, Camerata, all watched cautiously. No one said a word. Gradually, eyes were raised from staring at the heart. They looked across the table at other sets of eyes, seeking confirmation, as if taking a vote.

All eyes agreed. On its own, the heart was beating strongly and with good rhythm. The blips skipped across the monitor with reassuring regularity. Slade was about to order Angstrom, "Close!" but McCandless said, "Let's give it a little more time."

He continued to watch. Kaplan continued to watch. Minutes went by. The heart beat on, gaining in strength and vigor. Finally McCandless nodded to Slade. Slade gave the order, "Close!"

Aside from the routine surgical steps in closing Jim Campbell's chest cavity, the operation was completed. Ten hours and nineteen minutes after he had been brought into the operating room, Jim Campbell had acquired a new heart, a healthy new heart.

If he followed the regimen prescribed for heart-transplant patients, he had acquired a new, a long, life as well.

32

MILLICENT FORREST ENTERED Jim Campbell's room, this time to find that Nancy had finally fallen asleep curled up in the armchair. Millicent took a blanket off the bed and draped it around the young woman carefully, so as not to wake her.

Poor Nancy, Millicent thought, *asleep from exhaustion. Who can blame her? Better she continue to sleep. Instead of worrying. Or crying. God knows, she's done enough of both tonight. She's right, though. Why no word? What happened after Allen was called up to the operating room? Why hasn't he come down? Or sent a message? Have things gone so badly up there? God, I hope not.*

So long a time. It must be daylight, she realized.

Silently as she could, she drew back the draperies that shut out the night. The first faint light of dawn could be seen in the east. The rain and mist of last night were gone.

Having made sure that Nancy was comfortable and covered, Millicent Forrest started back to attend her husband. Before she reached the door, it was thrust open. Short, stocky Dr. Kaplan entered, beaming. Behind him, Allen McCandless's broad smile reinforced the old man's delight and relief.

Before he was aware that Nancy was asleep, Kaplan exclaimed, "Nan, darling! It's done! Jim is fine! It couldn't have gone better! Oh, I'm sorry . . . I didn't realize she was . . ."

But she was no longer asleep. She shook her head trying
to absorb what Kaplan had said, trying to make sure she had
heard it correctly.

"Darling, he is fine! That Slade is a magician! And this
McCandless, he's no slouch, either."

The old man punched McCandless in the bicep in
comradely enthusiasm.

"Can I . . . can I see him?" Nancy asked, as tears
welled up in her blue eyes.

"Of course," McCandless said.

"Where? What floor?" she asked, starting for the door.

McCandless caught her, held her. "He's up in CPOR."
At her look of puzzlement he explained, "Cardiac Post
Operative Recovery. Ben, maybe it would be better if you
took her up."

"My pleasure," the old man said, holding out his arm for
her to grasp.

Before she could take it, Millicent Forrest intervened.
"No, he should see you at your best. Let's wash away those
tearstains. And we'll do something about your hair, too."

Millicent Forrest used one of the towels in the rack over
the sink to wash and wipe Nancy's face. As she combed the
young woman's hair, she studied her face.

"No," Millicent decided, smiling. "You don't need any
makeup. The happiness in your eyes is enough."

As if the news seemed too good to be true, Nancy asked,
"He *is* okay? I mean, honestly okay?"

"He is fine," McCandless replied. "A little time to
recuperate, and if he follows the routine we'll lay out for him,
he can live a perfectly normal life. In fact, you'll probably
have him home in a few weeks."

Reassured, clinging to Kaplan's arm, Nancy hurried out.

Millicent Forrest and Allen McCandless were left alone.

After a tenuous moment of silence, he said, "You can
say it now."

"Say what?" she avoided.

"You no longer have to be the diplomatic government

wife," he said. "So say it. That heart could be beating in Winston's chest right now. I'm sorry that it isn't."

"So am I. But I understand."

"Does he?" McCandless asked.

"He doesn't know how the choice was made," she admitted.

"You're right. That's my responsibility. I'll look in and see how he's doing this morning."

"He's been sleeping peacefully."

"Good," McCandless said.

Up in CPOR, Nancy Campbell was being given the usual visitors' instructions by one of the nurses. First, she had Nancy wash her hands thoroughly. Then the nurse held out a sterilized isolation gown of yellow cloth. Nancy slipped into it. The nurse made her put on a pair of plastic gloves, explaining, "To fight off rejection, his immune system has been severely depressed. These precautions will protect him from infection." She handed Nancy her final piece of ICU equipment, a mask to cover her mouth and nose.

Ben Kaplan watched the entire procedure with great satisfaction. When it was completed, he urged, "Now, my dear, go to him!"

"Can I kiss him?" Nancy asked.

The nurse reluctantly shook her head.

Nancy Campbell approached the door to the room, hesitated on the threshold to steel herself. She promised, *No matter how bad he looks, I'll keep smiling. I won't let on.* Ben Kaplan watched through the transparent glass wall that exposed each ICU room to constant surveillance by the nursing staff.

Nancy approached Jim's bed. Slightly elevated, with an intravenous affixed in his arm, he lay there, eyes closed. Above his head a monitor reflected the strong healthy action of his new heart. The blips streaked across the screen in a steady pattern that seemed to defy all the previous faulty electrocardiograms taken of Jim Campbell in recent months.

Timidly, in a shy whisper, she asked, "Jim? Honey?"

He opened his eyes. He smiled.

"Thought you could get rid of me, did you?" he managed to say softly. "Well, I'm going to be around for a long long time. So get used to me."

Smiling, she began to cry.

"Oh, Jim . . . Jim, you look so good. I never expected . . . I mean, you really look terrific. Your face is so pink and healthy. Even your lips. I never expected it would happen so soon."

"I can feel it, darling. It's hard to describe. But I can feel the difference already."

"I'd love to kiss you, darling. But they said no, not yet."

Despite his post-op fatigue, he made a special effort to comfort her. "It's enough for me just to see you standing there. I love that gown."

"Silly," she said. "It's an isolation gown. All visitors have to wear them."

"But yellow is such a nice color for you. 'Course, I wouldn't exactly wear those gloves to church on Easter Sunday, but right now they look great. Even that mask can't hide how pretty you are. And your hair, I like it that way."

"Mrs. Forrest," she explained.

"You're crying. I've never seen you cry like that before. But I like it."

Her smile broadened. Her tears increased. Jim noticed Ben Kaplan through the glass and raised his left hand slightly to wave. Kaplan waved back.

"The old man been here all night?"

"Like he said he would."

"I'll bet he'll be a tyrant when it comes to making me follow my new routine."

"So will I!" Nancy replied. "Your medication every day, at exactly the right hour, your diet, your exercise . . ."

"Exercise. Next you'll have me running in the New York Marathon," he joked.

"Dr. McCandless said that once you recover, you can

live a normal life, do anything you want. He even said you might be home in a few weeks."

"The kids . . . do they know?"

"I'll be calling soon as it's time to wake them for school."

"Just imagine, a couple of weeks and I'll be home. Waking up the kids for school. Sleeping upstairs in our bed. Even . . . even making love to you again," he said softly. "It'll be like old times."

"No, new times," she corrected, smiling. "God, how I wish I could kiss you."

"We'll do a lot of kissing. Now it will mean more. A lot more. I can't tell you how it feels. Just before you go under, you think, 'I may never wake up again, never see her face again, never feel the kids' arms around me again.' There's no way to describe that feeling. No way. All those people who think they're living dull unexciting lives ought to thank their lucky stars every night."

McCandless was stethoscoping Winston Forrest's chest, concealing from his patient the concern caused by the weak, erratic sounds that reached his ears.

"How am I doing, Doctor?"

"Better than last night."

"The oxygen did it, I guess."

Forrest glanced at his wife, who stood at the foot of his bed, awaiting the doctor's findings. She kept trying to smile encouragingly. It proved too difficult.

McCandless shifted the area of his examination to Forrest's back, moving the shiny, flat stainless-steel diaphragm of his stethoscope from area to area.

"You haven't told me," Forrest said suddenly, causing McCandless to stiffen in anticipation of the one question he expected. "How's my gin partner? Come through the surgery all right?"

"Came through fine."

"Good! I'm glad," Forrest said with all the enthusiasm

he could muster in his weakened condition. "Nice young man. And that wife of his . . ." He had to pause to regain breath. "Very sweet girl. He going to be here long enough for me to win back some of my losings? I was down four hundred and ten thousand dollars last count." Forrest tried to laugh. The effort was too much.

"If everything goes okay," McCandless said.

"You're afraid he might reject that new heart?"

"We always expect some minor episodes of rejection. But unless he suffers a really acute one, he should be going home in two weeks, three possibly," McCandless said, his mind distracted by two divergent thoughts. His concern about what his stethoscope revealed, and Forrest's avoidance of the one question McCandless would prefer not to face.

"When do *I* go home?" Forrest asked.

Poised behind Forrest, McCandless had no need to disguise his dismay at being confronted by such a direct request.

Millicent Forrest's eyes pleaded, *Be gentle with him, lie if you have to.*

"You're top of the list. But we can't predict when a heart will become available," McCandless said. Frustrated by Forrest's refusal to pose the crucial question, McCandless finally asked, "Aren't you going to ask, 'Why? Why Campbell? Why not me?' "

"Even before I arrived here, Admiral Crider explained all the factors. Blood match. Tissue type. Size. Weight. Degree of damage. I assume Campbell proved more compatible."

"It wasn't that clean-cut," McCandless said.

Forrest reacted with puzzlement.

Because he felt he had to, McCandless continued, "All the clinical findings were equal."

"I see," Forrest said.

"Even Baldwin's test," McCandless said.

"Baldwin?"

"My old chief, the man who got me interested in

transplant work. He had one final test. Will to live. He used to say, if the patient doesn't exhibit a strong will to live, all our work can turn out to be so much plumbing.''

"Will to live . . ." Forrest considered, then recalling that last examination McCandless had made before deciding, said, "Do you search for that with a stethoscope?''

"I was searching for tone, attitude, spirit. Both patients exhibited a fierce will . . . *both*. So a choice had to be made . . . I had to make it.''

"I know the feeling," Forrest said.

"Believe me, you can't," McCandless said.

"I've been there myself," Forrest said. "Primitive countries . . . war-torn . . . so many hungry mouths . . . so many swollen bellies . . . and so little food. You have to choose. *I* had a test, too. A rule. Vote for tomorrow. Choose the future. Choose youth.''

"You *do* know," McCandless agreed.

"One man in his fifties. One in his thirties. You had to choose as you did," Forrest said.

"It wasn't made any easier, knowing that while I was deciding, a dozen perfectly good hearts were being buried in this country," McCandless said. "I could promise there'll be another heart for you very soon. But I won't demean our friendship with little lies. I'm sorry. Very sorry.''

"Strange," Forrest said, forced to pause to regain breath before explaining. "You've just given new life to a man. Twenty years ago that would have been considered an impossible miracle. Yet, here you are apologizing for it. Feeling guilty about me.''

"I felt I owed you an explanation.''

"Doctor, if it's any consolation, since the responsibility for making those decisions has to be in the hands of doctors, I'm glad it's in the hands of a doctor like you. Someone with integrity. God, how this nation needs people with integrity now.''

Weak as he was, Forrest put forward his hand to McCandless. As they shook hands, the younger man assessed the older man's grip. The hand was icy cold and even weaker than he had anticipated.

"I can confess now, much as I wanted to live, I didn't come here with great expectations. Crider had told me, 'If anybody can help you, McCandless can.' That was the telling line, '*If* anybody can help you' . . . I knew then it was hopeless. So I don't blame you. No need. You're blaming yourself too much as it is."

"As long as you understand . . ." McCandless said. He released the older man's hand and left the room without another word.

McCandless had been gone only minutes when Millicent asked, "Win, have you felt that way since we arrived here?"

"Yes."

"But all the plans you made, the things we were going to do?"

"At first, I was trying to hide from you how discouraged I was. Then, for a time, I actually began to believe it myself. Until I realized they weren't plans at all. I was only trying to rewrite our personal history. Our life together. As I wish it could have been."

"Yes, Win, it could have been so different."

"Millie, one thing you learn in government. There is never time or opportunity to go back and undo the mistakes. You have to deal with the situation that exists. So, don't you go back and try to relive the past. Our marriage. Or Paul's death. Live with today. And for tomorrow. And if, from time to time, you think of me, be tolerant and forgiving. That's all I ask."

"Win—" she tried to protest.

"I'm a little tired now, Millie. Talked too much. And you could do with some sleep yourself."

She took his hand, kissed him on the cheek, aware that he had begun to run a fever. She must report that to the floor nurse on the way out.

*   *   *

It was early morning. The sun was coming up from behind the buildings to the east of the hospital. The daytime shift of nurses, orderlies, maintenance workers and staff physicians was arriving, drawn as if by a funnel into the front entrance of the hospital.

Allen McCandless emerged to stand on the top of the broad steps and inhale the morning air. The heavy rains having washed out the impurities, the air smelled fresh and clean. As he was about to start down the steps toward the physician's parking lot, he heard his name called.

"Mac!"

He turned to find Ben Kaplan and Nancy Campbell coming out into the daylight. She rushed to him. "I saw him! He looks so great. So terrific!" She threw her arms around McCandless, stood on tiptoe to kiss him on the cheek. Embarrassed, she drew back, blushing.

"I'm sorry, Doctor, I didn't mean—"

"Why not?" McCandless said. "Doctors like to be kissed when they do something right. God knows we are blamed enough when we're wrong."

Kaplan said, "Allen, you fellows saved four lives last night, not just one."

"Thank you, Ben," McCandless said. "We have to discuss Jim's follow-up treatment once he goes home. I'll give you a call."

He watched as old Kaplan shepherded Nancy Campbell toward the parking lot. From behind him McCandless heard a voice he had come to know quite well by now.

"Dr. McCandless . . ."

He turned to face Millicent Forrest.

"Allen . . . if there is anything in the world you can do for him—" she started to say. The words caught in her throat. Her eyes filled with tears. She struggled to regain control. "Sorry. I know you've done all you can. But he's been such a strong man. It's painful to see him so . . . so resigned. To see him accept death . . ."

She turned away to hide tears. McCandless realized he had

never seen her cry before. Throughout, she had been strong, calm, almost majestic, in keeping with her striking beauty.

How she must have loved that man in years gone by, he thought. *And still loves him. She is loyal unto death. Maggie wasn't. Because she is Maggie? That's not fair. Because I am me. Given a second chance, I'd do it all differently.*

She recovered sufficiently to ask, "Is there anything in the world you can do for him?"

"We could keep him going with a pump, a mechanical heart," McCandless suggested.

"Would he be tethered to it, like I've seen on the television news?" she asked.

"One day there may be an implantable mechanical heart, but not yet."

"Winston tied to that machine like some imprisoned animal—he wouldn't like that. Not with his sense of dignity, his need for freedom. Even if freedom only means being able to walk across the room on his own," she considered aloud.

"He'll need full-time hospital care," McCandless pointed out.

"If you had to assess his chances, getting a heart in time, surviving the surgery, what would you say? Honestly?"

"Not good," he said.

"Just 'not good'?" she asked, staring at him through her sensitive, tear-filled hazel eyes.

"There's always a chance—" he started to say.

She interrupted, "Meaning there's virtually no chance at all."

"Slim. Very slim"

"Then I'd like to take him home. Back to Georgetown. He should be among familiar things. Books he loves. Memorabilia of his government service. Friends. Old colleagues. I'd like to let him relive his best days. He deserves that. He's really a fine man. With his own sense of duty and integrity. You two are more alike than you know, Allen"

"I'll run another series of tests on him. If they show what I suspect, I'll discharge him."

"Thanks," Millicent said.

"I'll . . . I'll miss seeing you every day," he confessed softly.

"Who knows. We may meet again. Sometime," she said, extending her hand.

They shook hands, and he held hers longer than he intended. She pulled back her hand gently. He watched her start toward her car in the parking lot, get in. He saw the backup lights go on. Saw the car pull out and start away.